MASTER *of* ALASKA

THE SAGA OF ALASKA'S FIRST RUSSIAN GOVERNOR, ALEKSANDR BARANOV

ROGER SEILER

A Historical Novel

Master of Alaska is written as historical fiction with a mixture of historical and fictitious events, people, and places. No currently living people are depicted, and any resemblance to any living person or current event is purely coincidental.

TRUE
N★RTH
PUBLISHI

Published by True North Publishing
Imprint of Motivational Press
1777 Aurora Road
Melbourne, Florida, 32935
www.MotivationalPress.com

Manufactured in the United States of America.

ISBN: 978-1-62865-329-8

To Sally

and her million-dollar smile

that brightens every day.

ACKNOWLEDGMENTS

Making this book into a story worth reading happened thanks to suggestions from many excellent guides. From Barry Sheinkopf, an accomplished historical novel writer, I learned how to blend "showing" and "telling" the story for best effect. John Davenport, an experienced historian and eloquent writer who knows something important about nearly everything that has ever happened, offered useful ideas for strengthening the story structure. Three able writers, Lita Oppegard, Sally Seiler, and Pat Schneider, tirelessly critiqued the text, helping to improve clarity and flow. Allan Engstrom provided expert insights into the Russian language and the historical background of Russian America. David Rutledge gave many hours early on as a sounding board to help focus character development. Peter Danish and his Writing Academy enlightened my efforts to get *Master of Alaska* into a shape that could actually get published. Justin Sachs, of True North Publishing, had the vision to see this story's potential to gain wide readership and courageously chose to publish it. Finally, the excellent work by True North Publishing's editor, Victoria Nunnenkamp, refined my writing so that the story could be better enjoyed. To all of them, I say a heartfelt, "Thank you!"

CONTENTS

PREFACE

When my daughter Diana first started to read this story, she commented, "This is just for macho guys, so it doesn't interest me." I encouraged her to read on, because after K'asasee, Anooka, and Irina come into the story, it is much more than just a guy story. It involves the kind of relationships and character depth that my daughter would find interesting. She did read on, and agreed.

Intertwined with Aleksandr Baranov's story, beginning in 1790 when he became Russsia's chief manager in Alaska, is that of the Tlingit chief Katlian, Baranov's main antagonist whom he learned to respect for his bravery and intelligence. They were archenemies since early in Baranov's tenure, and yet the watercolor portrait of Katlian (shown in the Appendix), painted in 1818, near the end of Baranov's 28-year rule, tells us that something important had changed. Something happened between them that enabled peace between the Russians and the Tlingit, which in turn enabled the Russians to hold onto Alaska and keep it out of British hands until they sold it to the U.S. in 1867. That "something" is a key element of this book.

Each of these men had a strong woman in his life: Baranov's Anooka (renamed Anna) and Katlian's K'asasee, plus Baranov's daughter Irina. These women influenced the men's important choices, and did so in surprising ways. I guarantee you'll enjoy getting to know these women.

The big question often asked of historical novels is how truly they represent actual history. In this case, there are a wealth of letters written by Baranov and people who knew him, as well as portraits, which have been relied on here to develop the characters, their motivations, the dynamics of their interactions, and the fabric of events in which they operated. Some of these fascinating source documents are excerpted in the appendix so you can see for yourself how they were used as the foundation for this story.

Aleksandr Andreievich Baranov is a controversial figure today. Some believe he was a brutal and ruthless tyrant. His statue in Sitka has been attacked with an axe multiple times. Others see him as a heroic figure. Baranov-the-Brutal-Tyrant was the view held by Russian colonial clergy, who wrote to the home office demanding his replacement. But his own letters, and those of many who knew him firsthand, show a man with empathy for others. These letters show that he worked under the stress of enormous challenges, doing the best he could with what he had to achieve remarkable results. The historical record in these letters, and in the Baranov biography by the only author who actually knew him personally, Kyrill Khlebnikov, testify to many instances when Baranov's empathy broke through his necessarily tough exterior in ways hidden to most.

We should note that during Baranov's rule in Alaska, 1) he never resorted to capital punishment, and 2) there was not a single jail in all of Alaska. He had chosen not to use these two requisites of truly brutal and ruthless tyrants. If he had been a real tyrant, he would have had Chief Katlian hanged for leading the massacre of Russians at Sitka in 1802. Instead, he eventually made peace with Katlian and gave him an Allies of Russia silver medal, as seen in his Russian portrait. That portrait of Katlian is itself an amazing testament to the ability of powerful enemies to find peace if they really want to.

That subtle portrait, with its many underlying messages, is one of the most important pictures in the history of Alaska. Were it not for the story told by that picture—which resulted mostly from Baranov's choices and leadership—Alaska would almost certainly have never become part of the United States. Instead, Alaska would probably now be part of Canada, and the non-Native people living there today would be very different individuals, with few of USA origin.

The story in this painting is the inspiration for much of this book. And the core truth in the painting is that Baranov's greatest achievement was not his victory at the 1804 Battle of Sitka, but his success in making peace with the Tlingit afterwards. Please view this portrait and an analysis of its story in the Appendix, along with excerpts from letters of that time, etc. that address the issue of his being an alleged tyrant.

I was most attracted to the Baranov story by the complexity of its real-life characters, the challenges they faced, and how they often reacted to situations in unexpected ways that exposed the depth of their values. These values drove their conflicts and evolved in ways that are thought-provoking today.

How was I introduced to the saga of Aleksandr Baranov? My father, Ed Seiler, was a bush pilot on the Alaska Peninsula where he and my mother, Josefina, had built Enchanted Lake Lodge. He had read a biography of Baranov, and after I graduated from the UCLA film school, he suggested that the Baranov saga would be a great subject for a fascinating adventure film.

Years later I started researching Baranov. Especially interesting was his dilemma of being essentially a good man with a bad job. How does one navigate this situation and stay morally intact? It's a question I thought worth exploring.

I wrote this story first as a screenplay, but the first draft was about 240 pages—twice the ideal screenplay length. I cut it down to the ideal length but was dissatisfied with dropping so much strong material. So I decided to convert my original, too-long screenplay into this historical novel.

In recent years, many reality TV shows with Alaska venues have been highly popular, because Alaska is loaded with exciting true-life stories outside the realm of most people's experience. When people ask, "Who would be interested in the story of Alaska's first Russian governor, Aleksandr Baranov?" I point to the millions of viewers of these Alaska reality shows and to the millions of travelers who have taken cruises to Alaska as a positive indicator. The appetite of these viewers and travelers for Alaskan adventure will be well fed by the saga of Baranov and the Russians in Alaska, a story that is among the most engaging and unique of all real Alaskan adventures.

Baranov's reputation for ruthless brutality may have been deserved for a short time early in his administration, as shown in this story. Lashings had been routinely used to discipline tough and misbehaving Russian hunters, many of whom were burly ex-convicts who came to Alaska by way of Siberian prisons. But he found lashings were a disaster with Natives. In a letter excerpted in the Appendix, that he wrote to his boss in Russia, Grigori Shelikhof, he shows that he had begun to sympathize with his Native hunters. Later, in guidelines written to one of his managers, also in the Appendix, he specifically forbade corporal punishment of Natives. This was probably due to incidents of Native suicides, noted by historians. These resulted from the extreme humiliation to them of being whipped by a Russian.

The contrast between the depiction of Baranov by some as a ruthless tyrant allegedly responsible for the deaths of thousands of Natives and the reality of the man seen in Baranov's letters and the testimony of people who actually knew him (excerpted here in the Appendix) is striking. These documents describe a strong and intelligent man who was a capable problem-solver, who could be tough but who also had empathy for the people with whom he worked, especially the Natives. Again, the painting of Chief Katlian wearing the Allies of Russia Medal tells a story of Baranov the peacemaker, a story that is written largely between the lines of history. It is a story that deserves to be told, and also considered by Baranov's current critics. It is a story from which we have a lot to learn.

Some early readers of this book have even noted similarities between the Russian-Tlingit conflict and the current day Israeli-Palestinian conflict—except that Baranov's gift for empathy succeeded in achieving an acceptable accommodation with his Tlingit adversaries, which has so far eluded the Israelis and Palestinians.

A note about the depiction of various languages: The language of the protagonist, Baranov, and the people with whom he interacted the most was Russian. But other languages—Native Alaskan, German, and Spanish—are also spoken in this story. All of them are shown in English, but to distinguish the story's primary language of Russian from other languages, the others are represented here in italics.

A second linguistic factor regards the spelling of names and places when translated into English. There are a variety of spellings for even the name Baranov, which also appears on maps and in literature as Baranof or Baranoff. I chose Baranov because it appears most consistently in his many biographies. Chief Katlian's name has a half dozen spellings, including Kal'yaan and Kotleian. I chose Katlian because this is the spelling for one of the main streets in Sitka that is named after him, and so is likely to be more commonly recognized. Captain Becharof's name also has multiple spellings. I chose to spell his surname the same as the lake named after him, the second largest lake in Alaska.

There is a third linguistic factor I want to point out. When Natives are shown in this story speaking Russian as a new language, they speak with gaps in vocabulary and grammar, as one would expect with anyone learning a new language. But as time goes on, they become fully proficient and speak fluently. When speaking their own Native language, they are shown as fluent speakers using a language that is as capable as our own at facilitating sophisticated conversation—a fair assumption, in that their languages have been around for thousands of years.

Growing up in Alaska, I knew many people of indigenous ancestry, and they usually referred to themselves as "Native." Those I met from the far North called themselves "Eskimo" with pride. I knew a lot of these people and I never heard any of them refer to themselves as "Indigenous" or "Inuit" (used mostly in the Canadian Arctic), so I don't use those terms in this story. One commonly used term is the name of the Natives' large sea-going open boats: *"baidar."* I don't use that name here because it is too similar to *"bidarka"* (two-man kayak) for non-Alaskan readers to easily distinguish. So I use the alternate but perhaps less familiar Aleut/Unangan name for these boats, *"nigilax."*

This book is a historical novel, meaning that it mixes historical people and facts with fiction. Why? A chronological recitation of the facts, portraying only people who are known to have been involved in recorded history, often doesn't tell us enough about why things happened. What motivated these people? What were they thinking? Why did they think that way? How did their motivations and ways of thinking make them do what they did? The insights of good fiction offer answers, showing the motivations, thoughts, and spoken words of people in the river of history, based largely but not entirely on documented facts, to give history more meaning and to offer us a better understanding of the human condition in which we ourselves are actors. Good historical fiction does an effective job of helping us read between the lines of history in order to learn from it. So, let us keep in mind the Native American proverb, "This story may or may not have happened this way, but it is true."

Roger Seiler
Nyack, New York
January 6, 2016

Scale of Mile
Miles   0   100   200
Kilometers 0   200   40

Russia

Russian
Alas
1790 –

Bering Sea

Yukon Riv

Susitna R

Fort St. Nicholas

Kenai Bay

Lake Illiamna

Pribilov Islands

Bristol Bay

Becharof Lake

K
Thre

Unalaska Is.

Pacific Ocean

Map 1

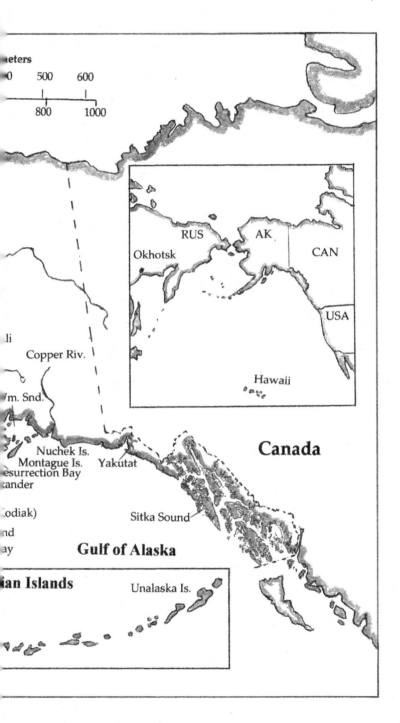

eters

0   500   600

800   1000

RUS   AK

Okhotsk   CAN

USA

Hawaii

li

Copper Riv.

m. Snd.

Nuchek Is.

Montague Is.   Yakutat

esurrection Bay

ander

odiak)

nd

ay

Sitka Sound

Canada

Gulf of Alaska

ian Islands   Unalaska Is.

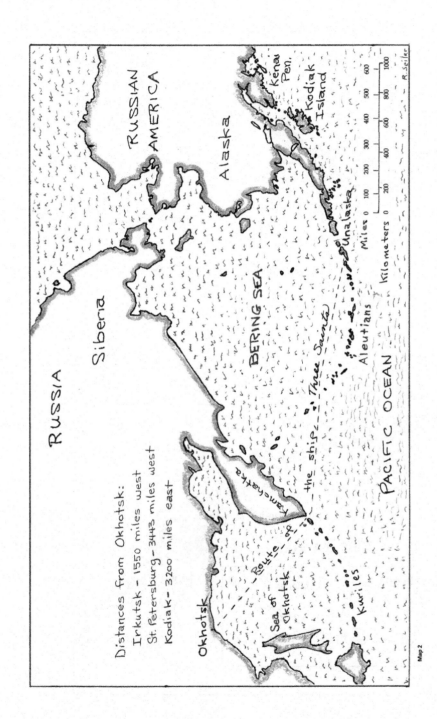

RUSSIA

Siberia

RUSSIAN AMERICA

Alaska

Kenai Pen.

Kodiak Island

Unalaska

Aleutians

BERING SEA

PACIFIC OCEAN

Kamchatka

the ship *Three Saints*

Route of

Sea of Okhotsk

Okhotsk

Kuriles

Distances from Okhotsk:
Irkutsk – 1550 miles west
St. Petersburg – 3443 miles west
Kodiak – 3200 miles east

Miles   0   100   200   300   400   500   600
Kilometers 0   200   400   600   800   1000

R. Seiler

Map 2

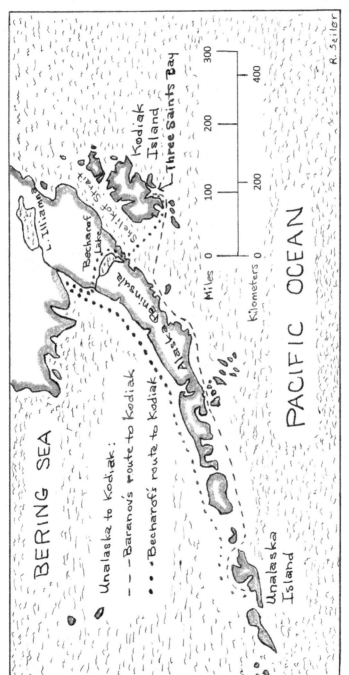

BERING SEA

Unalaska to Kodiak:
--- Baranov's route to Kodiak
•••• Becharof's route to Kodiak

L. Illiamna

Becharof Lake

Shelikof Strait

Kodiak Island

Three Saints Bay

Alaska Peninsula

Unalaska Island

PACIFIC OCEAN

Miles   0   100   200   300

Kilometers   0   200   200   400

R. Seiler

Map 3

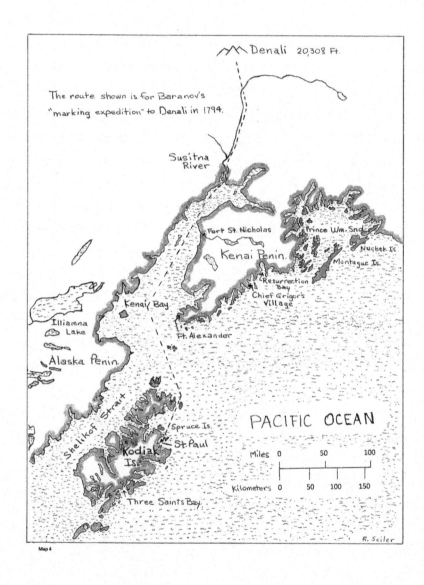

Denali 20,308 Ft.

The route shown is for Baranov's "marking expedition" to Denali in 1794.

Susitna River

Fort St. Nicholas

Prince Wm. Snd.

Kenai Penin.

Nuchek Is.

Montague Is.

Resurrection Bay

Chief Grigor's Village

Kenai Bay

Illiamna Lake

Alaska Penin.

Ft. Alexander

Shelikof Strait

Spruce Is.

St. Paul

Kodiak Is.

PACIFIC OCEAN

Miles 0   50   100

Kilometers 0   50   100   150

Three Saints Bay

R. Seiler

Map 4

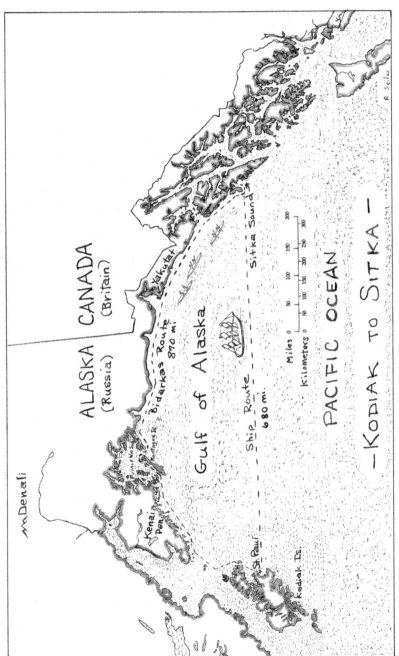

ALASKA (Russia) | CANADA (Britain)

Denali

Kenai Pen.

Montague

Bidarka's Route 870 mi.

Gulf of Alaska

Yakutat

Sitka Sound

Ship Route 680 mi.

St. Paul

Kodiak Is.

Miles 0   50   100   150   200

Kilometers 0   50   100   150   200   250   300

PACIFIC OCEAN

— KODIAK TO SITKA —

R. Seiler

Map 5

xix

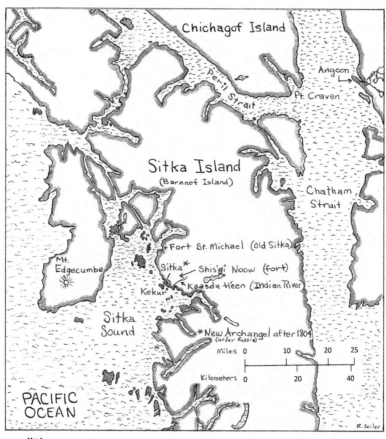

Map 6

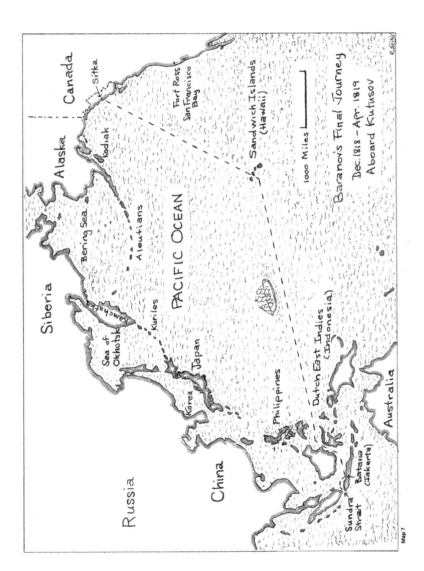

Canada

Sitka

Alaska

Siberia

Kodiak

Bering Sea

Aleutians

Kamchatka

Kuriles

Sea of Okhotsk

PACIFIC OCEAN

Fort Ross
San Francisco Bay

Sandwich Islands
(Hawaii)

1000 Miles

Baranov's Final Journey

Dec. 1818 – Apr. 1819
Aboard Kutusov

Korea

Japan

Philippines

Dutch East Indies
(Indonesia)

Australia

Russia

China

Sundra
Strait

Batavia
(Jakarta)

Map 7

C. Reiley

CHAPTER 1

FINDING UNALASKA

October 1790. . .

George Washington was President of the United States;
Catherine was Tsarina of Russia; and Aleksandr Andreievich
Baranov was sailing across the roaring Bering Sea near
Alaska's Aleutian Islands. (See Map 2, maps section.)

Baranov had never been at sea before, but that didn't scare him. He was accustomed to controlling fear with calculated reason. At age forty-three, with a short, wiry build, he exuded an impatient energy. Now he was headed across a fierce ocean to what he'd been told was a wild land of volcanoes, glaciers, giant bears, and savages. *No matter*, he thought. He would do whatever must be done. Entrusted with a mission for Catherine the Great and for mother Russia, in his strong and able hands he now held the chance to prove he was a greater man than his lowly rank of *mestchannin* in the merchant class. Even more, it was a chance to bring honor to his family back home and to rebuild his plundered wealth. He was sure all the challenges he'd faced for years had uniquely prepared him for this assignment.

Sailing east 3,200 miles from Okhotsk to Kodiak in the blustery fall of 1790, Baranov (Bare'ah·noff) sat at the map table below the ship's deck. He dipped his quill in ink and continued writing his first report to headquarters, despite the lurching shudders of the ship. In the din of the ocean pushed aside by the hull, he was surprised by a sound that should never be heard far out at sea. Listening intently in the early dawn, his mind's eye saw the ship he was riding, the dark green bow of the two-masted Russian galiot, christened *Three Saints*, pounding through waves in the gray fog of early dawn. Its square sails billowed, and its yellow bowsprit lunged eastward toward "Alaska," what the Aleutian Natives called the mainland of Russian America. But could he have just heard the sound of surf?

Then he remembered that the captain wanted to find an island, so he could send men ashore in search of fresh water. Nearly out of drinking water, they were each rationed just one quarter of a cup a day. Everyone was anxious. A few parched and spent sailors seemed about to go crazy. They had to find fresh water. Baranov realized that the ship was groping through thick Aleutian mists near some island, seeking a safe harbor.

Again, he heard the surf's warning growl, growing louder. He stuffed his report in a pocket, threw open a hatch, and burst up on deck into the fog to investigate. A gusty, wet wind slapped his clean-shaven face, and his sandy hair was blown about as he stuck his arms in the sleeves of a black rain jacket that whipped around him. His intense eyes, set in a rugged, triangular face, glowed with tough, pragmatic intelligence. The roaring surf was close, and he rushed to look over the side for rocks. He saw only swirling mist. The captain, Dmitry Becharof (Beh·share'off), spun the wheel hard to starboard to turn away.

"Becharof, where the hell *are* we?" Baranov yelled.

The captain shouted back, "Unalaska, Baranov. Unalaska Island!"

At that instant, the ship struck a fist of protruding rock with a deafening crash, and the port bow was thrust up toward the fog-gray sky. The bitter smell of loosened caulking filled the air, and the bow lurched farther into the granite teeth that tore through the hull. Baranov grabbed hold of the rigging as he saw men fall and slide across the deck, arms and legs flailing for a hold, amid the thunder of cracking timbers, shouted curses, shrill orders, and raging breakers washing over the sinking deck. Both masts broke and fell, dragging flapping sails and tangled lines with them. Baranov lunged toward a lifeboat tied near the stub of the main mast. With three sailors, he struggled to untie and launch it. One of its ropes got tangled in ship's rigging. He pulled out the hunting knife he always wore from a sheath on his belt and cut the line.

"Launch it, men! *Launch it!*" he shouted.

The splintering deck tilted steeply as a wave surged over it, sweeping him and the others over the side with the lifeboat. Flying through the air, he grabbed an oarlock of the little boat and his powerful arms pulled him into it as it dropped upright onto the sea. He fell on the planking with a bone-jarring thud, and two sailors rolled in on top of him. A sheet of cold salty spray soaked them through.

They all scrambled up, and Baranov pointed to bobbing heads and flailing arms in the foaming water. He barked, "On the oars! Get to those men! I'll pull 'em in."

Just as he said it, the wrecked ship broke in two with a shuddering crack that made his stomach lurch. Crashing waves tossed the lifeboat as he hooked his feet under the gunwale of the boat, reached into the surf, and pulled desperate men out of the water as quickly as he could. He threw a rope and shouted, "Grab the line!" to one floating by, who struggled toward him in the streaks of foam sweeping over angry waves. The man lunged for the rope as if for salvation itself, and Baranov pulled him in and hauled him aboard. He saw the terror in his eyes and in those of the others still in the water. Something inside Baranov said he must save them—must save them *all*. He pulled in another, and another. In just minutes, the lifeboat was full of men soaked to the skin by frigid water.

"Row to shore!" he ordered the sailors on the oars, and they instantly obeyed, making for the rugged nearby coast of the island. The surf helped propel them toward a gravel beach through a narrow channel between jagged jaws of rock.

The boat flew onto the beach and ground to a halt in the gravel. All the men climbed out—except Baranov. He called to the strongest, "You four stay here on oars! We're going back for the rest of them."

And so they went for two more trips. On the last, Baranov saw someone clinging to a broken beam—it was Becharof. "Captain!" Baranov called out in a voice growing hoarse as he threw him a rope. It missed. The captain caught it on the second try. Baranov pulled the exhausted man aboard just as a huge wave nearly capsized them and sent the lifeboat hurtling toward jutting rocks.

"Pull to starboard!" Baranov barked at the oarsmen.

But the surf, too strong, hurled the rowboat headlong into the rocks. With a loud crunch its hull was punctured by holes too big to plug with shirts and the men were thrown about in the boat as it spun around. Before they could react, the next wave pulled them off the rocks, and they fought the sea to row through the channel toward shore. But water came in through the holes faster than they could row. The lifeboat sank beneath them, and the icy surf seized them all. They were tossed and dragged toward the beach.

Out of the pounding waves, Baranov pulled himself onto the gravel shore where he heard the hollow clatter of small round stones rolling up and down the beach in cadence with the surf.

The battered, worn-out, gasping men crawled in torn clothes toward the crest of the beach. Ahead, a tan, earthen overhang formed a low wall covered by thick green moss spilling over it. The wall had been shaped for centuries by relentless tides that had undercut the layers of alluvial earth behind the beach that held back the sea. The men huddled for shelter under the overhang.

They included sailors and several *promyshleniki* (prom·eh·sh-len·ee'kee)—Russian frontiersmen. Most Russian colonists were these rough and ready men, many of them trappers and hunters who had made their living in the Siberian fur trade. Half were bearded, and all were tough and crude mannered, wearing the sturdy dark clothes of the backcountry. They were accustomed to privation on the edge of survival, and Baranov knew he could count on their hardiness to see them through the disaster.

That none of the fifty-four men onboard had been lost was a miracle. The fierce sea had coughed them up and spat them out in the shallows before any were drowned—but banged up, scraped, and nearly frozen they surely were. Their wounds oozed blood and were aflame with pain. In the thundering, rocky surf, the wreckage of the broken ship loomed like the bare bones of a washed-up whale ripped open by scavenging grizzlies. The waves pushed and pounded crates of cargo toward shore. *Disaster had struck so fast,* Baranov thought. One moment they were whole and the next wrecked. What a goddamned mess in a God-forsaken place.

"How the hell did this *happen,* captain?" he asked. "I heard you're the best navigator east of Okhotsk."

The older man's face was slack with exhaustion. Under bushy eyebrows and heavy lids, he gave Baranov a steely look. The captain's gaze fell to the ground as he muttered, "We weren't where I thought we were."

"Such treacherous waters," Baranov quickly observed. Better to be understanding of an able man who had just suffered defeat. He himself had been in that position more times than he wanted anyone to know. He turned and called out to the others, "Save the gear! Let's grab it!" He was responsible for this cargo, as the new chief manager of what would eventually be called the Russian American Company, and he wasn't about to forget it.

Baranov and others dragged crates out of the roaring surf onto the beach while the captain led another party on a search for fresh water on higher ground beyond the shore. To slake their long thirst, they looked for hollows on top of big outcrops where rainwater might have gathered. They found many small pools, thankfully, and everyone came to drink. Exhausted, many hopelessly discouraged, they returned to the mossy overhang.

"Come on, men!" Baranov urged as he started making a lean-to under the overhang with salvaged wood from the wreck.

Those who could helped. When the crude shelter had been thrown together, they all climbed in. Most fell asleep immediately—except Baranov, who was battling within himself to cling to hope, and thinking hard to find a way out of this mess. He had to. He was in charge.

He stared at the sea, contemplating his predicament and the savage winter that would soon be upon them.

It would serve no purpose to blame Becharof, he told himself. Charts of the Aleutians were notoriously inaccurate. The man had, after all, shown great seamanship just getting them as far as he had—2,600 miles east of Okhotsk—in what had become a worn-out vessel. Along the way, he had deftly navigated a tough passage from the Sea of Okhotsk into the North Pacific and then the Bering Sea. The two men didn't get along, but Baranov knew he would need Becharof's skills to somehow get them out of there and cover the remaining 600 miles to Kodiak. He would go easy on him.

Baranov's mind had long before been shaped into a problem-solving engine. By habit, he surrounded a problem with cold logic and a huge reserve of practical knowledge. He would consume the facts of a problem, its dimensions, and the resources at hand, digest them, and the solution would emerge. They were stranded on Unalaska Island without adequate clothes, food, and shelter. Surviving the coming winter would be an awesome challenge. But the more difficult a problem, the more it animated the mind of Baranov until he found the solution, which he always believed to be somewhere within his reach.

His mind wandered to another time and place as desolate as the Aleutian cove. Here, the desolation was physical. There, it had been spiritual. He thought of the May over a year before in the frontier town of Irkutsk (Ear'kootsk), Siberia. Spring had just begun to blossom in that northern place, and the flat ground with low shrubs had just lost its lingering residue of hard-caked ice patches.

He had walked to the transit station with his wife Matrona, his pretty, beloved ten-year-old daughter Afanassya, and two younger adopted children. They were all wearing open, fur-trimmed black wool coats and carrying bundles of belongings.

Matrona, forty then, had dark hair secured under a green scarf. About Baranov's height, she was tending toward a middle-aged, stocky build on her way to becoming a *babushka*. Matrona was a good-looking woman who could be quite jolly, especially with her women friends and children. But on that occasion, he recalled, she had been consumed with heartache, frustration, and worry about the 3,000 miles of overland travel back to their hometown.

"Matrona, I'll send money to you in Kargopol. You can be sure of that," he had said.

"I can be sure of nothing except that your eye and something else will wander, Aleksandr Andreievich," she answered.

". . . Sometimes I drink too much vodka."

"Irkutsk is too wild," she went on. "I can't spend every night waiting, worrying, wondering, and crying."

When they reached the wagon depot, a ramshackle cluster of buildings set apart from a wide corral of oxen with their great horned heads buried in hay that had been forked out for them, Baranov threw the family's bundles onto an ox wagon. He leaned over to hug and kiss the children goodbye.

"Appolonii, little angel, and Afanassya, God be with you."

Afanassya, with blonde curls framing her face, had pleaded, "Why aren't you coming with us, Papa? You must come, too. Please come!"

He remembered lifting each child onto the wagon. Then he and Matrona had stared at each other a moment; her eyes had teared up, the bitterness of their parting giving way to the realization that she might never see him again. She leaned forward and kissed him on one cheek. He kissed her too and helped her up.

"After Peter and I make our fortune at Anadyr in the fur trade, I'll come home to you in Kargopol," he told Matrona.

Turning to the children, he had sighed, "Goodbye, my darlings! Do as your mother says."

The wagon pulled away, leaving him standing alone.

The crash of a rolling wave yanked Baranov's mind back to the Aleutian cove. The sky was still a muddy gray and strewn with strands of low-lying fog. He stared at frothing stretches of black and white sea agitating dark green seaweed. Just what had brought him to this hostile place that sought to devour him and his men?

He reached in his pocket again, pulled out a small, flat ebony box, and opened it. His eyes fell on the glistening rectangular brass medal inside that bore the emblem of his sovereign—a double-headed eagle, one head facing left, the other right—that bound him to his empress, Tsarina Catherine the Great. He remembered the honor he had felt when they chose him to carry this hallowed symbol of Russia and the greatness of its empire to their part of the new world.

Two months before, in August 1790, he had been walking along the wharves of the Siberian port of Okhotsk (Oak'hotsk) to what would become a decisive meeting. Due to the summer heat, he had worn just a tan smock and trousers tucked into his high leather boots. He had hoped to find work in a shipyard at the end of the line of dockside warehouses and had been staring at the ground ahead of him as he plodded, absorbed in worry over his overwhelming debts.

Suddenly, a church bell chimed three doublets so loud that he looked up toward the source. He saw that the harbor church was just on the other side of a warehouse. On the outer wall of the warehouse, he saw a large Cyrillic sign: *Shelikhov Company.* He stopped, remembering that, a few days before, a friend had told him he'd heard that Shelikhov had a job for him, and that he should see the man as soon as possible. But Baranov didn't like Shelikhov, whom he knew from Irkutsk—he thought his business dealings too unreliable. Curiosity got the better of him, though, and he turned toward the wide cargo door of the warehouse that was yawning open, the mystery of its dark interior beckoning.

He entered the warehouse and strode past piles of boxes and barrels of supplies marked to be sent to Kodiak, and musk-smelling stacks of seal and otter pelts from Alaska. In back, he found an office door and stopped a moment to look at it. It was made of heavy, well worn oak. But its rich blonde color and heavy grain, finely carved with figures of seals, otters, and foxes, expressed an importance that seemed out of place in a warehouse.

Facing this door, he had wondered, *What does Shelikhov have in mind for me?* Baranov knocked on the door, opened it, and looked in. The tall, slender military commander of Okhotsk

District, Ivan Gavrilovich Koch, and the portly businessman Grigori Ivanovick Shelikhov, were standing side by side at the far end of a deep, narrow room. They were talking above a map of Alaska draped over a table. Behind them, a large window with nine panes overlooked the harbor and its bustle with its forest of masts. As was the custom, the men addressed each other initially by their first name and patronymic middle name based on one's father's name.

"Commander Ivan Gavrilovich! My old friend!" Baranov declared.

"Come in, Aleksandr Andreievich! You know Grigori Ivanovich from Irkutsk."

Baranov nodded and shook hands with both men.

"Have a seat," said Shelikhov, and the three sat around the table. *Shelikhov must be doing well*, Baranov thought then, because he had certainly been eating well— must have gained twenty pounds since Irkutsk.

Koch explained to Shelikhov, "Four months ago, I've heard, Baranov's entire stock of furs—sables—was stolen from his Anadyr trading post." He turned to Baranov and used his nickname. "Right, Sasha? So now I think he needs a job to pay his debts. And you need a new manager at Kodiak to replace Delarov."

Shelikhov already knew Baranov's story, and he nodded quickly. His otter-like face, plump, dark, with Kirghiz eyes and ears pressed tightly against his head, was half in shadow. "Look at this, Aleksandr Andreievich," he said rapidly as he handed a pelt to Baranov. "From Russian America. The Natives call the place 'Alaska.' Have you ever felt a fur so exquisite?"

Baranov handled the pelt, stroking it knowingly with his fingertips. "Otter. Exquisite indeed!"

Shelikhov continued, "There's a huge fortune to be made selling otter and seal furs in China. You're a smart manager, Aleksandr Andreievich—I saw your work in Irkutsk. I offered this job to you then, and you turned me down. But now, maybe you'll see things differently. Manage our fur company in Russian America, this Alaska, for five years, and you'll be well paid."

Baranov remembered staring at the man. Both were smart, energetic businessmen, so it would seem they were kindred spirits. But Baranov distrusted Shelikhov from prior dealings. As desperate as he was for a good-paying job, he had lingering doubts, so he said, "Tell me about your colony."

Shelikhov pointed a plump index finger at Kodiak Island on the map. "We built a village here, with some outlying forts for trading, to get the fur business started. Three hundred men on Kodiak, mostly otter hunters. But there's no Russian navy there to protect us from the British, who are also in the area. So Tsarina Catherine, instead of making official ownership claims that would provoke them, has companies like us building settlements there unofficially."

He handed Baranov a pine box with several rectangular copper plates embossed with the imperial seal—a two-headed eagle. Below the seal was the declaration *Property of Empire of Russia.*

Baranov examined the plates, his brow furrowed with interest.

Shelikhov continued, "And with these, we quietly stake Russia's claims to the colony. We bury them at scattered locations, and we give them to Native chiefs to announce their inclusion in the Russian empire. All this to outfox the damn British, who'd like to take the place away from us and add it to Canada. They've already taken a big chunk of coastline to the south. Hopefully, we can keep them satisfied with that."

As Baranov handled a six-by-eight-inch copper plate, he shook his head and commented, "Amazing. No navy, no troops, just copper plates for protection."

"It's sovereignty, Baranov, *sovereignty*. That's what it's all about. The basis of all colonization is sovereignty, based on divine right from a monarch and the monarch's power to back it up. That power can be in ships and guns, or in cleverness. We don't have a lot of ships or a lot of guns over there, but under the circumstances we have enough power if we are clever."

"... Sovereignty?"

"That's right. We have it, and the Natives don't. But the British have it because they have a monarch. The Americans have it because they *had* a monarch, from whom they took *their* sovereignty. So it's our sovereignty against other sovereign nations, especially Britain, and against the Natives' lack of sovereignty. That's what those copper plates are all about. It's what all wars are about—whose sovereignty rules. Think about it, Baranov, and you'll figure it out."

A bit puzzling, but he would think about it more later. "How do you run the business over there?" he asked.

Shelikhov shrugged, and an uncharacteristic silence fell, during which the third man, Koch, opened his snuff box with a muted click and took some.

"Natives do most of the fur hunting for us," Shelikhov said at last, with a faint, unintended note of apology in his voice that Baranov sensed rather than heard. "They're much better hunting otters in the sea than Russians. Tsarina Catherine made the Natives citizens of Russia and wants them treated well. But Her Majesty also wants us to make a profit, because she owns part of our company. So we do what we have to with the Natives to make a profit, because that's why we're there."

Baranov considered his other options. There weren't any, aside from some low-paying job at the shipyard.

"Take this job, Baranov, make a success of our colony, and you'll earn ten shares in the company. Enough so you'll never have to worry about money again."

Baranov gazed long and hard at the otter fur, stroking its thick, brown softness.

"I've got debts to pay, and a wife and three children to support in Kargopol," he said. "I need an advance to pay debts and to send money to my family. And you must continue to send my family money from my earnings."

Shelikhov leaned toward him, staring intently. "All right, but under one condition: Make our part of Russian America profitable! If you don't, we'll take the money we've sent to your family out of your hide."

"Agreed. I'll take the job. But I leave in five years—or sooner, if I'm cheated!"

"You won't be cheated, Aleksandr Andreievich. We'll send you over on our supply ship next week. In just five years, you'll be out of debt and back home with your family."

They shook hands, Shelikhov delighted that he had snared an able man to take charge of his operations in Alaska, Baranov resigned and uneasy in his distrust of Shelikhov but confident in his own capabilities.

———

Baranov had been halfway to the door when his new employer again spoke. "One more thing." He'd picked up a small ebony box from his desk, strode over, and handed it to him. "Go ahead, open it. It's yours."

Inside, gleaming in a shaft of sunlight that fell at a sharp angle across the room, Baranov found a brass medal engraved with the same emblem as the copper plates, but much more finely rendered.

"Your commission," Shelikhov had said dryly as Baranov stared at it. "Keep it with you always as a reminder that you represent Her Majesty Tsarina Catherine—and our company—and that you must always carry forward the best interests of her empire in our New World colonies. That means *outsmart the British!* Keep them from grabbing Alaska. Her Majesty is depending on you, Aleksandr Andreievich, and so are we. Good luck.

"Oh, and one last thing, Baranov. We're bringing God to the Natives. We've done lay baptisms for hundreds of them. But no priest and no church is over there yet."

"Well, I'm no priest. With no priest and no church, what makes you think God even knows or cares where Russian America is?"

Shelikhov shrugged, wishing he hadn't brought up the subject. He hadn't wanted to give Baranov any excuse to back out.

As Baranov left Shelikhov's office, at that very moment, the church bell next door had chimed again. . . just once.

Huddled with the other shipwreck survivors in their lean-to on the Aleutian seaside cove, Baranov finally fell asleep, the ebony box back in his pocket.

Early the next morning, a stick slid through a crack in the lean-to and poked Baranov in the ribs. He looked up through the crack into the angular, stoic face of an Aleut hunter and whispered loudly, "Becharof! Kuskov! Natives are here. Keep still. Keep quiet."

CHAPTER 2
THE ALEUTS

Baranov kept a wary eye on the round, beardless faces of the Natives standing on the beach—six Aleut (Al'ee·oot) men holding seal hunting spears. He knew "Aleut" was the Russian name for them, though they called themselves "Unangan." They were dressed in the tan, loose-fitting Native *kamleika*, foul-weather gear made of tightly sewn seal gut. Their jacket hoods were folded back, and their black hair stuck down flat on their heads even as the wind blew. Other Aleuts stood behind, above the mossy bank, silhouetted by the dismal, dark-gray sky. They seemed wary, but not threatening—certainly not the savages some sailors had told him to expect. Baranov crawled out of the lean-to as the Aleut hunters stared at him impassively.

"You speak Russian?" he asked.

No response. They just stared at him.

"Lost our ship," Baranov continued as he pointed to the wreck. "We go to Kodiak. Kodiak?" (Koe'dee·ack.)

"Kodiak," replied the first Aleut, expressionless.

"Yes, Kodiak!" Baranov exclaimed, glad that there was now a glimmer of communication.

The first Aleut turned and pointed toward the northeast, repeated, *"Kodiak,"* and turned slightly bow-legged toward his beached *nigilax*. It was a large, tan open boat made of walrus skin stretched over a wood or whalebone frame that could carry about 20 people. Mostly propelled by paddling, some *nigilaxes* also had a sail for longer trips. It was called an *umiak* by the Eskimos to the north. The Aleut soon returned with sticks of smoked salmon, which he called *yukola* (yoo'koe·la), and a sealskin bag with fresh water to share.

Baranov looked into this Aleut's calm, youthful brown eyes that seemed to have a permanent squint to protect against sea glare, then pointed to himself and said, "Baranov. Baranov."

The Aleut stood ramrod straight, pointing to himself in turn, and said, "Kuponek. Kuponek." (Koo·pon'eck.) He laid the stress on the second syllable. He was of an athletic build and a shade under five and a half feet tall, about Baranov's height. However, Kuponek's erect posture made him seem taller and gave him an air of confident authority.

Baranov smiled eagerly and thrust his hand to take Kuponek's. They shook hands awkwardly, as Kuponek seemed unsure about this white man's custom. Baranov's enthusiastic friendliness seemed to make him accept it, but with a blank face.

Captain Becharof crawled out of the lean-to and stood next to Baranov. Eyeing the Natives, he told Baranov, "We're lucky. The right Aleuts found us, from a controlled village."

"Controlled?"

"Controlled, because we probably hold the chief's children hostage in Kodiak."

Surprised, Baranov said, "We hold *hostages*?"

"Yes. Here's how we run things: Guns rule. We have all the guns. And by taking Native hostages, just a few hundred of us can rule thousands of Natives. They'll take good care of us."

Kuponek set down his bundle of *yukola* sticks and the bag of water on a flat rock near the lean-to. All of the Russians crawled out, grabbed the salmon, and guzzled the water. They sat on nearby rocks as they eagerly chewed off chunks of savory fish meat, a welcome breakfast.

The Aleuts put down their spears, sat across from the Russians, and stared at them in silence. As the Russians finished eating, they stared back.

Kuponek spoke to the Natives in their guttural tongue, something short and decisive. The others seemed to reply in agreement as they got up, picked up their spears, and headed for their *nigilaxes*. Kuponek turned to Baranov and spoke words sounding like soft, guttural clicking and clacking. He pointed to the Russians and to his group's *nigilaxes*, suggesting that the Russians should get in these 20-man open boats to go with the Aleuts.

The shipwrecked had no choice. Everyone crammed into the vessels with some of the salvaged gear.

The cloud cover became a high overcast as they swiftly rode the sea offshore by the strong paddling of the Aleuts. To the north, Baranov could see a tall cone-shaped volcano rising from the seacoast up to what looked to him to be about 5,000 feet. Its summit was covered with snow and ice, and it appeared as if some prior eruption had blown off the top of it, giving it a flat-topped silhouette. Some steam could be seen rising from vents far up its conical sides. He tapped Kuponek on the shoulder, pointed to the mountain, and Kuponek said, *"Aigagin."*

There was barely a tree anywhere, just mossy light green tundra with low bushes here and there, and large patches of snow up the sides of the volcano.

It was nearly midday under a brighter gray sky when the *nigilaxes* rounded a coastal promontory and headed into a cove with a village nestled in its protective recess. As the vessels landed on shore by other beached craft, several Aleut men came toward them from the village.

Kuponek loudly announced, *"Rooska! Rooska! Umiakpak piyaqquqtuq."* The news that they were shipwrecked Russians was met with little enthusiasm. Baranov met the village *toyon* Putuguq (Poo'tu·guck), the chief called "Big Toe," who nodded a greeting with cold but polite formality.

The Russians had crashed their way onto Unalaska Island, 600 miles southwest of Kodiak, their destination. It was obvious to Baranov that with winter storms soon upon them, they would be stuck there for some time. He wondered, *How will we survive?* He had over four dozen men to be housed and fed. Would the *toyon* cooperate? But considering the beat-up condition of his men, there was no choice but to assume the best—and no time to lose in getting them housed.

His always-inquisitive eyes scanned the treeless terrain. He could see for miles across the mossy tundra to barren granite mountains rising from the sea on the other side of the cove. About ten miles distant, against the high gray overcast, he saw the steaming, snow-capped volcano Aigagin, mostly asleep, with long patches of snow streaming down its shanks. Out to sea was the familiar dark gray water, constantly in motion, constantly a threat. Below the sky, there were just three colors here: dark gray, white, and olive green, carelessly spattered about everywhere on a landscape dominated by mossy green tundra.

He walked with the *toyon* and Kuponek into the small village of earthen huts called *barabaras* (baa'ra· baa'ras). Aleuts poked their round, curious faces out of the squat huts to stare at the strange newcomers. Clearly, there was no housing to spare. Toyon Putuguq spoke to Kuponek, pointing to an area a couple of hundred yards away. Baranov understood from their hand motions that the area could be used to build *barabaras* for the Russians. Now he just had to figure out *how* to build them. Kuponek indicated that he and other village men would help, and he left Baranov, to get something or someone.

It was both. In a few minutes, Kuponek returned with two Russian shovels bought in trade, and two of the Natives who had been part of the rescue party. Immediately, Kuponek and one of his tribe started vigorously digging out a ten-by-ten-foot rectangular shape in the green mossy tundra that would form the below-surface part of a *barabara*.

With hand motions, Baranov beckoned to several of his more able men to come over, watch, and learn.

After the outline was made and a hole dug to a depth of six inches into sandy soil below the top layer of spongy moss, Kuponek handed his shovel to the third Native, who dug down another six inches. Kuponek took the shovel from the second Native and handed it to Baranov, looking him in the eye with a sort of challenge, a look that said, "Now show us what you can do, white man." Baranov smiled, eagerly took the shovel, and began digging faster than the Natives. He liked the fresh, musky smell of the uncovered earth and glanced up at Kuponek, expecting an expression of approval, but there was none—just a stony face waiting to see an outcome. Then Baranov's energetic digging ran into a rock that upset his rhythm for a moment. He grabbed the foot-long rock, lifted it and heaved it away. Back to digging, he kept at it until he reached a depth of three feet.

Kuponek motioned to stop and signaled to Baranov to follow him. They walked to a brush thicket where Kuponek began cutting branches about five feet long. As soon as Baranov realized what he was doing, he took out his hunting knife and began cutting branches also. When they had a pile of branches about waist high, they carried it to the building site.

Kuponek dug a smaller round hole in the tundra, near the first one, and he and one of the other Natives brought over a sealskin vessel and poured water into it. With a long, thick stick, the third Native began stirring the water into the earth to make a thick mud. Kuponek stuffed the branches he and Baranov had cut into this slurry, plying them back and forth until they were thickly coated. He stuck the thickest branches into the ground around the rim of the *barabara* hole, overlapping and roughly weaving them, arching them over the base until he had formed a roof. More mud was caked over the sides, and an opening was left in the center of the roof, both for campfire smoke to escape and to serve as a doorway accessed by a ladder inside.

After the *barabara* was completed, it had to be furnished. The three Natives hauled over rocks and a few prized whalebones and set them around the interior perimeter to serve as rudimentary seats and tables. The whole procedure had taken less than five hours.

Baranov nodded to indicate that he and his men now knew how it was done.

———

"All right, men," Baranov said to the Russians. "Let's get started making our Aleutian castles."

In the cold fall weather, there was no time to lose. Some Natives helped the Russians begin to build their *barabaras* and gave them small helpings of food—dried berries and fish. Baranov eagerly involved himself in building more *barabaras*, leading the Russians after Kuponek and the other Natives left for a tribal meeting.

Kuponek stepped into Toyon Putuguq's *barabara*, where the village men had gathered and solemnly sat around the central fire. Kuponek listened to Putuguq and the others speak in Aleut while all stared into the sacred flames. *"Not enough food to feed ourselves and Russians, too. Before long, they will fight us for our food supply."*

Kuponek said, *"We must hunt more seals to feed them."*

Putuguq answered, *"Storms coming fast. In storms, we will not be able to kill enough seals."*

Another man, sitting next to Kuponek, spoke up. *"Then we must kill Russians before they kill us for our food. They have no hostages from us, so we can do it. We must kill them while they sleep."*

"No," objected Kuponek. *"With just a short break in the weather, we can hunt enough seals. Maybe the Russians will help."*

Another man replied, *"They are too weak! If we wait until the Russians regain strength, we will not be able to kill them. We must kill them tonight."*

"If we kill them, Russians from Kodiak will come and kill us," said Kuponek.

"We will drop their bodies near the wreck, so it will look like they died there."

Putuguq held his hand up for a moment, then said, *"Go. I will consult the sacred fire for an answer. Then I will tell you what we will do."*

Kuponek and the others got up and left, leaving Putuguq still seated, contemplating the fire.

A few of the Russians were building *barabaras;* the others, recovering from their injuries, were huddled under sealskin blankets, resting. Kuponek sat on a rock and watched the builders.

He was fascinated by Baranov, whose eyes never seemed to rest, examining everything. Just from his manner, it was obvious to the Native that Baranov must be the *toyon* of the Russians. Kuponek noticed that Baranov never sat still if something needed to be done. He seemed smart as a fox and tough as a bear. Yet though he was the Russian *toyon,* Kuponek saw that Baranov worked harder than any of the rest. He'd never seen a *toyon* do that. It would be too bad if he would have to kill him, but Kuponek knew that if Toyon Putuguq decided to kill the Russians, Baranov would have to be the first to die.

Kuponek got up and went to his parents' *barabara,* where he still lived. At twenty-two, he would soon have to choose a wife, make his own *barabara,* and start to raise a family. Some villagers thought he was already late in this. But he didn't feel ready. He was restless in a way that made him just want to hunt or do. . . something else—he knew not what. When he was out on the sea, whatever was beyond the next cove, or over the next horizon, somehow called out to him. He needed to see more.

Baranov knew that feeding the Russians would stretch the village's food supply. This would be a great problem for Toyon Putuguq, a problem Baranov knew he had to solve.

As he moved gear into his *barabara*, a box in the pile caught his eye. Could it be what he thought? He opened it. It was the box of copper plates. He removed one from the box, went out, and called, "Kuponek, Kuponek!"

The Native emerged from his parents' *barabara* and came to him.

"I will give this to Toyon Putuguq," Baranov said in Russian, pointing to the plate, then himself, and then to Putuguq's *barabara*. Kuponek seemed to figure it out and accompanied him. At the door to the *toyon*'s barabara, Kuponek motioned for the Russian to wait outside, and he went in.

After a few moments, Kuponek reemerged through the rooftop doorway and invited Baranov in. So, he climbed up the slanted exterior wall of the *barabara* and then entered it via the roof door and its ladder. Putuguq was still seated where he had been contemplating the sacred fire and the Russians' fate. He looked up expressionlessly at the white chief.

Baranov entered holding the copper plate out toward him. He explained in Russian what it meant, with hand gestures and jabs of sign language, and gave it to him. Putuguq took the plate and examined it closely. Copper was very valuable to Natives, and from the inscribed emblem of the double-headed eagle, he could see that it came from a great power. As his expression turned respectful, Baranov got the impression that the chief saw the plate as some kind of sign about a decision he must make.

On the wall of the *barabara* hung a seal-hunting spear, and on the floor below it a sealskin blanket. Baranov pointed to the spear, to the sealskin, and to himself as he spoke. "I will hunt seals to feed the Russians. We must not take your food. Kuponek can teach me to hunt by your ways, and I will get the food we need."

With a lot more hand gesturing, he made himself understood. Then Toyon Putuguq pointed to Kuponek, the spear, Baranov, and the sealskin, speaking in the Aleut language that Baranov did not yet understand: *"Yes. Kuponek will teach you to hunt seal. You feed the Russians. Then we will not have to kill you."*

Putuguq and Kuponek grinned broadly, and Baranov saw that his proposal had been understood and accepted.

"Good!" he said, nodding enthusiastically.

***

Over 1,200 miles east of where Baranov had landed on Unalaska lay a thick chain of long, narrow islands pressed together against the lower mainland of Russian America. (See Map 1 then Map 6.) These mountainous islands, heavily wooded with dark green firs and Sitka spruce, with massive white and blue glaciers pushing through many mountain valleys and dumping ice in the sea, were the domain of the fierce Tlingit (Klink'it) Indians. One of their villages was Angoon, on what the English called Chatham Straight on the west side of Admiralty Island.

Here lived a young Tlingit named Katlian (Cat'lee·aan), who was seventeen. He was a strong hunter of medium height. Under a shock of thick black hair, he had a square, dark face with big, intense eyes set under thick, angular eyebrows. A long nose, thin and straight, thrust over firmly set lips with a slightly protruding chin. He spoke in a medium pitch, but always with the clarity and strength of a man who had thought things through and made up his mind. Katlian was a member of his mother's Xutsnoowú Kwáan, her clan.

Her older brother Deiyik (Day'yik) had raised Katlian with a skilled, wise, and stern hand. It was the custom among the Tlingits that one of the mother's brothers had the primary training responsibility for a growing boy. This was because the brother was of the same clan as the child in that matrilineal society, where the family descended from the mother's line. It was the brother who would guarantee the continuity of the mother's clan customs and unique spirit. Deiyik had seen to it that Katlian was tough and worldly—an excellent hunter, skilled in combat, and a persuasive leader.

"You must be the best in all things," Deiyik had sternly told Katlian again and again. *"And you must be fearless."* Now, as Katlian was about to leave their village to embark on his new life, Deiyik recalled the long trail over which he had led the boy.

When Katlian was just six, Deiyik had taken the boy through the spruce forest to a pond that was a good walk southeast of Angoon, to teach him to swim. Swimming would be the first rigor the boy must master. Initially Deiyik just played with young Katlian in the water, to get him used to being in it. It was a shallow pond, warm in the summer and perfect for learning to swim. He knew that though he himself was not a good swimmer, he could teach it. Gradually, he pushed the boy to swim farther and farther until finally he could cross the pond. He made the boy swim in an ocean bay to get used to cold water. In a canoe in calm weather, he took Katlian a hundred yards from shore and made him swim to shore. Then two hundred yards. Then three. Then in a storm and rough seas. Katlian liked it. He relished challenges.

"Why don't you swim with me, Uncle Deiyik?" Katlian asked his mentor.

"I would hold you back. You must do many things I can't do. But I can show you the way. Then you can go where I can't go, where only you can go. For it is you, and those you will lead, who must save our people and our land from the white invaders."

Deiyik had seen in Katlian a bright boy of great promise. And he saw to it that, through swimming and running and lifting logs, Katlian developed an athletic physique as he grew. Further, he had put the boy through mental training to make him quick of mind. Deiyik constantly asked questions about their surroundings to push the boy's powers of observation. Then he had made Katlian answer questions quickly about how to deal with sudden dangers in the wilds or in battle. And there was marksmanship with bow and arrow, wilderness navigation, and wrestling. Finally, there was leadership.

As mentor uncle, Deiyik trained Katlian to be cool under stress and impervious to pain. But as with swimming, the boy was always given greater challenges by degrees. Deiyik also had gradually disciplined the boy's emotions so he would never weaken or soften amid the horrors of battle. Deiyik was proud that, at seventeen, Katlian had grown into the most formidable Tlingit warrior of his clan, with the knife-edged mind of a compelling leader.

One day Katlian asked a question that made Deiyik realize that he had overlooked an important part of the boy's education. They were sitting next to their training pond at the edge of the Angoon forest with wind gusts whistling through the towering firs.

"Why do we have moieties?" the boy had asked.

What a basic question about the most essential element of Tlingit society, thought Deiyik. He had concentrated so much on building the boy's supremacy as a warrior that he had forgotten to teach him about the complex structure of Tlingit society. He had work to do. But he must not shake the boy's self-confidence by saying anything that implied Katlian was lacking important knowledge.

"Our people use moieties to build alliances between tribes and keep the peace between them," said Deiyik.

"How does this work?" asked Katlian.

"The Tlingit people are divided into two moieties—the Ravens and the Eagles—and each moiety is a collection of many clans. But you know that already."

"Yes, but how does that build alliances and peace between the clans?"

"Our rule is that every man who marries must marry a woman in a clan from the opposite moiety. Then he must go to live with that woman and her family, because with us, the line of a family follows the line of its mothers. This way, every village has men from many clans, so that any village is not likely to make war against any other village that also has men from the same mix of clans. Also, a woman is protected because she always lives near her own clan."

"So when I marry, I will have to leave Angoon?"

"Yes. It is your father's job to find you a wife, and he will probably look in Sitka, because he came from there and knows those people."

"Sitka," mused Katlian.

Katlian's father made arrangements and indeed sent him to a village on Sitka, a large neighboring island (Map 6), to marry the daughter of his female cousin there. In this way, Katlian would be eligible to inherit from his great-grandmother's wealthy family in Sitka.

He arrived by kayak in the bay leading to the main Sitka village, *Noow Tlien* ("Big Fort"). Most of the village was built in a fort atop a rock outcropping, a *kekur*, in Sitka Sound near the shore. The sixty-foot height of the *kekur*, flat on top and surrounded by water, made it easy to defend from attack.

In front of the *kekur* in the Sound, Katlian saw several clusters of small islands holding up clumps of spruce trees. And beyond them, looking west across the Sound, he saw the dormant volcano reaching for the sky, L'uz (known by Whites as Mount Edgecumbe). Studying the land behind the *kekur*, he saw yellow and orange fall colors beginning to spread through seaside brush. Behind the shore stood green hills covered with dense stands of Sitka spruce, and behind them rose a range of mountains with steep, spruce-covered slopes topped by barren granite peaks covered with patches of snow.

However, the family of Katlian's prospective wife lived not on the *kekur* in the bay but in an extension of the village on the flatter shore lands nearby.

His paddle lightly splashed the calm water as he headed for shore. Katlian brought with him the payment from his mother's clan to be given to his bride's family. After he was accepted by the bride's father, the wedding would be planned, and his family would come for the event. But first he had to face the prospective bride's father alone, one on one, for that acceptance.

It had been three years since Katlian had been to Sitka on a visit, and he now came as one coming to claim his birthright. Katlian believed that all good things were rightfully his, insofar as he was surely the greatest hunter and warrior of his clan.

Laying his eyes on K'asasee for the first time, he was pleased to see the great beauty of her round face with warm brown eyes and smooth skin. Her beauty was enhanced by a flat disk carved from whalebone, called a labret, inserted in a slit in her lower lip and protruding forward. This labret was indeed a sign of high family status and wealth.

But there was a problem. Due to a misunderstanding in inter-clan mating negotiations, another young buck, Naawan, from a northern clan, had arrived at the same time for the same purpose—to marry her.

The two muscular young men were called before the clan chieftain and father of K'asasee, Aakashook.

"Only one of you can marry K'asasee, so I must give you both a test to decide which one. Go out and hunt a brown bear before they den. Whoever brings back the largest bear skin will win K'asasee. Now go."

***

At Unalaska, Baranov wanted to learn the Native way of hunting seals immediately and asked this of Kuponek, using impromptu sign language to communicate. Kuponek agreed and they got in a two-cockpit kayak, a *bidarka,* with Baranov sitting in the front cockpit. As they took off, he clumsily worked at paddling with the same rhythm as Kuponek. They went out into the heavy surf under a cold gray sky, with wisps of fog rolling in. Kuponek steered them out about a quarter of a mile from the rocky shore, and then followed a course paralleling the shoreline, heading toward the extinct, snow-streaked volcano in the distance.

They passed two small inlets and a barren rocky promontory. Baranov saw a pile of rocks poking up out of the sea. As they approached, he heard the din of barking seals and saw dozens lying on the rocks. Kuponek motioned to Baranov that they must each turn around in their cockpits so that Kuponek would have the front hunter's seat as they turned the *bidarka* around. Clumsily, Baranov almost flipped the vessel as he reversed position. Some seals saw the craft approaching and slid into the sea. Kuponek paddled forward slowly and quietly, Baranov's eyes riveted on him. Kuponek motioned toward three seals on the nearest rock, about thirty feet away. Baranov saw them and nodded.

They approached stealthily, and just as the seals started to slide into the water, Kuponek launched his spear and snagged one. They pulled the thrashing animal alongside the *bidarka* by the gut line connected to the spear, and Kuponek slit its throat with his knife and pulled the carcass aboard. The happy hunters turned back toward the village, Baranov remaining rear man in the *bidarka.*

The next day, the weather held, and they went hunting again. Baranov made his first kill. He was sure Kuponek was pleased that he was a fast learner. This was going to work.

***

Katlian, high on a Sitka mountain ridge, broke out of the spruce. He was on a grassy slope above the tree line. Spear in hand, bow over his shoulder, he moved parallel to the tree line. He closely examined the ground signs of his prey. It didn't take long. He soon found bear prints crossing a muddy patch—but they didn't look big enough. He kept looking.

Nearly a mile away, on the brow of the same mountain, Naawan was also intently searching for a bear. But he was still in the woods below the tree line.

Two hundred yards behind Naawan, a big brown nose sniffed the man's footprints and began to follow.

***

Baranov and Kuponek began teaching their languages to each other. As they paddled along, Baranov pointed to a mountain rising up from the shore.

"Mountain."

Kuponek replied, "Muntin," followed by the Aleut word for it: "*Iebbiq.*"

Baranov picked it up: "*Eebiq.* Mountain." Then he pointed to the sea and said, "Ocean."

Kuponek responded: "Ochen." Then in Aleut, "*Tabuiq.*"

"*Tabik.* Ocean."

***

Naawan heard a twig snap behind him. He turned to see the brown beast charging uphill. The young hunter held his ground and aimed his spear. The bear stopped about fifteen feet from him and then started walking around Naawan in a circle, eyeing him warily. Naawan slowly set down his spear and grabbed his bow, loading an arrow and taking aim just behind the bear's massive shoulder for the heart. He let the arrow fly.

He was only slightly off. The arrow bore into the bear's shoulder and was stopped by heavy bone. The bear immediately erupted in rage, swatting at the arrow in his shoulder and bounding toward the young man as Naawan launched his spear. It grazed the bear's chin as it plowed into the animal's upper chest, but the bear kept coming and, with a roar, jumped on top of him. Under the enormous pain of the bear biting and tearing his shoulder, he let out a terrified scream.

Katlian heard both the roar and the scream. He knew immediately what was happening and ran toward the noise, leaping over hillocks and jumping from boulder to boulder. He soon reached the scene. The bear was down on its haunches, still ripping Naawan apart. Katlian loaded an arrow and yelled at the bear. The beast immediately turned and rose up eight feet on his hind legs, the broken spear still hanging from its chest. Katlian aimed for the heart, let the arrow fly, and reached for a second arrow as the first slammed into the bear's chest exactly on target.

The bear let out a pained growl and fell over on its side. Katlian again took rapid aim, now at the bear's neck, and released his second arrow. It severed the animal's spinal cord just below the skull, and the bear died instantly. He cocked a third arrow and aimed it warily at the bear as he slowly walked toward it, looked at it a moment, then kicked its head. There was no response. He laid down his bow, pulled out his hunting knife, just in case, and looked at Naawan. His face became stiff with determination not to be overcome by what he saw. The bear had crushed the man's head with its jaws. Features of the face were barely discernible in the ball of coagulated blood. Muscles had been ripped from limbs. Katlian turned away.

The words of Deiyik rang in his head: *"In battle, see what has to be done, and then don't think, just do it. That is the way of the wolf. Think about it, and you're dead. There is always time to think about it later, when it doesn't matter."*

Katlian began skinning the bear methodically as twilight fell upon him and both of his dead. He knew he had to return to the village that night, before the scent of all the blood from Naawan and the bear attracted other hungry predators. He built a small fire for light and made a litter sledge from the trunks of small trees lashed together with strips of evacuated gut from the bear. He tied the hide onto the sledge, then arranged the remains of Naawan on the bed of bear hide and folded the hide over to decently secure the mangled body. He tied his gear to the front of the sledge, where he could quickly reach it, doused the fire with soil, and began his trek back to the village, dragging the heavy sledge behind him.

A full moon illuminated the clouds above, so a dim light suffused the forest, making it possible for him to proceed with care. He was aching with fatigue, but whenever he stumbled, he immediately stood up again and resumed putting one foot in front of the other toward the village. He knew that if he lay down to rest for even a moment, he would fall asleep. He kept going, his muscles aching even more. But the more they ached, the more determined he was to keep on going.

Finally, he saw the fire of a village through the woods. It was the Kiksadi Kwaan. He dragged his sledge into the village toward the shore near the *kekur,* heading directly for the longhouse of K'asasee's father. There he stopped and sat outside the doorway. In a hoarse voice, he called out, *"I have the bearskin."*

Aakashook emerged. In the moon-glow and firelight, he saw Katlian sitting there with bear blood smeared over his arms, legs, and face, and behind him, the sledge with the huge bearskin and head of the beast. Something was wrapped in it, he could see.

"This is the bear that killed Naawan," said Katlian.

Aakashook lifted up an edge of the bear skin and beheld the horrible story it contained. He looked over at Katlian just as the young man slumped forward, sound asleep.

The father said to himself, *"Katlian, the great bear killer, now sleeps."*

***

With the Russians' food cache in fair shape, Baranov turned his attention to salvaging more from their ship's wreckage. Together with some Russians, he and Kuponek made several *nigilax* trips to the broken wreck strewn across rocks and washed up onshore. They retrieved more cargo, equipment, belongings, and guns before the other Natives could get them.

As a sign of his trust, Baranov gave Kuponek a musket. Kuponek felt greatly honored, but out of respect for protocol and to Baranov's surprise, he passed the musket on to Toyon Putuguq. Once the chief had the musket, Baranov kept careful control over all gunpowder supplies, doling out powder to him for just one shot at a time. Trust would only go so far.

He liked Kuponek, but something bothered him about their friendship, and he had to get to the bottom of it. Was Kuponek's cooperation motivated by hostages? The Aleut knew just enough Russian now for Baranov to ask him a question. On their next hunting trip in a *bidarka*, he asked it. "Kuponek, how many of your village women and children are held hostage in Kodiak?"

It seemed that Kuponek got the gist of the question, which he obviously didn't like. He turned his head sideways, so Baranov, sitting behind, could hear him.

"None. None from Kuponek village."

"None? Then why did you rescue Russians and take us in?"

Kuponek didn't want to answer. He ignored the question and looked out to sea.

With great enthusiasm, Baranov continued to learn seal hunting, going out twice again with Kuponek. Then he tried training the other Russians—but those burly men, great hunters on land, were mostly inept at spearing seals in the ocean. Not as athletic as he was, their timing and precision of aim were often poor when throwing the spear. Altogether, however, the Russians brought in six more seals for the food supply. It would be almost enough.

Toyon Putuguq kept an eye on the Russians, especially Baranov. *This is a special man,* he thought. *A strong leader and also a strong worker with exceptional skill as a hunter.*

Soon winter came, with ferocious storms and hard living for the Natives. Between blizzards, Baranov slogged out to hunt with bow and arrow for chicken-sized ptarmigan or blue foxes to help feed his men and the village. On one such occasion, he stuck his head up out of the *barabara* door and crawled out into the blowing snow, dragging a bow and sheaf of arrows behind him. He wore the ever-present Native *kamleika*, its hood pulled tight over his head and around his face. He rose, leaned into the cold, and trudged toward a hill where he had seen ptarmigan before. He took off his gloves and set an arrow in his bow, knowing he had to be ready for instant action if he came upon a flock of the birds. With their white winter plumage, he likely would not see them until he was practically on top of them.

He was barely out of camp, plodding on into the whiteout of snow against fog and cloudy sky, when above the howl of wind he heard a sudden beat of wings. As the ptarmigan took to the air, he aimed and let his arrow fly. His luck was as good as his aim. A bird fell onto a white drift, a couple of drops of red blood marking its place. Dinner for one.

That night in the dark, two young, round-faced Aleut women came into the *barabara* and slid under the blankets with two Russian hunters they liked.

***

It seemed to Baranov as if spring would never come, but finally the storms subsided in April 1791. As he and his men prepared to leave for Kodiak, Toyon Putuguq invited him into his big *barabara* next to a ceremonial fire, along with Kuponek and some other Aleut men. The room was quiet as the men entered and took their places around the central fireplace. Baranov saw this was going to be an important ceremony and payed close attention.

They all stared at the fire for a long moment. Then the chief began singing and chanting, with Kuponek joining in—a ritual song describing a seal hunt. After another long and silent moment, Toyon Putuguq spoke to Baranov in the Aleut language, which Baranov by then knew well: *"Baranov has learned Native ways. Baranov is the only Russian who learned to hunt well with Native ways and speak our language well. And Baranov worked for the village, not just himself.*

"Now Baranov is part Aleut," he continued. *"So now, as toyon, I give Baranov an Aleut name: Nanuq, blessed by the sacred fire spirit. Nanuq is the polar bear, the great white hunter.*

"With your Native name, I give this skin of Nanuq. I got it from an Eskimo up north. It has great powers."

The chief unfolded the big white bear skin and solemnly draped it over Baranov, who admired it with a smile. The bear head was awesome with its snarling white teeth. The top of it lay above Baranov's head, with the ferocious gleaming canines thrust forward under the bear's black nose. The lower jaw and teeth projected under his chin. His face was then framed by that of the bear, and the full length of the nanuq's white fur fell over his shoulders and arms, down to his feet.

"Toyon Putuguq, I accept with pride."

The chief looked again into the sacred fire and spoke solemnly: *"But now your Native part will fight your white part.*

"Not a good fight.

"Sometimes your white part will win. Sometimes your Native part will win.

"How these fights will end, I don't know."

CHAPTER 3

NANUQ AND KATLIAN

I n May 1791, the Aleutian sunflowers, beach fleabane, welcomed the spring with yellow petals along foggy coasts. The skies were alive with cackling Aleutian geese in long, undulating V formations returning from their winter retreats. The weary winter was finally at its end, and the Russians were able at last to continue their journey to Kodiak. They borrowed four Aleut *nigilax* boats and the men to paddle them. As they climbed into the open boats with their gear, Baranov wore an Aleut *kamleika* rain suit and hat, looking very much like the Native he had become.

Toyon Putuguq stood on shore with all the villagers. A drummer stood beside the chief, beating an energetic send-off. The *nigilaxes* were pushed into the low surf. The men paddled vigorously and looked intently ahead, as if there was not a minute to waste before the next storm hit. With memories of their shipwreck still vivid, the prospect of being at sea in a skin boat during an Aleutian storm made some Russians anxious.

Baranov and a dozen Russians, including his assistant, the young bookkeeper Ivan Aleksandrovich Kuskov (Koos'koff), rode in the lead *nigilax* with Kuponek as guide. A second *nigilax* followed with more Russians and an Aleut crew, and the last two boats, skippered by Dmitry Becharof, headed for a different track. They would explore the northwest shore of the Alaska Peninsula and seek a trans-peninsula portage toward Kodiak. (See Map 3.)

"Kuskov, let me tell you something," said Baranov. "Surviving the shipwreck and spending the winter with the Aleuts forced me to become as much like a Native as any white man possibly could. And that is good, because from now on, it seems my life will be intertwined with Natives in ways I'd never imagined."

"I think you're right, sir."

Baranov's group paddled northeast with the mountainous, olive-green coast of the Alaska Peninsula on their left. As each evening approached, Kuponek looked for a coastal island where they could camp for the night. They avoided camping on the mainland to prevent attack from hostile peninsula Natives. As their food supplies dwindled, Kuponek and Baranov used the *bidarka* towed behind their *nigilax* to hunt seals on the many coastal rookeries they passed.

During part of the trip, Baranov was sick with chills and fever, and lay in the bottom of the boat rolled up in a sealskin blanket. He spoke to Kuponek in Aleut. *"Again, my Aleut friends take care of me. And to think that your village looked after us even without hostages in Kodiak."*

Kuponek replied, *"When we first brought you and your Russians to our village, Chief Putuguq knew we could not feed so many. Some thought all Russians must be killed at night while sleeping. But before we could do that, you agreed to hunt seals to feed the Russians. That made Putuguq decide to let Russians live."*

"Would you have helped kill us?"

"Putuguq is our chief. We do what the chief says."

Baranov was astonished, but only for a moment. He had not known how perilous his people's situation had been. But he knew it made sense. *"I understand,"* he said. He knew that the Aleuts lived in a dangerous environment with limited resources. Sometimes they were faced with life-or-death decisions as a community, and sometimes they relied on superstitious influences. But within their context, a context that white men could rarely comprehend, Putuguq had shown they could make important decisions on a rational basis. *These people truly are not savages,* he thought. He knew he would have to keep this in mind as he dealt with Natives in his new job. That would be the challenge of his *Nanuq* role.

After a few days, Baranov recovered and was back at his paddling station.

It took two months for the men to reach a point along the Alaska Peninsula opposite Kodiak Island, where Kuponek saw something new to him: tall trees, absent on the Aleutians. He watched their dark green branches waving in the wind in unison, and they fascinated him. It seemed that the whole wooded coastline was somehow alive, and was speaking about some great truth through a secret whisper in the wind. To Kuponek, there was somehow something magical about these tall trees—an idea suggested by a belief in animism common to many Aleuts.

At this point they turned their boats east to cross the dark blue ocean straits and navigated along the island's lofty mountainous southern coast, interspersed with fiords. Onward they paddled toward the Russian settlement at Three Saints Bay.

Standing watch in the bow of the lead *nigilax*, Kuponek saw a pod of white beluga whales about a hundred yards ahead. *"Kilalugak! Kilalugak!"* he yelled as he pointed to the whales.

The Natives paddled fast to catch up with the belugas, racing to see which boat would reach them first. The air was full of excited shouts from men in pursuit.

"What's going on?" Baranov asked Kuponek.

"*Kilalugak!*" he exclaimed, pointing ahead.

Baranov saw whale spouts as they surfaced ahead. Then he too got caught up in the excitement of the chase. As the *nigilaxes* drove into the rear of the pod, Baranov saw the graceful white shape of a whale rise to surface beside his *nigilax*, its eye scanning the boat and men. Then it blew, took a deep breath, dove with white tail up, and glided below. As the opening to the Three Saints Bay fiord appeared ahead, the boats left the pod and headed for the bay.

As the *nigilaxes* paddled into Three Saints Bay, Baranov could see the tiny Russian seaside village come into view below steep, snow-capped mountains. They approached the small harbor where two sailing ships lay at their moorings and where many kayaks had been pulled up on the beachfront.

Then the *nigilaxes* were spotted from the shore, and a commotion went up as villagers ran down to meet them. In a moment, both *nigilaxes* of the Baranov group had landed and were quickly surrounded by an impromptu welcoming committee.

"I'm Aleksandr Andreievich Baranov, here to be the new chief manager. And this is my assistant, Ivan Aleksandrovich Kuskov," Baranov announced as he climbed out of his boat onto the beach.

The man Baranov would replace, a clean-shaven, middle-aged fellow a bit taller than Baranov, stepped forward and held out his hand. "Yevastrate Ivanich Delarov. Where's our supply ship?"

"Wrecked in the Aleutians," Baranov answered, shaking the hand. Looks of dismay immediately spread across the villagers' faces.

"And our supplies?" Delarov inquired.

"We salvaged what we could. There's no food left."

Delarov was crestfallen. "We've had no supplies for a year, nothing to trade to Natives for food. I've been rationing now for three weeks. One meal a day. Many are sick. Most want to go home."

Baranov stared at him for a moment, then looked at the anxious faces of the hungry villagers staring at him.

"But supplies are shipped regularly," Baranov said.

"But not received," Delarov told him. "Many ships sink. What gets here is less than we need."

Baranov looked back toward the sea and got an idea. He pointed seaward and then shouted to the Natives who had brought him, *"Kilalugak! Kilalugak."* Kuponek didn't understand at first. So Baranov jumped into a beached boat, pantomiming the action of spearing a whale, calling out, *"Kilalugak!"*

Then Kuponek understood and he yelled to the others, *"Afuniaqtuq kilalugak!"*

They quickly launched the *nigilaxes* into the bay and paddled back toward the white whales, with much excited chatter.

In the first boat with Kuponek, Baranov looked ahead, still wearing his *kamleika* with his sandy hair blowing in the breeze. The hunting party found the beluga whales and chased the nearest spout. In just minutes, they had speared and killed their prey. Jubilant at their good fortune, they tied a rope to the carcass and towed it to the village. It trailed a stream of bright red blood in the blue ocean. Baranov looked toward the village, proud of his Aleuts' accomplishment.

The Natives danced around Baranov and the whale as it was carved up, chanting his Aleut name: *"Yi, yi, Nanuq! Yi, yi, Nanuq!"*

Delarov came over to inspect the whale, and Baranov asked, "Can we celebrate with a *praznyk*?"

"Of course! You know, we tried often, but we had no luck hunting whales. Good work!"

"I do what I must. A man is his job."

As at many company towns everywhere, meals were communal. The dining hall was at the center of the village both physically and socially. As the village's main building, the dining hall was long and narrow and made of logs. Inside, its furnishings and equipment were frontier utilitarian. That evening, after a satisfying whale blubber dinner, a *praznyk* celebratory party erupted. Baranov, mug of vodka in hand, boisterously led the men in a song, a favorite Russian drinking tune about a *Kretchma*, a Russian pub:

And there is singing, and there is dancing,

And the Russian vodka is all right.

Come to the Kretchma, that's where you'll ketchma,

drinking vodka every night. . . .

Singing with gusto, Baranov carried a keg of vodka, doling out drinks to each man, both Russian and Aleut. How he loved a *praznyk!* With every mug he poured, he took a swig himself, singing right along.

Three Russian seal hunters were drinking together in a corner. One of them, Gorsikov, commented indignantly, "Look at him. He's got no rank, not a military commander or sea captain! Just a stinking trader, a merchant! What was Shelikhov thinking, sending Baranov to run this place?"

His friend Popov replied, "Tell me something, Gorsikov. Is your belly full? Who got the whale?"

"Well, I'll give him one thing," offered Gorsikov. "He holds his booze—what an iron stomach!"

The following morning, Baranov came out from a log bunkhouse, unshaven, put on his shirt, and strolled steadily past two men snoring loudly on the porch. He heard loud growls on the beach below, beyond his line of sight, and turned toward a grassy shoreline bluff to investigate. About a hundred yards away, on the beach, he saw three large Kodiak bears arguing over the remnants of the whale carcass. The biggest bear won, chasing off the other two a short distance, where they stood and sulked as the dominant bear went back to get first pickings.

Delarov came from behind to join Baranov. "Our garbage collectors," he said. "But we have to be careful. We should have buried those whale remains to avoid attracting bears. They come like flies. And when they finish picking those bones, they'll start sniffing around for where we stored the rest of the meat."

"What do we do then?" asked Baranov.

"Throw rocks first and yell a lot. And if that doesn't work, then we shoot 'em."

"How often is that?"

"Not often. When the salmon are running, there's no problem. They stay away. But in the spring and fall, we have to keep a sharp eye on our livestock. Once in a while, we lose a cow or a goat."

Delarov saw a Russian hunter, still a bit tipsy, stumbling toward the bunkhouse and called out to him. "Andre! Watch those bears! Get your gun and a pile of rocks. Don't let 'em get near our whale meat cache." Then, to Baranov, "I'll show you around. By the way, where are you from?"

"I was born in Kargopol, near St. Petersburg."

"I know the place. What did your father do?"

"A storekeeper," answered Baranov.

"Merchant class?" asked Delarov.

"Yes, a *mestchannin*," replied Baranov.

"But that's the lowest of the merchant classes."

"Yes, way below the fourteen ranks of nobility decreed by Tsar Peter the Great."

"Why'd you leave Kargopol?"

"No future there. When I was fifteen I ran away from home and made my way to Moscow. I got a job with a German merchant and taught myself to read, write, and do arithmetic."

"Got a family?"

"Yes. I married Matrona Ivanova, and we have a daughter, Afanassya. When I was thirty-three, we moved east with my brother Pyotr to Irkutsk—almost to the Pacific. I built a successful glass factory there, and Matrona and I adopted two more children, a little boy and a little girl."

"So Irkutsk was a good move?"

"Yes, until Pyotr and I lost nearly everything by investing in the fur trade in the Anadyr region of Siberia. I knew Shelikhov, and he liked how I'd run my glass factory, so he threw this job my way. There you have it, my life story."

"Hopefully it's prepared you to run this place."

The two men walked on to the edge of the settlement, where Baranov said to Delarov, "I heard we've got Aleut hostages."

"Yes—to get the villages to send us otter hunters. But we do pay the hunters. Even so, we must keep the hostages to make the hunters really work. They understand hostage taking—they themselves keep peace by holding hostages from neighboring tribes. It protects us from attack, too. We just do what they do."

Baranov commented, "So they're turning us into savages? I thought we're supposed to be civilizing them."

"Civilizing them? A nice ideal, Aleksandr. But here, ideals are worthless. To survive here, practicality, resourcefulness—and balls—are everything."

"How ironic," Baranov observed. "Shelikhov holds my family hostage to make *me* perform, and I must hold Natives hostage to make *them* perform! Amazing. I had no idea what I was getting into here."

Delarov added, "And to get Aleuts to do what you want, you must get them to *want* to do it. That's an art, my friend. It's called leadership." He pointed to a building. "That storehouse has 300,000 rubles' worth of otter and seal pelts, to be shipped next spring after we get the furs from our outlying forts."

"I need to explore Kodiak," said Baranov. "I have to get to know this place."

Delarov waved his arm toward the steep, rugged mountains surrounding them and observed, "What a place. Wild Alaska, testing you at every turn. And each test always asks the same question: 'Do you have what it takes to survive here?' The worst tests come when you hunt along the southeast coast and have to face the Tlingit."

The next day, Kuponek loaded a few belongings into his village's *nigilax* as he and the other Aleuts from his village prepared to return to Unalaska. Baranov walked over and said, *"Kuponek, I need an interpreter. Stay—I'll pay you."*

Without expression, Kuponek stared at Baranov, then reached into the *nigilax* and took his things out. In the Native manner, actions speak.

Delighted, Baranov exclaimed, *"Good man, Kuponek!"* as he grabbed Kuponek's right hand and shook it in vigorous appreciation. Kuponek beamed from ear to ear. Now he would see what was over the next horizon.

The exploration led by Captain Becharof along the Alaska Peninsula finally reached Three Saints Bay. As the two *nigilaxes* approached the shore, the bell was rung, and everyone stopped whatever they were doing to run down to the beach and welcome the arrivals. Baranov was there when Becharof's boat landed. "Welcome to Three Saints!" he yelled.

"Hello, Aleksandr Andreievich," replied Becharof.

"Did you find the portage you were looking for?" asked Baranov.

"Indeed we did!" answered Becharof. "We made a map. I'll show you where." (See Map 3.)

"Shelikhov said we need it as a back-door escape route if the British attack us," Baranov commented. "Or to escape from John Henry Cox, that English pirate who's sailing for the Swedes, and his dreaded *Mercury*."

Becharof unrolled a hand-drawn map and spread it over the bow of his boat. "Here it is. Right here we came to a Native village called Egegik, at the mouth of a big river. So we went up the river and found a big lake, about twenty-five miles long and ten miles across."

"That big! We'll name it after you."

"At the east end of that lake, it narrows and ends just a few miles from the Pacific."

"Then what did you do?"

"Well, we climbed a mountain on a clear day and saw a low-lying pass through the mountains toward the Pacific. But we practically had to rebuild our boats before we could continue. They were starting to rot. Then we went through the pass and headed across the straits to Kodiak. So here we are!"

"Good job! We *will* name that lake after you: Becharof Lake."

"Thank you, sir. I hope I never have to see it again."

"Now if the Swedes, or the Spanish, or the English attack us, we can escape by your back door. The trouble is, we never really know who Russia is at war with, because news takes so long to get here. But that's just the way it is. Here, Russia has no navy and no army to protect our empire. Will the copper plates with the imperial seal do the job instead? I wonder."

Baranov and Kuponek launched a sea canoe filled with gear to explore Kodiak. In a second canoe, they were accompanied by a big, bearded Russian hunter, Yuri Karloff, and an Alutiiq guide—in case Baranov needed to be backed up by some muscle. As they paddled along the island's coast, he made entries in his journal of what he saw, including his observations of wildlife, topography, Native villages, and chiefs.

The small party reached a seaside Native Kodiak village and approached a cluster of *barabaras*. Villagers came out of their huts and watched them approach.

"I've come to talk with your toyon," Baranov said in their language.

The *toyon* stepped forward and motioned for them to enter his large *barabara*, where some village elders joined them. Inside, Baranov sat down cross-legged to negotiate with the Natives for a levy of hunters to be provided the next summer. In a circle around a fire, chewing sticks of smoked salmon, they spoke at a slow, deliberate pace, with Baranov speaking mostly in the Native tongue. *"I am Nanuq, the great Russian hunting leader you have heard about. And I am the assistant to the Empress, the Great Mother and protector of this country. She has blessed you by accepting all the people of this land as citizens of Russia. We sit in the protection of her shadow. And I am here to collect your tribute to her. As tribute, she needs you to hunt otters for her."*

"We have heard of the great Nanuq, and of your bravery," said the *toyon*. *"But what proof have you that you came from the Great Mother?"*

"This," said Baranov as he pulled one of the copper plates with the imperial seal out of a pocket in his jacket, and sent it around. Each of the Natives handled the plate respectfully and passed it on.

"Never see before," said the second Native. *"Yes, plate must come from Great Mother."*

Baranov continued, *"Next summer, each village must provide half of its men and their bidarkas to hunt for two months. We pay one piece of iron for each otter fur, and one iron for each three seal skins. Payment will come at the end of the season."*

The *toyon* looked briefly at each of the other elders, then said, *"Too many men. Not enough pay."*

The negotiations continued for a couple of hours, during which Baranov was patient and tireless. Eventually, a deal emerged.

"All right, Great Nanuq," said the *toyon. "We will send half our men to you for the hunt. We will get one iron piece for each otter fur, and one iron piece for every two seal pelts. We also get to keep two of every ten pelts we catch."*

"No, one *of every ten pelts,"* Baranov insisted.

"Yes," replied the *toyon* quietly, seeing that his last-minute gambit to up the ante had mostly succeeded.

Baranov's two canoes crossed Shelikof Strait to the Alaska Peninsula. The barren, razorback granite peaks, spotted with snow, were thrust toward the sky above steep slopes of green grass and bushes flowing down to rocky coasts. Among the high peaks stood a few steaming volcanoes. At a village along the Peninsula coast, Baranov sat on the beach across from the *toyon*—who could speak Russian—trying to negotiate a deal.

"I must think about this. Need time to think," implored the *toyon.*

Baranov's patience was worn out. "As you wish. But if you don't agree, then your whole village will be punished. *Severely* punished. I will leave Yuri Karloff here to bring me your answer tomorrow."

Baranov got up with a frown and left with Kuponek without the usual ritual of goodbyes to the chief, and paddled away.

More than an insult, this lack of protocol conveyed a sense of foreboding to the chief. But that feeling didn't last long. In a few minutes, the chief got in his *bidarka* with his son and headed in the opposite direction to go fishing for Chinook salmon.

A few hours later, a volcano several miles away suddenly erupted, spewing a huge column of billowing gray clouds tens of thousands of feet up into the atmosphere. Within minutes, the prevailing wind blew the hideous cloud over the village, where it fell and started throwing volcanic ash everywhere. The chief, fishing just a couple of miles away, wondered if this was a sign of Baranov's power and his threatened punishment. He raced back to his village and found it under bombardment of volcanic ash and pumice, causing chaos and hysteria. *Definitely a sign!* he concluded.

As he got in his *bidarka* to find Baranov, a terrified Karloff stumbled through the dark ash cloud enveloping everything and gave the *toyon* a note for his leader. The *toyon* paddled off at top speed to catch up with the great Nanuq. He found him and Kuponek, just beyond the black cloud, standing on the shore and looking back toward the eruption.

"We give you what you ask! We give it! Just stop the mountain, great Nanuq! Stop the mountain!" pleaded the chief, and he handed him Karloff's note. Great Nanuq opened it, glanced at it, then read it out loud to Kuponek.

A mountain has blown up and turned day into night. I'm very sick because I can't breathe. We expect death at any moment. Of course, do not be alarmed. —Yuri Karloff[1]

---

1   Griggs, Robert F., 1922, *The Valley of Ten Thousand Smokes*, Washington: The National Geographic Society, p. 19.

Then Baranov asked the chief, "What did the mountain look like when it exploded?"

In broken Russian the chief replied, "Me no look. Me paddle like hell."

***

In October 1791 on the island of Sitka, K'asasee had given birth to her first child with Katlian. Five days later, her father Aakashook summoned them to his longhouse.

She wore an ankle-length dress and carried their baby bundled in a small blanket as she and Katlian reached her mother and father's longhouse. Katlian wore his best deerskin shirt and pants, decorated with raven and eagle drawings. Bear claws and teeth from the bear he had killed hung in a string around his neck. His long black hair was tied up in a knot in back, and raven feathers dangled from it. He now had a thin mustache and short goatee.

Katlian's expression was solemn as they entered and sat side by side on a blanket in front of the fire in the center of the house. Soon, her parents joined them and sat across from them on the blanket.

"*K'asasee has had a child,*" said Aakashook to Katlian. "*So now I give you back your marriage payment.*" He handed a package to Katlian wrapped in sealskin. "*According to our law, with the birth of her first child, K'asasee's marriage to you is now ended, unless she decides to continue it. What is your decision, K'asasee?*"

"*I want to keep Katlian,*" she replied.

Aakashook looked at Katlian for his reaction.

Katlian nodded. He was happy with K'asasee, who sat next to him, cradling their baby boy. *"I want to be with K'asasee forever,"* he said softly as he passed the marriage payment package back to her father.

Aakashook smiled. *"Good."* His demeanor quickly turned serious again as he said ceremoniously, *"Now, as the father of the clan, and as father of K'asasee, I agree. You two are now married again."*

After a long moment of silence, Katlian looked directly at Aakashook and spoke in a firm voice. *"Our clansmen of Yakutat were attacked by the Kenaitze who want to prevent the Yakutats from fishing for salmon in the rich waters of the Copper River that have long been the waters of the Yakutats. The Yakutats want our help in a war to come. I ask your permission to go, Father Aakashook."* (Yakutat: mid Map 5.)

Aakashook looked sternly at Katlian for a long minute, then said, *"You may go, only because if I say 'no' the great bear killer will go anyway. You were born and raised to fight and to kill for the rights of our people. K'asasee and baby Aanyaanax will stay here with us. I know you will come back. But remember, your seed is only for K'asasee. Break that rule and any of our clansmen can kill you anywhere, anytime, without threat of vengeance from your clan. Now go."*

***

Baranov's party returned to Three Saints Bay just as the first flurries of approaching winter arrived. Paddling into the harbor, Kuponek said, "You learn much, Baranov. But you still must learn much more."

"I know," answered Baranov. "And you'll teach me."

Soon winter arrived at Three Saints Bay in full force. The first blizzard swept in with pounding seas and driving snow, rocking boats in the harbor. Men and women ran from building to building as window shutters banged against walls. A Kodiak bear dug his den in the mountains nearby as snowdrifts built up.

CHAPTER 4

NATURE RULES SUPREME

Two months later, it was dark, when the nights were at their longest, and in the dining hall a *praznyk* party was again underway. Everyone was there. Most of the Russians had beards, baggy smocks, and leggings. The Aleuts were included too—the hunters and female hostages and consorts, some of whom were pregnant. And of course, Baranov was there with his slender and clean-shaven young assistant, Ivan Aleksandrovich Kuskov.

An able fellow, Kuskov had a quiet and forthright manner. From Tot'ma, in Russia, about four hundred and fifty miles from Moscow, he had come thousands of miles east to Okhotsk to seek his fortune, and there had been recruited by Baranov in August 1790 to keep the company's books. He was glad that, at Kodiak, Baranov had discovered his management strengths, and was giving him greater responsibility. Of a more serious bent of mind than most of the Russians, Kuskov was more an observer than a participant at *praznyks*. But he quietly enjoyed watching and listening to the antics of others.

At a table to one side, two burly Russian hunters sat arm-wrestling, with several onlookers cheering them on. Suddenly, one contestant threw over the other man's arm, pinning it to the tabletop. Amidst the cheering, Baranov came over and took the loser's seat, challenging the winner to a new contest. With elbows on the table, they locked hands and began a strenuous contest. Baranov looked intently into the eyes of his bearded opponent as he slowly began to have his way with the other man's arm, both men huffing and puffing as they strained. Then all at once, the other man's arm gave way and Baranov pushed it down to the tabletop, to a loud cheer.

Nearly everyone by then was singing and dancing in a circle to the folksy twang of balalaika music. Most had a vodka mug in hand. They alternated between the *kazatsky* squat-kick dance and the rapid-tempo *chastushka*—humorous songs that got everyone laughing.

The occasion was New Year's Eve, and as the year turned, a loud bell rang. Kuskov saw the cook set down his big brass hand bell and then, with a wide grin below his ample curled mustache, hold up a board on which he had written *January 1, 1792*.

There was much cheering in front of a hot fireplace. Boisterous singing followed as all the other Russians again danced in a circle that undulated in and out as it turned and wheeled around the room, as first one, then another, dancer took the center to dance the *kazatsky* to applause. The faster the tempo, the greater the applause. Kuskov saw Baranov cheering as he downed yet another vodka. *What an astonishing capacity for liquor*, Kuskov thought.

Baranov came over grinning and singing. He had a vodka keg tucked under his arm and filled Kuskov's empty cup. Then he set down the keg and wandered back to rejoin the dance. Unnoticed by Baranov, Kuskov—a teetotaler—poured the vodka from his cup back in the keg and filled his cup with water from a pitcher.

A Russian who didn't drink vodka seemed a contradiction. Kuskov's father had been an abusive drunkard whose early death from alcohol had persuaded Kuskov to foreswear all of it. But he could still enjoy a good time.

That winter passed without the stress of heavy storms, and the spring of 1792 arrived. In March there were still patches of snow spotting the hillsides nearby. A *nigilax* arrived from one of the Kodiak villages, filled with Alutiiq women and children hostages to exchange. Baranov came outside to supervise. A big Russian hunter, Belonogov, chased a departing hostage woman and grabbed her.

Baranov commanded, "Let her go! She's being exchanged."

"Shut your face, merchant!" Belonogov sneered.

"Kuskov, seize him! Three lashes!" ordered Baranov.

Several men quickly grabbed the man, bound him to the whipping post, and Kuskov administered the lashes as Baranov, with crossed arms, looked on disdainfully. Belonogov looked up in pain, surprise, and submission. Then Baranov strode back to his log house with an air of command as others looked on, impressed. The obvious message was that the chief manager's discipline could be depended upon to be administered instantly, harshly, and mercilessly. Baranov knew that, in a distant outpost of the empire manned by *promyshleniki*—Russian wild men—It was the only way to stay in control. He slammed his cabin door for emphasis, and the hostage exchange proceeded without further interruption.

As Ivan Kuskov rolled up the whip, he told Belonogov, "Get back to your barracks, fool. And remember: 'God is high, and the Tsar is far away.' In this place, Baranov is the law."

***

The Yakutat Kwaan was home to Tlingits along the southern shore of the Pacific Ocean's large Yakutat Bay. Like most of the high-rainfall regions of southeastern Alaska, the bay's shoreline alternated between dark green spruce forests and light green marshy areas surrounding meandering streams flowing out of the tall snow-capped mountains behind the bay. At its northern extremity, Yakutat Bay narrowed into Disenchantment Bay, having been given that name by the Spanish explorer Alessandro Malaspina, who was looking for a Northwest Passage and had been disappointed there. At the northern rim of that bay, a white mass of ice was continually calving icebergs into the ocean. The Tlingit village was in a spruce forest on the south side of the bay, near its wide mouth on the Pacific Ocean. Looking toward the northwest from the village on a clear day, one could see the spectacular snow-topped Mount St. Elias. Rising almost straight up from near sea level to 18,008 feet, Elias was second in height in Alaska only to Denali.

Katlian had been in Yakutat for several weeks. Because of Katlian's high maternal family status, Chief Ish-Kah of the Yakutat people had listened to his urgings to prepare for war with the Kenaitze. The cost of the Kenaitze's attack on a Yakutat hunting and fishing party some months before at the mouth of the Copper River must be avenged ten-fold. Only then would the Yakutats reign supreme over the lands and rivers to the near north. So the chief had allowed Katlian to begin training the Yakutat warriors for battle.

Katlian had seen that the young men of Yakutat were soft. He had to harden them the way his uncle had hardened him. So he embarked on a rigorous program of physical training, enduring hardship and withstanding pain. After weeks of this, he trained them in the rudiments of battle tactics developed long ago at Angoon. The same tactics had scared away the first Russians when sailors came ashore near Sitka in search of fresh water and were captured, tortured, and killed.

But Katlian had encountered an unexpected challenge. Unlike the Kwaans he knew to the south, the Yakutat Kwaan had Wolverines, a council of tribal women that had the power to veto any decision of the council of male chiefs and sub-chiefs. Going to war against the Kenaitze would require the approval of the Wolverines, because it was their sons who would go into battle. Katlian was dismayed—the power of these women could prove fatal to an effective war plan—but there was no getting around it. He would have to convince them.

***

On a typically overcast spring day of 1792, the dock was busy as the sloop *Archangel St. Michael* was loaded for its voyage to Okhotsk. Baranov came down to bid farewell to Delarov, Becharof, and the other Russians going home. He knew that, with Delarov gone, he would be completely on his own as chief manager. But that would not be a great burden, because Delarov had been quite content to turn over all control to Baranov soon after he first arrived. Nevertheless, he would miss Delarov's confidential advice and intelligent companionship.

As the men boarded ship, their Native women and children, left behind on shore, cried in despair. Many were heartbroken, knowing that their men would likely never return.

"Well, Delarov, so you're out of here," said Baranov. "Three and a half more years for me. Then, God willing, I'll be out of here too and on my way home to my family, free of debt and with a good profit."

"Good luck, Aleksandr Andreievich," said Delarov as they shook hands in farewell. "Oh, and I have something for you that Shelikhov gave me. You may need it." He handed Baranov a small box.

"You know what, you slippery bastard?" exclaimed Baranov suddenly. "You never taught me how to navigate! Neither did Becharof, and I can't get Izmailov to teach me anything either! You skippers guard the knowledge of navigation like it's the Holy Grail. Are you members of a secret society?"

Delarov smiled at him sheepishly. "As I said, I wish you all the luck in the world, Baranov. Goodbye." He turned up the gangplank with a duffel over his shoulder.

Captain Becharof had come back onto the dock briefly for a last word with Izmailov. Baranov knew that Becharof, like most of the North Pacific navigators (as ship captains were sometimes called), thought him the wrong man for the job. They all believed the chief manager should be an experienced sea captain, insofar as the business of the colonies had mostly to do with the sea. And they weren't about to teach him how to be a navigator, either. That was their exclusive realm. *No matter*, thought Baranov, *as long as they sail when and where I tell them.*

This would be Captain Becharof's first ship command since the wreck over a year before, and Baranov wondered whether his self-confidence was fully up to facing the rigors of the sea again. As the captain turned to climb back aboard, Baranov held out his hand.

"Goodbye, captain. Have a good sail. Your passengers and crew are lucky to have the best navigator of the North Pacific guiding their ship."

As they shook hands, Becharof replied, "I know. I pray to Him every day. Goodbye, Aleksandr Andreievich." He turned and bounded up the gangplank.

Delarov boarded the ship, and it cast off, pulled by a jib, then set sail and went with the wind. Baranov waved for a moment, then looked at the box in his hand and opened it. It contained a Bible. He wondered what use a book written halfway around the world, and such a long time ago, would be to him in this savage backwater.

In early May, Baranov awoke early, opened his cabin door, and looked outside to see the pink glow of sunrise begin to spread from the eastern sky to the still-snowy mountaintops. He saw lanterns being lit in a few buildings. A flock of honking geese flew by heading north. The sloop *God's Friend Simeon* was tied to the wharf. Suddenly, the ground shook violently. He saw men running from the bunkhouse next door in nightshirts, including Kuskov, who yelled, "Earthquake! Earthquake! Get out!"

People scrambled for a safe place, but there was none. Boulders shook loose from the mountain above, rolling down into the village. Baranov, still in the open doorway of his cabin, clutched the doorframe. He saw Kuponek run toward him, calling out, "Get clothes! Climb hill! Big wave coming!"

"*What?*" exclaimed Baranov in confusion.

Kuponek yelled, "Get *clothes!* Get *boots!* Climb hill! *Ocean* coming!"

Baranov saw the urgency and conviction in the man's eyes and instantly reacted, barking orders to everyone: "Grab some clothes! Grab your boots! Climb the hill! The ocean is coming! Move! Move! *Move!* Pass the word!"

He dashed back into his cabin as the ground continued to shake. He grabbed clothes and boots, was nearly knocked off his feet by the ground's sharp tremors, and lunged outside. Clouds of dust rose all around him, and he heard the banging of rocks tumbling down the mountainside toward the village and splashing into the bay.

"Follow me!" he yelled as he ran toward the slope, dodging careening rocks. A scattered group of men followed as he ran toward the mountain slope behind the village, charged up fifty feet, and changed his boots, which he'd put on the wrong feet. He looked downhill at the helpless people below and ran down again, jumping from boulder to boulder, to help the women and children.

Rumbling aftershocks continued. Then the roar of a huge wave from a tsunami, rolling from the ocean into the fiord, added raw terror to everyone's panic. Baranov ran back up the slope as the giant wave crashed ashore and swept away people who were still trying to escape toward the hill. It lifted the sloop and carried it, along with tangled clumps of debris from crushed buildings, up the narrow bay. Then the waters rushed out, carrying its struggling victims out to sea. Baranov ran down the slope again, jumped into a kayak that had escaped the wave, and quickly paddled out to rescue whomever he could reach. Fortunately, a long coil of rope had been tucked into the kayak. He tied it around his waist and trailed it in the water for survivors to grab, then towed them to shore. He made five quick trips out into the water this way and saved a dozen people. On his sixth trip, he only found floating dead bodies.

After that he beached his kayak and wandered around where the village had been. All the buildings had been destroyed. But, somehow, the sloop remained upright at the edge of the shore.

Baranov climbed the hill to the huddles of stunned survivors. Though fear was all around him, his mind coolly and methodically analyzed the situation, defining the problem and the possible solutions to it. He walked to each knot of terrified people, checked for injuries, and offered reassurances. As he moved among them, his calm self-assurance and purposeful attitude did indeed calm their terrors. Meanwhile, the sloop's skipper, Gerasim Alekseevich Izmailov, grabbed a kayak that had washed up, dragged it to the water, and paddled to where, *God's Friend Simeon* rested haphazardly.

Baranov called out, "Who's missing? Kuskov, make a count."

Kuskov asked, "What will we do?"

"We can't stay here," Baranov replied. "This place is too dangerous."

Kuskov made a count while Baranov paddled a kayak toward Izmailov and the sloop, where he asked, "How is it?"

"Little damage. We can fix it quickly."

"Good. Then get her ready to sail," Baranov told him. "We'll move everyone to Chiniak Bay." He pointed toward the northeast.

"I think twenty were lost," said Kuskov as he joined him.

"Some may have made it to the shoreline along the bay," said Baranov. "Let's get all the *bidarkas* we can find and search for them. Now!"

"Yes, sir!" Kuskov replied.

A rapid search was made along the shoreline for people swept out to sea who might have made it to shore. One woman and a child were retrieved alive, and four bodies found.

Izmailov finished repairing the sloop. Baranov gave the order, and about a third of the survivors climbed aboard for the trip along the jagged, mountainous coast to Chiniak Bay, including Kuskov.

"Kuskov, at Chiniak Bay you're in charge until I get there," said Baranov. Kuskov nodded.

Baranov got many more loaded into two *nigilaxes* that had been retrieved from wave-swept debris. Once they were off, he turned his attention to another problem.

"All right, men," he said to a group nearby. "Let's scour the wreckage here and salvage as much useable gear as possible. We're going to need it at Chiniak."

The sloop and *nigilaxes* reached a protected cove at the new settlement site untouched by the tsunami. Kuskov oversaw their initial encampment. Those on the sailboat were ferried to shore in a *nigilax*. Above them, just a short way back from the shoreline, rose spruce-forested hills with plenty of timber for building a village.

Just one more sloop trip from Three Saints Bay, accompanied by *nigilaxes and bidarkas,* got everyone, including Baranov and the salvaged gear, to the new site.

It was dusk there on the grassy bluffs above the rocky beach of Chiniak Bay. All the survivors were still in shock, huddled in groups, waiting for direction. Kuskov said to Baranov, "Shouldn't we say a prayer?"

Baranov was a religious man, though not in any formal way. He was puzzled at first, but realizing his responsibility to his people in a moment of spiritual need, he nodded and said, "All right. Let's gather."

They all came and bowed their heads, as Baranov paused for a moment to collect his thoughts. Then he spoke: "Thank you, Lord, for saving us from the earthquake and tidal wave. . . . Please accept the dear souls of those we lost. And help us, Lord, to build a new village here. . . . And we pray that this will be a place where we can live in safety and peace."

The others all said, "Amen," and sobs rose from the grieving. Campfires were lit, and makeshift tents from sails were put up; the exhausted survivors crawled in, got under wet, salvaged blankets, and went to sleep.

The next day was clear and brilliant, and Baranov led all the Russian men with axes into the nearby forest of spruce that would soon become log buildings. Kuskov heard the air quickly fill with the chopping clatter of axes and the crashing of tall trees. And he saw a shirtless Baranov swing his axe, setting an energetic example.

A few weeks of rapid construction brought several new log buildings along the grassy bluffs overlooking the ocean. Kuskov and Kuponek walked from project to project, checking on progress and making sure each building team had whatever they needed. Kuponek marveled at how well they all worked together. He, like all the others, was swept up in the great camaraderie to do the job and do it well. And he saw that Baranov was both a conspicuous leader and the hardest worker, gaining unquestioned respect from his people.

Finally, with construction mostly complete, they all gathered for a dedication. Baranov unveiled a sign with the name *St. Paul* and announced, "Here it is, the first great city of Russian America: St. Paul! And tonight *we have a praznyk!*"

In their new dining hall just hours later, Kuponek sat next to Kuskov as they listened to *balalaika* music filling the room and a folk tune being joyously sung.

"I've never seen a better reason for a *praznyk,*" Kuskov told Kuponek with a satisfied smile. Then he sang with gusto along with the others as the one surviving *balalaika* led them in a favorite Russian folk song.

There was lots of dancing and drinking, and Baranov had a fine time winning arm-wrestling contests, always with a glass of vodka in hand.

The next day, he hauled his belongings into his new cabin with its sparse furnishings and put things in order as best he could. When finished, he sat down and noticed the Bible from Shelikhov. He stared at it for a moment, opened it, and started to read.

CHAPTER 5

CHIEF CHOKTA

I n mid-June on the hillside above the village, a trim and athletic Kuponek stood ramrod straight, looking like a statue. Scanning the new village of St. Paul, he saw that they had got it mostly finished—just in time for the beginning of the 1792 otter and seal hunt.

A Russian hunter hiked up, joined him, and said, "Nice view, eh?"

"*There* is where I want to be," Kuponek said, pointing out to sea. "I want to hunt again. That is where I am happy. That is where I belong. Out there is the real world. Not on land with all *this*," he concluded as his hand waved over the buildings below. "I want the wind and salt spray in my face. I want to ride waves. Big waves! I want to outsmart animals I hunt. That is where I am a man. Not here."

"You are our most able hunter, Kuponek," said the Russian, nodding.

A steady stream of Native hunters arrived below in *bidarkas* from scattered villages of Kodiak, the Alaska Peninsula, and the Aleutians. A fleet of three hundred two-man *bidarkas* filled the bay.

Someone running from the beach below caught Kuponek's eye. It was Kuskov, hurrying to Baranov's house. What could have gotten him so excited? Kuponek started down to find out.

In his new house, Baranov was sitting at a rough-hewn table looking at a coastal map, thinking of the route they would take to hunting grounds in Chugach Bay. His wiry build was full of pent-up energy, and the intensity of his eyes, darting from the map to his view of the bay where hunters in bidarkas were gathering, said it was time to get going.

Just then, Kuskov burst in fuming. "Trouble," he declared. "Chief Chokta of Aklonek has refused to send his levy of men. And we have no hostages from them. If he doesn't send his, other villages will refuse, too. Then many men already here will leave, crippling the hunt, and we won't make a profit."

Baranov jumped up in a flash of anger, grabbed his leather jacket, and said to Kuskov, "Come on, and bring the whip." He marched out and down to the beach, signaling Kuskov, Kuponek, and others to follow. "Nobody gets in the way of our profit!" he barked. Then he asked Kuskov, "Why did Chokta refuse?"

"He said the families of his men need them at home."

"My need is more important."

Baranov and Kuponek got in the lead *bidarka*. Kuskov and seven bearded and burly Russian hunters armed with muskets shoved off with them, and they all paddled toward Aklonek. Yes, this rebellion had to be stopped before it could spread, and Baranov was determined to stop it. His jaw was set firm as he paddled hard.

In just an hour, they landed on the beach in Aklonek. They leapt out of their *bidarkas,* and Baranov led them toward the village. Chief Chokta and a few of his men, wearing pale leather garb decorated with feathers, approached with solemn faces. In a line splayed out behind him, Baranov's big Russian hunters stood, muskets at the ready, opposite the more slightly built Natives armed only with spears. Baranov looked the Natives over, sure that he had the upper hand.

He demanded, *"Where is your levy of hunters?"*

Chief Chokta replied, *"No hunters."*

A few more Native village men joined the Chief's lineup. All were able-bodied, ranging in age from twenty to forty.

"No hunters? What about these *men?"* Baranov challenged.

"No give *hunters,"* was Chokta's adamant reply.

Baranov turned to Kuskov. "Tie him to that tree and pull his shirt off!"

"You heard him, men, let's go! You, you, and you, and the rest of you cover us," said Kuskov.

Four Russians raised their muskets toward the villagers as Kuskov and the three other hunters grabbed the chief, ripped off his shirt, and hauled him toward a tall, thick tree. Chokta's men were intimidated by the raised muskets. As he was dragged, struggling to maintain his dignity, he glanced at Baranov's waist and saw a long hunting knife hanging in a leather sheath on a belt.

The chief, tied to the tree trunk with his bare back toward Baranov, saw his people standing about fifty feet away, stoically watching. He looked at Baranov's knife again. Kuskov stood on one side of Baranov. Kuponek stood on the other, taking no part in the dragging and binding of Chokta. Baranov took the whip from Kuskov.

"Baranov, no," implored Kuponek softly.

Baranov glanced at Kuponek for just a moment, then stepped forward, uncoiling the whip and slapping it alongside his high black boots.

"Eight men not provided," said Baranov. *"Eight lashes!"*

His jaw set with a look of grim power, he tossed the whip's tail behind him and then snapped it forward to smash onto the bare back of the chief.

Chokta recoiled and groaned from the burning pain of the lash—again and again. The Russians with muskets warily eyed the stoic Natives. Kuponek stared at the ground.

After the eighth lash, Baranov stood back as Chokta was untied, quietly weeping with unbearable humiliation. As Baranov turned to look at the villagers, Chokta looked again at the knife on Baranov's belt and suddenly lunged for it. He grabbed it before anyone could react, fell to his knees, plunged the knife into his own heart, and fell over.

Baranov jumped back and stared at the dying chief in disbelief. A Native woman screamed and wailed. All seven Russian hunters aimed their muskets at the village men, who just stood still. "No! Back!" said Baranov with a wave toward the beach, signaling his men to lower their muskets and leave. They all backed away, stunned, heading for their *bidarkas*. As Baranov neared his, Kuponek came from behind him.

"Baranov's knife," Kuponek said, as he held the knife out toward Baranov, who turned and stared at the blade dripping with blood.

"Clean it," Baranov said.

_____

Kuponek didn't respond as he glared into Baranov's eyes. His outstretched arm held the bloody knife toward his leader, turning the handle toward him. Baranov saw a defiance in Kuponek's eyes and quivering chin that he'd never seen before. Slowly, Baranov took the knife, contemplating what had come over Kuponek. He turned, took a couple of steps toward the water, and washed the blood off in the surf. Still hearing the wails behind him, he knew this was a moment on the brink of disaster, and he had to proceed with extreme care. He glanced again at Kuponek and headed for his *bidarka*. Kuponek stood where he was, the Russian hunters waiting behind him to see what would happen next.

"Kuponek?" Baranov called softly but loud enough to be heard above the sea. Did he know his man well enough? He would soon find out.

After a long pause, Kuponek came forward, and they all took off quietly and paddled back to St. Paul.

That night in his cabin, Baranov took the knife from his belt, dropped it on the table, and stared at it as he spoke to himself in anguish. "How could this happen? Where was my Nanuq? I should have remembered! Whippings—not in their culture. Too humiliating to bear."

He wrapped the sheathed knife in a rag and buried it in his clothing trunk. It was hiding a sin. Then he grabbed his vodka bottle and took a long swallow. His old liquid friend would surely help.

A hundred yards away, Kuponek entered Kuskov's small, sparsely outfitted cabin.

"Tell Baranov tomorrow: I go."

"You go? Go where?" asked Kuskov.

"Home. Kuponek go home."

Kuponek stepped out of Kuskov's cabin and walked away.

Baranov, meanwhile, had poured himself another shot of vodka and gulped it down. "I should have *listened* to him!" he snarled, as Kuponek walked by, heard, and stopped.

Kuponek had a determined look on his face. How could the great Nanuq have done this? He was no longer worthy of the name. Kuponek listened as Baranov continued in a loud, vodka-strained voice.

"Why didn't I listen to Kuponek? What a *fool* I was! A damned *fool*!"

Kuponek's expression began to soften, and he walked on to his bunkhouse.

The next morning in the village of St. Paul, when the breakfast bell rang, both Russians and Natives took the footpaths to the dining hall. Kuponek was among the first; he got his porridge and tea, and took his place at a table. Kuskov soon came in and sat at another table near Kuponek. A moment later, Baranov sat next to Kuskov. None of them said anything. Kuponek could see that Baranov was agitated, as he looked only at his porridge. Finally, Baranov spoke to Kuskov. Kuponek heard him, too. "When Toyon Putuguq made me part Native and named me Nanuq, he said my Native part would fight my white part. That is the curse of Nanuq. A curse!

"This job is impossible. On the one hand, I must make the company a profit, or my family in Russia will suffer. On the other hand, my Nanuq part says I must be fair to the Natives—but that can hurt our profit! How am I to deal with these damn contradictions? That is my hell. That is my hell!

"Kuskov, this morning I will write an order that you will make sure gets delivered to all our managers and supervisors. The order will say that Natives must never be whipped. Any supervisor who does it will be whipped himself."

Kuskov wanted to ask if Baranov planned to be whipped, but he thought better of it.

Baranov finished his breakfast, got up, took his empty bowl and cup to a sink, and left. He was followed shortly by Kuskov. Kuponek waited a minute to again contemplate his decision. Then he too left and went looking for Kuskov on the dirt trail through the alder bushes to the warehouse.

He came up behind him, tapped his arm, and said, "I stay."

"You're not going home?" asked Kuskov, turning around to face him.

"Kuponek stay."

For Kuponek, loyalty was a precious thing he could only give to someone he respected. He saw that Baranov had not only admitted his wrong, but would forbid further whippings of Natives. Only a man of great inner strength could do that.

Chief Chokta's men did not come to St. Paul to join the Russian hunt. Baranov let them be.

In the following weeks, as hunters went ashore to camp for the night during the annual hunt, Kuponek would speak to men from many tribes who knew the story of the chief's humiliation and suicide, which had quickly spread. He puzzled over an irony: The story had actually increased the awe in which Natives viewed Baranov, though Baranov himself thought of it as one of his greatest failures.

Each evening in camp, Baranov walked among the Natives, speaking to many of them and going out of his way to treat them with respect and appreciation. Kuponek now thought that the Chokta tragedy had planted a seed in Baranov's soul that would slowly grow into a great tree bearing a single berry—a fruit that might one day save Baranov in a time of great spiritual trial. And for Baranov's humble and honest acceptance of that seed, Kuponek would be eternally loyal.

CHAPTER 6

BARANOV MEETS ANOOKA

I n the dining hall, Kuskov sat down next to Baranov and reported, "We got a message from the Fort Alexander outpost."

"Where is that, again?"

"At the tip of the Kenai Peninsula. They say men from our competitor, the Lebedev Company of Fort St. Nicholas, on the Kenai River, are raising hell with our people there and with the local Natives, the Kenaitzes. Our man there wants you to do something."

Baranov shrugged. "What can *I* do? I have no authority over the Lebedev Company outposts."

The next day, he was standing on the wharf in his Native *kamleika*, looking at the crowded harbor. There he saw the sloop skippered by Gerasim Izmailov and a fleet of four hundred and fifty two-man *bidarkas* paddling around in circles, waiting for his signal to start. And he was in command. He savored the sight for just a moment, then raised his hand and looked at the bell ringer up the hill to see if he was ready. He dropped his hand as a signal, and as the bell tolled loudly, the fleet began to move northeast.

Using a wooden ladder fastened to the side of the wharf, Baranov climbed down into his *bidarka* with Kuponek, and they took their place amid the first squadron of the fleet.

Baranov looked back. On a grass-topped bluff above the harbor he saw families waving, crying, and cheering. The great moment he had been waiting for had come—leading his first big hunt. Out of St. Paul harbor they cruised toward Prince William Sound, south of the Kenai Peninsula. There they would find their sea otter hunting waters.

To their right was the endless blue Pacific that could erupt any moment with white-capped swells before which the men in *bidarkas* would be helpless. To their left were the gray coastlines of the Kodiak Islands, backed by steep green mountains. Onward paddled the 900 men, stroke after stroke, mile after mile. Their muscles tired, then ached, then numbed as they paddled on automatically, following Izmailov's sloop ahead stroke after endless stroke. (Map 4.)

Baranov turned his head and said to Kuponek in the rear cockpit, "I know that years ago, when there were still lots of otter along the Aleutians, the hunts were easy. Then our hunts thinned the herds, and we had to move up the peninsula. That was still easy hunting. But we thinned that out too, so now we have a long way to go to find numbers worth hunting. Do you think the number of otter in the Aleutians will ever come back?"

"No."

"No? Why not?"

"Overkill. Your people left nothing to grow back."

"Nothing?"

"Nothing."

"Isn't there something we can do?"

"No."

Baranov was stunned by the man's frankness. He stopped paddling and turned his torso around more so he could look at him, almost upsetting the *bidarka* in the process. Kuponek's quick and expert paddling stabilized the kayak, and the two stared at each other for a moment. "There must be a way," said Baranov. "I must find a way," he added, He turned forward again and resumed paddling. He knew he had to find a way to conserve and rebuild the otter populations, or his company would eventually be doomed.

He turned his head and spoke again. "Another problem: The furs of southern otter, where we're going, are not as good—not as dark and rich as those from the hunted-out areas. In fact, the darkest and finest pelts come from Kamchatka and the Kuriles, far to the west, but those waters have also been hunted to nothing."

"Bigger problem," said Kuponek. "Over-hunting along the Aleutians and Peninsula. Cut food supply of people there. Some villages even starve."

"But they have seals."

"You're killing their seals, too."

"It's that bad?"

"Yes."

"Well, we found huge numbers of seals on the Pribilof Islands in the Bering Sea, so we can stop all hunting of seals in the Aleutians. That should help those people."

"Good."

It occurred to Baranov the businessman that, if he could develop a method for controlled hunting to stabilize the supply of furs, it would ensure long-term profits. "I need a scientist to help me figure out how to balance otter hunting with reproduction rates. In the end, it's all about profit."

Doing this would involve risk, of course. But as he well knew, profit was the reward for investing in a risk that led to success, whereas loss was the punishment for investing in a risk that led to failure. This was indeed a risk he would have to take. Still, dealing with it, even thinking about it, would have to wait until after the hunt. "All for another day," he said as he looked ahead, thrust one blade of his paddle into the water, and pulled it back with a determined burst of strength.

He saw the *bidarkas* ride the waves with ease between Kodiak and the Kenai Peninsula, even with swells rising several feet. The Aleuts took to it as naturally as the seal and otter they hunted. At Prince William Sound, they camped overnight on an island where they would be safe from attack by the Tlingit, the fierce Natives of the south.

The following morning at dawn, as Baranov and Izmailov ate breakfast by a campfire, they decided to break the fleet into two groups in order to best exploit the hunting grounds. After breakfast, the larger group took off and headed south with the sloop. Baranov and Kuponek launched their *bidarka* and led three hundred men north. They hunted from *bidarkas* in small bays teeming with sea otter, and Baranov was pleased with their catch. Then the squadron passed the end of the big, heavily wooded Montague Island and headed for a Kenaitze Native village near the middle of the Kenai Peninsula's southeastern shoreline, with a snow-capped mountain range seen in the distance. (Again, Map 4.)

Baranov and his men beached their *bidarkas* inside a narrow bay. Tall spruce rose behind the shoreline on either side of the bay, and at its apex there was a grassy meadow. The Russians walked across this meadow toward the village, backed by a forest. Baranov saw log longhouses with cook-fire smoke spiraling up from mid-roof. As they approached, he saw a portly Native, apparently the chief, step out of the center lodge with some warriors at his side.

"I am Baranov, the Nanuq from Kodiak, leader of the Russians." Kuponek translated Baranov's words.

To their surprise, the chief responded in Russian. "I am Grigor, chief of the Dena'ina in this region, or Kenaitzes as you call us, and I speak Russian. I captured a Russian and kept him until he taught me your language."

"Then what did you do with him?" asked Baranov.

With a wave of the hand, Chief Grigor said dismissively, "Oh, I ate him," as he tapped his ample tummy with his fingers. Seeing Baranov's shock, he chuckled. "No, I let him go. Your people name me Grigor, because my real name tangles their tongues: Razkazchikuka."

He invited only Baranov to enter his lodge. Inside, women were huddled in groups of three or four, already working on clothing for the following winter. The smell of open fish oil lanterns permeated the place. But Baranov was used to that odor from Unalaska. A fire was in a central fireplace, where the two men sat near the low, crackling flames.

"So you are the famous Nanuq, who leads with a whip," said Grigor, eyeing Baranov to see if he'd rise to the bait.

The Russian *Nanuq* pretended not to hear, determined that

he, and not Grigor, would control the direction of the talk. He pulled from his pocket one of the engraved copper plates and handed it to him. "This is the seal of the mighty Tsarina of Russia, the royal mother of this land. Her great armies have thousands of rifles and cannons. I am here as her assistant, to bring her rule and her protection throughout this land."

"You bring us her protection?" said Chief Grigor. "Then why do you let your Lebedev people attack my people? When they went to visit our hostage children at the Lebedev fort, they were attacked, some were killed, and their girls, who were with them, were stolen and raped! What will the mighty Empress, the Great Mother of this land, and you, Great Nanuq, do about *that?*"

Baranov paused a moment, looking Grigor steadily in the eye, then said, "I'll see about it."

"You'll see about it," Grigor replied, unconvinced, as he examined the copper plate again.

"Just as this country has many Native tribes," said Baranov, "Russia has many tribes. Just as Native tribes here sometimes fight, Russian tribes sometimes fight. But the great Empress rules over all the tribes, and they all obey her. I will make sure that the law of the Empress solves this problem. Then no Russians will attack your people again."

Chief Grigor stared at Baranov for a long moment, and Baranov stared right back.

"I believe you, great Nanuq."

Chief Grigor's eyes widened in amazement as he examined the copper plate closely. "This is important," he said.

It was exactly the reaction Baranov wanted. He continued, "I look for a long future of friendship between us. We can help each other in many ways. I must explore Montague Island, over here, and need some of your men as guides."

"Great Nanuq, do you have a woman?"

Baranov was taken aback. "I have a wife in Russia."

"In *Russia?* What good is that? Take my daughter for wife. Then I be your father, and we work together as one. This way we make powerful alliance."

Before Baranov could react, Chief Grigor turned and called out to his daughter in his Native tongue, *"Anooka, come here!"*

From a dim recess of the lodge, a slender seventeen-year-old in deerskins approached with unusual youthful dignity. She had glistening long, black hair flowing over her shoulders, and set in an oval face were the high cheek bones common to many Natives. Her big, warm, brown eyes looked out from under lovely arched eyebrows. Clear, tan skin, a straight, pretty nose, and a mouth with soft lips completed her. To Baranov, Anooka was strikingly beautiful. Though reserved, the self-confidence of her rank allowed her to glance at the strange Russian in front of her, and then she faced her father.

In the Kenaitze dialect of the Alutiiq language, the chief told her, *"Turn around and face the great Russian Nanuq."* She did so. With no hint of shyness, she looked Baranov right in his eyes. Her intelligent dark eyes held his stare as an equal for a long moment, until she yielded a slight smile, revealing perfect white teeth, and looked down.

Nanuq quickly collected himself and, wanting to get back to the negotiations for guides, replied, "Chief Grigor, your offer is most generous. But as I said, I already have a wife in Russia."

Grigor insisted, "But not here. How long has it been, great Nanuq, since you've had a wife at your side?"

Baranov stared at him in silence. He didn't want to offend the man, but the proposal was absurd.

The chief tried once more. Certainly an alliance with this Russian Nanuq would greatly benefit his own stature in the eyes of his people—and especially their southern enemies, the hated Tlingit.

"I see. Well, you need a wife here! And we need a strong alliance."

"A Russian can only have one wife."

"Poor man! Poor man!" said Grigor in mild disappointment. He knew that making such alliances, especially with one as strong as Nanuq, could take time and much negotiation. But just how strong was Nanuq, anyway? Maybe he should be tested. There was more than one way to impress the Tlingit with Kenaitze power. Grigor motioned to Anooka to return to her work.

"Well, then, the least I can do for you is give you the guides you need."

Anooka sat on a blanket in the back of the longhouse, where she had been making a bear claw necklace for her father. Why did Father want to give her to this man? Though short, he looked strong and intelligent, but strange. Could she ever want him? She knew what she wanted would count for nothing. Her father would decide, and she had to trust him to choose well for her. She would ask one thing: that her father wait until he really knew a man before he made his choice. As his daughter, she deserved at least that, and the chief had only just met this Nanuq.

Baranov looked into the shadows for Anooka, straining for another glimpse of her youthful beauty. Grigor noticed.

Baranov's fleet headed toward Montague Island and found an English schooner, *Phoenix*, limping with broken masts into Prince William Sound. He and his men went to its aid. Their fleet of *bidarkas* surrounded the ship like Natives coming to trade. Not knowing who Baranov's group were or their intentions, the ship opened its gun ports as a precautionary measure, revealing several cannons. But to facilitate talks, a rope ladder was thrown over the side.

Baranov, wearing his *kamleika* and Aleut rain hat, climbed up to meet the British Captain Hugh Moore. The first mate was Joe O'Cain, an American. As Baranov stepped on deck, he took off his rain hat to reveal his fair hair; Moore and O'Cain were surprised that he was a white man. On deck Baranov saw boxes of beads and glass—typical items of trade with the Natives. *So*, he realized, *this is a trading ship*. At first there was a communication problem: Neither Moore nor O'Cain could speak Russian. But after some experimentation, they found a common language, German, with which Baranov had at least a basic fluency.

In German, Baranov introduced himself. *"I'm Aleksandr Baranov, chief manager of the Russian Shelikhov Company from Kodiak, at your service."*

Moore and O'Cain introduced themselves, after which Moore said, *"We're very glad to see you! We ran into a wild gale that broke our masts, so we pulled in here to make repairs. We could indeed use help getting new masts from the forest."*

"We'll be glad to help," said Baranov, anxious to make a better acquaintance with these men and to learn what he could from them about lands, seas, and trade to the south.

Continuing in German, Moore asked, *"Aleksandr, will you join us for a glass of brandy in my cabin?"*

Baranov answered, *"Ya."* He had never refused a drink in any language.

As the three walked toward the cabin, Moore asked, *"You're in the fur trade, I presume?"*

Baranov nodded.

In the captain's quarters, a Bengalese cabin boy named Richard served them brandy.

"What is your business in these waters?" asked Baranov.

O'Cain replied, *"We're trading goods to the Indians for otter pelts that we'll sell in Canton."*

Then Moore continued, *"But we've found this is too far north for good trade. Much better about 500 miles south."*

"Really?" commented Baranov, somewhat surprised.

O'Cain spoke up. *"Oh yes. In fact there are many more otter south of there, all the way into California. We should have stayed down there."*

"Interesting," said Baranov. *"I don't know much about that. In fact, when I first saw your boat, I was worried you might be a pirate. Cox, maybe."*

"Oh, don't worry about Cox. He died in Canton last year," said Moore. *"Now it's the Americans we have to worry about, competition from their trading ships—three times more than a couple of years ago."*

"My problem with 'em is they trade muskets to the Indians for furs," said Baranov. *"Muskets that the Indians can then use against us."*

Moore and O'Cain looked at him without comment. They too had been trading muskets, albeit antiquated ones, to the Natives for furs.

———

"Another problem is food for our settlements here. Shipments from Russia are few."

"You should do some trade with the Hawaiians," suggested Moore. *"Their islands are full of foodstuffs, and their King Kamehameha is a very smart fellow who is open to trade."*

"I've never heard of him," admitted Baranov.

"Oh, he's big in the mid-Pacific," said O'Cain. *"You should get to know him. He's right in the middle of the best route from here to Canton, which is the best market for furs."*

"You can tell him I sent you," said Moore with a grin. *"Now, let's see what we can do to fix our masts."*

Baranov and some of his men went with Moore's crew into the forest of Montague Island to cut down two tall spruce for new masts. As they walked through the woods, O'Cain stumbled and fell. Baranov offered a hand to pull him up. *"What's the matter with you, Joe? Your sea legs no good on land?"*

With a mischievous grin, O'Cain took Baranov's hand to be pulled up. As O'Cain started getting up, he suddenly pulled Baranov while pushing his foot away so that the Russian fell over. But Baranov didn't let go of O'Cain's hand, so that O'Cain fell back down in a heap next to him. The two sat up side by side, looked at each other, and then broke out in laughter. The other men laughed, too. Then, in good spirits, the two men got up, and they went about the business of chopping down trees.

The repairs were made to the ship, during which Baranov and O'Cain struck up an easy friendship. After the work was finished, Baranov came back on the deck of *Phoenix* to bid farewell to Moore and O'Cain.

"Baranov, thank you for all your good help," said Moore.

"Here's a going-away present for you—some furs and a kamleika to keep you dry," said Baranov.

"And I have a present for you too, in gratitude for your great help in repairing our masts: Richard, my Bengalese cabin boy. He'll serve you well, especially as an English interpreter."

"Thank you! Thank you, Hugh and Joe," said Baranov. *"And good sailing to you!"*

They shook hands before Baranov and the boy climbed down the rope ladder into one of the ship's rowboats. *Phoenix* crewmen rowed them ashore to the Russian campsite, where Baranov's men had waited.

Baranov had a tent set up for Richard. *"You can sleep here. I keep thinking about O'Cain—what a funny, friendly fellow. I like him a lot."*

"Yes," said Richard. Then, in a low voice, he continued, *"He's the last person you'd ever guess is a spy, isn't he?"*

"He's a spy?"

"An American spy watching British naval activities from that English ship. And every time he returns to America, O'Cain reports what he's seen directly to President George Washington," Richard answered.

". . . Does Captain Moore know this?" Baranov asked.

"Oh, yes. But he's Irish too, so he allows it."

The next morning, they broke camp, mounted their sea craft, and paddled several miles along the north shore of Montague Island, examining the forests, until they came to a cove with the tallest and thickest stand of spruce Baranov had seen. *What wonderful lumber for any kind of building use*, he thought. He decided they should climb the mountain behind the cove, to survey the supply and accessibility of spruce across the island. So he motioned for the squadron to land in the cove.

Kenaitze guides led him and his men through the woods of Montague Island to a high overlook from which both mountain fronts of the island could be seen. Baranov looked at the panorama before him. As he turned he could see, far below, a meadow near the beach where their *bidarkas* were waiting. He admired the impressive stands of fir on all sides, so valued for building, and then signaled a return down the trail to the beach where they had landed. Single file, they made their way through the woods until they reached the beach.

"We'll camp here, Kuponek," Baranov declared. "You and Kuskov set up the falconet, aimed at the beach, to protect against an attack. We'll make a fire, have our meal, and then sleep. One man on guard at all times."

Kuponek nodded, and Kuskov moved to set up the falconet as others gathered driftwood for the fire.

CHAPTER 7

FIRST BLOOD

In the early dawn of the following morning, everyone was asleep, including the watchman. Kuponek stirred, nudged Baranov, and whispered, "Something not right."

The young Tlingit warrior Katlian, his face decorated with fearsome red-and-blue war paint, had moved stealthily and eagerly through the dark woods with a spear in one hand and a knife in the other, eyes wide with the anticipation of finally proving himself in battle by killing a man hand-to-hand.

He turned briefly and saw several other tall, muscular Tlingit warriors in war paint, wooden helmets, and body armor moving stealthily alongside. Through low-hanging branches, he saw the encampment ahead. In just a few moments, he knew, he would be plunging his knife into the heart of an enemy and feeling hot, red blood spurting over his hands. It excited him in a way he had not expected. He could hardly wait, fearless as he was—and in that wild land, Katlian prized fearlessness above all else.

At the yelping signal of a Yakutat leader, they suddenly attacked with knives, spears, and muskets. Katlian saw that the enemy were Russians and Aleuts. That was a surprise—a good one. The Aleuts, the first he'd ever seen, were small and slight of build compared to the Tlingit. He would have to kill two of them to count as one of his own. But he saw that without the fierce battle skills of the Tlingit, they were instantly terrified. Good, he thought, that will make it easier to kill a lot of them. Like killing rabbits in a nest.

Baranov jumped up, understood the situation in a flash, and grabbed for his musket. A spear thrown by Katlian pinned his shirt to a tree. As he tore loose, Baranov wheeled around and shot an attacker. He saw four Kenaitze guides run to the Tlingit and get captured. He wondered, *Why did they so quickly surrender to the attackers?* Kuskov fired the falconet, killing two Tlingit.

The battle continued inconclusively in the advancing dawn for well over an hour. Suddenly, musket fire raked the Tlingits from the sea as a Russian whaler from Nuchek Island came in with guns blazing. Katlian glared at them.

"Katlian! Come! We go. Katlian!!" yelled a Tlingit warrior.

The Tlingit vanished into the woods, but three were taken prisoner.

Baranov mused to himself, "So this is battle and death."

Katlian reluctantly retreated through the forest to their landing place. The battle leader of the Yakutat Tlingit had ordered the retreat, and he had to obey. But he complained to another warrior, *"I killed two Aleuts and one Russian, and now I have no scalps to show for it, not even one!"* Feeling great frustration, he and his companion got into a brightly painted Yakutat dugout battle canoe to escape with others carrying two bloody wounded warriors.

This canoe could carry up to forty warriors and their gear. It had been carved out of a single cedar log and had a large eagle figurehead brightly painted black, gold, and white. This head thrust forward over the water, beyond the prow designed to cut through the waves. The canoe's tail also had a high overhang to protect against swells from behind.

Katlian had assumed there would be plenty of time to collect his scalps after they defeated the enemy. *"I made a big mistake!"* he said to the other warrior as they picked up their paddles and started to help propel their battle canoe out to sea. *"Next time I will cut the scalp from each enemy right after each kill."*

"Our Yakutat Tlingit don't take scalps," said his companion.

"I know, but it's our right. And why did we retreat?" continued Katlian. *"Just because a boat of Russians with guns arrived and killed two Tlingit. How cowardly. We should have just made a partial retreat to the woods near that beach for cover and then shot the Russian reinforcements when they were most vulnerable—as they beached their boat and ran up the shore."*

These Yakutat Tlingit cousins are not bold enough, he thought. *"Your people do not understand Oondikat."*

"Oondikat?" asked the companion.

"Yes. That is the burning inner spirit that ruthlessly protects the right of the Tlingit to live on this land forever. And Oondikat means that, when attacked, you must not retreat but must turn back and fight even harder to kill the enemy—and kill them all. The Russian enemies are filthy rats that can take over the land by contaminating it with their diseases that kill more Tlingit than their guns!"

The other warrior grunted in agreement.

"And I noticed today," Katlian went on, *"that these rats even have the putrid smell of disease. They do not smell clean like the*

Tlingit. We Tlingit smell like the land that is rightfully ours. And these rats are destroying the otter and seal that are the wealth of the Tlingit. Only by Oondikat can the Tlingit rid the land of these rats and survive. You Yakutat do not understand this."

"I've never heard of Oondikat."

Katlian glanced at the wounded moaning in the bottom of the canoe. *"This is not the way to fight,"* he muttered as he paddled. *"We should throw these overboard. They are contaminated with the awful spirit of defeat."*

Kuponek reported, "Nine Aleut hunters killed. Two Russians dead." Then he went back to where the Tlingit prisoners were being held.

Baranov saw three Russians from the reinforcements join his group, headed by Egor Purtov, who said, "We were scouting for otter nearby and heard the shooting."

"Thank God," said Baranov.

Kuponek quickly returned with more information about the prisoners.

"These are Tlingit. We can make them tell us why they attacked."

Baranov nodded. The bound prisoners were carried to a fire, and their feet were pushed toward red-hot coals to make them talk. Baranov looked sternly at them, impressed that they merely grunted and didn't scream as he smelled the searing of their flesh. He quickly had enough. "Go ahead, question them," he told Kuponek.

Kuponek interrogated them in rudimentary Tlingit. *"Why you attack our camp?"*

A Tlingit answered, *"We came to attack Kenaitze. We did not know this camp had Russians."*

"Why you attack Kenaitze?"

"Yakutat council make war on Kenaitze. Ten war canoes will attack soon. We are a scout group."

Kuponek told Baranov, "Yakutat Tlingit make war on Kenaitze. These men were sent first. Soon ten Tlingit war canoes will attack the Kenaitze village."

"We must warn Chief Grigor! And I saw four Kenaitze guides taken prisoner."

"They thought the Tlingit were Kenaitze and ran to meet them. They know the Kenaitze plan to attack our camp. So they now are Tlingit prisoners."

"The Kenaitze planned to attack *us?"* Baranov was incredulous.

"Yes. A Kenaitze guide just told me. Grigor want to show Tlingit he can beat Russians."

"We'll take these prisoners to Kodiak and make them teach us to speak and think more like Tlingit. But first, let's go have a talk with Chief Grigor!"

That evening, Baranov and his men strode across the tidal flats to Grigor's village. The chief and his men came out to meet them in front of their longhouses. When Baranov saw Grigor, his fury came to a boil, but he quickly restrained it; he wanted to wait for the right moment to blast this perfidious chief.

Standing face to face with him, he murmured in a low undertone, "The Tlingit from Yakutat attacked us on Montague. They killed eleven of my men and took four of yours prisoner."

"How could that be, great Nanuq?" replied the chief. "You guaranteed my men's safety!"

What a slimy, fat bastard, thought Baranov. Now was the moment to unleash. "Because they thought the attackers were *your* warriors and ran to join them! They expected *you* to attack! Only the Tlingit got to us before you could!"

". . . You think *I* would do such a thing, to the great Nanuq?"

"When my ship comes back, I'd like to sail it into this bay, aim its cannon at your lodge, and blow you to bits!"

"You would do that with Anooka inside?"

Baranov replied softly, "No."

Chief Grigor flashed a knowing look—he'd found a weak spot.

But Baranov's toughness quickly recovered. "Those Tlingit thought we were your people! Ten more war canoes are coming to attack you."

Grigor immediately snapped an order to two of his warriors, who ran off to carry it out.

Baranov took another step toward the chief. "Next year, when I come back, you'll give me a hundred men in *bidarkas* for my hunting fleet, and twenty hostages! If you don't, I'll find you when Anooka isn't with you, and like a grizzly takes down a moose, I'll rip you to pieces and feed your guts to the wolves. . . *Chief Grigor!*"

"I think you would," observed Grigor as he stepped back.

Baranov turned quickly and strode away seething, his men rushing to catch up. Through the open door of the lodge, from the shadow within, Anooka watched.

CHAPTER 8

TO BUILD A SHIP IN WILDERNESS

God's Friend Simeon, sailing in light wind, led its flotilla of *bidarkas* at the end of their hunt, with only a thousand otter pelts but with no men lost. The yield was low because the Aleuts had feared going into better hunting coves deep in Tlingit territory without escort from an armed ship. Baranov and his group met them, and together they headed back to Fort Alexander, the Shelikhov Company's outpost at the south end of the Kenai Peninsula. Baranov went ashore and, inside the stockade rampart of the log fort, saw the manager, Vassili Molokhov, who said, "Grigor Konovalov, the Lebedev Company leader at Fort St. Nicholas, wants to force us off the mainland. He says his company has exclusive authority to settle the mainland, and that our company is authorized only on the islands."

"How does he think he can push us out of here?" asked Baranov.

"By turning the Natives against us."

"…I'll go and have a word with him. So I have two troublesome Grigors!"

***

Katlian and the Tlingit raiding party returned in their war canoes to Yakutat. Several men and women quickly gathered around to hear of their exploit. It was immediately seen as a defeat. Mothers and wives of slain warriors filled the air with wailing. The expedition battle leader went to report to Chief Ish-Kah in his longhouse, and Katlian insisted on tagging along.

The three men sat on the floor in a semicircle, and the battle leader drew a map on the dirt floor as he described the battle and its outcome. The chief listened and said nothing. When the battle leader finished, Katlian spoke. *"We could have defeated the Russian reinforcements. They were vulnerable because they were coming from the sea. We could hide in the woods and easily shoot them as they landed. It was a mistake to retreat."*

Then Chief Ish-Kah spoke. *"We didn't go there to fight the Russians. We went to fight the Kenaitze. We should have broken off the fight as soon as we saw there were Russians there. We're not strong enough to beat the Russians and their big guns. It's the Kenaitze we must fight and defeat."*

"Then let us go back," urged Katlian. *"From the prisoners we took, we know where they are now. Let us go back."*

"You will have to convince the Wolverines, Katlian. It is their sons who die in battle."

Katlian and the battle leader waited a week before asking for a meeting with the Wolverines, to give grief a chance to subside. At the meeting with the seven women in the tribal lodge, the battle leader had little to say, deferring to Katlian to make the case.

"We have to fight for what is rightfully ours or it will be taken away," he said. *"The Copper River and all of its rich bounty of fish has long been ours. We cannot let the Kenaitze take it away from us. We must chase them from the Copper and push them back into the midlands where they belong. If we don't fight for our rights, they are lost forever."*

For a long moment, the women stared at Katlian. Then their leader said, *"You made a big mistake attacking the Russians instead of the Kenaitze you were supposed to attack. How can we be sure you two won't make another stupid mistake that will waste the lives of more of our cherished sons? How can we be sure you will know what you're doing this time?"*

"We won't make that mistake again."

"So what new mistakes will you make? Katlian, you should go back to Sitka, where your mistakes won't cost the lives of our sons."

***

Baranov, Kuponek, and six other men approached Fort St. Nicholas in their *bidarkas* and pulled up on the shore below the log fort. Baranov ambled up to its main gate. Konovalov was perched with two of his men on top of a rampart looking down at Baranov.

"I'm Aleksandr Baranov, and I want to talk with Grigor Konovalov."

"That's me. What do you want?"

"I hear you claim an exclusive government license to settle the mainland. Show me written proof of that claim."

"You'll see no such thing until it suits me to show it to you, which it doesn't. Now get out of here before I have you drawn and quartered and fed to the bears."

"You know, my boss, Shelikhov, is a part owner of the Lebedev Company."

"I don't care if he is. Get out of here, and get your straggly mob off the mainland. Any that I find on the mainland in thirty days will be shot."

Baranov, seeing that he was outgunned, went back to his *bidarka,* humiliated, and said to Kuponek, "They have us outnumbered and outgunned, so we can't pick a fight here."

Baranov's group headed back down the Kenai Peninsula and then crossed the straits to Kodiak.

The hunt of 1792 ended in mid-summer, and the hunting fleet returned to Kodiak just as a boat from Okhotsk arrived, named *Orel.* As the small schooner's sails were furled and it glided in, Baranov jumped onto the dock from his *bidarka.* Finally, a supply ship!

The boat was tied on, and its skipper, James Shields, threw over the gangplank as he yelled to the men on the wharf, "Where is Aleksandr Baranov?"

The short, red-headed, wiry Shields wore a scant shirt revealing tattoos over every inch of his arms and chest. He had an unusual facial expressiveness that grabbed attention and distracted from what would otherwise have been a face of remarkable ugliness. *What a curious-looking person,* thought Baranov, who said from the foot of the gangplank, "I am Baranov."

"Aha! I'm James Shields. My crew and I are English, sailing for Shelikhov."

He charged down the plank enthusiastically to shake hands.

"I just broke the record—only six weeks from Okhotsk!"

Shields' infectious enthusiasm delighted Baranov, who announced to all, "Tonight we have a *praznyk!* We celebrate our hunt—and the arrival of our supply ship!"

One of Shields' crewmen handed a packet of mail to Baranov. He opened it eagerly and quickly fanned through its contents. There it was, just what he'd been waiting for—a letter from Matrona. He opened it and, tucked inside, found a letter from Afanassya. He read this one first, and a slight smile spread across his face. His daughter had been fourteen when she wrote it the year before, and it was full of bubbly descriptions of her activities and desires, in which he delighted. In his mind's eye he saw a pretty, vivacious girl with long, blonde curls prancing about, laughing with her friends. But there were four words that jumped off the page at him: "Papa, I miss you!"

He read Matrona's matter-of-fact letter, full of news of Kargopol and of their family from the prior year. She ended it, "I pray that you are well and safe and that you will come home to us."

He put the letters back in the envelope and put it in his pocket, deep in thought about the uncertainties of his future. Just three more years until he could return. However, as yet there was no replacement for him anywhere in sight.

Soon those thoughts were pushed aside by his imagining of Afanassya's girlish activities, and he smiled again. One day, he hoped, he would walk down the aisle of a majestic Russian church in St. Petersburg with Afanassya on his arm in a flowing white wedding dress carrying a bouquet, while the organ and chorus performed the soaring hymn "The Joy of Elysium" by Mikhail Sokolovsky, Baranov's favorite hymn.

That evening in the dining hall, a *praznyk* was in full swing, and so was Baranov. He grinned as he walked the hall with a small vodka keg, filling every man's cup. Aleut women quickly got drunk and giggly. A circle of men, arms linked, performed a Russian folk dance. A tipsy Baranov got his usual drunken yen for warm female skin next to his and led a laughing young Aleut woman to a side room.

The next morning, Shields and Baranov walked through the hung-over village as Baranov spoke about a letter he had received from the home office via Shields's boat.

"Shelikhov's letter says you'll help build a ship here. Wonderful! A third of our ships sink in savage seas from here to Siberia. Now we can build replacements."

Shields replied dismissively, "Shelikhov is full of grand ideas."

"You built *Orel* in Okhotsk. Why not build another ship here?"

"Where's your timber? Where's your sawmill? Where are your ship's ways? Where are your tools?"

"Shelikhov says your cargo has the tools and rigging."

"Barely."

Baranov persisted, "The best timber is on Montague Island. Unload, and we'll sail over there and you'll see for yourself." Shipbuilding was now not a hallucination, but a practical possibility that only needed resourcefulness and perseverance to be realized—two requirements he had in abundance.

As the schooner *Orel* sailed between the Kenai coast and Montague, Baranov was delighted to be at the wheel, learning navigation from Shields. "Finally, I'm being taught to sail," he said. "None of the Russian captains would teach me."

"Yes," the captain agreed, "a closed club, those Okhotsk navigators."

"And they knew I'd be hamstrung here as manager without this knowledge."

Shields shook his head with a teasing grin. "No, the real reason is that only an English master of the sea, like me, could possibly make a sailor out of a landlubber like you, Sasha." His grin disappeared as he continued, "Where's all the great shipbuilding timber you promised me?"

"Just around that point."

In the woods of Montague Island, Baranov, Shields, and two armed crewmembers trekked through the woods examining trees, which met Shields's enthusiastic approval. "Sasha, you're right! Excellent timber!"

"And a perfect shipyard site lies just across the bay," Baranov promised.

Later that day they sailed to Resurrection Bay, where

Orel anchored. Baranov and Shields went ashore and climbed the tidal slope. Shields observed, "Many things are still missing. But at least you have good timber and a fair place for a shipyard."

Baranov, glad he was overcoming the man's reluctance, insisted, "We *have* to build our own ships. Then we'll sail to California and Hawaii for supplies, trading furs for what we need to survive. No more at Shelikhov's mercy, shipping supplies from Siberia when he feels like it."

Shields rolled his eyes skeptically.

Baranov continued, "We'll bring the men and tools we need from Kodiak, and we'll get started. How long to build the first ship?"

"If all the problems are solved, which is very doubtful, maybe in just over a year," Shields told him. "But, my friend, I'm sailing back to Okhotsk in six months."

Two months later, they entered the Kodiak warehouse and went to a table where the design was spread out for the ship that Baranov wanted to build. For weeks, he had been completely absorbed in every detail of the project. His mind worked that way—he had a rare ability to focus doggedly on something important until it was accomplished. Baranov said,

"I've made some changes to the boat plan."

Shields took a quick look at the revision, shook his head, and exclaimed, "Two decks and three masts? Too big."

"We need it! More cargo capacity."

"You think you're a naval architect? Baranov, you're the strangest brew of intelligence and stupidity I've ever seen. Well, do whatever you want, because I return to Okhotsk in April."

"No, you won't. I can't build this without you."

"True. But I'm leaving anyway."

"I order you to stay. My letter of authorization from Okhotsk gives me command over all captains of the Shelikhov Company in these waters!"

"Command *me*? Never!" In a flash of anger, Shields grabbed Baranov by the collar and threw him across the room. Baranov sprang back and slugged him. A furious fight ensued. Shields knocked Baranov down and went out the door. Baranov quickly got up and pursued him.

"*Damn!* I'll sail right *now!*" Shields barked.

"Like *hell* you will!"

Shields pushed Baranov, who slugged him again. They rolled around wrestling in the dirt, got up, and slugged it out some more, bloodying each other. Kuskov and Kuponek rushed over to break up the brawl and restrained Shields. Others grabbed Baranov, who calmed down quickly and was released as he ordered his men, "Lock him in his cabin on *Orel*. And chain and lock the wheel so he can't sail away."

"You *bastard*, Baranov!" Shields spat as he was immobilized by four big Russians.

"Take him away," Baranov whispered.

From the wharf the next morning, Baranov boarded *Orel* carrying a document. He had black eyes, a bandaged head. Kuskov followed. Baranov marched up to Shields's cabin door. Kuskov unlocked it. Baranov opened the door and looked in. Shields, who was sitting on his berth, also had two black eyes, and he stared at Baranov as he entered.

"You look as bad as me," Baranov said.

Shields had no reaction.

Baranov waved a sheet of paper. "My authorization from the Commander at Okhotsk to control sea captains here in the Russian service," he said, and handed him the document. He had to convince Shields that there was no choice but to obey him, and he had to somehow persuade Shields to want to do it, which was going to be harder.

Shields glanced at it. "Can't read Russian much."

A moment of silence followed as the beat-up men stared at each other. Baranov saw he'd achieved his first objective, but getting Shields to willingly cooperate would be harder. He pulled over the one chair in the cabin and sat facing Shields. "Another reason to stay: You'll get rich here, with a share of the hunt plus a salary bonus of over 2,000 rubles for each hunting season."

"Hm!" Shields' eyes opened wider, pleasantly surprised by the prospect of making real money. "But you still lack many materials to build a boat," he continued in a matter-of-fact tone. "Not enough caulking, and no iron nails."

"We have iron," said Baranov. "We'll scavenge it from old wrecks along the coast. We've paid Aleuts with iron. We'll borrow it back. We'll make our own nails."

"What about caulking?"

"We use moss to caulk our cabins."

"It'll wash right out on a ship!"

"I'll think of something," said Baranov with customary self-assurance in his own resourcefulness. "Whale oil! Mix it with whale oil, so it'll stick."

Shields shook his head in disbelief.

The chief manager went on, "We can start our ship building this fall and build right through the winter when our men can't hunt anyway."

Baranov got up and walked out. Kuskov started to re-padlock the door. But with a wave of the hand, Baranov said, "No," and the door was left unlocked.

***

Looking over the bow of his war canoe, Katlian saw his family's Sitka village ahead. How would K'asasee feel about him, he wondered, after so many months' absence? What would their baby boy look like now, almost a year old?

As Katlian and some companions beached their canoe, he turned toward Aakashook's longhouse, and there he saw them. K'asasee and little Aanyaanax were there, K'asasee outside watching the baby as he crawled around examining blades of grass and little sticks. Katlian smiled, jumped out of the canoe, and hurried to her. She had not yet seen him.

He called out, *"K'asasee!"* She turned and looked up at him, and for an instant didn't recognize him. Then she did, and began to cry as she scooped up Aanyaanax and then Katlian took them both in his arms, beaming with happiness.

After a long moment, tough as he was, he had to admit, *"I'm glad to be back."*

CHAPTER 9

CATHERINE, TSARINA OF ALL THE RUSSIAS

In the St. Paul dining hall at night, a raucous *praznyk* was in session. On the wall hung a hand-scrawled sign: *NEW YEAR 1793.* To the right of it, Kuskov nailed a crudely drawn map of European Russia, Siberia, and Alaska.

"Here's where we are, boys," he said, pointing to Kodiak Island, "and there's home!" He drew a circle with his index finger over Russia and Siberia.

"Mother Russia!" someone yelled. Others called out as well, and it became a chant, *"Mother Russia! Mother Russia! Mother Russia!"* Then someone grabbed a *balalaika* and started playing "Mother Russia." Soon everyone was singing it.

When they were finished, Kuskov said, "Look, Alaska and eastern Siberia are like two bears about to rub noses over the Bering Straits."

Baranov spoke up as he stepped toward the map, pointing. "The stretch of these two bears covers great distances. From Kodiak across the North Pacific, Siberia, and Russia to our capital at St. Petersburg is 8,000 miles. *Think of it!* It takes a whole *year* to travel that distance. A whole year for a letter to travel. That's why, my friends, most of the time when we have a problem, we're on our own. But we can do it, can't we, boys?"

The answer was a loud cheer with vodka mugs held high.

***

Tsarina Catherine the Great was a charismatic and Machiavellian German princess who had married Tsarevich Peter, heir to the Russian throne. He had been quite unpopular, whereas she was loved by the masses (literally, it seemed—she had a constant parade of lovers). And within two months of her husband becoming Tsar Peter III, she had conspired with the palace guard to engineer a coup, forcing him to abdicate in her favor. Shortly after his fall from power, he had mysteriously and conveniently died.

Besides being a ruthless power seeker, Catherine was also a Renaissance woman who invigorated architecture and the arts in St. Petersburg. The magnificent Winter Palace, the most sumptuous palace in all of Europe, was where she held court. And it was there in the spring of 1793, at the age of sixty-four, that she had consented to an audience with Grigori Shelikhov and his wife Natalya.

Prior to the meeting, the Tsarina received a preparatory briefing from a new assistant, the twenty-nine-year-old Nikolai Rezanov, in an anteroom off the imperial audience chamber. He was a tall, square-faced young man with a shock of curly blonde hair, dressed in a dark blue suit.

The Tsarina wore a flowing dark red and gold silk dress, her graying brown hair pushed up in a high bun surrounded by a pearl and diamond tiara. Around her neck, she wore seven layers of pearl necklaces, each with a teardrop-shaped diamond pendant. Her earrings were large, round diamonds surrounded by clusters of pearls. The air was filled with the sweet floral scent of her Rallet perfume, "Imperial Rose."

"So we review the new map with the partition of Poland, and then meet with the Shelikhovs about Russian America?" she asked.

Rezanov bowed. "Yes, Your Majesty."

"What do the Shelikhovs want from me?"

"Not much. They want to report on their progress in our Russian America colonies, to ask for a priest to be sent and for permission to use serfs for farming over there."

"No one ever meets with me who wants 'not much.' It's a game, you know. What will they say they want? But what do they really want? What will it cost me? What good can they do for me? Being the empress means always being surrounded by people who want something from me."

"Ah, yes, Your Majesty."

"And people often ask for something that is a *mask* for the real thing they want. Sometimes that real thing can cost much more than what they seem to be asking for. The trick is to see through them, give them something that will satisfy them and cost me next to nothing, and benefit me as much as possible.

"As for the Shelikhovs' serfs, well, as you know, serfs are a problem. My proposed Nakaz proclamation would have mostly eliminated the slavery of serfs, but the Senate wouldn't agree, and at that time I couldn't overrule them. But in Russian America, the Senate has no power, so if serfs go there, it won't be as slaves. All right, let's go."

She rose with a burst of energy and headed for the double doors—constructed, like so much of her surroundings, in the French style—which were opened by two soldiers elaborately uniformed in blue with gold trim. As she entered and mounted the raised dais of the audience chamber, four trumpets announced her regal entrance with a vigorous, triumphant fanfare matched by her smile of command. With that, Catherine the Great, Tsarina of all the Russias, approached an ornately carved red mahogany table at one end of the dais. Rezanov followed her and unrolled the map of Poland on the table as she sat in a gold-trimmed white chair behind it. Twenty luxuriantly dressed courtiers stood on a red carpet around the perimeter of the chamber, a vast, high-ceiling hall with marble columns and two gigantic paintings of Tsar Peter the Great, at the battles of Lesnaya and Poltava, on the side walls.

Having just entered the palace, Grigori's eyes were enraptured by the extravagance of the ornate interior. An ordinary subject of the Tsarina would likely have been intimidated by such grandeur, but not Grigori Shelikhov. It emboldened him. He saw it as a call to be grand himself. "Magnificent!" he whispered to Natalya.

"Indeed!" she whispered back. They were led by an elegantly suited usher down endless halls decorated with heroic paintings, and through countless sets of giant double doors manned by blue-uniformed guards, until they finally reached the cavernous imperial audience chamber.

Grigori saw the Tsarina seated behind a table on the raised dais. She was looking at a map of Poland on the table in front of her. Her hands flattened the map as if she were holding Poland down to keep it from rolling up and bouncing away from her (as well it might, insofar as King Stanislaw of Poland-Lithuania was a former lover). The Shelikhovs were led forward by the usher to face the empress, and they bowed deeply before her when she looked up. Behind the Tsarina, Grigori saw a clutch of her ministers and courtiers. The scent of powdered wigs filled the air.

"Your Majesty," said Rezanov, "I present Grigori and Natalya Shelikhov of the Shelikhov Company, who have colonized Russian America at Kodiak in your name."

The Tsarina motioned for them to come closer, with a slight smile and look of complete self-possession. They took three steps forward to just below the royal platform. She looked them over with some interest, knowing they were adventurers from the Far East.

At her signal, the chamberlain murmured, "You may approach the table."

The three climbed the two steps of the platform and drew close. Shelikhov glanced at the chamberlain for permission to open the map, and the aide whispered something to the Empress.

"You have something to show me, Mr. Shelikhov? Something as important as the partition of Poland?" she asked in her strong contralto.

"Your Majesty, I'm sorry, but I know nothing of Poland," answered Shelikhov. "My attention has been on your eastern realm of Russian America."

"My *realm*? I thought it was just a string of foggy and windy islands with a lot of seals, otter, and Aleuts."

The chamberlain moved the map of Poland to one side of the table. Shelikhov rolled out his map there, and the Empress rose from her chair for a better view. She was taller than Shelikhov expected. Standing ramrod straight, she could be quite intimidating, but not to Shelikhov.

"It's much more, Your Majesty," he said. "The islands lead to a large mainland about the size of Spain, France, and Germany put together." His hand swept over the map, from the end of the Aleutians toward the mainland interior.

"That big! And how many Natives live there?" she asked.

"About 20,000 along the islands and coast, and perhaps another 30,000 farther inland. Right now, about four hundred Russians are there."

"What an empty place! But it's part of my realm, like Siberia?"

"Yes, Your Majesty."

"As you know, three years ago I declared that the Natives are Russian citizens. But I wonder. . . What does that really mean over there? Yes, what does that mean to them? Here in Russia, sensible social changes are thoroughly resisted and can only be achieved little by little. But perhaps Russian America is a place without strong traditions, where we may create a society as it should be."

She examined the map for a moment, then asked, "Are any of the Natives Christians?"

Shelikhov replied, "We have performed many lay baptisms, Your Majesty. However, Chief Manager Baranov has asked us to send a priest."

His wife Natalya added, "So we can properly baptize many more into our faith, Your Majesty."

"Yes! They have souls that need saving too, so we must get

priests over there. See to that," replied the Tsarina. "I hear you have a proposal regarding serfs. What is it?"

"We have thirty serf families we want to take to Russian America to grow food for the colony at Yakutat," said Shelikhov as he pointed to Yakutat on the map.

"Splendid idea!" exclaimed the Tsarina. "But be careful with serfs. Let's not have another Pugachev Revolt from sending them to a wild country. And in Russian America, I don't want serfs used as *slaves*."

Both Shelikhovs responded in unison with fawning overemphasis, "Yes, Your Majesty!"

They were delighted—out of the Tsarina's sight they would, indeed, use unpaid serfs as slaves.

The Tsarina, unsure of their sincerity, gave her order.

"Really. Not slaves. All right, you may do it, but just at Yakutat."

CHAPTER 10

THE VANCOUVER CHALLENGE AND BATTLES OF WITS

Back in Alaska in the fall of 1793, at Prince William Sound near Montague Island, a full load of Russian and Aleut workers were sailing aboard *Orel*, with Baranov at the wheel learning navigation from Shields, toward a lumber harvest for building a ship.

Timber was felled and trimmed. Rafts of logs were lashed together and pulled across the sound by *bidarkas*. Buildings and the ship's ways were put up at Resurrection Bay. Wooden planks were made. Iron was melted in a forge and poured into molds for nails.

Baranov and Shields stood amid it all as snow began to fall. Surveying the scene, Shields nodded with admiration and exclaimed, "Amazing. You're doing the impossible! But how are we going to *feed* these men?"

Baranov replied, "I'll make a deal with Chief Grigor."

"To get food in trade for *what?*"

"I'll think of something," Baranov replied.

Some days later, Baranov and Kuponek returned to Resurrection

Bay in a *bidarka* followed by four Kenaitze canoes loaded with fish and deer meat.

Shields asked Baranov, "How'd you get all this?"

"I thought of something he wanted," Baranov answered, turning away to avoid further explanation.

The shipbuilding proceeded as winter set in with a blinding blizzard, and a frigid New Year's Day 1794 came and went. Intense labor continued on the construction of the vessel.

***

In April, as snow fled and meadows turned green, Baranov headed back to Kodiak in the thirty-foot sloop *Olga* to shift his attention from boat building to gathering men from the villages for the hunting season. Egor Purtov, in a *bidarka* with another man, caught up with him at the Barren Islands on the way to Kodiak, where *Olga* was anchored for lack of wind. Purtov brought his *bidarka* alongside and climbed aboard. "Sasha, a British warship is here. Twenty-gun man o' war. It's called *Discovery*—and a second ship is on the way."

"Where is *Discovery* now?"

"In Kenai Bay, heading for Cape Elizabeth and Fort Alexander."

"Any idea what they're up to?"

"They seem to be on a mapping expedition."

"Aha, map it and it's yours!"

"I told them everything in sight around here belongs to Russia."

"You *talked* to them?"

"Yes, I went onto their ship and met their captain, one George Vancouver. Doesn't speak Russian, and I don't speak English, but we both speak a little French, so we got by with that. I brought him some fresh halibut as a gift for him and his men."

"Excellent, Egor! Excellent."

"He said, just like Captain Cook, they're still trying to find a Northwest Passage. But now he doesn't think it's there to be found."

"What kind of questions did he ask you?"

"Whether we had any maps or charts to show him."

"What did you tell him?"

"Yes, of course, I said, but that you had them. So he'd like to see you, and our charts."

"I see. The problem is, if we show the British our charts, they can dispute them—insist they are incomplete, and that therefore Russia doesn't really own what we claim. Based on Captain Cook's maps, they'll say *they're* the true owners here. What is he like?"

"Every bit a gentleman. Very polite."

"The worst kind of Englishman. I've heard about them. They disarm you with politeness and charm while they plot how they're going to stab you in the back."

"What should we do?"

"I should meet with him, and I crave to see the inside of a British man o' war. But I have to continue to Kodiak first to check on preparations for the hunt. Then I'll head back to the Kenai. I should be able to meet Vancouver in five days. So paddle back, take the British some more fresh halibut, and tell the good captain I'll try to get there to meet with him then. But don't get involved in any discussion about who owns what. Just act like a gracious host on our own territory. I will bring only my local Kenai chart to show him. I'll tell him the chart of our whole colony is back in Kodiak, which is true. I don't think he'll want to go that far out of his way to see it, so I can dodge the issue of who owns Alaska."

"Very well. Goodbye, Sasha."

Baranov became too busy in Kodiak to meet with Vancouver in the Kenai, though he sent messages asking Vancouver to wait a few more days. But Vancouver had to take advantage of tides and wind, and he headed south.

Egor Purtov returned to Kodiak and met Baranov at the warehouse, where he was taking inventory, to tell him the news.

"I see," said Baranov. "Couldn't wait. . . . It's just as well. This Englishman might have gleaned something from me and my local chart, despite my caution, that they could use to undercut Russia's claim to Alaska."

"I understand."

"To tell you the truth, Egor, just *thinking* about this international chess game makes me a little nervous. But at the same time, I find it invigorating. Here I, the son of a *mestchannin*, am playing my very own hand in a gamble of wits over the fate of Her Majesty's colonies."

Baranov returned to the shipbuilding at Resurrection Bay, which went on through the spring and summer, with great intensity and the constant clatter of hammers, as the boat took shape on the shipway that held it up like a big hand. And Kenaitze food was continuously delivered in canoes.

Then the food shipments stopped, and the mood of workers at the building site turned ugly.

Baranov and Kuponek visited Chief Grigor to find out why. They found the portly leader in his lodge.

"Why have the food deliveries stopped?" asked Baranov.

"You lied about your power," Chief Grigor said flatly. "The Lebedev men say only *they* have power over this area, not you. They shoot at my men delivering food to you, so we stop. They say Konovalov chase you away from Fort St. Nicholas. They say Nanuq a coward. So I stop food."

"They lie."

"How can I know what is true?"

"I'll show you."

Baranov and Kuponek turned away and left. As they paddled back, Baranov puzzled over how to finally resolve the problem with Konovalov.

The next night, in his small cabin, Shields and Kuponek met with him. Shields said, "Sasha, you have a serious morale problem here. You've lost a lot of the men's respect because you've let this Konovalov get away with his bullying."

"So far, I haven't found a way to take action that doesn't create more problems than it solves. For us simply to attack Fort St. Nicholas would be illegal. It would get a lot of people killed, and I'd risk getting myself hauled back to Okhotsk in chains. Yet we've seen what happens if I do nothing."

"All the shipbuilding work has stopped," Shields pointed out, "so doing nothing is no longer a choice."

Kuponek had an idea: "Maybe make *Konovalov* do something so *he* will be put in chains and go to Okhotsk."

"What was that?" exclaimed Baranov. "Say that again."

"Make Konovalov do something so *he* can be put in chains and sent to Okhotsk."

"Interesting idea! But what?"

Shields offered, "Lure him to attack us here, while we're ready for him. We would ambush him, taking him captive. He'd be blamed for attacking us, and then we'd arrest him and send him to Irkutsk for trial."

"But how could we do it?" asked Baranov. "How could we be sure to win with no serious injuries or loss of life?"

"He'd have to come with a small group, not a large war party," said Shields.

". . . I have an idea, but I'd have to tell a lie, and he'd have to fall for it."

"Like what?" asked Shields.

"I could send him a message saying I've received a letter from the Governor General of East Siberia authorizing me to settle the dispute between the Shelikhov and Lebedev companies. And I'd insist that he come here for a meeting."

"You think he'd believe it?"

"He might think that a claim like that is too serious, that I could get into too much trouble for making it up. Hell, I could get hanged if he could prove it!"

"So you'd have to use it to get him here, and then destroy all proof that you'd done it."

"Exactly."

"So you'd have to write two letters—one to Konovalov, and a fake letter from the governor general to you. But you can't write both, or he'll recognize the handwriting."

Baranov nodded.

"Even the *paper* has to be different," said Shields. "I have paper on my ship that's different from yours."

"There's no one else here who can write in good Russian. I'll have to do both. I'll do the letter from the governor general in script, and for my letter to Konovalov, I'll use print in block letters."

Baranov got out a piece of paper and started to write.

The next morning, he handed Kuponek the letter. The Aleut got in a *bidarka* with another Native and headed for Fort St. Nicholas.

Near the mouth of the Kenai River, Kuponek walked up to the main gate of Fort St. Nicholas. It opened, and a belligerent-looking Konovalov stepped out. Kuponek handed him the letter, which the other immediately opened and read. Kuponek stood there waiting for a verbal reply. When Konovalov finished, he grunted and sneered at Kuponek. "He expects me to *believe* this rubbish? Ha!"

Konovalov went back inside, but just before closing the door, turned to look Kuponek in the eye for a moment, searching for truth. Kuponek was steady and impassive. Konovalov's gaze fell to the ground for an instant, then rose again, and he slammed the door. Kuponek stood there for a moment before he returned to his *bidarka,* and he and his companion started back.

On the evening of the next day at Resurrection Bay, Baranov sat writing a report. There was a knock at the door, and Kuponek entered.

Baranov looked up. "You did it! Well, did he believe it?"

"Not at first. Then he thought about it."

"So we don't know if he'll take the bait."

Shields entered and listened.

"Big fish circles bait," said Kuponek. "Big fish not afraid because it is big fish. But curious. Then big fish bite."

Baranov replied, "Kuponek, make sure we have a watch day and night up the bay, so we'll know if he's coming, and how many are with him. James, we don't know for sure, but Konovalov could show up any day, and we must be ready."

"Yes. I've been thinking about that. My old army training will help."

For the next couple of days, the men of Resurrection Bay were consumed with preparations. A watchman hid in the brush overlooking the bay about a mile from the shipbuilding camp. Shields trained the Russian hunters and the Aleuts to ambush and seize Konovalov and his men. There was a changing of the guard at the watch station.

But when dusk set in, the watchman on duty fell asleep. Konovalov and his party of four *bidarkas* paddled by unnoticed, landing in the unsuspecting scene at the shipbuilding camp. He motioned to four of his men to hide nearby with their cutlasses, ready to spring to action if need be. Then, with three other men, he started toward the buildings, his hand on the handle of his sheathed cutlass.

"Baranov! Where are you, Baranov?"

In his cabin near the shore, Shields heard the man, looked out his window, and saw the big Russian, about fifty feet away, coming up the embankment with his men. He doused his lantern, grabbed his cutlass and a pistol, and slipped out the door on the opposite side of the cabin from Konovalov. He sprinted up a trail through brush to the hunters' bunkhouse a hundred yards away, and ran inside.

"Konovalov is here! Grab your weapons, and take your positions. But don't let him see you. He's coming up the central path. When you're in position, remember, wait for my signal. Go, men, go! Singers, get started!"

Three men in the bunkhouse started singing a popular drinking song to create the illusion that everything was unremarkable. The others sneaked out a back door to take up their ambush positions. Shields ran down a trail through the brush to Baranov's cabin and burst inside. He found Baranov so intently studying the plans for the ship they were building that he was oblivious to what was going on.

"Konovalov is here!" the Englishman whispered.

Baranov immediately became alert, thought for a second about what to do, then jumped up and grabbed the fake governor general letter. He stuck it in his pocket, grabbed his cutlass, strapped it on, and led Shields out the door. They headed toward Konovalov's voice in the dusk.

"Come on out, Baranov, wherever you're hiding!"

"Konovalov! I'm glad you came. We need to talk."

"We're not talking about anything until I see written authority from the governor general!"

"Oh? *You* refused to show me your authority to exclusively occupy the mainland, but now you must see *my* letter from the governor general."

"Give it to me right now!"

Baranov reached into his pocket and handed the forged letter to him. Konovalov unfolded it with a frown, and as he started to study it, Shields gave a hand signal to Baranov's men to attack. Shields and two other men (who jumped forward from behind buildings) grabbed Konovalov, who dropped the letter as he shook them off, pulled out his cutlass, and lunged for Baranov. Baranov pulled out his own and defended himself. He was quicker on his feet than the big Russian, evading Konovalov's slashing thrusts.

A general melee ensued as Baranov's men ambushed Konovalov's companions up the trail. When the Konovalov men who'd been hiding by the shore ran up to assist, they surprised and wounded some Baranov men. A ship builder killed one of Konovalov's men with a musket shot.

Baranov and Konovalov remained in a desperate cutlass duel until Baranov managed to slash one of Konovalov's arms and, almost simultaneously, Shields hit Konovalov's cutlass hand with the backside of a swung axe, forcing the man's weapon to fall clattering to the ground. Baranov, Shields, and two other men immediately jumped Konovalov, who was quickly subdued and tied with hands behind his back and legs hobbled. Konovalov's men were also quickly caught and tied up. The prisoners were hauled into the dining hall with much commotion.

"Take these men down to their boats, strip them of their weapons, and send them back to Fort St. Nicholas."

"You'd send us back in the dark, without food?" one of them asked.

"There's a full moon and a clear sky. You'll find your way. And we'll give you some dried salmon to take with you."

Baranov paused for a moment, looking the prisoners over, then barked, "Get them out of here!"

Commotion followed as they were led away.

"You'll never get away with this," Konovalov snarled. "Ambushing me with a forged letter!"

"What letter? *I* don't see any letter," Baranov told him.

"So? What are you going to do with me?"

"Send you to Kodiak in chains. You'll be kept in a cabin there until the next ship to Okhotsk, where you'll be sent to stand trial in Irkutsk."

". . . Trial? For *what?*"

"I'll think of something. Murder, mistreating the Natives, bad manners, bad breath—something that will get the old Judge of Irkutsk all worked up."

Baranov headed back to his cabin.

Two days later, at the beach of Resurrection Bay, *nigilaxes* bearing Kenaitze food supplies arrived, in recognition of Baranov's arrest of Konovalov. Rapid activity resumed to complete the construction of the ship.

CHAPTER 11

ANOOKA BECOMES ANNA AND LEADS THE BLIND TO DENALI

Finally, the ship was ready for launching, and a delegation of Kenaitzes arrived to witness it, including Chief Grigor, his daughter Anooka, and many of their Kenaitze tribe.

Next to the shipway, a large mixed crowd of Russians and Natives took seats on the embankment as the tide came in and Baranov stood by the new ship to address the crowd. He looked them over, beaming with an intense sense of pride he had rarely felt before. "This is a great day for us all," he declared. "Today we launch the first ship built in Russian America, a ship that can sail across the Pacific, taking our furs to market, then bring back supplies, new settlers, tea, and yes, *vodka!* We can all be proud of what we built here, and we did it by working together. Thank you, everyone! Now, let's christen her and get her wet!"

Turning toward the ship, he pulled out his cutlass and tapped the bow three times. "I hereby christen thee *Phoenix!*"

He had named it after the English ship sailed by the Irishmen Moore and O'Cain, which he had helped two years before in Prince William Sound, and upon which he had roughly patterned this ship.

The blocks holding the boat on the shipway were knocked away, and *Phoenix* slid down into the bay to much cheering. Then Baranov led the singing of a favorite Russian folk song, accompanied by balalaikas.

The time had come—no escaping it now. Baranov walked to the beach, where Chief Grigor's clan was gathering for a wedding. Baranov saw and heard ceremonial drummers begin to beat out a tune to accompany chanting dancers in a circle around nineteen-year-old Anooka, exotically beautiful in her pale, deerskin dress. Once he caught sight of her, he couldn't take his eyes off her.

In preparation, her father had spent the last few months teaching her basic Russian to speak with her new husband. Chief Grigor, across the circle from Baranov, looked on and bellowed cheerily to the great Russian Nanuq, "Months of food for your men have bought us a powerful alliance and gotten Anooka a husband! I wish her mother was still alive to see this! She was from Kodiak, you know, near your village."

Baranov nodded, his eyes still enthralled by the girl.

Moving to the rhythm of the drums, Anooka danced to her father, and at his command she obediently knelt. He draped a bear claw necklace around her neck. It would certainly be a great honor to be married to the great Nanuq. And she would serve both husband and tribe by doing for him whatever he wanted. This was what she had been raised to expect.

But there was one thing *she* wanted. She rose, then danced to Baranov and placed the necklace around his neck, signifying their bond, and the drums beat louder and faster. She looked Baranov straight in the eyes for the second time. What was he like? Would this strong man give her the one thing she wanted, the one thing that would guarantee her undying loyalty forever? *Gentle kindness. Always.*

He was struck by the warmth, intelligence, and innocence in her eyes. As his wedding gift, he gave her jade earrings; she put them on, still looking him in the eyes as she did.

"Now, my dear, I give you your Russian name: Anna Grigoryevna."

She didn't understand, so he pointed to her as he said, "Anna Grigoryevna. . . . Anna."

Then he pointed to himself as he said, "Aleksandr Baranov. . . . Aleksandr."

Smiling, she pointed to herself and said, "Anna." Then she pointed to him and said, "Al-ek-san-der."

The drummers and dancers led the wedding party to a potlatch celebratory dinner, during which Baranov took Chief Grigor aside to discuss a delicate matter. "There is no place here at this rough construction camp for us to have our wedding night. That must wait until we reach my home in Kodiak. We will sail there tomorrow. And so I must ask you to keep Anna with you one more night."

The chief felt immediate trepidation, fearing a bad omen at such a departure from tradition. Among his fears was the possibility that Baranov might try to get out of the marriage by sailing off in the middle of the night.

Baranov saw his hesitation and understood it. "You can put guards on our two sailing ships, so that we can't leave without Anna."

With misgivings, the chief agreed. "All right, great Nanuq. But if you somehow leave without her, I'll show you how easy it is for me to scalp a white man, no matter where you go, if it's the last thing I do."

The next day, *Phoenix*, with a small patchwork sail, and *Orel* left for Kodiak. The Baranovs rode on *Orel*.

Baranov enjoyed Anna's reactions to new things, like sailing on a ship. They were a mixture of surprise, curiosity, and amusement. If he smiled at her, she smiled back, watching him with interest. He started teaching her more Russian, pointing to objects and giving her the Russian words. She learned eagerly.

Early that evening, they reached St. Paul on Kodiak Island, and Baranov led Anna into his house. She looked all around this strange place. Why was there no hole in the center roof for a cooking fire? She looked out a window, then touched it, amazed by the glass.

He carried the moose-hide duffel containing her few belongings and put it in the bedroom. She followed him there. He hammered a nail into the bedroom wall and hung the bear claw necklace on it. Then he took a blanket and pillow for himself, and looked at her for a long moment. He smiled at her gently and left the bedroom, closing the door behind him.

Anna sat impassively on the edge of the bed. She looked up at the bear claw necklace. She knew her duty. She had been trained from an early age for this moment—a moment she kept trying to delay.

She thought of how at the age of ten, after her mother drowned at sea on a trip from Kodiak to the Kenai, she had become especially close to her father. This devotion had made her accept her mission, as awful as it was. Her Aunt De'ina had been assigned to prepare her for it. In the shadows of a private corner of her father's log longhouse, sitting on a blanket on the floor, Aunt De'ina had said, "When you grow up, you will have a very important purpose. It is to give our tribe the greatest advantage in getting the best alliance through your marriage."

"What does that mean?" she had asked.

"It means your father will choose someone from another clan to be your husband who will strengthen our tribe among all tribes. And to attract such a husband, you have to be taught how to act, how to dress, how to talk, and what you must not do."

"What I must not do?"

"You must not give yourself to a man until you are married to the husband your father chooses for you."

She remembered that when she was sixteen, her father had banished a boy who had shown too much interest in her. He was sent off as a hostage to the Russian outpost on the Kenai River.

Her aunt also said, "Being raised for your mission as a girl with intelligence and sensitivity, you have to be taught to hide your feelings and innermost thoughts beneath a look of dignity and reserve. Because you are sensitive yourself, and so aware of the feelings of people around you, you have an unusual gift of caring for others that makes others like you. This will help make you attractive to the right man."

Anooka recalled that, after a long pause leading up to something that must be very important, her aunt had said, "You will have a special duty on your marriage night. It is very important for the future of our tribe. If not done right, you could be sent back to your father by your husband and the disgrace to our tribe would be so great that you would have to be put to death. If done right, our tribe will be honored by a great alliance enjoyed by no other tribe."

She remembered how strange and threatening this had sounded, and then her aunt continued, "On the first night of your marriage, you must remove all your clothes and present yourself to your husband so he can enjoy your body. You should not expect to enjoy this yourself at first, but eventually you probably will."

This sounded horrible to her then, and even more so now—especially because of what some other girls had told her about Russian men. They spoke when they were in the woods by themselves at their special hiding place, under the boughs of a large spruce. Her friends had been hostages to the Russians, and they secretly told her of their experiences. "They raped us," one friend said, the others nodding in agreement. "The Russians were rough and strange and made us do awful things. And the first time was so *painful*."

Now she thought of Baranov. He was not at all the kind of man she had expected to marry—not the handsome young son of a Native chief. Instead, Baranov was white, much older than she, and from a totally foreign culture. And he smelled like stale sweat. But she had no choice but to obey her duty. Completely separated now from her tribe, family, and friends, she knew that for the first time in her life she was totally on her own, and that there was no refuge for her if things went badly.

She had never been undressed in front of a man before. What would he think of her body? What would he want to do with her? What would it feel like? All of this frightened her to her core. And deep inside, despite all she had been taught about this moment, what was happening now to her and her life somehow seemed wrong. Again she remembered being told that Russian men did strange things with women, things that scared her. But her courage and sense of duty to her people were now pushing her in the one direction she knew she must go.

The time was now. Slowly her eyes moved to the door. Aleksandr had appeared to be kind to her, a man who would not want to hurt her.

She did as she had been taught and undressed herself. Her hand and bare arm reached forward, grasped the bedroom door latch, and opened the door to the parlor. She saw Baranov across the room on the floor, lying on a bear rug under a wool blanket, as she took a step into the room. He stirred and looked with arousing awe at her naked, innocent beauty in the doorway. A tear rolled down Anna's cheek.

"Please, no hurt me," she asked softly.

Baranov had a compassionate streak that, despite his willful toughness, could be triggered by vulnerability. And when his compassion came to the fore, he too could have empathy.

"I will never, never hurt you, Anna," he promised gently. "Come here and lie next to me, and we'll just keep each other warm for awhile. Then we'll just see what happens. . . . But I won't hurt you. And we won't do anything you don't want to do."

She came the rest of the way, the door shutting behind her, and they began to create their own private world.

A few days later, as Baranov entered the parlor, he found Anna sitting at his desk, wearing a red-and-beige Russian print dress in which the contrast of her Native coloring and features made her look particularly lovely. He had been forced into this "marriage" in order to feed his men, but it was turning out to have a silver lining. And as long as she wasn't a baptized Christian, living with her wasn't a sin. It didn't count. At least, he didn't think it did.

Every day he saw something new in her that delighted him. He thought how lucky he was that the chief's daughter was such a beauty, and had such a gentle, responsive manner. And her curiosity about things suggested that she might even have a keen mind! What a wonderful surprise that would be. Of course, she was totally uneducated, but he could fix that as far as was necessary for her to be a good housemate and companion.

At his desk, she was thumbing through a book with prints of Russian scenes. He looked to see which one it was.

Anna pointed to a picture and asked, "What this?"

"The Tsarina Catherine's Winter Palace in St. Petersburg."

"What this say?"

"'The Imperial Cossack Guard arrives at the Winter Palace to parade before the Tsarina.'"

"I want learn how read."

"I will teach you!" Baranov said enthusiastically.

He found a piece of paper and quill pen, sat next to Anna, and wrote the alphabet, naming the letters aloud.

A couple of weeks later, Baranov and Shields stood talking on a hill looking out over St. Paul toward the ocean, with the Russian flag flapping in the breeze on a flagpole in front of them. Baranov told him, "In two days, we go to Kenai Bay for a marking expedition."

"*Marking* expedition?"

"Yes. We have copper plates to mark our colonial claims of sovereignty. British explorations here worry me. If they try to take Russian America away from us, I want our colonial markers hidden far inland to prove our sovereignty claims. There's a big mountain called Denali, north of Kenai Bay. I'll put our markers next to it."

"Who will guide you there?"

"Anna. She went there with her father. She knows the way."

At the mouth of the Susitna River of Kenai Bay, the sloop *Orel,* skippered by Shields, was moored. (Map 4.) A small expedition departed from the boat, led by Baranov with both Native and Russian men, and Anna. She wore her tan deerskin outdoor clothes, with a blue scarf over her head that Baranov had given her. One of the Russians was both a hunter and an artist, and would paint a picture of Denali to prove they had seen it. Leaving *Orel,* they started upriver in two tan *nigilaxes,* each carrying about fifteen people, nearly all manning paddles to push the boats upstream. *Orel* would wait behind, where the water was deep enough for its draft. Baranov sat in the first *nigilax* with Anna while strong Russian and Native hunters paddled.

On both sides of the muddy gray Susitna River there were lush, green spruce forests with the fresh smell of sap in the air. Occasionally, the forests bordering the river on one side or the other gave way to a swampy, light-green meadow through which a tributary stream joined the river. And in a few places, dirt and gravel cliffs rose alongside where the meandering river with multiple channels separated by sandbars had cut its way into a hill eons before. The river made a constant gurgling sound that would give way to a roar whenever they went through rapids. Looking ahead at the wild country upriver, he asked her, "Natives tell of dangerous spirits around the mountain. Is that right?"

"Yes," she replied without expression as she loosened her scarf and slipped it down around her neck.

"What happens?" he asked.

Looking straight ahead, she said matter-of-factly, "Many men go to mountain, then no come back."

"What happened when you and your father went there?"

"Two men die."

"How?"

She shrugged. "They scream and die."

"Just like that?"

She looked straight ahead without answering. He studied her impassive face, looked forward again, and said with fatalistic determination, "Well, here we come."

They paddled many miles up the Susitna fighting through rapids where the Natives would get out in cold, waist-deep water and pull the boats upstream. When Anna recognized the place where they had to leave the river, she pointed and turned to Baranov. "Stop at beach ahead. Trail there. Must walk."

He told the paddlers, "Land on that beach. We catch a trail there."

Later that day, on the trek north through the woods, one of the Russians unknowingly came between a grizzly sow and her cubs. The enraged sow galloped toward the man and leapt on him, knocking him over. She swatted him with the slashing claws of her front paws. His terrified screams increased her ferocity and with a roar from her wide open jaws, she grabbed his neck, sank her three-inch canines into his throat and then shook her head from side to side throwing him back and forth like a lifeless doll. She tore him apart with vicious anger and wild power, his blood spraying all around, and he was killed before others could react. The bear dropped him and turned back to her young. The Russians shot wildly at the sow without effect as she ran into the woods with her cubs trailing behind. The man's bloody body lay crumpled on the moss, his head nearly torn off. Baranov ran over and stared at the blood still dripping from the slashed carotid arteries, and repeated to himself, "'They scream and die.'"

The dead man was quickly buried with a brief ceremony, and the rest wanted to leave as fast as possible. Anna, pointed and said, "Denali that way."

Baranov studied where she was pointing and said, "I don't see a trail."

She looked at him indulgently and replied, "Big trail. I lead blind men."

He shrugged and chuckled. She led the way, and he soon learned from her how to recognize the trail. The sky was overcast, so only the low foothills of Denali could be seen as they approached the base of the great mountain. For food, they killed a bull moose, butchered it, and pieces of meat were apportioned for each person to carry. At the foothills in the evening, the party made camp on a hilltop with a scattering of tall spruce silhouetted against the sky and ate their moose dinner as they became engulfed in fog.

At dawn the next morning, a bald eagle screeched as it took flight from the top of a nearby tree, waking Baranov. He opened his eyes just as the sun began to rise in the east. The fog started to clear and the eagle circled overhead. Baranov looked for Denali, hoping to finally see it. In the pink dawn glow, he sensed something significant was about to happen. It was an eerie feeling. In his mind, he could hear faint Russian orchestral music, sounding like a mysterious wind blowing from Denali. It was music he had once heard in the courtyard of the Winter Palace, the only time he had ever been there.

He got up, put on his boots, and climbed a few feet to a better vantage point. As the fog lifted more, the tune in his head got louder, and the eagle flew up toward the mountain. A strong gust blew the remaining fog away, and the huge majestic grandeur of snow-covered Denali suddenly appeared with glacial fingers in its lap. 20,320 feet high at its summit, it was the highest peak in North America and a magnificent sight. Other Russians awakened and joined him to admire Denali in awe, but he paid no notice of them. Baranov wished he could see Denali as the eagle then saw it from above. Just a few powerful beats of the bird's wings propelled it up over a ridge of one of the mountain's massive snowy arms and it grabbed an updraft to soar with the wind. As Baranov stared at the mountain, he heard the music of his mind erupt into the roar of a full-throated orchestra trumpeting Russian imperial majesty.

Anna had awakened in the early twilight before the others and had been picking berries for breakfast. On returning, she was glad to see Baranov and the Russians so transfixed by the sight of Denali. Her work in getting them here had been worth it.

The Russian artist quickly set up his easel to paint Denali to document not only Russia's reach, but the most awesome sight he had ever seen. The day was spent burying copper plates in locations carefully plotted on a map. Let mad King George try to deal with that!

After supper, Baranov laid out blankets for a bed and climbed in. He looked at Anna, sitting across the campfire. Denali was lit behind her by a sunset glow. She poked the fire with a stick, well satisfied with her achievement in guiding the expedition. He stared at her for a moment, then said, "You're amazing."

She looked up and, though not sure, sensed a compliment and smiled a bit shyly.

"And you're mine. Come here, Anna."

Her smile disappeared, and she looked back at the fire.

"I not *belong* to you. We *part* of each *other.*"

He pondered that for a moment, nodded as she looked up again, and held up the corner of his blanket. She crawled over and slid in. As he put his arm around her, he asked, "And what part of you am I?"

She looked up at him, amused by the question, hesitated a moment, then said, "You are *toyon* of my heart."

"I am the chief of your heart?"

With a big smile, she answered, "Yes."

He kissed her and said, "And you are *toyon* of my heart, too."

CHAPTER 12

BARANOV FACES THE CHURCH

The next month, a ship arrived in Kodiak from Okhotsk. As its billowing sails were furled in the harbor, bell gongs marked the arrival. Baranov and Anna came out of their house and walked to an overlook where they watched the ship tie up at the dock and passengers disembark.

He said, "Travel between Alaska and the Russian capital of St. Petersburg takes a year in each direction. So a request from Alaska requires at least two years to get a reply. Let's see what kind of answers I'm getting to requests I made two years ago."

They continued watching the unloading. Kuskov came up from the wharf to join them, carrying a mail satchel. Baranov pointed to a group of clergy coming off the ship. "Look, I asked Shelikhov to send us a priest, and he sends me a monastery of eight. To impress the Tsarina, I guess. But just what does he expect me to do with all of them? How am I going to feed them? I know they won't lift a finger to grow their own food. And look at those rough men coming off now."

"A letter from Shelikhov," said Kuskov, handing it over.

Baranov opened it, skimmed the first part, and was appalled. He shook his head. "Added to the priests, he sends me seventy paroled convicts from Siberia who are the scum of humanity with no useful skills. While I'm busy here solving problems, Shelikhov busies himself with creating *new* ones."

"We'll wear out the whip on these men," observed Kuskov.

Baranov read more of the letter and exclaimed, "Unbelievable! Shelikhov bought thirty serf families that he's sending to us—just because serfs don't have to be paid! Supposed to be used for farming at Yakutat, and Yakutat *only*, according to an order from the Tsarina."

"*Yakutat?*" Kuskov exclaimed. "A crazy place for farming."

"But he secretly says to use the serfs to work wherever we want. Well, I'm not going to disobey her majesty the Tsarina! The serfs will farm at Yakutat, no matter how stupid it is. Is Shelikhov out of his *mind?*"

Anna asked, "What are serfs? Are they people?"

Baranov and Kuskov glanced at each other and chuckled at the unintended irony of her question. Then Baranov replied, "Yes, they are people. They work on farms."

"Here's another letter for you," said Kuskov.

It was a letter from Matrona. Again, a letter from Afanassya, age sixteen when it was written, was tucked inside, plus a short, one-page letter from his twelve-year-old adopted son, Appolonii. He slid them back into the envelope and carried it in his pocket for three days before he sat down alone on an overlook of the sea, took it out, and read them. Again, Afanassya had written, *Papa, I miss you!* He put the letter back in his chest pocket, stared across the sea to the western horizon, and softly wept.

A month later, when Baranov heard the big bronze bell announce another ship arrival, he jumped from his desk and went outside to look. In the harbor below, he saw a ragged-looking schooner limping in with torn sails and rigging. He ran down the trail to the main dock as it landed. Kuskov joined him, and together they watched the ship tie up and begin the disembarking of its survivors. That's what they looked like: worn-out survivors of a near disaster at sea. The ship's supercargo jumped off and brought Baranov the manifest. He quickly read that the boat was from Okhotsk and skippered by Gavriil Pribilof, discoverer of the Pribilof Islands. Several *promyshleniki,* Russian frontiersmen, came off—a tough bunch.

True to Shelikhov's alarming earlier letter, they were followed by thirty serf families overseen by a company supervisor named Polomoshnoi. These people came with chickens, cows, goats, and sheep. They were a pitiful lot, nearly starved, looking like lost souls—and filthy from a long journey with farm animals.

Baranov shook his head, incredulous. "Looks like Noah's ark!"

"They can move into the new dormitory until we send them to Yakutat, as the Tsarina has ordered," Kuskov suggested.

Winter soon fell upon them with a blizzard and darkness most of each day. As was usual at that time of year, Baranov became aware of a morale problem among his hunters—but he always had a ready cure for morale problems. Tucking a keg of his berry vodka home brew under an arm, and with cup in hand, he sauntered down to the main bunkhouse. Inside he found sullen men milling about or sitting on their bunks.

"All right, get out your mugs," he called out. "Let's sing in the New Year!" He filled his own cup and began singing.

The atmosphere quickly brightened as men scrambled for their mugs. Someone hammered up a hand-written sign: *Hello,*

1795! Baranov filled their mugs. Soon they were enjoying an uproarious party, he most of all.

The next morning, men slept on the floor or crossways on bunks, snoring. A disheveled Baranov leaned against a wall, the vodka keg next to him, and a young Aleut woman asleep on his lap. He awakened, startled by the girl, and he pushed her off. He looked around, shook his head vigorously, picked up the keg, and walked out crookedly.

Later that day, after he had sobered up, he got a message that Father Nektarios wanted to see him. *What for?* he wondered and headed to the man's cabin.

The priest was sitting behind the desk in his quarters. At fifty-five, bespectacled and with a gray beard, he wore his long, black Orthodox vestments as a statement of power.

Baranov knocked on the door. "Come in," said the priest.

Baranov did and took a seat across from the cleric, sizing him up as the man stared at him sternly. "You must stop holding hostages and levying Aleut hunters," Nektarios said. "Those practices are un-Christian!"

Just as I expected, Baranov thought. *The man has his head in the clouds of liturgy.* "Father, you speak of matters outside your authority. You were sent here by the company. Our purpose is to run a profitable business here. As chief manager, I'll decide what practices are necessary to make a profit."

"The business is secondary. It is merely a means to an end. The real purpose here is to bring Natives to Christ and save souls."

"You think that by sprinkling a little holy water on them and reciting a jumble of Russian words that mean nothing to the

Natives, you are saving souls? How can you possibly save them without speaking their language? How ridiculous."

Nektarios glared at him. "You're outrageous! Simply *outrageous!*"

"Well, saving souls may be your job, but it's not mine. Your demands are impractical. Also, with our limited resources, all priests must help hunt and gather food. Everyone must do their share to earn their own keep."

". . . Everything I heard about you in Okhotsk is true, Baranov. You have a wife and family in Russia, yet you live with a Native woman here. You abuse the Natives. You are the greatest sinner in Russian America! Whether you can be saved remains to be seen."

"Fortunately, as chief manager, I have the privilege of choosing who gets to save me," Baranov snapped as he got up, turned, and started toward the door.

"Only Christ can save you, if you have repented your sins and deserve saving. But I see no sign of repentance in you, Baranov."

Baranov stopped, thought for a moment, and turned around. "I have a question for you, Father. The Bible is the word of God, right?"

"Of course."

"Then why does the Bible contradict itself?"

"It doesn't."

"The Book of Acts, Chapter 9 Verse 7, contradicts Acts Chapter 22 Verse 9. The first place says the men with Saul on the road to Damascus heard the voice of Jesus, and the second says they didn't. How do you explain that?"

"You have the arrogance to read the Bible *yourself?*" admonished the cleric. "You have no business reading the Bible. Only clergy can properly read and interpret the Bible. The parts of the Bible read in church tell you all you need to know."

"So what's the answer to my question?"

"If you keep questioning the Bible, you'll end up going straight to hell. Give me your Bible, so you won't be tempted to play priest."

"So you'll be free to play God?" asked Baranov softly.

"How *dare* you!" sputtered the graybeard.

They glared at each other. Baranov turned again to leave, saying, "Good day, Father." And he was out the door.

CHAPTER 13

NANUQ RULES YAKUTAT

It was a beautiful day in May 1795 as Baranov looked out the window while he pulled on his sealskin jacket, a good omen for the beginning of the hunt. He saw a bustle of activity filling the alleyways of St. Paul as hunters prepared to depart. In the harbor, a fleet of three hundred *bidarkas* was milling around, waiting to leave. He emerged into the soft air and stopped briefly to watch Anna, in her overalls, planting rows of potatoes and cabbages nearby. She rose to face him, holding her trowel and wiping her brow with her sleeve. "I learn from serf woman to grow potatoes and cabbage for our table," she said to him.

"Good! Very good, Anna. I leave for the hunt this morning. I'll come back to pick up my gear and say goodbye before I go."

As he turned to leave, he felt her pull on his sleeve, and he stopped to look back at her.

"I come, too," she said firmly.

He considered that for a moment, couldn't think of a good reason why not, and nodded. Then he rushed off quickly down a trail to join Kuskov and four burly Russian hunters on their way to the serfs' barracks. There he had a tough job to do. He steeled himself for it by making up his mind that there was only one way out of the situation—his way. They marched up to the barracks, and Baranov motioned to the hunters to wait outside. He and Kuskov climbed the three steps to the door. They entered, and Baranov jumped up on a stool in front of the milling serfs. He announced, "You people must grab your things and board the ship, *now*."

Ruslan Lukin, a tall, slender serf of thirty, jumped up, shouting, "No! We're not going to Yakutat. It's suicide. Yakutat is surrounded by Tlingit who will kill us."

"Lukin, you'll be protected by a strong fort. Now, go!"

Nobody moved. So Baranov winked at Kuskov, who nodded, and they both left. The hunters then stormed into the barracks, grabbed Lukin's young wife Natasha, who was holding a baby in her arms, and dragged her outside. This got the expected effect: The enraged serfs charged out of the building to free her and the baby. When they had all run out, Kuskov slammed the door and padlocked it. Then hunters with clubs came from behind the barracks and chased the serfs to the wharf and onto a ship. Baranov turned to Kuskov. "Now go back with some men and get their gear."

In a few minutes, they emerged, carrying bundles of serfs' belongings, and trudged off toward the ship. From the wharf, the hunters threw the bundles onto the ship over the loud protests of the serfs on board. Several other hunters with big sticks were on the dock, beating back those who tried to escape.

The captain ordered, "Cast off!" and the docking ropes were untied by hunters and thrown aboard as the jib was hoisted and the vessel started to pull away.

As it departed, Baranov's expression softened in sympathy for the serfs. He saw Lukin break loose from a sailor trying to restrain him and run toward the side of the ship, where he jumped up onto the rigging. The ship kept drifting steadily away from the wharf. Lukin held on, glaring at Baranov, shaking his fist, and cried out in indignation tinged by the sorrow of losing yet another crucial battle for his beloved family.

"Baranov! You will burn in *hell* for this!"

Baranov stiffened, pretending to ignore the curse. He turned and saw Anna and an Aleut servant bringing their gear to the dock. Then he, Kuskov, Kuponek, and Anna boarded the sloop *Olga*. The lines were cast off, the sails raised, and they were off.

As the ship departed with Baranov at the tiller, he said in a rising, sarcastic voice, "Let's sail on to. . . that most feared place on Earth, with fork-tailed devils that breathe fire—*Yakutat!*"

They headed north into the Gulf of Alaska along the lower side of the Kenai Peninsula, leading the hunters in their squadrons of *bidarkas* across the deep blue waters into Prince William Sound, then turning southeast. (See Map 5.)

All along the coast, high mountains stood out against the sky with dark green forests of evergreens reaching up their slopes. Snow sat on sharp peaks, and steep rock cliffs slanted down from the mountains toward the forests below. An occasional valley was filled with a massive glacier calving with crashing rumbles into the waters below.

In an early afternoon, under a high gray sky, they sailed into Yakutat Bay toward the Russian settlement's green island. It was covered by mossy meadows surrounded by spruce thickets. Baranov saw the serfs' ship at anchor. He heard a strange quiet and saw that the fort construction had barely begun. They moored *Olga*, went ashore in *bidarkas*, and met the builders who had been sent out earlier. "What's *happening* here?" he demanded. "There's hardly any construction."

The construction foreman answered, "The Tlingits said we can't build here. They're taking the island back because we won't sell them guns."

With rising anger, Baranov said, "You're damned right we won't—because they'd use them against *us!*"

Kuponek advised, "If you challenge them quickly, they'll back down, because the Tlingit chief can't go to war without a formal council."

"All right, men! Get your guns, all of you," Baranov ordered. "We're going to pay our neighbors a visit." To Kuponek, he added, "Bring my friend in the burlap bag."

In *nigilax* boats, Baranov led his men and Anna across the narrow strait to the mainland. He knew the risk was huge, but it was one he had to take, or the crucial strategy to move their influence south would unravel.

As always when facing a confrontation, he focused on how to instantly intimidate his adversary. He had a plan—tricky, but he was sure he could pull it off. He knew he must be smarter than these Tlingit—he was a Russian *mestchannin!*

They landed, and he motioned for everyone to gather round. The Russian hunters, mostly bearded, were wearing their usual dark baggy outfits; the Aleuts with them wore tan seal leather shirts and pants, as did Anna.

"Listen to me carefully. We have to move fast and look fearless, with no hesitation—so fast that they won't have time to think. Here is what we're going to do." He rattled off a list of instructions.

Baranov saw a few hunters look at each other dubiously, and he knew he couldn't give *them* time to think about it either. "All right, then. Let's go!"

He set his jaw, looked straight ahead, and briskly started off with his phalanx of big-armed Russian hunters toward the Yakutat Tlingit village. Kuskov, Kuponek, and Anna followed immediately, motioning to the others to come along.

They passed rows of fierce-faced and winged totem poles lining the trail. Kuskov glanced at them and whispered to Kuponek, "See? 'Fork-tailed devils that breathe fire.'"

Suddenly, Baranov vanished amid his men, according to his plan. Several Tlingit warriors, all much taller than him and looking fierce, with painted faces, were alerted and came forward, ready for a fight, stepping back slowly as the lead Russians continued to move forward without missing a beat. One warrior held up his spear to block their way, but the enormous Russian in front of him contemptuously shoved it aside.

The Russians took full advantage of the Natives' indecision, marching right into the village of about ten log longhouses nestled in a clearing and surrounded by high, dark green firs. As the lead Russians came before the main longhouse in the village center, presumably the chief's, they stopped, and all the Russians quickly took their assigned positions. Some Russians pointed their muskets at the door of the longhouse, and the others aimed theirs to the side and behind at the encircling Tlingit warriors. Kuponek and Anna were immediately behind the two big Russians in front and faced each other as they went down on one knee. Their level forelegs provided a platform for Baranov, and he stood up on them as they grabbed his lower legs to brace him.

When he came into view above the hunters, he was wearing his polar bear Nanuq cape, with the toothed bear head as a crown. Kuponek and Anna were completely out of sight behind the big Russians screening them front and back. Baranov looked much taller than he actually was.

His arms were crossed in front of him, and he wore a stern expression, with the gleaming ivory teeth of the polar bear's upper jaw menacing forward just above his forehead. The teeth of the lower jaw jutted out beneath Baranov's chin, and the white fur flowed over him like a waterfall. He was an amazing sight to behold, especially to the Tlingit, who had heard of the polar bear but never seen one.

The big Russians kneeling in front held their muskets at the ready. This whole assembly was right in front of the door of the village's main house, the chief's lodge. Chief Ish-Kah, a muscular six-foot-tall Native of about forty, came out bare chested in long deerskin pants and with a warrior from Sitka at his side: Katlian, who was visiting his Yakutat relatives again. The chief was actually several inches taller than Baranov, but Baranov was looking down at the tall Native standing impassively a few feet in front of him. Then he spoke to the chief in Tlingit. *"I am the great Nanuq, assistant to Her Majesty Catherine the Great, the Empress of Russia, who rules all of this country."* He spoke with a sweep of his hand indicating all of the land.

The chief took a step forward, and there was a loud set of clicks as all the Russians cocked the hammers of their muskets.

"Step back, chief," Baranov advised him.

Chief Ish-Kah stepped back.

"All right," said Baranov, and his men uncocked the hammers of their muskets. *"When your warriors tried to attack me on*

Montague Island," he went on, "*I showed that I knew how to kill them, and they went away. Last year you agreed to sell us the island for our peaceful settlement and now you want to take it back. What is this nonsense?*"

"*Before your man left, I learned you won't sell us guns and powder, so I told him I changed my mind.*"

"*Your memory is wrong. If you had told him that, he would have told me. That is our island because you agreed to sell it to us, and I'm not selling it back.*"

"*Why won't you sell us guns and powder?*"

"*What have you done that would make us trust you with guns that you could use against us? Was it not your men who attacked me without reason on Montague? And is it not you who now wants to go back on your sale of the island?*"

"*If you stay there, we must have hostages.*"

"*No. It is you who must give us hostages because it is you that has given us so many reasons to distrust you.*"

"*We don't want you to have the island because your people there will hunt all of our seals and otters.*"

"*The people who will live here are not hunters. They are farmers, just farmers. Listen, if you take back the island, I, Nanuq, will call in my warships with their mighty cannons. They will blast your village into a thousand flaming pieces that will tumble over that mountain and set the forest on fire. Then nothing will be left of your land or your people. So what will it be? Do we keep the island, or do we blow you to your dog-heaven hell?*"

There was a long moment of silence as Baranov and Chief Ish-Kah stared at each other. Baranov's jaw was set resolutely, and his intense eyes under the polar bear teeth were unblinking.

He knew this argument would be settled by the single issue that always settled arguments with Natives: firepower. The warriors looked at their chief and at Baranov for some sign.

As Kuponek had said, the Tlingit were not used to making decisions on the spot without consultation, and Baranov would allow no time to think it over. All of the Russians stared resolutely at the chief.

Katlian whispered something to Chief Ish-Kah, who shook his head and then finally, with a slight smile, said, *"We celebrate our agreement with a potlatch."*

Baranov nodded approvingly, and at his signal there were cheers from the Russians.

That night, there was a celebratory bonfire in the center of the village, and everyone sat around it in a big circle. A ceremonial potlatch dinner followed. Baranov, still wearing his polar bear skin, had himself carried in on the shoulders of Russians, who set him down with folded legs on a large rock, so the Tlingit could never see just how short he really was. The Russians all sat around him. There was a sumptuous amount of food—deer meat, salmon, seal, and more, cooking on the fire—and they ate it, followed by Tlingit dancing and chanting. Then Baranov led the Russians in some favorite folksongs.

Throughout, Baranov noticed the chief and Katlian studying him intently as they sat across the circle. He believed that, as Nanuq, he must look formidable. They seemed to be watching him closely for any telling sign of the real man, but he wasn't going to give it to them. They kept whispering. Finally, it seemed as if Chief Ish-Kah had decided Nanuq was a powerful monster indeed and not to be trifled with.

But Katlian, though impressed by Baranov's cleverness, wasn't intimidated by it. In fact, he concluded the day would surely come when he would have to defeat this man and kill him.

CHAPTER 14

TWO WIVES AND TWO LIVES

In the early spring of 1796, three Russian men were on the roof of the first Russian Orthodox Church built in Russian America, completing the installation of a two-foot-tall bronze bell. As customary in Russian churches, the bell was stationary, and only the clapper would move. It would ring to call everyone to worship, and again, during some services, at the moment of elevation of the host. The men climbed down, and then the bell rang to call the community to worship for the first time.

A procession formed in the village heading toward the little church, singing the hymn of St. Vladimir. A gold-painted cross atop a six-foot pole was held high and carried at the head of the procession. Just behind the cross followed the priests, and behind them Baranov, as secular leader, his hands clasped reverently in front, leading the congregation of Russians and Aleuts.

The unbaptized, both Natives and Russians, were allowed to attend the first part of the liturgy. Baranov sang the Russian hymn with great gusto.

Inside, the church had no pews or benches, and as the procession entered, the priests went forward into a private sanctuary, where the *Proskomedia*, the pre-communion ceremony, was performed at the Table of Preparation, singing throughout. The rest of the congregation waited in the main room of the church. Then the priests brought the *prosphora*, the holy communion bread, from the sanctuary into the main room and distributed it. Four icons hung on the walls, depicting sacred scenes. Father Nektarios gave a short sermon, acknowledging the achievement of building the church.

"Finally, we have our church, which we should have had long ago, but now we have it. Thank you to Manager Baranov, who gave fifteen hundred rubles of his own money to build it, plus the community's contribution of five hundred rubles. Now the word of God and the salvation of Jesus Christ can be properly celebrated."

After the service, Baranov returned to his house with Kuponek, who asked some questions about the service he had just witnessed.

"Who is this Jesus they speak of?"

Baranov didn't want to get into a religious conversation with him. He wasn't interested in converting Natives to Christianity, because he knew that would give the priests power over them at his expense. So when questioned about religion, he tried to give answers satisfying enough so the interested Native wouldn't start questioning a priest and be pulled into the cleric's orbit. He was reluctant to have a vigorous missionary effort for fear that it would upset the delicate balance of relationships he maintained with the Natives, crucial to the success of his fur-hunting operations.

"Oh, he lived a long time ago a long way from here. He was an important leader of his people. The Russians, and people of many other countries, believe in his spiritual leadership."

"What does this mean, 'spiritual leadership'?"

"Mostly it is about how people should treat each other and how they should worship God."

"And what is God?" asked Kuponek. He had heard of the Russians' God long before, of course. But he wanted to hear from Baranov himself, the man he respected most.

"The great spirit who made the world and everything in it, and who made the rules for how the world works and how people should behave. . . . Kuponek, do you know yet how many men the lower island villages will send for our next hunt?"

"No."

The next day at a construction project at the edge of town, Father Herman was watching a small, one-room schoolhouse being put up. Baranov came over to see the work in progress. "Well, Father, your school will be finished soon."

"Thank you, Aleksandr Andreievich, for your contribution of money to build it. Now both the Russian and Aleut children, side by side, will learn how to read and write!"

"But it is a school with no books yet," Baranov replied.

"I will have a slate. That is all I need right now. God will provide the rest, as we need it."

"Good work, Father," said Baranov, and he walked on.

***

Baranov greatly enjoyed *praznyks*, but Anna found them distasteful and avoided them. He needed only the barest of excuses to hold a *praznyk*, like the end of the salmon run of 1796. One *praznyk* soon became even more raucous than most.

Baranov got very drunk, grabbed a Native girl, and led her off to a corner where they began engaging in giggling foreplay. Just then, Anna came in looking for him. Unnoticed, she saw him cavorting with the young woman, ran outside, and collapsed weeping on the back steps, her heart aching with betrayal.

It was not in Anna's upbringing to confront Baranov with what she had seen. She assumed that it was her fault, that only some shortcoming in herself could have caused him to reach for another woman. And so she plied him with special kindnesses to win him back, which he noticed but didn't understand. He, of course, had no memory of his drunken betrayal, and his true, sober feelings for Anna were unchanged.

***

On the evening of November 5, 1796, in St. Petersburg, the sixty-seven-year-old Empress Catherine was wearing an ornate bathrobe as she moved down a hall of the Winter Palace. Three maids accompanied her as well as her much younger lover, with whom she was speaking animatedly. She passed a guard at attention by her bathroom door. The door was opened by a butler, and she stopped momentarily. She faced her boyfriend, touched his lapel, and winked at him. "You'll come in and visit me at my bath in a minute, won't you?"

"Of course, my darling."

The empress and her maids entered, the door closed, and the boyfriend waited in the hallway, looking admiringly at the soldier standing stiffly at attention.

The door flew open. "Her Majesty has *collapsed! The Tsarina has collapsed!*"

As the maid ran down the hall to get help, Catherine's lover started for the door, but the soldier coolly barred his entry.

Empress Catherine II died of a stroke the next day, and her estranged son Paul became Tsar of all the Russias.

***

In May of the following year, just before the beginning of the hunt, Baranov again entered a bunkhouse during the late afternoon with a keg of vodka under his arm for a last fling with his men before the season's main work began. He looked out a window and saw Anna on a trail from one of her vegetable gardens to the Baranov house. She was many months pregnant, ripe in fact, and that bothered him.

At the bunkhouse *praznyk*, he started pouring and drinking, ushering in another drunken party. Baranov told Kuskoy, who was drinking water instead of vodka, "Tomorrow I leave for Fort Alexander."

He sailed *Olga* to the fort on the Kenai Peninsula to deal with some problems there, leaving Anna home alone. Soon, she went into labor and, in the Native way, knelt on the floor to deliver the baby, stoically holding back cries of pain. She was enduring not only the pain of childbirth, but also the fear that Baranov didn't want the child. With a surprisingly short labor for a first birth, she delivered a son. Afterward, she lay exhausted on a floor mat next to the baby, then pulled a blanket over both of them. She worried how her *toyon* would react to the baby. Would he hate it and want to kill it?

Two days later, on the beach in front of Fort Alexander, near the southwest extremity of the Kenai Peninsula, Baranov and

Kuponek were talking with the fort's supervisor when Kuponek pointed to an approaching *bidarka*. Baranov looked at it with a puzzled expression. As they turned to meet it, the man in the front cockpit, Kupreanof, called out, "I bring news! Anna has had a boy. Both are healthy."

Baranov nodded and wandered down the beach by himself. In his mind, he saw the scene in Irkutsk that continued to haunt him. Again, he saw Matrona and their children on the ox wagon leaving Irkutsk. But mostly he saw ten-year-old Afanassya pleading with him: *"Why aren't you coming with us, Papa? You must come, too. Please come!"*

As he turned back to the others, his mind returned to the present. He was greatly troubled by this new complication tying him to Alaska. Having a Russian family meant he couldn't take his Alaskan family to Russia. And how could he himself leave Alaska with a young child here dependent on him?

He immediately boarded *Olga* with Kuponek and headed back to St. Paul.

They returned at dusk. Baranov rushed up to the house and into the bedroom. He saw Anna in bed. . . but where was the baby? He got down on his hands and knees, touched her face gently, and slipped the blanket back, revealing the baby. "What a beautiful boy!" he said. Anna felt an immediate wave of relief. "He is us," she whispered.

He marveled at how she always said exactly the right thing in the fewest possible words. He kissed her forehead. "Antipatr, that's what we'll call him. Antipatr was a heroic general with Alexander the Great. A good name to live up to."

Anna didn't know anything about Alexander the Great, but

the name was fine with her if it would make Baranov love the child more.

Two Natives ran into Chief Grigor's village, having paddled from Kodiak. The old man came out of his lodge to hear the news that Anna had delivered a baby boy. He threw up his hands over his head and let out a whoop. "Now Baranov is really my son-in-law! Now he can't leave our country. That is good for us."

In St. Paul at that very moment, Baranov was strolling along the wharf, talking to Kuskov.

Kuskov commented, "Your boy sure is a cute little fellow."

"He is a joy," replied Baranov. "But he is also a heavy chain binding me to this place. Damn the Shelikhov Company for not replacing me on time two years ago! If I had been replaced then, I wouldn't be bound here now by this child, this wonderful child. I am caught now in a prison of the heart."

A supply ship docked in mid October after an unusually fast North Pacific crossing that would bring news earlier than usual. Baranov was on the dock with Kuskov and Kuponek, overseeing the unloading. A sailor handed him letters from Irkutsk. He opened and read a letter from Madame Shelikhova. His expression grew dark, and he summarized it to his companions.

"Shelikhov died two years ago, and his wife now runs the company. Tsarina Catherine died in November. Her son Paul is Tsar. My title is now 'Governor'—hmmph. A Frenchman, Napoleon Bonaparte, wages war all across Europe, and the Tsar opposes him."

Amazed, Kuskov said, "Paul is Tsar? Many say he is crazy."

"Better keep that to yourself!" murmured Baranov. "More bad news. The company is out of money, so they can't hire anyone to take my place. Now I'm stuck here! When will I ever see my Russian family again? To hell with big titles—'Governor'!"

Kuskov tried to console him. "Natalya Shelikhova is smart and well connected. She'll find money, and then she'll hire your replacement."

At the bottom of the packet of letters, Baranov found a letter from his brother Pyotr, reporting first on the mixed status of their various business ventures—the glass factory in Irkutsk failing, and the trading post in Anadyr barely holding on. Then Pyotr announced that, in place of Aleksandr, he had given nineteen-year-old Afanassya permission to marry Vassily Belayev, a government secretary.

A wave of sadness swept over Baranov. His beloved Afanassya was to be married, and he would have no part in it! He was not there to be asked for permission by Belayev, and he would not be there to give her away at the wedding. In fact, she was already married, because the news from Russia traveled so slowly.

He had two lives, and his Russian one was slipping away from him.

Pyotr's letter fell from his hand. He made a half-hearted effort to grab it before a gust swept it out to sea. He watched it disappear in the waves, then turned back toward shore, shook his head, made fists that he knocked together, and trudged up the hill to his house and Anna.

In a few days *Phoenix* returned from Okhotsk, pulling into the wharf on October 25, 1797. Baranov and Kuponek reached the wharf just as the ship was tying up. Midshipman Gavril Talin came down the gangplank, followed by two other newly minted midshipmen, and came up to Baranov. "Where will I find Chief Manager Baranov?"

"That's me."

"You?" Talin said dismissively, surprised to find such a scruffy little man in so august a position.

"Yes. And who are you?"

"Midshipman Gavril Terentyevich Talin."

"Glad to meet you, Midshipman Talin," Baranov said, offering his hand.

After a slight hesitation, Talin took it. "Where are my quarters?"

"Up on the hill," answered Baranov. "Kuponek will show you the way."

From the outset, it was obvious that the young midshipman had an attitude problem. He was quite class conscious and sized up everyone by their social class, regardless of their official functions. Because Baranov was a *mestchannin,* despite his title, Talin as a midshipman outranked him in the Tsar Peter the Great's fourteen-level Russian table of rank.

Shields handed Baranov a letter. He opened it, quickly read it, then closed it. "They've sent Emelian Larionov to be in charge at Unalaska, and they say I can have him replace me when I think he's ready."

"I know him," said Shields. "He may be too soft."

"We'll see. One thing is certain—I want to get out of here so I can see my family again in Kargopol!"

A few months later, in early 1798, Baranov held a big *praznyk* to honor Russians about to sail back to Siberia. Father Iosaph, the eldest of the clergy, was being recalled temporarily to be consecrated as Bishop of Russian America. He was a kindly cleric who had mixed relations with Baranov, sometimes seeing him as a demon, and at other times as just another lost soul trying to make the best of things. James Shields would skipper *Phoenix* to Okhotsk and back. There was, of course, the usual party uproar, much to the clerics' distaste. Iosaph spoke out. "Baranov, I hope you won't allow this to degenerate into another drunken brawl."

Baranov, quite tipsy with yet another full cup of vodka in hand, answered, "Oh, no, Bishop-elect. We will be quite controlled."

Then he stumbled, tripped, and had a terrible fall, breaking a leg. There was much commotion as he was tended to, bewildered. But he wasn't in much pain, and wouldn't be until he got sober.

The next day, in the parlor of the Baranov house, he sat quite miserably, gazing out at the harbor as his beloved *Phoenix* departed. His broken leg, set in a narrow wood box, rested on a stool. Meanwhile, Anna played with the baby crawling on the floor.

Baranov said to her, "There goes the great *Phoenix* we built ourselves. May God guide her safely to Okhotsk and protect her return with our new bishop next year."

He watched the sails fill with wind and pull the ship away toward the far horizon. What a wonderful sight, he thought. And what an excellent decision it had been to build it, to be independent of his supply stream from Russia. Now that the company's fur profits were up, should he build more like it to increase that independence, or buy a ship or two from the Americans? Should he start planning now to take Captain Moore's advice and trade for supplies in Hawaii? Now that he was tied down by his leg, he had plenty of time to think of such things—and write letters.

Yes, letters. He had just sent a twenty-page report via *Phoenix* to St. Petersburg. Now he would use his healing time to write to his managers at each outpost. to inform them of developments and let them know he hadn't forgotten about them. But first he needed something for that aching leg—just a swallow or two.

He looked out the window and saw the ship getting smaller in the distance. Meanwhile, Anna picked up a samovar full of boiling water off the stove and carried it toward a table next to him. For just an instant, she looked at the ship sailing away—then tripped and spilled boiling water over much of Baranov's body. He screamed in excruciating pain. Anna was horrified, and the baby across the room broke out in hysterical cries.

CHAPTER 15

EMPIRE BUILDING

Two months later, Baranov was again staring stoically out to sea, his body and outstretched leg covered by a seal blanket. There was a knock at the door. Baranov looked up, and Kuskov burst in.

"A message from Ft. Constantine, on Nuchek Island. They were attacked by Tlingit, who killed many men, including the manager there, Konstantin Samoilov. It seems Samoilov and others had kidnapped some Tlingit women and raped them. So the Tlingit retaliated. When they found him, they strung him up and tore off his genitals, saying, 'He'll never know pleasure with our women again.'"

"How did they force their way into the fort?" asked Baranov.

"They had better guns than our men, guns they got in trade from the British and Americans."

"Get me out of here!" yelled Baranov as he threw the blanket onto the floor and started ripping the wooden cast off his leg. "We've got to stop them from arming the Tlingit and from stealing our wealth of furs! The only way we can do that is to build a fort on the southern coast, right in the middle of Tlingit country."

"Are you going to avenge Samoilov?" inquired Kuskov.

". . . No. Horrible, but it seems he asked for it," Baranov replied matter-of-factly.

Now he had to think about how to build a fort along the southeastern coast. One thing he knew: It would take a lot of planning in order to build *anything* in Tlingit country.

As Baranov sat at his desk working on accounts, Father Nektarios knocked on his door. Baranov got up and opened it. Upon seeing Nektarios, he stared for a moment, then motioned for him to come in and take a seat as he went back behind his desk—all without saying a word, such was their enmity.

"I fear an outbreak of smallpox among the Natives, and so I want to go into the villages and inoculate them," said Nektarios.

"You have the means to do that?"

"For the inoculations, yes. But you will need to assign some of your men to take us around to the villages—perhaps two Russian hunters, and three or four Native men."

Baranov stared at him for a long moment, weighing the pros and cons of the proposal. "I think it's a splendid idea. I'll see to it that you get the men, the boats, and the supplies that you need."

Nektarios was shocked. He had expected a refusal and was prepared with a blistering counter-argument. So, for a moment, he fumbled before responding. "Well. . . . Thank you, Baranov," he finally said, and he got up to leave. "Maybe there is some hope for your salvation, after all."

Nektarios let himself out the door. Baranov smiled knowingly. He had expected the man to say something like that. He shook his head and returned to his accounts.

Nektarios set out along the coast of Kodiak in a *nigilax* paddled by four Natives. Accompanying them were two *bidarkas*, one with two Russian hunters and the other with two Native men. They approached a seaside Native village and beached their craft. The tall, stately Nektarios passed among the short Natives, truly looking like a shepherd dressed in black among his sheep. He briefly explained to the chief in the Alutiiq language (which he had learned at Baranov's prodding) why he was there.

"I come to stop great sickness from attacking this village. I come to give your people a shield that goes in their bodies to protect against the terrible smallpox." The chief nodded. He had heard of this already from his returning hunters. *"I must give it to you first, so your village will take it. I need your arm."* The chief cooperated, and one of the Russian hunters inoculated him.

Speaking to his people, the chief said, *"I have taken the shield into my body so I will not get sick. You must do it now."*

The village people lined up, and they each got inoculated in turn. Nektarios took the chief aside to talk to him confidentially, insofar as this chief could speak basic Russian.

"How many hunters does the chief manager levy from you?"

"Who is this chief manager?" asked the chief.

"Aleksandr Baranov."

"Oh, you mean the Great Nanuq?"

Nektarios hesitated. "Yes."

"He levy sixteen hunters last summer. Two drown. Village very sad."

"Then don't send him a levy next year," Nektarios urged.

Incredulous, the chief replied, "Nanuq work for great Tsar, and levy is for him. If no give levy, then great Tsar will punish us."

"No. Tsar Paul wants fair treatment for your people. Nanuq is treating your people badly. Tsar Paul doesn't want you to work for Nanuq unless your people are treated well. You must be paid before you work for Nanuq again. He hasn't paid you for the last hunt yet."

"That true. No pay last hunt."

"Then don't give levy of hunters again until paid for last hunt. And don't give hostages."

"Then I will get whipped by Nanuq. To get whipped brings great shame. One chief kill himself from shame of being whipped."

"Don't worry. I won't let him whip you."

"You can *stop* him?"

"If all the chiefs agree to hold back their men, I can stop him."

"I think about it."

Nektarios visited many villages, giving smallpox inoculations and talking to many chiefs.

In late September 1798, Baranov was sitting at the desk in his parlor when Kuskov came in, quite disturbed. "Father Juvenal was murdered up north."

Baranov looked up, attentive for details. "His journal was brought back to us by a Native boy who saw and told us what happened. Apparently Juvenal criticized the chief's polygamy up there, so they cut him to pieces and threw his parts into a lake. It's awful."

Kuskov dropped Juvenal's journal on Baranov's desk. Baranov picked it up and started to thumb through its pages. Just then there was a commotion at the door as Father Nektarios brusquely entered.

"Give me that, Baranov. That is Juvenal's private journal. What's there is just between him and God."

"And you," answered Baranov as he handed the journal to him.

"You must bring this vicious chief to justice, Baranov."

"Yes, this is tragic. I'm sorry. But do I detect a note of vengeance, Father? I thought you were only interested in converting Natives, not imposing our ideas of justice on them. How would that win you souls?"

"That's ridiculous."

"It is indeed an awful tragedy, Father. But going over there to arrest the chief presents great and dangerous risks."

"If you don't, what's to stop them from killing other Russians?"

"I know. But I can't take the risk of wasting the lives of more Russians on this."

"You don't think Father Juvenal should get *justice*? What an abomination!" Father Nektarios stomped out.

Inside the main dining hall at Kodiak, a general meeting had been called by Midshipman Gavril Talin. The hall was filled with Russian hunters, Aleuts, and the clergy. The attitude of everyone was very grave, especially because rations were short, and no new supplies had been received in a year. Talin stood on a chair and started to speak. "I was in St. Petersburg when Tsar Paul took command of the empire. He plans to transfer control here from the merchants to the navy, probably next year. I have secret instructions to prepare for the transfer of power here. Because I am the only person here of noble rank, and to end the corrupt and inefficient rule here, I will take control in the name of the navy."

Suddenly, people were aware that Baranov had entered the hall, and they made way for him as he, still limping with a cane, made his way to the front. He pulled over a chair next to Talin and climbed torturously onto it, facing the audience. Then he turned to look Talin over from head to foot with sheer disdain.

"Your Excellency! Surely you have your orders in writing? Something so important wouldn't be left to mere verbal recitation, and with no witness to vouch for it. If you have such orders, why haven't you knocked on my door and shown them to me?"

"The word of a gentleman is enough."

"Yes, that is true, gentleman to gentleman. But as you have made clear, except for you there are no gentlemen here."

Suddenly, there was a cry from the hillside outside, signifying the approach of a ship. The schooner *Zachary and Elizabeth,* with Becharof as skipper, was approaching. The meeting immediately dissolved, and nearly everyone hurried from the hall to the wharf. Talin remained standing on his chair, dumfounded. Baranov was the last, aside from him, to reach the door, limping with his cane. He turned to face Talin for a moment, staring at him with contempt.

***

On the driveway to the Tsar's Gatchina Palace in St. Petersburg, an ornate closed carriage drawn by two horses was driven to the main palace entrance. Thirty-five-year-old Nikolai Rezanov, now son-in-law of the Shelikhovs, stepped out and climbed the steps to the entrance.

Still a tall, square-faced man with a shock of curly blonde hair, he was finely dressed in the formal clothes signifying the high noble rank of Imperial Chamberlain. His blue eyes conveyed an intensity of mind to anyone he encountered. As he walked with a loud patter down an exquisite, gold-trimmed hallway with a polished, basket-weave parquet floor, his strong gait suggested the confidence of command. Heroic paintings of Russian royalty hung on the wall. Rezanov seemed to sail through a double door on the other end of the room onto a stone balcony overlooking a parade ground.

A small, well dressed forty-five-year-old was standing there looking over the railing at the parade ground below, where a hundred soldiers were drilling in precise Prussian style. This was Tsar Paul I. Just behind him stood two aides. Rezanov came smartly to the side of the Tsar and knelt.

"Ah, Rezanov."

"Your Majesty."

"This is my best drill team. How they have mastered the Prussian drills! I could watch them all day."

Rezanov straightened up and observed, "Yes, Your Majesty, they are magnificent! I have never seen such precision!"

"What do you have for me today, Nikolai Petrovich?"

"Good news from Russian America. Thanks to the very shrewd business management there by Chief Manager Baranov, the company has made a multi-million-ruble profit for the last two years."

"Multi-million?"

"Yes! In his dealings with the American traders who carry our furs to China, he is a genius. We're now making more money from Baranov each year than we made from all his predecessors combined!"

"Excellent!"

"I have the order for your signature that you approved regarding the Russian American Company, run by Baranov, granting it a twenty-year exclusive contract to operate in Russian America."

"Yes, Russian America, as you've said, key to the North Pacific. . . . Have we purchased the two frigates yet for our around-the-world navigation and for the protection of Russian America?"

"Being built as we speak, Your Majesty."

"Good. I'll sign the order inside. Just look at those men. . . magnificent indeed. If only I could get our entire army to march like that! If only I could get the nobility to live by the code of knighthood and chivalry."

CHAPTER 16

TRAGEDIES AT SEA

Spring 1799: After the birth of Antipatr, an office had been built for Baranov and a couple of assistants in a corner of the main warehouse. That way, he was able to move most of his work out of his home so that he, Anna, and Antipatr could have greater privacy. The office was strictly functional and practical in its appointments, without a trace of elegance or pretension. Baranov sat at a simple, rough-hewn table, used as a desk, with Kuskov across from him.

"This year we're going to build a fort on Sitka Sound, right in the heart of Tlingit country—right in the midst of where the Brits and Yanks have been trading guns with the Tlingit. We're going to put a stop to that."

"How will we do it, and when?" Kuskov asked.

"This year, the fur hunt will be of secondary importance. Building that fort will be our number-one project. We'll take our whole *bidarka* fleet down there to give us the manpower we need for construction. Included will be the wives of a few men who will be among our new Sitka fort's settlers."

Anna and little Antipatr entered the office.

"I'm hearing about problems getting the fleet together this

year," said Kuskov, "because many still haven't been paid yet for last year's hunt."

"I'll solve that," replied Baranov.

"How? We haven't received a shipment of iron yet to pay them with."

Anna spoke up. "Pay off their debts at the commissary for the long winter supplies bought on credit. That will satisfy them."

"Yes," Baranov agreed. "It should indeed. Thank you, Anna!"

"What about Father Nektarios?" asked Kuskov. "He has appointed himself as spokesman for the Aleuts."

"Oh, I don't worry much about Nektarios. He doesn't understand the Natives the way I do. You can't understand the Natives while your head is in the clouds."

". . . Do you think the company will pay you back for this?"

"Of course not. But as long as I have enough money left to support my family and pay my taxes in Russia, I'll just do what I have to do to keep the Natives with me."

***

A month later Nektarios was in his cabin when a monk entered with an alarming announcement. "Father Nektarios, come down to the beach and see. The Aleut *bidarkas* are arriving for this season's hunt just as before."

"*What?* They all swore they wouldn't!"

The two went outside and looked down at the beach. Scores of bidarkas were arriving.

"Baranov paid off their commissary debts, so now they're willing to hunt again," said the monk.

"Baranov! That snake!" Nektarios exclaimed.

***

At the Russian-American Company wharf of Okhotsk, *Phoenix* was about to put to sea. It would return to Russian America with the newly consecrated Bishop Iosaph, his staff, and Shields as skipper. A solemn ceremony was held as the bishop and his staff proceeded to the ship and the bishop performed a blessing for their voyage. Then *Phoenix* set sail into the Sea of Okhotsk.

***

The hunting season of 1799 arrived in Kodiak, and a fleet of two hundred and thirty *bidarkas* headed southeast toward Yakutat and Sitka Sound, including both Aleuts and Russians. They were escorted by the forty-foot *Olga*, skippered by Baranov, with Kuskov, Richard, and Kuponek crewing. The larger escort *Orel* was skippered by the disdainful young Russian midshipman Talin.

The weather was fine, and Baranov could see that his hunters were in good spirits. The clear skies seemed an omen of a great hunt to come. On a day like that, how proud he was of his huge fleet moving southeast. Soon he saw the snow-capped peaks of the Kenai Range thrust up into a blue sky like giant spectators watching a naval parade. They camped the first night at the mouth of Resurrection Bay. (Map 4.)

The next morning, the fleet separated into two groups in the harbor, one to be escorted by *Orel* and the other by *Olga*. Before departure, Baranov handed a written order to Kuponek. "Take this sailing order to Talin. We must all follow the coastline closely to Yakutat. It's a longer route, but safer if a sudden storm kicks up."

Kuponek, in his *bidarka*, took the order to Talin, who quickly read it, crumpled it, then tossed it overboard. Talin pointed southeast, toward the direct route far from shore, and yelled to his squadron, "To Yakutat! Straight across that way!"

Kuponek paddled back to *Olga* and lashed his bidarka onboard as he reported, "I gave it to him, but he threw it away. Looks like he's going straight across."

Baranov frowned, shook his head, and then led his squadron on the longer, more circuitous course that hugged the shorelines of a string of islands along Prince William Sound, taking more time than Talin. But the midshipman's reckless choice of the more direct route turned out to be lucky—his flotilla reached Yakutat before a gale with high waves swept in.

Baranov's fleet was traversing open water between Nuchek Island and the mainland when the gale hit them. Winds rose from ten knots to thirty-five in less than twenty minutes, blowing with a frightful roar past *Olga's* sails. It took him by surprise, and with yells and urgent arm waving and pointing, he signaled the kayaks to head straight to the mainland. His hat was blown away, and the wind ripped at his kamleika rain coat. Waves quickly rose to four and six feet high. Stretched to the limit of his skill, Baranov steered *Olga* windward, holding the tiller firmly with both hands, while Kuskov manned the main sail sheet, spilling just enough wind to avoid capsizing in gusts.

Kuskov yelled, "Sasha, we have to reef the main sail!"

"Right, let's do it. Reef it!" replied Baranov.

Kuskov, Kuponek, and Richard jumped to the task, and in short order they had the main sail reefed about four feet lower.

Some yards off to starboard, two *bidarkas* struggled with the battering of the waves. Baranov watched with dismay as a frothing roller came from behind, lifted the sterns of both kayaks, and drove them headlong into a rising wave—it flipped them, spilling three men and a woman into the angry sea, with no flotation.

"Throw them a line!" Baranov yelled to Kuskov, who was already reaching for a life-saving rope.

But it was no use. In just seconds, the terrified faces of all four, with their arms thrashing desperately in the cold blue, slipped below the surface and were gone, just as the rope was tossed.

Baranov decided to turn his tack more into the wind to seaward, to be able to rescue others. "We'll head more upwind. Ready about?" he yelled. Then, "Hard a lee!" He tried to time it when *Olga* was at the top of a roller, but his timing was slightly off, and the bow burrowed into the water of a rising wave, creating huge drag up front and causing the rest of the boat to suddenly swing left from its momentum and begin to flip over.

Kuskov, Kuponek and Richard jumped at once to the top edge of the boat and leaned way over the side to create a counterbalancing weight. The boat was sliding down toward the trough between rollers. If it flipped over, they would all be dead. As they were nearly in the trough, Baranov pushed the tiller away to suddenly right the boat. His crew jumped back to the center, and then, moving slower in the trough, he pulled the tiller back all the way and headed nearly into the wind as the bow was lifted up the side of the oncoming wave.

He couldn't have done it better, but he nearly collided with a *bidarka* heading for shore. As *Olga* reached the crest of the next wave, another *bidarka* just ahead broke apart, leaving its two Aleuts in the sea thrashing and gasping for air. Baranov swung *Olga* toward them and Kuponek threw a rope at them. They both caught it and then were swung back, trailing behind. As they desperately clung to the rope, Kuskov and Kuponek pulled the line in and grabbed hold of the first man. Just then, the second man lost his grip, fell away and sank, never to be seen again.

One man saved. Baranov realized that the chances of making successful rescues were almost nil, and the risk of continuing on this tack out to sea too great. If he continued to attempt rescues he would likely lose control of *Olga* and get capsized in the raging waters. So, as *Olga* started to ride up the side of another advancing roller, he yelled, "We can't do this! Gotta tack toward shore. Ready about?" Then, "Hard a lee!" Just as they reached the wave crest, he swiftly turned the boat toward shore on starboard tack, still heading upwind and southeast. They hammered through wave after wave toward shore.

The ocean crushed many more *bidarkas* on both sides of *Olga,* throwing Russians and Aleuts into the frigid sea to drown just out of reach. The wind pummeled Baranov, and his face was contorted with the grim frustration of helplessness.

Nearing a rocky coast, he headed for the safe haven of a cove, and most of the remaining *bidarkas* followed. Sailing into the inlet, he was nearly blown onto rocks. The sails were quickly furled and Kuskov set the anchor. "Take me in," Baranov told Kuponek, who untied his *bidarka*, launched it, and paddled him ashore. Baranov ran up a seaside bluff, and in the howling wind, he waved his arms overhead to draw others still at sea toward the cove.

As he stood there, leaning hard into the gale, he yelled, "Alaska, hear this, you savage beast! I will not be defeated! Not now, not ever. Never! Never! Never!"

He glared at the angry sea and sky. The raw power of nature was awesome indeed. Even beautiful, though his enemy.

That evening, in the small cove, they roasted seal meat over driftwood campfires, and the survivors ate. Just one hundred and forty-four men and women had made it safely to shore. Many of the Russian hunters had their Native wives with them, expecting to settle in the new Sitka community that they would help build.

Sadness gripped them all after dinner. Baranov knew he had to say something. What? What words of solace could he offer? He was nearly at a loss. After a few moments, he collected his turbulent thoughts and prayed aloud for all: "Dear Lord, surely we have sinned and thy mighty fist has come down to punish us. Forgive us, Lord, for we know we are not worthy of thy grace. Save us from this most terrible day. Show us the way, and we will follow. Thou art the master of all, and we ask now for thy protection as we continue. Please still the raging waters and let us pass in safety. King of Heaven and Earth, we pray that those friends we lost at sea today are all with thee now, and that their souls rest in thy care, as we now speak their names."

Someone called out a name of a friend he had seen go down, and they all repeated the name in unison. This proceeded through sixty names. Then Baranov said, "Amen."

There was still a glow from some campfire embers as the exhausted men and women drifted off to sleep on the beach under their sealskin blankets. Suddenly, from the strip of brush and forest just above the beach, the dreaded ululation of Tlingit warriors on the attack exploded.

Baranov had not yet fallen asleep, and he reacted instantly. "Load your guns and shoot! Load and shoot," he called out. The Tlingit fired at Baranov's people from the protection of the nearby woods. Baranov took aim at a bush where he'd seen movement and fired. Some terrified and confused Aleut men ran to the forest to escape, but went right into the lunging knives of hidden Tlingit.

As Baranov's men fired back at their attackers, they scrambled for cover behind driftwood logs. Only the Russian hunters had guns, and many had two muskets for more rapid firing. The virtually unarmed Aleuts, who just had hunting spears, helplessly hid behind logs and rocks. The Russian men with wives had them reload so they could keep on firing, aiming at flashes in the woods.

Kuskov ran over and dove down onto the ground next to Baranov as he reloaded. "What the hell is this?" Kuskov asked.

"Must be Tlingit. Damned if I know why."

Both men took aim and fired again.

These northern Tlingit couldn't capitalize on their many tactical advantages, because of the heavy cloud overcast. It made the dusk dark and hard for the attackers to see Baranov's people, who were hidden behind driftwood logs on the beach.

After half an hour, the much more experienced marksmanship of the Russians paid off. The Tlingit took unexpected losses and retreated.

Baranov saw the column of retreating Tlingits crossing

the barren bluff where he had stood before, silhouetted in the moonlight against the snowcapped peaks beyond.

In the aftermath, he ordered a rotating watch and tried to get some sleep. In the early dawn, he arose and counted the people he had left. Eighteen more were missing. As his people stirred, he found that eight had been killed where they lay on the beach. Kuskov and Kuponek got up and joined him.

"We lost sixty at sea, and another twenty-six here," said Baranov. "A tragic and awful way to start a work season."

"A terrible loss of good people," said Kuskov.

"My prayer brought us nothing," answered Baranov.

* * *

In the North Pacific at the end of May 1799. *Phoenix*, skippered by Shields and returning from Okhotsk to Kodiak, was sailing at night under full canvas in moonlight. The ship was a beauty.

The lookout sailor in the crow's nest heard something, turned, and saw the frothy glimmer of a huge fifty-foot high rogue wave approaching fast from behind and yelled to the helmsman.

"Big wave aft! Turn to the wave!"

The helmsman saw it and turned the wheel hard. Shields ran on deck and froze with a sense of helplessness. The wave came in as the ship slowly swung about into the onrushing wall of water that rose up over it and hammered it with a deafening blow. The boat rolled over, breaking apart, with Shields and his men flung into the sea and helplessly thrashing about as hungry death attacked from the darkness to consume them. Bishop Iosaph was in the water with his gray-bearded head barely above water.

"Father, into your hands, I commend my—"

Before he could finish his prayer, a wave heaved a hunk of wood debris from the ship at the holy man's head, killing him instantly and as casually as a squashed bug.

CHAPTER 17

A FOOTHOLD ON SITKA

Baranov reached Sitka Sound on *Olga* leading a flotilla along a circuitous route with about four hundred and fifty Aleuts and Russians. (Maps 5 & 6.) He had come to Sitka Island to build a fort, from which he would be able to control British and American fur trading, and also reach south toward California, Hawaii, and China. *Orel* and *Olga were* moored by a small island where some men went ashore to set up a temporary campsite for the fleet. Meanwhile, Baranov and a few of his men paddled in *bidarkas* to inspect a building site for a fort that Baranov knew was second-best. They had passed the best site a few miles south on an easily defended rock outcrop—a *kekur*. But it was already occupied by the Tlingit, who had named it Noow Tlien. He knew they wouldn't give it up, so this site would be the best he could get.

But first, he had to persuade the Sitka Tlingit to sell him the land for his fort.

At the chosen site, Baranov and three of his men examined the ground and paced it off for various buildings.

Some muscular Tlingit warriors, all over six feet tall, stepped out of woods at top of the glade to observe this curious behavior.

"Baranov. Tlingit come," said Kuponek, pointing up the rise.

Baranov took a moment to study the Tlingit body language for clues to their intentions as a few more Tlingit joined the initial group. "We're going to need a meeting with their chiefs. Go up there and ask for one here this afternoon. But don't get too close to them, so they can't grab you—or worse."

Kuponek unflinchingly went to do as he was told.

On closer inspection, these Tlingit made the Yakutat warriors look tame. All were huge and fearsome, conveying a sense of commanding power in their rippling muscles, wooden armor, and carved eagle-and-raven helmets, the menace of their facial expressions accentuated by face paintings. Kuponek concealed his fright as he delivered the message. The Tlingit said nothing, but turned and left. Kuponek returned to Baranov. "They say nothing."

"But you gave them the message?"

"Yes. They understand." Otherwise he would have been killed or captured and tortured.

"Well. . . . Then we have just a few hours to get ready. Let's get back with the others quickly. This meeting is very important, and we have to make a good impression. So we have to prepare."

That afternoon, sixty Tlingit were waiting at the top of the shallow slope as Baranov's men climbed it in two long columns, led by two hundred and fifty Aleuts followed by a hundred and fifty much taller Russians with muskets.

From his vantage point behind his men, Baranov saw that the Tlingit were drawn up in two lines at the top of the slight incline. Warriors and sub-chiefs stood on either side of their top chief, Ska-outlelt—another Katlian uncle. This chief was around fifty years old and the tallest of all the Tlingit men. He had a weathered, rectangular face and wore a ceremonial cape decorated with brightly colored animal heads. The Tlingit presented a fierce wall of tall, muscular men, all exquisitely dressed and decorated in Native garb. Some had muskets; others bows, arrows, and battle-axes. Baranov was unafraid and invigorated by the challenge of the moment.

Twenty-six-year-old Katlian, standing with a musket next to Ska-outlelt, looked at the impressive formation of Baranov's troops, lined up in ten rows. When they were fully in place facing the Tlingit, a murmur arose from the Russians' rear, growing louder into a thundering drum-beat of a chant: "Nanuq! Nanuq! Nanuq!" They thrust muskets overhead in cadence with their call. An aisle opened amid the Russian rows, and Katlian saw Baranov come briskly forward. He was unarmed, dressed in tan trousers and a smock with no ornamentation, and he radiated compact, irresistible power. With an air of command, he bounded onto a large, flat rock just in front of Katlian and Ska-outlelt. The Russian chants moved into a rousing cheer. Kuponek came up and stood near his boss to assist, if needed. Baranov raised his hand, then dropped it, and the noise instantly stopped.

This is impressive, Katlian concluded. *So this is the Nanuq without his cape. What will he say?*

So these are the fearsome Tlingit of Sitka, Baranov was thinking. He had long heard of their reputation. But more than their strength on the battlefield, he knew of their cruelty to prisoners. Any enemies so unfortunate as to be defeated alive were tortured simply because they were the enemy. Those who survived were enslaved and set to hard labor with meager rations and scant shelter. Indeed, he had heard that the Sitka Tlingit were expert at bringing hell on earth to their captives. In the Tlingit language, he said in his deepest voice, *"I am Baranov, Russian Nanuq and chief of these men."*

The Tlingit stared at him with evident curiosity. *"We come in peace. I represent His Majesty the Emperor, Tsar Paul, ruler of all this country."*

Ska-outlelt then spoke. *"I am Ska-outlelt, chief of the Sitka Kiks.adi Kwaan. Why are you here?"*

Kuponek came closer and explained, "He's the chief-of-chiefs of the Sitka Island Tlingit, the group of clans they call their 'kwaan,' or community."

Baranov turned back to the Tlingit chief. *"We know British traders have behaved badly to your people. We want to build a fort here to protect you from them. We alone will trade with you for furs. Then British can't take your women hostage and rape them."*

". . . How much will you pay for this place?" asked Ska-outlelt.

Some Russians came forward and set down boxes with colored beads, glass bottles, scraps of iron, and rolls of colored cloth—things of value to the Tlingit.

"This land has been ours for all time. Many say only Tlingit should be here."

"The Tlingits will gain much in trade with a Russian fort here. Especially cloth and iron and tools, and we can teach you how to build better houses."

"What is wrong with our houses?"

"You will know when you see our houses."

The chief saw that his men were looking over the boxes of Russian trading items and seemed pleased. *"Well, we do not use this part, and maybe you can help us with the British devils. We will trade this place to you."*

Baranov was pleasantly surprised that the negotiation had gone so quickly and well.

"Good. We have a deed for you to sign."

He took a pre-written scroll out of his pocket and handed it to Kuponek, who walked it over to Ska-outlelt along with a quill for signing it.

Ska-outlelt seemed a bit surprised by this formality, but he clearly liked formalities. He especially liked formalities that only he as chief could perform. So he minimized his befuddlement about exactly what he was supposed to do as Kuponek held the scroll, pointing to the place to make his mark. He made a small mark with the quill on the edge of the document to show it worked, and then handed the quill to the chief. With great solemnity, the chief made his mark, which looked like a grizzly bear print, in the appointed place.

Kuponek carried the scroll back to Baranov, who rolled it up, put it in his pocket, and then stepped forward with hand outreached to shake hands with Ska-outlelt.

The chief grasped the hand as they stared into each other's eyes and saw each other's strength. Baranov gave a slight smile of satisfaction, which Ska-outlelt returned. Then he turned and shook hands with the chief's nephew, the stern sub-chief Katlian, and only then realized he'd seen him before.

Under Baranov and Kuskov's supervision, the Russians went into the woods and cut timber for construction. With long ropes they dragged the big Sitka spruce logs to their building site, stripped off the bark, and set up the frame for their fort. Boards were cut from logs, and the walls went up quickly. They began building a stockade wall around the fort with parapets set in two corners.

Soon winter fell, and New Year's Day 1800 came and went. Baranov sat in his small cabin, looking out the window across the fort's inner yard now full of snow, and thought of Anna and two-year-old Antipatr. He was missing them. How big was his little boy now? What could the little fellow do?

The coming of spring 1800 was welcomed by all. In April, the fort was completed, and Baranov and his people celebrated Holy Week. In the back of the storehouse, they had built an altar with a wooden cross on it. Carrying lit candles, the Russians paraded around their fort, singing hymns accompanied by a drum and flute. The procession, with Baranov in the lead, hands piously clasped in front of his chest, passed through the storehouse to the altar, where they all kneeled and prayed, took up the cross, and carried it outside the fort, parading down to the shore and back.

From the woods, the Tlingit watched the celebration with misgivings. Katlian wondered if the Russians were calling upon evil spirits to destroy his people.

Other Tlingit interpreted the procession as preparations for an attack. So when Kuponek coincidentally visited the Tlingit village to interpret for a Russian hunter buying smoked salmon, they took him prisoner. The Russian ran away before he could be caught, straight to Baranov. "They took Kuponek!" said the hunter breathlessly.

"Why?" asked Baranov.

"I don't know."

"Kuskov! Come here," Baranov ordered. "Kuponek was captured in the village. We must get him out fast! Bring two dozen men with muskets to the kayaks, and two falconets."

Kuskov issued orders, and men raced to *bidarkas* with their muskets, others into the fort for their weapons, including the two small cannon, and then to the beach.

"Load up, and let's go!" Baranov barked.

One *nigilax* with the cannons and five men, plus four *bidarkas* with sixteen men—twenty-one in all—paddled quickly toward the village three miles away. Baranov knew that Chief Ska-outlelt had built a new longhouse for himself below the kekur in the main village on flat land near the shore. That would be his target.

The five craft beached in front of the village, and the men got out and surrounded Baranov, who was carrying the burlap bag with his "special friend." Immediately, three hundred men in the village stirred and came out to see what was happening.

"Mount the two cannon right here, aimed at the chief's longhouse," Baranov ordered. "You four stay here with the cannon, load them, and do nothing else except on my command. The rest of you—load your muskets with blank charges."

The men did so.

"See that lodge with the two guards?" Baranov asked. "That's where their chief is. We're going right over there. When I signal by dropping my hand, you ten men fire into the air for surprise, and then the rest of you grab those guards and tie them up. Ready? Let's go."

Baranov used the same formation around him as he'd used in the Yakutat confrontation, and the Russians marched forward. The hundreds of Tlingit men stared astounded as Baranov and his men marched right into the village toward the guarded lodge. Ska-outlelt emerged from his lodge with some curiosity, giving no signal to his men. The Russians were too outnumbered to be any real threat.

And yet their behavior was so *brazen*. To top it off, Baranov was standing on the thighs of two of his men with a screen of others kneeling around them, as at Yakutat. Again, he wore his sparkling white polar bear head and fur cape. As he and his men reached the two guards, he raised and then dropped his hand, and the ten muskets were fired into the air with a great noise, frightening some women and children, who cried out.

Immediately, the two guards were seized—to their surprise— quickly subdued, and tied up. The Tlingit turned to their chief for some sign, but he started to laugh. Then Baranov laughed, and so did the rest. The chief invited Baranov into his lodge for a negotiation. Baranov was carried into the lodge cross-legged on a board carried by four of his men. Four of the chief's warriors accompanied them. The chief and Baranov sat down inside facing each other, Baranov on a thick cushion brought by one of his men so he would appear taller. The chief offered him *yukola*, smoked salmon, which he took and chewed. Both men spoke in the Tlingit language.

"You are Baranov."

"Yes."

"So this is Nanuq," said the chief, reaching out to touch and stroke the white bear fur. *"The great Nanuq."*

"Now, give me Kuponek, and I give you your two."

Ska-outlelt laughed. *"I can take them away from you any time."*

"If you try, my cannon will blast this lodge to bits."

"With you in it?"

"No, just you. Tied up."

The chief suddenly turned serious, studying the man now staring at him resolutely and with no sign of nervousness or fear. He thought that what Baranov had just done was outrageously fearless and self-confident—so much so that Ska-outlelt sensed that he might have met his match, and so chose caution.

"Can you walk on your own feet now, like before?" asked Ska-outlelt.

"Yes. On my own ground."

"You must be crazy or have powers I don't know." The chief stared into his eyes for a long moment, then laughed again, lightly.

"Were you planning an attack on this village? Is that what you were preparing this morning?"

"No. If we were, we would have done it then with all our men and all our cannon, without warning, without parading around, and you, my friend, would be dead. But because you are my friend, we have no such plans."

"How much smaller than me are you? I remember much smaller."

"Who is the more ferocious fighter, the bear or the wolverine?" After a silent pause, Baranov continued, *"If you are taller than me, does that mean you can shoot straighter?"*

The chief gave no answer, and Baranov went on. *"The Tlingit are a great people. You have made this island your home for hundreds of years. Except for land we buy from you, we don't want to take anything from you."*

"What about our seal and our otter?" asked Ska-outlelt. *"They belong to us. But you have Aleuts hunting for you, taking them away from us."*

"There are many more seal and otter here than your people could ever hunt by yourselves. And we will gladly trade for whatever furs you get. But all the seal and otter here don't belong to you, and they don't belong to me. They belong to His Majesty the Tsar, and you and I hunt them with his permission."

"Will you sell us guns and powder?" asked the chief.

"That is too dangerous for us, because those guns could be used against us later, by someone else who somehow acquired control of them. . . . Give me my man, and I give you yours," said Baranov as he smiled slyly, as if to say, "Aren't we smart. Let's make a deal."

After a moment's thought, Ska-outlelt returned the sly smile. "Yes. Let's do it."

Two weeks later in the Tlingit village, an argument erupted between Ska-outlelt and his nephew Katlian. Kuponek, while visiting the village, overheard it and reported it to Baranov when he returned to the fort.

"Tlingit argue. Some want Russians off of Sitka Island."

"Why?" asked Baranov.

"Not sure. Chief Katlian hates Russians. He is a powerful sub-chief."

Just a few days later, Baranov and some of his men boarded *Olga* to sail to Kodiak. Vasilii Medvednikov, who was to be left in command at Sitka, rowed a *nigilax* with others out into Sitka Sound to see them off.

Baranov instructed him, "You're in charge while I go back to Kodiak and tend to the Aleutians. Until I return, be wary of the Tlingit, especially Chief Katlian. Finish building the stockade."

Medvednikov nodded and waved as the ship departed.

He's an able man, Baranov assured himself. Respected by his men. And he'd had experience with the Tlingit at Yakutat. Medvednikov should be able to handle Sitka. His mind quickly turned to navigating out of Sitka Sound and on to Kodiak.

He knew the distance from Sitka to Kodiak was 700 miles, not a trivial distance, and could take a week of sailing in changeable weather—the distance from Moscow to Warsaw, or from Rome to Paris. And the distance from Kodiak to Unalaska, near the beginning of the Aleutians, was nearly the same. Alaskan distances made his job especially challenging.

Olga arrived safely at St. Paul. Baranov had been away almost two years. As he hurried from the wharf to his house, he saw Anna standing in the yard, holding the hand of three-year-old Antipatr, who was watching him closely. Baranov climbed the hill and entered the yard. They looked at each other, each seeking a sign from the other. In her eyes, he saw a shy joy. Then she spoke to their son.

"This is your papa, Antipatr."

Baranov hugged Anna, and her happy face beamed over his shoulder with tears of relief. Then she carried Antipatr into the house, Baranov singing a favorite Russian children's song.

Inside, Anna set the boy down on the parlor floor. He stood there, sucking the fingers of one hand while he held onto his mother with the other, and stared at this strange man. Baranov sat down on the floor and started to play peek-a-boo with Antipatr. Soon the boy was laughing and let Baranov pick him up and set him on his daddy's lap. Baranov was grinning with delight. Anna sat on the floor next to them with a happy smile.

***

Along the Alaska Peninsula coastline, debris from the *Phoenix* wreck washed up on many beaches. Natives found a box of church candles, part of a spruce deck beam with Alaska-forged nails, pieces of clerical clothing, and brought them to Baranov.

He was devastated. He sat down and put his elbows on his desk, and his face sank into his hands. This wreckage proved that *Phoenix,* with Captain Shields and the new bishop, had been lost returning from Okhotsk. How could he bear the loss of Shields and the great ship they had built together?

But hoping against what must be the truth, he suddenly got up, grabbed some gear, issued orders to Kuskov and Kuponek, and launched *Olga* with a small crew in search for survivors.

Hugging the coast, entering every bay and scanning the shore with his telescope for some sign of survivors, he finally had to admit the futility of it. They returned to Kodiak as winter arrived.

The following spring, in 1801, Baranov sailed away from St. Paul to inspect villages and visit with chiefs along the Peninsula.

One morning after he left, Anna let little Antipatr play in the yard of the Baranov house. An Aleut servant stood nearby, watching for any wandering Kodiak bear that might look upon the small boy as a tasty morsel. About twenty feet from the yard, the priest Nektarios also stood watching the boy. Anna looked out a window, saw Nektarios, and wondered what had so captured his attention. Then, out another window, she saw little Antipatr.

CHAPTER 18

ANNA'S FAITH AND THE TSAR'S DEATH

Anna attended church many times while Baranov was away, enthralled by the ceremony and music. It awakened a spiritual place deep within her that needed nurturing. After one service, she found Nektarios as he supervised a young male acolyte, Stefanov, who was storing service items. Haltingly, she spoke to Nektarios. "Father, I want to become Christian."

"You can't, because you are living in sin," Nektarios replied. "You are living with Baranov, a man married to someone else. That is a sin. He has children with her, too."

"If he is married to someone else, where is she? I am with him for years and see no other wife. If he has another wife and children, they would be here."

Nektarios couldn't respond to that logic, so he changed the subject. "Your son is a child of sin. You must give him to us, so we can raise him in Christ, away from the evils of Baranov. Then the boy will be saved."

"The boy belongs with me, his mother."

"Then leave Baranov to save yourself and the boy. At least save the boy by giving him to me."

Very troubled, she returned to the Baranov house. She had read the Sermon on the Mount in Baranov's Bible and felt the call to follow that preacher, so distant and yet so close. He had said what she had always believed but could never put into words. And he had seemed willing to welcome her. But now Nektarios said no, she was not worthy. Worse, she was a terrible sinner. Yes, she knew all were considered sinners in this religion, but she'd just been told her sins were so grave she could not be accepted. How could that be? She had always tried to be kind and faithful to those around her, the friends and family she saw every day. And she tried to be a friend even to strangers, like the Good Samaritan.

Worst of all, the Church wanted to take her dear little son away from her. How did she deserve such punishment? Why did Nektarios really want Antipatr?

The next evening, in the front yard overlooking the sea, she sat watching the ocean while little Antipatr played at her feet. She picked him up and held him on her lap, pondering her dilemma.

A few days later, she again went to a church service, and amid other worshipers, she was again spiritually engaged by music and holy ritual. Afterwards, as she left the church, Nektarios followed her outside and said, "I will come to get the boy this afternoon."

Anna saw his determination and hurried home. She entered the house, moving in a panic, and found Antipatr playing, watched by the Aleut servant.

"Come," she said urgently to the boy.

She picked him up and wrapped him in a sealskin blanket,

pulled on a jacket and a belt with Baranov's hunting knife for protection in the wild, and headed out the door with Antipatr.

She carried him swiftly on a foot-trail along the coast above the oceanside cliffs. How she wished Baranov were here to protect them from the priests. She would have to do it herself.

"Mama, where we going?"

"I take you to my mother's village. You will be safe there. When Papa comes back, we will bring you home."

She ran up an uneven part of the trail, climbing a bluff next to the ocean. At the top of the grassy bluff, she tripped on a stone and fell, dropping Antipatr. Wrapped in sealskin, he rolled down over a cliff and toward ocean rocks about thirty feet below. A big wave washed over the rocks just in time to cushion his fall. Anna gasped, pulled herself up, scrambled to the edge of the cliff and looked down. She threw her arms up in horror.

Nearby hunters in kayaks had seen the boy fall and seeing her arms thrown up, thought she had tossed him over the cliff. When she tried to climb down to the boy, a hunter fired a warning shot toward her, and the men rescued Antipatr. The boy was stunned and didn't move. Thinking he was dead, she ran into the forest consumed with grief and guilt.

The hunters returned to the harbor. Stefanov, the church acolyte, had been fishing from the dock with a few other villagers and saw the hunters carry the whimpering boy onto the wharf. Before Stefanov could ask, a hunter said, "Anna threw the boy in the ocean."

Then Baranov arrived in his sloop, hopped onto the dock and tied up alongside. The boy was brought to him.

"What happened?" Baranov asked.

Stefanov pushed forward to explain.

"I heard Anna tell Father Nektarios she wanted to become a Christian. He said she can't while living in sin with you. He also said the boy is a child of sin, and she must get rid of this sin before she can be baptized. So she took the boy up there and threw him in the ocean. Hunters pulled him out. Then she ran into the woods."

Baranov looked to the rescuers for confirmation, and they murmured, "Yes."

Furious, he handed the boy to Kuponek and marched toward Nektarios's cabin with an entourage of angry hunters. He threw the cabin door open, pulled Nektarios outside, slammed him against the outside wall, and barked, "You *bastard!* You made Anna try to kill our son, an innocent child. If there is an Antichrist, it is *you!*"

"*No!* It is *you* who are from the devil," Nektarios replied.

Baranov threw him back into his cabin and ordered Kuskov, "This demon shall be confined to his cabin. Guard him. If he tries to set even a toe outside, shoot him! We won't let him out until he is converted. Completely converted."

From where he sat on the floor of his cabin, Nektarios called out through the open door, "Converted? Converted to *what?*"

Baranov spat out with seething anger, "*Christianity!*"

He slammed the cabin door and marched off, muttering, "You stiff-necked, pea-brained, murderous fool."

He went home to look after his son and saw Kuponek heading for the woods to look for Anna. "No! Leave her alone," Baranov yelled. "She can survive out there. Her spirit is split in two. She must put herself back together the Native way. If she does, she'll be back. If not, I never want to see her again."

Inside the rustic parlor of his house, Baranov poured himself a mug of vodka and sat down to ponder the situation.

A priest whom Baranov liked, Father Herman, came to offer comfort and sat by Baranov who stared for a moment at Herman in his hooded deerskin monk's robe. Then Baranov cried out angrily, "There is no God. . . . *There is no God!* How could God let a priest do this to an innocent child?"

"I don't know what Nektarios did or told Anna," replied Herman. He got up and said, "But come with me. There is something you should see."

Baranov followed Herman outside and down to where Antipatr had fallen below the cliff. Herman pointed to the top of the cliff thirty feet above as the surf roared behind them, looked at Baranov, and said, "How could he fall from such a height, into the jaws of certain death, and yet survive? Who saved him?"

"Then why? *Why?*"

"There is a reason for *everything*," Herman replied, as he clasped Baranov's shoulders in his hands. "But sometimes it is not in this world."

Baranov went back up the trail, looked back, and saw Herman kneeling and praying below. He found Antipatr sleeping on his bed at home, with the servant sitting at his side. As Baranov entered, the servant left. Baranov got on his knees, and as he took the boy's small, tan hand in his, he spoke softly to a great ear that he then believed surely must be listening.

"Thank you."

About a mile away, Anna was sitting on a hillside rock, staring at the sea, tears streaming down her cheeks, holding in sobs. A Kodiak bear walking nearby stopped, turned to face her, and rose on hind legs to look. It dropped to all fours and came a few feet closer. Anna ignored it, staring seaward, still seeking a reason for what had happened. The bear grunted and ambled off.

She had killed her son. In the darkness of her fathomless grief and guilt, she turned to the forest for comfort. Her heart cried out to sea and sky to make sense of it. For her people, nature was the source of all reason.

Baranov's knife was on her belt. In her misery, she could hold in the sobs no longer. Her hand came down, unsnapped the hasp, and grasped the knife handle.

In the house, Baranov poured himself a shot of vodka while he tried to comprehend what had happened. He sat down looking out the window at the sea.

There was a knock at the door. "Come in," he shouted.

Kuskov entered. "The priest has no food in his cabin."

"Good. Make sure he gets none. He must work for his dinner. Tell him he gets no food or water until he writes down exactly, word for word, the Sermon on the Mount—every day! And I must approve the accuracy of it before he gets even a bread crumb."

"How long will you lock him up?"

"Jesus went into the wilderness and wrestled with the devil for forty days and nights. Let the priest wrestle with his devils for forty days and nights."

"Have you heard about Father Herman?"

". . . Heard what?"

Kuskov replied, "Father Herman has left St. Paul and gone to Spruce Island. He will build a cabin there for himself."

"Why?" demanded Baranov.

"He didn't say."

Baranov thought about this, at first puzzled. Then he realized Father Herman was refusing to take sides in Baranov's dispute with the other priests, and so had physically distanced himself from both parties.

"I see," he said, as he sipped his vodka.

The next morning, it occurred to Anna that maybe the boy had in fact actually survived. She hiked back to where she could see the house and saw little Antipatr playing outside with toy soldiers until taken indoors by a servant. Weeping for joy, she headed for the house.

Inside, Baranov was reviewing paperwork at his parlor desk when he heard her enter the front door. He had already chosen to confront her in the Native way. A Native does not ask an obvious question, but instead waits patiently for the answer to come naturally.

"I saw Antipatr playing outside. I want to see him."

"Get cleaned up first, so he won't be frightened. And get something to eat. Then you can see him."

When she was ready, he took Anna to the boy's room. Antipatr ran to her happily, and she embraced him in tears.

"I'm sorry I fell and dropped you, Antipatr," she said softly.

". . . You *fell?*" Baranov said in surprise. "You didn't throw him in the ocean?"

"You think I threw him in the *ocean?*" she asked, incredulous, as she stood quickly. She turned to face him, saying firmly, "I'm his *mother!* How could I throw him in the *ocean?*"

She saw confusion in his eyes. He saw truth in hers.

"But the hunters said—"

"They did not see me fall on the trail. Nektarios wanted our boy, so I tried to take him to Mother's village to be safe."

For a moment, his eyes were wide with surprise, and his mouth hung open. Then he exclaimed, "Anna, what are we doing to you?" He took her in his arms, where he knew she belonged.

The next day, Kuskov came up to Baranov's house just as Baranov came out to tend to business. Kuskov reported, "Nektarios won't do as you say. Says he'd rather starve than take orders from you, and that you have no ecclesiastic authority."

"He's right, you know. I can't tell the priests what to do. That's my *problem.* All right, let him go."

***

On the night of March 23, 1801, in the hallway of Tsar Paul's Mikhailovsky Palace in St. Petersburg—a palace specially built to protect the Tsar from conspirators—the reverberating clatter of military boots moving forward in the ornate, candle-lit hallway shattered the quiet. Three middle-aged Russian generals moved forward at the head of it, all recently fired by the Tsar for failure to adhere to an ancient code of knighthood and chivalry that he was trying to impose on them. For many in the military, these firings had been a final insult.

The imperial guards were all off duty, as arranged. Behind the generals, half a dozen army officers advanced toward the door to the Tsar's bedroom. General Bennigsen was carrying a document, and General Yashvil a rope.

Paul was alone in his ornate bed under sumptuous blankets and gold bed covers, wearing a white nightcap and gown. He stirred awake as he heard the commotion in the hallway. Long afraid of assassination, he immediately sensed something was wrong, especially as he heard no guard challenge the oncoming boots. His eyes grew wide with terror as he looked at the crack under the door, seeing the candle glow growing brighter and the noise of approaching death growing louder. He slid out of bed and, in the moonlight, glanced around for somewhere to hide.

The assassins reached the bedroom door and burst into the room. The bed was empty. Bennigsen saw a small movement behind a drape.

"There he is!" he shouted.

Three of his cohorts rushed to the drape, pulled the terrified Tsar Paul from behind it, and pushed him down on his knees in front of the two generals.

"Guards! *Guards!*" he screamed.

"There *are* no guards," Bennigsen sneered. "Sign this abdication! Sign it *now!*"

In wide-eyed terror, Tsar Paul whimpered, "You're going to kill me, aren't you?"

"Yes!" declared Yashvil as he jumped forward with the rope, threw it over Paul's head, and began strangling the Tsar. He was pushed, gasping, gurgling, to the floor, his attackers' boots holding him down.

Finally there was quiet in the room. The assassins stood up and looked down at the lifeless body of the Tsar.

Sarcastically, General Yashvil said, "Good night, Your Majesty."

"Not so majestic now!" observed General Zubov.

"We should ship his carcass to Malta," said Bennigsen.

"Grand Master of the Knights Hospitaller indeed!" Yashvil replied.

"Yes, where were your glorious knights when you needed them? Grand Master. . . ." Zubov shook his head.

They stomped out of the room, taking the rope with them. They went down the hall, out the front door of the unguarded palace, and down the front steps toward their three black carriages. Tsar Paul's eldest son, Alexander, having heard the commotion, ran out the front door to the top of the steps, peering down toward the carriages in the dimly lit darkness.

"What is this?" he demanded.

Zubov called out from the darkness, "You are now the Tsar, Alexander! Time to grow up! Go and rule!"

The carriages raced off down the driveway into the night, leaving the new young Tsar Alexander I wondering, at age twenty-three, what had happened. He ran back inside.

"Help! Is anyone here? *Help!*" he cried out into the vast echoing hall.

CHAPTER 19

BARANOV HONORED AMONG WHIPPED DOGS

Baranov, in the warehouse with Kuponek, walked past the shelves to check their inventory of supplies. He was appalled. "Almost out of everything. Three years since the last supply ship! If food runs out, the colony fails."

Kuponek offered, "I could take men to try a whale hunt."

The bell rang, and a commotion went up. Outside they saw the American ship *Enterprise* sailing in. They jumped up and bounded out the door.

Baranov and Kuponek paddled out to meet the ship as it anchored. Joe O'Cain, first mate, threw a rope ladder over the side. Upon seeing his old friend leaning over the side of the ship, Baranov was instantly delighted. *"O'Cain, you son of a bitch! Glad to see you!"*

"Baranov, you rotten bastard! Glad to see you, too!"

Baranov raced up the ladder, jumped over the side, and he and O'Cain embraced excitedly, as the captain walked over.

"Sasha, meet my skipper, Ezekiel Hubbell."

Baranov and Hubbell shook hands as Kuponek climbed aboard.

Hubbell said, *"From the stories I've heard about you, Governor Baranov, I thought you'd be ten feet tall."*

"I get smaller when I'm out of vodka."

"And you're losing hair, too, without vodka to feed it," O'Cain kidded him.

They laughed heartily. Then Baranov turned to O'Cain. *"Say, Joe, who is your president now?"*

"Thomas Jefferson, a Virginian."

"Are you spying for him, too?"

O'Cain grimaced.

Hubbell got down to business. *"Joe said you need supplies we could trade for furs, which we'd sell in Canton—so here we are."*

He handed Baranov a manifest, which Baranov read with great interest but with a nonchalant poker face. The list had everything he needed in foodstuffs, plus muskets and cannon that he must not let Hubbell trade to the Natives.

"What do you want for it all?" asked Baranov.

"One thousand otter pelts," answered Hubbell.

"I'll give you two thousand red and silver fox pelts," offered Baranov.

"One thousand otter."

"No. Two thousand fox," said Baranov firmly.

"I have an idea!" said O'Cain. *"Sasha, you're famous for holding your liquor. Let's drink it out. You against the two of us. If either of us is the last man standing, then payment is in otter. If you are the last one, then fox."*

"What do you say, Hubbell?" asked Baranov.

"Up the ante, and I'll go for it. Twelve hundred otter versus twenty-five hundred fox."

"And if we win," said O'Cain, *"I get your famous polar bear hide thrown in."*

In a flash of anger, Baranov turned to leave, muttering, *"Forget it."*

"Never mind! Never mind, Sasha!" said O'Cain quickly. *"Just joking."*

Baranov returned, looked down, collected himself, then looked up and exclaimed, *"It's a deal! I'll send for Richard—you know him, Honest Joe. He'll stay sober as our witness."*

"Good. Now, will you join us for dinner first?" offered Hubbell.

"Delighted!" replied Baranov as he turned to Kuponek. *"Go get Richard."*

Kuponek went over the side to the bidarka.

Inside Captain Hubbell's cabin on *Enterprise*, the captain and his guest, plus O'Cain, took seats at a table set for dinner and started swapping sea stories—tall stories all, enjoyed with great hilarity. Richard appeared, the dinner dishes were cleared, a bottle of rum was placed on the table, and a glass was set in front of each of the three contenders. A ship's man poured rum to fill each glass. Baranov raised his glass in a toast.

"May the best son of a bitch win!"

"Here! Here!" O'Cain and Hubbell agreed, as each took a swig.

O'Cain blurted out, *"Baranov, you old fool, you should know better than to try to out-drink two Irishmen."*

As each contestant's glass was emptied, the ship's man was there to refill it. On every refill, the three clinked their glasses together. Before long, O'Cain's and Hubbell's arms started to weave from side to side, their heads bobbing back and forth. But Baranov remained nearly steady as a rock.

After a few hours, O'Cain and Hubbell were peacefully asleep under the table, as Baranov sat wobbly in his chair. He struggled to stand and just barely made it to his feet.

"Lasht mun shtanding! A vodka drinkin' Russian!" he declared.

In a congratulatory tone, Richard announced, "Fox pelts it will be, sir."

The next day, as a consequence of the drink-out, Kuponek and Kuskov supervised both the unloading and loading of *Enterprise*. Baranov, though a bit hung over, inspected the precious cargo they had just bought in trade with furs. He said to Kuskov, "Ivan, this cargo saved us. And we traded at a profit!"

"The priests say their prayers got these supplies," Kuskov replied.

Baranov had little inclination to give the clerics credit for anything, except maybe Herman.

"Hmph. Now, if only their prayers to get me replaced here would be answered, then I'd know God really listens to them, and I'd be a happy man."

***

Henry Smith, master of the Hudson's Bay Company expedition to the Pacific, was standing above the shore near British Columbia's Metlakatla looking out to sea toward Hecate Strait. He watched a fleet of Aleut *bidarkas* under Russian command hunting otter near a small island a couple miles away. He shook his head as he turned to Stuart McKay and said, "Somehow we've got to get rid of the Russians, or they'll wipe out all the furs in the northwest."

"How?" asked McKay. "We don't have anybody with us to do that."

"Right, but maybe we can get somebody else to do it for us. Someone who wants them out as much as we do. We *do* have guns. We can trade guns for furs with Natives who want the Russians out—they'll do our fighting for us."

". . . And what will keep them from using those guns against us?"

"Gunpowder. They'll need a continuing supply of gunpowder and musket balls, so they'll need us. I've heard of a young chief named Katlian who hates the Russians. See if you can get a meeting with him."

***

The year 1801 seemed to be passing like so many years before. There was the otter and seal hunt; Chief Grigor came for a visit to check on the great Nanuq and his family; many men were engaged in repairing ships damaged by the rigors of Alaskan seas and storms; Baranov, Anna, and Antipatr took outings down the Kodiak coast on *Olga* when the weather was fine, seeing awesome scenes of nature—including Kodiak bears standing knee-deep in the outlets of rivers, fishing for salmon they caught with their powerful jaws.

One day in midsummer, Baranov heard that Anna had left Antipatr to play at a friend's house and gone blueberry picking by herself. He knew that her favorite blueberry patch was on the mossy, hilly meadow just southwest of the village. It was a sunny day under bright blue skies with a few wisps of high, white clouds—and being after mid-July, with a strong breeze, mosquitoes were hardly a nuisance. *A beautiful day indeed*, he thought.

Baranov's work was done for the day, so he decided to join Anna and hiked out to seek her in the hills. He went through the woods near town and then onto the slopes of open fields with spongy moss and low blueberry bushes. There, in a meadow ahead, he saw Anna, her back to him, kneeling and picking berries. On this island, Kodiak bears were also blueberry pickers, so he thought he would give her a playful scare by sneaking up behind her. But he hadn't counted on the acuteness of her Native senses. When he was twenty feet from her, she said without facing him, "Hello, my *toyon*."

She continued picking without turning around, as if to say, "I know where you are without having to look, so I win this game." He came up right behind her and got on his knees. Yes, he had to agree she was superbly aware of her natural surroundings, more capable at that than he could ever be. Then he noticed how lovely she looked as the sun made her flowing black hair glisten over her open blue jacket, which covered a pleated white blouse tucked into a long blue skirt. He realized there was another game he knew he could win.

He lifted the hair from her shoulders and leaned over and kissed the nape of her neck. That got her attention. They stood up, and with the berry basket hanging on one arm, Anna turned to face him. Looking steadily and warmly into his eyes, she put a ripe blueberry in his mouth. As he savored it, his playful mood changed into something more serious. He caressed the side of her face, and then put an arm around her.

"What do you want?" she asked softly.

"I want your berries."

He pulled her close and kissed her tenderly on her lips.

"My basket full of berries." She kissed him. "For you." She fed him a couple more berries as a tease, which he quickly swallowed, focusing on her.

"I want them all, my dear Anna." He kissed her.

"Every *round*. . ." (he kissed her) "*ripe*. . ." (he kissed her) "*delicious*. . ." (he kissed her) "berry."

He knew he wanted her right now, right here, in broad daylight, on this soft bed of moss and berries. His rising passion infected her, and she dropped the basket, spilling the berries. He felt her arms around his neck, and he lowered her onto the soft, green moss. From above, he unbuttoned her blouse as her hands gently held his face.

She lay back and looked up into the strong, good face that she adored, seeing above him the crisp blue sky that would ever after remind her of the glorious happiness of that moment. Looking into his eyes, she saw him as she always did. Though tough and powerful, never hesitating to use the whip or unleash a blistering tirade on unruly Russian hunters, he had never raised his hand to her, never spoken a cross word to her, and had always been kind and patient. There was something about his raw strength that others saw, and the contradictory inner gentleness that only she could see, that made this man so very special to her. Could he ever understand the depth of her love for him?

He paused to look into her loving brown eyes. Until then, the aim of his excitement had been gratification. But, now, as he looked into her eyes, it was as if the sun had come out from behind a cloud and bathed the whole countryside with its life-giving light. Now for him, this moment was no longer about the ecstasy of sex. It was about the ecstasy of love. As her head lay back on the green, sunlit moss, framed by a few leafy sprays of blueberries, the person he saw in her face was incredibly beautiful—a radiant beauty intended for just him to see. She was love itself. How had he not really seen it before? Maybe he had held himself back while he expected to return to Russia without her. Now that he doubted he'd ever return, whatever had been holding him back must have been released. At that moment, for the first time, Baranov knew that he truly loved Anna.

He said softly, "Anna.... Anna, I see your spirit... so beautiful."

He came down, kissed her ear, and whispered, "I want your spirit... to be part of me." He kissed her ear again. And then his heart made him say what he'd never said before: "I love you."

He spread open her clothing, opened his own, then slowly caressed her and kissed her, again and again, everywhere that could make her feel his love. So did she to him. Her smooth, warm, softly curving skin felt exquisite to his touch. And to her, his touch was heaven itself. So fluidly they moved, like water flowing over, under, and around stones in a wild brook. Lips and hands and bodies felt each other, warm skin on skin, all parts of them silently singing the soaring hymn of their caring passion for one another. And then they were one; the tempo of their loving rhythm increased, and their ecstasy was complete. He finished with a deep-throated sigh and a lingering kiss on the side of her smooth, soft, warm neck where he felt the pulse of her precious heart on his lips.

Afterward, they fell asleep, with Baranov partly on top of Anna.

Soon, a Kodiak bear wandered onto the field, saw them, and picked up their scent. The most formidable, most vicious killer of the North American animal world was with them. Cautious at first, having never seen people lying down like this, the beast became curious and slowly moved toward them.

Baranov awoke, and with one open eye, he saw the auburn fur of the front feet of the bear approaching with long, menacing claws. Immediately, adrenalin pumped into his blood. For an instant, he considered reaching for the knife on his belt. But protecting Anna made him dismiss that as too risky and probably useless anyway. So, with as little movement as possible to prevent provoking the bear, he pulled himself over to completely cover her, and she awoke.

"Shh. Bear. Play dead," he whispered. He brought his right hand up to cover and protect her throat, and reached behind with his left to shield his own neck.

The massively powerful bear came right next to them, and with its nose and mouth the size of a shoebox—a mouth filled with deadly teeth—It started sniffing all around. Their hearts raced. Then the bear, reeking of fish, took one huge foot-wide front paw and put it tentatively on Baranov's back, feeling his ribcage. That heavy foot terrified Baranov, but he kept still, knowing that a couple of swats from those dagger-sharp claws could finish them both. Were they just seconds from horrible, painful deaths? What could he do? If the bear grabbed him, he decided, he would swing around to face it, fight like hell, and give Anna a chance to escape.

Just then, the smell of the pile of picked blueberries spilled near the lovers' feet caught the bear's attention. Thus distracted, the bear moved over to lick up the pile of berries. Out of curiosity, it sniffed the lovers again briefly, lost interest, and slowly ambled off, picking berries as it went.

Baranov and Anna remained frozen. Silently, he kept asking himself, "Is it gone?" But he dared not look up to see, for fear that any movement could attract it again.

After several minutes, Anna whispered to him, "I think the bear is gone."

He ventured to look up and couldn't see it. Carefully, he sat up, his eyes scanning all around, and saw that the bear had truly gone. Then she sat up, pulling her clothes together. His rush of adrenalin began to subside, and he saw her look at him with a sigh of relief. With them still was the afterglow of the wonderful waves of emotion that had surged through them earlier, when they had expressed what it spiritually meant to be part of each other.

He stood and helped her up. She picked up her empty basket. They both glanced at it and smiled knowingly at one another, each thinking of what those berries now meant to them. They embraced, absorbed by all that had happened, and she pressed her face against his neck. They pulled each other close for a long moment. Then, hand in hand, they walked back to the village.

***

Contemplating the new year of 1802, Anna looked out a

window at the falling snow. She had more to contemplate—she was very pregnant again.

That spring, an urgently excited Baranov ran past a rainbow of wildflowers along the trail to his house. A female Aleut servant trailed behind, and they sped through the front door and on into the bedroom. There, he found Anna kneeling on the floor, delivering a baby. He stopped in the doorway, dumbfounded, looking on in awe. He heard the baby let out a healthy cry. A moment after the birth, he watched Anna lie down on a floor mat and the servant cut the umbilical cord and wrap the baby in a cloth. Then Anna took the baby in her arms and pulled a blanket over them. Baranov knelt and pulled back a corner of the blanket to admire his new daughter, taking hold of her little hand with its perfect tiny fingers.

He said softly, "What a miracle, that from our love has come this wonderful new life. Welcome to our world, Irina Aleksandrovna."

He smiled warmly at Anna, leaned over, and kissed her forehead as the palm of his hand gently held the side of her face. He saw her close her eyes wearily with a smile and fall asleep.

* * *

Nikolai Rezanov, in his formal dress as imperial chamberlain, made his way down a curved hallway with heroic paintings of royal scenes on the wall, eventually reaching the door to a large outdoor balcony, onto which he emerged and saw the young Tsar Alexander I—tall, handsome, and sandy-haired—standing alone, looking over the stone balustrade to the yard below. The Tsar saw Rezanov approaching and, as the latter bowed, impatiently signaled for him to rise. Two bright and charming young men, both quick, strategic thinkers, they enjoyed each other's company.

Back in 1799, all the colonial fur companies had been merged into one firm—the Russian American Company, with Count Nikolai Rezanov, a member of the Tsar's court, heading its board of directors. Then, in 1801, Tsar Paul had been assassinated, and his son, Tsar Alexander I became Tsar of all the Russias. Rezanov wanted him to expand Russia's Pacific empire.

"Good morning, Count Rezanov. Now my party is complete," said the Tsar as he motioned over the balustrade.

"Good morning, Your Majesty."

On the parade ground below, they could see a long table covered by a white and gold cloth, set for tea for twenty. At the far end, perpendicular to it, sat an ornate serving table with an enormous gold samovar; close to the middle of that table stood a huge world globe. On the other side of the long tea table, about fifty feet away, sat a concert grand piano with a pianist, a full symphony orchestra, and a conductor, awaiting their cue. The guests, all members of the Tsar's staff, half of them military, stood at their places by the long tea table.

The Tsar led Rezanov down the stairs and over to the globe. "My eye is on this all the time to keep track of what Napoleon is up to. What a pest, that Corsican. But now I want to see what we're up to in the Pacific. Show me, Nikolai."

"Here is Russian America, Your Majesty. As you can see, it commands the North Pacific."

"Yes, I see that. I've heard that the Natives call it something else. What is that?"

"They call it Alaska, sir."

"Alaska. I like the sound of that. That's what we should call it too. Alaska."

"But Your Majesty, calling it Russian America says that it's ours."

"Look, Nikolai," said the Tsar, smiling with a bit of irony, "If King George ever wants to know to whom it belongs, tell him to ask me, and I'll *tell* him it's mine! . . . I like 'Alaska,'" he said again, tapping his finger on the globe.

"Yes, Your Majesty."

"You worry the British will try to take it away from us, don't you?"

"Yes. But Napoleon is helping us over there. He keeps the British Navy so busy in the Atlantic that they have few ships in the Pacific. So it's easier now to expand our holdings southward toward California. We could even get into the Sandwich Islands—Hawaii. The trade value and the wealth to be gained for Russia in the North Pacific are incredible!"

Alexander nodded thoughtfully while looking at the places Rezanov pointed out on the globe.

"Tell me about this man Baranov who's running things for us there."

"There *are* some complaints about him, but all from people who don't understand his problems. He's doing an astonishing job in an almost impossible situation. He's only a *mestchannin*, but he's very smart. He turns a profit for the company every year—in spite of earthquakes, tidal waves, lost shipments of supplies, Native uprisings, and insubordinate naval officers."

"Doesn't sound like a mere *mestchannin* to me. Insubordinate naval officers? I know what we can do to fix that! And yes, let's take advantage of our opportunity in the Pacific."

The Tsar turned to his other guests. "Shall we have some tea?" He signaled to the orchestra. "Maestro!"

They all sat as the servants stepped forward to serve the Tsar, and the orchestra and pianist started to play a romantic and very Russian piano concerto.

***

It was a gray day with a high overcast on a narrow gravel beach at the extreme southern end of Sitka Island. A launch from an English sloop anchored offshore was beached next to a Tlingit war canoe. Five Tlingit men sat in their canoe, including Katlian. Alongside, Smith and McKay of the Hudson's Bay Company sat in their small launch, manned by a sailor on oars and a Haida man who spoke both Tlingit and English—their interpreter.

"If you agree to push the Russians off Sitka and trade only with the Hudson's Bay Company, we will provide you with two cannons, two hundred muskets, and plenty of gunpowder," said Smith.

"You will not hunt furs and will only have a trading post on Sitka," said Katlian.

"That's right. We won't bring hunters. You do all the hunting. We will just trade with you."

"Then we will do it," said Katlian. "When will you give us the guns to fight the Russians?"

"Right here in two months."

A *bidarka* approached St. Paul from the southwest, paddled

by Ivan Banner and an Aleut. They pulled up onto the beach next to the wharf. Banner was taken directly to Baranov's office at the warehouse. When they entered, Banner asked, "You're Aleksandr Baranov?"

"Yes."

"Ivan Banner, from the Okhotsk office. I left my ship at Unalaska for repairs and came ahead with important announcements. For you, all good news. But there are also announcements everyone should hear at once. Can you call a general meeting?"

"Of course. Are you my long-awaited replacement?"

"No, I'm not. They want you to stay—with a promotion, if you'll accept it."

Baranov didn't know what to make of that.

That evening in the main dining hall, the community assembled. Sitting in a row near the front were Midshipman Talin and the priests, with Nektarios sitting next to Talin.

Talin said to Nektarios, "I hear that this man Banner has orders from Okhotsk including the dismissal of Baranov. Today Baranov gets what's coming to him!"

"Oh, what a blessing!" said Nektarios. "Surely God has heard our prayers, and now we'll be rid of that devil."

A couple of benches were pushed together to create a makeshift platform, and Banner and Baranov stepped onto it.

"Attention, everyone!" Baranov called out. "Ivan Banner has just arrived from Okhotsk and Unalaska. He came directly here because he has important news for us."

"Tsar Paul died a year ago. His son, Alexander, is now the Tsar. Long live Tsar Alexander!"

The audience immediately replied, "Long live Tsar Alexander!"

"The new name of our company, merging all the fur companies, is the Russian American Company and is headed by Count Nikolai Rezanov. Tsar Alexander, in gratitude for Chief Manager Baranov's outstanding service and devotion, has awarded him the Order of St. Vladimir!"

Banner opened a box, took out a medal with a neck ribbon, and placed it around Baranov's neck, to great applause from the hunters. Talin and the priests were in a state of shock.

"Also, the Tsar has appointed Baranov as governor of all of Russian America, all the way to Kamchatka!"

This was followed by wild cheers from the hunters.

"And the Tsar now wants us to call all Russian America by the Native name 'Alaska.' He likes the sound of it."

Baranov stood up front, with the Cross of St. Vladimir shining under his throat. He bowed his head, briefly overcome with emotion. The audience, except the priests and Talin, burst into renewed applause.

Baranov collected himself and looked up. "Thank you. I'm overwhelmed. I have two things to say. Following the example of His Majesty's great generosity to me, I'm giving a thousand rubles to expand the school here for Russian and Native children. And second, tonight I host a glorious *praznyk*!"

The two men stepped down, and the meeting dispersed. Several Russian hunters came over to congratulate Baranov. Midshipman Talin and the priests, all except Herman, walked out looking like whipped dogs.

CHAPTER 20

THE SITKA MASSACRE

At night in the main village of the Sitka Tlingit Kwaan, Primary Chief Ska-outlelt and several secondary chiefs, including Katlian, sat in a conference circle by a campfire. Katlian was boiling with hate for the Russians as he leaned forward to speak in his authoritative voice. *"Big mistake letting Russians get land on Sitka. They often stop British and Americans from trading guns to us. Our clans at Hoonah, Angoon, and Kake ridicule us for giving in to the Russians and letting them have land here. The Russians' Aleut hunters steal all our furs, and we will be left with nothing! Our people will starve. We must push Russians off Sitka!"*

The ever-cautious Ska-outlelt asked, *"What if we anger the Tsar, who rules all this land?"*

A general hubbub among younger chiefs reflected their impatience with such cautious concerns. Katlian thought his uncle, having grown old, was becoming a dull knife. He responded, *"Who chose the Tsar for our chief? We cannot let the Russians take our wealth! We must destroy them on Sitka! We must destroy their hunters who steal our furs! We must destroy them at Yakutat! We must destroy them before they destroy us! Oondikat! Oondikat!"*

Sub-chief Naawushkeitl admitted, *"Katlian is right."*

There were sounds of enthusiastic approval from the young chiefs, then an expectant silence as all eyes turned toward Chief Ska-outlelt. Quietly and gravely he spoke. *"All clans would have to join together in this, in all the Tlingit lands. Attacks would have to happen all at once. Can we do this?"*

Tumultuous agreement provided the answer.

"And where will we get all the guns and gunpowder we will need for this?" asked Ska-outlelt.

"The British Hudson's Bay Company has promised guns and gunpowder if we trade only with them," replied Katlian.

"All right. But remember one thing," cautioned Ska-outlelt. *"We know how to shoot guns. However, we can't make guns or gunpowder. But the Russians can."*

"Yes," said Katlian. *"But we have the great mountains and the deep forests and wild storms, and with our shaman's spirits, we know how to use them. This is greater power than all the white man's guns and gunpowder."*

Soaring above their fire into the night sky and on to the stars high above went their chant: *"Oondikat! Oondikat! Oondikat!"*

On a typical gray morning in June at Fort St. Michael on Sitka Bay, most of the Aleut and Russian hunters had already left on a seal hunt at sunrise. Just a few were left to guard the fort.

A few miles away, at the Tlingit fort on the *kekur*, over a hundred warriors who had been bathing in Sitka Sound came out of the water and, according to ritual custom, switched themselves with spruce branches to toughen themselves before battle.

A Russian fisherman, Kosygin, opened the fort's main gate and carried a fishing net down to the shore of Sitka Sound, where he unrolled it. Carelessly, he left the gate open. On a low hill near the fort, Chief Ska-outlelt, War Chief Katlian, and two warriors climbed to the hilltop overlooking the fort. Below, they could see the Russian fort near the shoreline of Sitka Sound. It was a quiet, peaceful scene.

The fort was on a large clearing next to the Sound with a spruce forest behind it. It consisted of an unfinished ten-foot tall wall of vertical spruce logs mostly enclosing a large space with several weather-grayed log buildings of various sizes. The unwalled side had the natural protection of a deep marsh. The largest building was two stories with a dining hall downstairs and a company office upstairs. An octagonal building beside it was for Aleut ceremonial use. There was a barracks for the hunters and two smaller log buildings with quarters for married couples and families. One large building was a warehouse for storing otter and seal pelts. A small house had been set aside for Baranov when he was in residence. There was also a bathhouse, a large shop to support shipbuilding, a blacksmith shop, a barn, and two more log buildings under construction.

The perimeter wall facing the most likely line of attack had a large double gate facing the sound. Between the gate and the sound was a shipway framework upon which a sailing ship was under construction.

Looking down on the fort, the twenty-eight-year-old Katlian wore his multi-layered dark wood armor and black raven-head wooden helmet with large painted eyes and beak. He held a musket, and a long knife was sheathed at his waist. *"Our warriors are in the woods on both sides of the fort, ready to attack on our signal,"* he said to his uncle.

Chief Ska-outlelt took a long look at the fort below, largely surrounded by the high log wall, then said, *"We warned them many times to get out, and they did not."* He paused. *"They have left their main gate open. Our warriors should reach it before the Russians can close it."*

"Shall I lead the attack now?" asked Katlian.

Ska-outlelt stared at the fort impassively for a long moment, asking himself one last time if there was anything that could make this a disaster for the Sitka Kwaan. Then, still staring at the fort, he said, *"Start the attack."*

Katlian turned and ran down the hill into the woods toward the fort. His square face was elated and determined. Now he would kill Russians—all of them in this fort! He would finally rid Sitka of the hated Russians. Then Sitka would be only for the Native Sitkans! And he was sure he would fill his scalp bag today.

In a few minutes, he had run through the woods, jumping over rocks and low bushes until he came upon the left arm of his force. A phalanx of warriors was hidden behind trees, dressed in brightly painted wooden body armor and carved helmets shaped like the heads of bears, orcas, wolves, eagles, and ravens. They were standing at the ready, armed with muskets and bows and arrows. Five of them carried a long spruce log to be used as a battering ram. Katlian, looking adamant with a firm jaw, passed his men, then stopped, put his musket to his shoulder, and aimed it at a window on the top level of the fort. He squeezed the trigger, firing his signal shot and shattering the morning peace.

He looked at his men, pointed forward, and yelled *"Oondikat!"*

Then he turned toward the fort gate and led the charge at a run, all yelling, "*Oondikat!*"

On hearing the signal shot, another phalanx of warriors, hidden in the woods to the right of the fort, also ran toward the open gate chanting, "*Oondikat! Oondikat! Oondikat!*"

Katlian saw the fisherman Kosygin looking at him in surprise, and he signaled two of the warriors to get the Russian. They took him down with bows and arrows. He had no sooner hit the sand, convulsing, when one of the warriors ran over with a knife, stabbed him in the heart, grabbed his hair, and cut off his scalp.

Six Tlingit hostages held by the Russians ran from the fort and escaped out the open gate, followed by five bearded Russians running to close the gate. Katlian and several attacking warriors reached the opening, then aimed and shot their muskets at the Russians, killing two at once.

The remaining three, who had started closing the gate, were set upon by Katlian and several warriors and had their throats slit. Katlian grinned in triumph as the one he knifed collapsed, eyes wide in terror, blood spraying out of his neck as he let out a gurgling sound. His scalp was immediately collected and dropped into Katlian's scalp bag.

The warriors pushed the gates back open and flooded through the opening into the main yard. Katlian, body armor smeared with blood, signaled for them to attack the doors of the largest building, the fort's main barracks, with their battering ram.

Something else caught his attention—the forge with its many large iron tools visible through the open double doors of the blacksmith shop. He went inside and picked up various tools to gauge their potential as weapons. He settled on the blacksmith's hammer, banging it on the anvil with satisfaction.

At the beginning of the battle, the few Russian hunters left in the fort had run up to the top floor of the main building and shot down at the warriors in the yard from second-floor windows. Medvednikov, the manager, called out, "We have to use the cannon downstairs! Let's go!"

A small group of Russian men, Aleut women, and creole children in other buildings, hearing the erupting battle, ran into the back yard of the fort.

"Let's get out the back way," one of the men yelled, and they all ran toward the gap of the log wall in back. Two quickly looked around the corner to see if any attackers were there, and seeing none, waved to the others to follow them outside and into the woods behind the fort.

Medvednikov, still on the top floor of the main building, was heading for the stairs when a musket ball hit him in the right shoulder and knocked him down. As he got up, he saw a torch arrow come flying through the window and land on his bed, setting it on fire. There was nothing he could do. His shoulder throbbing with pain, he barely managed to get himself downstairs. He saw that Aleut women and their creole children had run into the big room on the main floor, all screaming in terror. Meanwhile, three Russian hunters and six Aleuts rolled a cannon into place aimed at the bolted main door, which warriors were pounding from outside with their long log battering ram. "Grapeshot!" yelled Medvednikov.

The cannon was loaded with grapeshot and fired at the door. The shot blasted through it and killed several attacking warriors.

"Reload!" ordered Medvednikov amid the rising roar of battle.

More torch arrows were shot through broken upstairs windows, and the upper floor was soon completely ablaze.

One of the women on the main floor yelled, "Into the basement, children!" Medvednikov saw them yank the basement hatch open, and with the children they rushed down the stairs into the basement like water down a drain hole and closed the hatch behind them.

The grapeshot had blown out the main door, and before Mevednikov and his men could reload, more warriors, led by Katlian, reached the open doorway and rushed in, firing arrows and musket balls at the defenders until all were downed. Medvednikov had gotten an arrow through a lung. Those still alive had their heads bashed in by the hammer, Katlian's new weapon of choice. The last thing Medvednikov saw was the Tlingit's dark, grimacing face, full of hate, as he swung the hammer and pulverized half of Medvednikov's head in an explosion of blood and brains.

The Russians' and Aleuts' scalps were immediately cut off and bagged. The wood floor was awash with blood and chunks of brain. The air was filled with the stench of cut-open guts. Flames from above began to penetrate the big room.

Katlian ordered his men, *"Drag the bodies out so we can cut off their heads, and bring the cannon out, too."*

Below, in the dim basement barely lit by a couple of small windows, one woman cried out, "We have to get out before we get burned alive!"

"Here—the stairs up to the outside entrance!" said another.

With two Aleut men, they ran up the stairs, pushed the hatch open to one side, and streamed outside, followed by the children.

Almost immediately, they were discovered by attacking warriors who, without a moment's hesitation, started slaughtering them with knives and hatchets. Then Katlian came around the corner of the building and ordered, *"Stop, stop! Take the rest prisoner!"*

All the dead Russian and Aleut men were scalped and beheaded, their heads mounted on sticks stuck in the ground around the perimeter of the fort. All of the pegged heads faced the shore, to greet any visitors as a warning. The headless bodies were thrown into the burning buildings.

The storage shed for seal and otter pelts had not yet been burned. Ska-outlelt had the furs removed and taken back to their fort on the *kekur*. Then he had the empty storehouse torched, along with the log wall, the ship under construction, and anything else still standing.

Twelve miles up Sitka Sound, one hundred and eighty Russian and Aleut seal hunters had set up camp with tents on a long, wide gravel beach backed by a tall spruce forest and mountains. The men had started making preparations for the next day's hunt.

Suddenly, there appeared a squadron of Tlingit war canoes that had hugged the shoreline so as not to be seen or heard until they were upon the encampment.

They quickly landed; warriors jumped out and ran with weapons ready toward the surprised Russians and Aleuts, immediately shooting them with muskets and arrows. The attackers yelled, *"Oondikat! Oondikat!"* as they killed terrified Aleuts. Most of the Russians were still trying to load their muskets when they were killed. All that the Aleuts had for self-defense were seal-hunting spears, of little use in this kind of combat. They were slaughtered like lemmings.

A few Russian hunters managed to fire muskets at the Tlingit and killed three. Seeing that defense was hopeless, the Russian manager, Urbanov, and his hunting partner launched their *bidarka* and made a run for it, followed by a few Aleuts.

Some other Aleuts tried to escape into the forest but were chased down and killed with arrows, knives, and hatchets. More tried to follow Urbanov's escape but were chased by Tlingit in war canoes and killed. The waters of the bay went red with blood.

In all, over a hundred and seventy hunters died and only twenty escaped, heading for the Russian fort—but seeing the smoke billowing above it, they turned north toward Yakutat.

For the Tlingit warriors, the day had brought a great and joyous harvest of scalps. Katlian was in his longhouse, counting his, when the leader of the attack on the Russian and Aleut hunters came in with his report.

"We killed nearly all," said the man. *"Of those who tried to escape, only a few got away."*

"Good," said Katlian. *"A great day for Raven,"* he added as he reached over to pat his raven helmet.

The next day, the English Captain Barber's fur-trading vessel, *Unicorn*, reached Sitka Sound. The rough-hewn, red-bearded Barber took one look at the ruins through his telescope and quickly deduced what had happened. He saw a couple of Russians signaling from shore who had escaped out the back of the fort. Barber sent a launch with armed sailors ashore to rescue them and the others hiding in the woods. He learned from them that the Tlingit had taken others prisoner and, more importantly to him, had stolen the Russians' store of otter pelts.

He invited Ska-outlelt onto his ship to negotiate the release of the prisoners, enticing him with commendations on his great victory and promises of valuable presents.

Ska-outlelt came aboard with two warriors as guards. He soon learned that Barber's manner of negotiation was to have his sailors close in and grab them, tie their hands behind their backs, and hoist them up on the masts. Barber had nooses put around their necks for all the Tlingit on the nearby shore to see. When the Tlingit shaman, Stoonookw, came out in a kayak to investigate, Barber gave him an ultimatum. "Turn over the captives and all the furs stolen from the fort by sunset, or your chief and his guards will be hanged!" An ethnographic scientist traveling with Barber translated what he had said into Tlingit for Stoonookw.

Stoonookw paddled back to the *kekur* and told Katlian what had happened.

"We have no time to organize an attack on the ship," said Katlian. *"And even if we did, at the first sign of force, they would hang Ska-outlelt. We have no choice but to give that captain what he wants. Ska-outlelt was a fool to go onto that ship!"*

The tribe complied, and the chief and his men were released, humiliated.

Barber decided he would sail to Kodiak to see Baranov and demand a reward for the people he had rescued.

***

Baranov sailed *Olga* along the Kodiak coast and approached a Native village. Behind, Kuponek paddled vigorously in a kayak to catch up. Soon, he came alongside *Olga,* and Baranov furled the sails so Kuponek could tie up and come aboard. One look at Kuponek, and Baranov knew the news was bad. "Fort St. Michael attacked by Tlingit. Kill nearly everyone. Half of hunting fleet also attacked and killed. An English ship came to St. Paul with survivors who told what happened."

"A massacre!" Baranov gasped. "My worst fear. I warned Medvednikov to be careful of the Tlingit. He must have been careless. What about our Tlingit hostages?"

"They got away right at the beginning. They knew."

"And the survivors were brought to Kodiak by the Brits?"

"Yes. But the captain of the ship, Barber, wants 50,000 otter pelts for them."

"Fifty thousand pelts? I've heard of this Captain Barber. A tough Englishman. I'll sail back to St. Paul right now!"

CHAPTER 21

BARANOV SEES HELL

As he sailed into St. Paul harbor, Baranov saw *Unicorn* anchored there with eight gun ports visible on each side. He moored *Olga* and, with Kuponek, kayaked over to the ship in their *bidarka* and climbed aboard.

Barber was waiting for them. *"Are you Baranov?"* he asked in German, knowing that Baranov spoke it.

"Yes, Captain Barber, that's me," as he held out his hand.

They briefly shook hands before Barber got down to business. *"I have twenty-three of your people, survivors of the massacre in Sitka. If you want them, I'll give them to you for 50,000 rubles' worth of otter pelts."*

"Let me see these people," Baranov said firmly.

Barber stared at him for a moment. *"All right, I'll bring some of them up, and they can tell you how many are here."*

Two Russians and three Aleuts, including a child, were brought on deck.

There was a lot Baranov wanted to ask them about the massacre, but this was not the place. "How many of you are there?"

"Twenty-three," answered one of the Russians.

Barber immediately had them returned below.

Baranov turned to him. *"Come ashore this evening, and we'll have dinner together and discuss this some more."* Before the other could answer, Baranov went over the side with Kuponek. As Barber looked down at them, Baranov called out, *"See you in our dining hall at the second bell,"* and he and Kuponek paddled off toward St. Paul harbor.

Soon after the second bell rang, Captain Barber, in his old British naval captain's uniform, appeared at the hall with two of his biggest sailors as bodyguards. Baranov and Kuponek were waiting for them outside the door.

"Welcome, Captain," said Baranov with a smile as he reached out to shake hands again. Then he led Barber inside, the others following. They sat at a table well apart from the others. A roasted lamb, a rare extravagance, was put on the table by a waiter and quickly served up.

"Where in England are you from, Captain?"

"Portsmouth."

"How long since you left there?"

"A year and a half."

"And where are you headed?"

"Canton."

Baranov nodded. *"Good cargo of furs so far?"*

"This is very good lamb."

"You asked for fifty thousand rubles' worth of otter pelts. I don't have that to give. The best I can offer is five thousand."

"Ridiculous! I put my ship and many of my men at risk to go ashore and rescue your people. And all you offer is five?"

"I greatly appreciate your heroic rescue of our people."

"I shouldn't have rescued them anyway, because our countries are at war! I should blast your little village off the map. Then I'd be doing my duty to King George!"

"You haven't been in England for a year and a half. If our countries were really at war then, what makes you think they'd still be at war today? Doesn't mighty England win every war now in a fortnight?"

"We are at war!"

"Why? For what reason did Russia and England go to war?"

". . . Pay my price," Barber said in a low, menacing voice, *"or my cannon will blow you to hell."*

"Not before my cannon in the hills over the harbor have broken your ship's masts so you can't go anywhere."

Baranov nodded to Kuponek, who rose from the table and stepped outside, where he picked up a loaded musket leaning against the building, and fired it in the air. Almost instantly, a Russian cannon in the hills fired a blank with a thunderous clap that echoed in the mountains behind the hills.

Barber jumped up with a start. Then another cannon sounded off, and another, and another, until all twenty of Baranov's pieces had been fired. The sound kept echoing in the mountains for a full minute.

"Sit down, Captain. We're not at war. Let's have some dessert," offered Baranov, smiling.

Barber, shaken, sat down. After a long silence, he again spoke. *"Twenty thousand rubles' worth of pelts, then."*

"Ten," said Baranov.

"Fifteen."

"Ten."

"Twelve."

"Ten," Baranov still insisted.

Blueberries in cream were served, and all dove in.

"All right Baranov, you'll get your people for ten thousand." He didn't mention that his ship contained a further two thousand Russian otter pelts liberated from the Tlingit. This would indeed be a very lucrative trip to Canton for *Unicorn*.

In March 1803, Baranov was seated at a table, studying a map of southeast coastal Alaska. Kuponek was sitting across from him. On top of one corner of the map, Baranov had a piece of paper upon which he was sketching a large raft with a couple of cannon.

"We must retake Sitka. With no fort there, we have no base for expanding our settlements to the south, and Russia will be squeezed out of Alaska by the British. We must get it back."

Kuponek pointed out, "We got enough men and guns? The Tlingit have many more men than we do. Many guns, too. Tlingit everywhere on Sitka Island."

"I know," agreed Baranov. "But we *do* have more, better, and bigger guns available to us. And we can get more gunpowder than they can. They just have more warriors." After a thoughtful pause as he rubbed his hands together and looked out the window and back, he said, "We'll have to move all our men, all our ships, and all our guns to Yakutat, and from there launch an attack to retake Sitka."

He looked at his drawing for a moment, frowned, and tore it up. Kuponek had gotten to his feet just as Kuskov and Banner entered, and he left.

"*Zachary* is leaving for Okhotsk soon, and we'll both be on it," said Kuskov.

"No, no, no!" Baranov cried out. "I can't lose my two best men! Not *now!*"

Banner said, "We've gotten no raises and no promotions from the company in years. For me in Okhotsk first, and then here. For Kuskov, his *whole* time here."

"I know what you want to do," said Kuskov. You want to attack Sitka and get it back. Right now, that's madness. We don't have enough ships, cannon, or ammunition. And I'm just sick of all the bloodshed. Sick of it. I'm going home."

"Yes, we have to retake Sitka, obviously. But not until we're ready. Not until I'm sure we will defeat the Tlingit." In utter sincerity, Baranov added, "The company should have promoted you both with raises long ago. If you stay, I'll give each of you enough of my company stock so that you'll be getting ten percent of the raise they recently gave me. Then you'd each have a substantial gain, now and in the future."

Banner said, "I can't do that. I can't take what is rightfully yours."

"You *should* have it, because without the work of the two of you backing me up, I would have achieved nothing. Take it and stay."

"Can Banner and I talk this over for a minute?" asked Kuskov.

"Of course," said Baranov as he got up and walked to the back of the warehouse. The other two sat, leaning toward each other, and conferred. Then they motioned for him.

"Your offer is most generous, so we accept," said Kuskov.

"Thank you, my two Ivans! I'd be lost without you."

He shook both their hands with relief and enthusiasm.

***

Katlian and Shaman Stoonookw stood on a slight rise overlooking a wide gravel beach at the edge of Sitka Sound. "The Russians will return," said the Shaman. "And they will be back with many boats and cannon. We must get ready."

"Yes, I think that is true. We need to build a new fort out of reach of most of their cannon but close enough to fight off any invaders. Their warriors will have to get off their ships and come up here to attack us. We will ambush and slaughter them. Yes, this is a perfect location."

Three of Katlian's warriors had hiked from the shore, where they had left their canoes, and joined the two.

"We must build a new fort right here," said Katlian. "A *big* fort, with many longhouses, protected by a high wall of thick logs."

"Why here, so far from the shore where we leave our canoes?" asked one of the warriors.

"This is better than our fort on the *kekur* in the bay, because when the Russians come back, they will not be able to reach us here with their cannon. When their warriors try to attack us, we'll have a big advantage. We'll wait until they are all well within range, and then, from high platforms behind our walls, we will shoot down and slaughter them. Just like slaughtering otters. We will scalp them all, and send the scalps to the Tsar."

"Then what will *he* do?" asked the shaman.

Katlian stared him for a moment. "Yes, you are right. So we *won't* send the scalps to the Tsar. We'll keep them."

***

It was the season again for the great hunt, and the fleet had departed Kodiak and gone to Prince William Sound. A sunny day had met them there with perfect wind and waves. Hundreds of *bidarkas* proceeded past Nuchek Island toward Yakutat escorted by *Olga,* skippered by Baranov, plus two other sloops. A joyful race broke out between *bidarkas* and sailboats heading to Yakutat, with all men feeling themselves masters of the sea. They reached Yakutat in fine spirits.

As Baranov and Kuponek covered the short distance from the shore to the fort, two male and three female serfs in their thirties ran toward Baranov from the fort and threw themselves at his feet, the women in tears. The first, wife of the serf Lukin, pleaded, "Governor Baranov! Sir! We live here in constant fear of death. Please take us out of here back to Kodiak."

The serf Andrei Plakov declared, "It's true! Death hangs over us every day! The Tlingit want to kill us. We can't work. We can't sleep. We are crazy with fear! Take us *out* of here!"

Baranov replied solemnly, "You are here to grow food for all of us by the order of the crown, which I must obey. Reinforcements are here. They will strengthen your fortress. The Tlingit cannot overwhelm this place if you stay alert."

He brushed past the serfs, heading toward Kuskov in the fort. When they met, he issued his orders. "Tomorrow, launch our fleet of hunters after otter and seal. But watch out for the Tlingit. I'm going to Sitka to see what happened."

"Just you, Dmitri, and Kuponek?" Kuskov asked with great concern. "That's crazy! The Tlingit will kill you. Then that will be the end, not only of you, but of Russian America."

"No. They won't get old Nanuq," Baranov assured him.

Olga sailed toward Fort St. Michael. When they reached it, Baranov scanned the field where the fort had been—only a few piles of burned-out logs remained. Behind that awful scene stood the indifferent forests and snowy mountains. Baranov anchored *Olga* near shore and pulled on a suit of mail, covering it with his regular outer clothes. "My suit of mail may be my best friend," he told Kuponek.

They kayaked to shore, where Baranov examined the ruins, seething with anger. *"We will come back!"* he shouted resolutely, in Tlingit. "We will rebuild. We will! We will! I swear it! God help me, I swear it!"

Kuponek took Dmitri back to *Olga*, leaving Baranov alone on the beach. He faced the ruins, hands on his hips in a determined stance. From the forest, an arrow whizzed toward him, hitting his chest and bouncing off. He recoiled a bit and glanced down at the arrow. Another hit his chest. It too bounced off the mail, but the impact pushed him back another step. He took a step forward, picked up the arrows, broke them over his knee and tossed them aside with contempt. In Tlingit, he called out, *"Go to your dog-heaven hell, you bastards!"*

He waded out to meet Kuponek in the *bidarka*. They returned to *Olga*, tied on the *bidarka*, and got the sloop under sail. Baranov sailed her past the *kekur* rising from the sound. He had not forgotten that the *kekur* was where he had originally wanted to build his fort. As they sailed past, he studied the fort the Tlingit had built there to see how it might be attacked. "If we can bring in cannon on a few good-sized boats, we could destroy that fort and push the Tlingit out of here," he said to Kuponek. "Then we can build our own fort there."

He turned west and headed out of Sitka Sound, toward the Pacific and the North.

Olga sailed on many tens of miles to rendezvous with the hunting fleet Kuskov commanded. They were on Icy Strait near the Tlingit village of Hoonah, with Kuskov's two ships at anchor and hundreds of *bidarkas* pulled up on shore. After mooring, Baranov paddled over to Kuskov on his ship, *Catherine*.

"Ivan, I've seen hell."

"Fort St. Michael?"

"Yes. We're going back. This time, we'll push the damned Tlingit off the *kekur* rock. That's the best place for a fort. We'll take it away from them."

"But we can't do it now," Kuskov objected. "We don't have enough ships or guns. And our men aren't trained yet for that kind of battle."

In a flash of resolute anger, Baranov replied, "We have to do it *now*, before the British or the Americans crowd us out. To control Sitka is to control the entire south coast. That's where our future lies."

Kuskov held his ground. "I tell you we're not strong enough yet to surely win, and if we lose, we'll never get another chance!"

"We don't have time to *fool around* any more! We have to do it *now!*"

Kuskov yelled, "It's too late in the *season*, damn it! The weather is about to turn against us! You can't fight the Tlingit *and* the weather!"

Baranov took another step toward him as he shouted, "We're going *now!* Weather or no weather, we're going to get it *done! Now!*"

Both men were seething, staring furiously at each other. Then Kuskov pointed ashore toward the rows of hundreds of *bidarkas,* the campground beyond, and the many men moving around. "Look at these men, Aleksandr," he said in a calmer voice. "Everything you've accomplished, you've done because of *them. Their* work, *their* blood! Don't risk their lives recklessly. Use this winter to build more boats and train our men. Then we'll have a better chance. The British and the Americans have all gone home till next year, so we have more time. Time to do it *right!*"

Baranov stared at Kuskov, his anger subsiding as he realized Kuskov was right. ". . . All right. Take volunteers to Yakutat for the winter. Build two new sloops there to carry cannon. You've got the plans. Train men for battle. I'll go to Kodiak. In the spring, I return. . . and we *retake Sitka.*"

Kuskov nodded, and Baranov climbed down into his *bidarka* and paddled back to *Olga,* where he climbed aboard and sailed back to Kodiak with Kuponek and Dmitri.

As he entered St. Paul's harbor on Kodiak Island, he saw a new schooner anchored there. He pulled out his telescope to read the name on the bow: *O'Cain.* A big grin lit up his face. He moored his boat quickly and had Kuponek take him to the schooner in a *bidarka*, where he scrambled aboard.

"*Honest Joe? Is this you?*" he called out.

Joe O'Cain came running out of his cabin to greet him. They hugged, danced a silly jig together, and settled down, laughing. Baranov said, "*You've got your own ship now! And you even named it for yourself!*"

O'Cain exclaimed, "*But of course! It* should *be named after the best skipper in the North Pacific!*"

They shared a big laugh.

Baranov asked, "*What brings you here?*"

"*I've come to trade,*" said O'Cain. "*Food, cannon, powder, muskets, rigging—you name it, and I've got it! It's all yours for twelve hundred otter skins, which I'll sell in Canton. And that's just the beginning, Sasha. I can make two round trips a year for you! Russia can't legally sell in Canton, but my American flag can!*"

Baranov suddenly became silent and almost sad.

O'Cain murmured, "*What's wrong?*"

"*I don't have it. Joe, I don't have the furs to pay for your load. The past year and a half have been so rough since we lost our fort at Sitka.*"

"*I know,*" O'Cain said. "*I saw the ruins. King Kamehameha heard about it also, and he's worried about you. He told me to tell you that, if there's anything you need, just ask, and he'll send it.*"

"*I need what you've got, Joe,*" said Baranov. "*I need it badly. What are we going to do?*"

"*. . . Let me think about it, Sasha. I'll think of something. Now, come have dinner with me. How long has it been since you've had* *corned beef and cabbage? And good old Boston rye?"*

In O'Cain's cabin, the two men were enjoying a sumptuous Irish meal, liberally washing down the food with rye. *"Sasha,"* the Irishman finally said, *"I have an idea! Let me take fifty of your Aleut hunters to California for the winter with their bidarkas. The coast there is teeming with otter! Your men will hunt them for us, and we'll split the profits fifty-fifty. Then you pay for my cargo from your half, and we'll be square."*

"A terrific idea! But there are problems. . . . The crown has set strict rules on the use of Aleuts. They can't be treated like slaves. You'll have to pay them for every fur. And I must send a Russian with you to give the Aleuts all their orders and look after them. And if one of them is killed or seriously injured, his family must be paid."

O'Cain mulled this over while Baranov poured himself more rye. *"My cargo. I'll have to leave it here. No room to take it with me. But it's still mine until I get back in the spring. Is that a deal?"*

"Yes, indeed. We have a deal!"

They clinked mugs and shook hands on it.

At St. Paul a few days later, the ship *O'Cain* pulled away from the wharf with many *bidarkas* lashed on deck and its crew of Aleut hunters leaning over the side, waving goodbye to their families. Piled high on the wharf sat the ship's off-loaded cargo, including ten sizable cannon. As the schooner sailed away, Baranov instructed his Russian hunter-stevedores, "Put this gear in the warehouse, men."

It was a mild winter, with only three feet of snow. The following spring of 1804, Anna gave birth to her third child, a little girl whom Baranov named Ekaterina. Soon after, *O'Cain* returned to Kodiak. Family members of the hunters ran down onto the wharf to greet them. Everyone had made it back safely. Baranov came onto the wharf and through the crowd and, as soon as the ship was tied on, climbed aboard and greeted O'Cain. *"Welcome back, Honest Joe! Well, what's the word? How was the hunt?"*

"We did well, Sasha!" said O'Cain. *"You earned enough to buy the cargo!"*

With mock seriousness, Baranov said, *"What cargo?"*

They erupted in laughter. *"This calls for a* praznyk!*"* Baranov exclaimed.

O'Cain chuckled, *"That it does. . . . And it's on you, old friend!"*

The two were sitting at a table off to one side of the party uproar, chatting. Baranov asked, *"Did you encounter other ships with news of Europe?"*

"Yes, a couple."

"What's going on in the world?"

"Napoleon is still tearing up Europe. But here's something really interesting—the Russians bought two new frigates from the British to sail around the world on a goodwill cruise. And they're coming here to help you out! They're named Neva *and* Nadezhda.*"*

"Two frigates! Coming here! When?"

"It seems they're now sailing different routes. But the first could show up here within just a few months—late spring or early summer."

"I could sure use them at Sitka."

Kuskov said, *"I've heard that the British and Americans are arguing about who owns a lot of the coast north of Alta California."*

"Oh, yes."

As they finished talking about English-American relations, Baranov got up and headed for the nearest vodka keg. After refilling his mug, he joined in an arm-wrestling match among some Russian hunters at a table in the back.

CHAPTER 22

A NOBLEMAN PREPARES FOR BATTLE

Baranov and his third assistant, Ivan Banner, were conferring in Baranov's Kodiak office when Kuponek came in with a packet of mail and handed it to Baranov. "A *nigilax* from Unalaska brought this mail from a Russian ship that got wrecked there," he explained.

Baranov found an official letter sealed with wax, which he opened. He was struck speechless. He handed it to Banner, who read it quickly and, in a stunned voice, repeated aloud, "Tsar Alexander has decreed this: 'By order of his Imperial Majesty, Tsar of all the Russias: for meritorious works in the face of great privation, for unbounded courage in service of his country, the noble rank of Collegiate Counselor is hereby granted to Aleksandr Andreievich Baranov.' Signed: Alexander the First."

Baranov stared out the window, overcome with a tearful mixture of pride, joy, and humility. Finally, he spoke. "What a great day. Honored by my sovereign! To be raised from lowly *mestchannin* to the middle of noble ranks, equal navy captain-lieutenant! Now those navy boys will have to obey and call me 'Your Excellency'!"

This realization brought him a broad smile. "Ivan, get me some paper. I've got letters to write. One to the Tsar, to humbly thank him for this great honor, and another to the company, declaring that my duty as a nobleman demands that I retake Sitka for my country."

Banner handed him the writing implements.

In the ripening spring of 1804, the time had come to begin solving the Sitka problem. Baranov stood on the end of the wharf, energetically directing hundreds of Aleuts below who were organizing a fleet of *bidarkas*. Banner stood nearby. Also standing by him were Anna, Antipatr, and little Irina; baby Ekaterina was strapped to her mother's back.

Banner asked, "Why not wait for one of the frigates to get here before launching this attack?"

"I don't know when they're going to get here," said Baranov. "But I do know that I must take Sitka this season, before the British make a move along the south coast. I'll never have another chance."

"I see your point."

"Banner, if any of the frigates sent to help us arrive, send them to Sitka."

"Right."

Baranov leaned down to kiss Antipatr and Irina. Then he kissed Ekaterina and Anna, and she had parting words that would make a mark on him: "*Toyon* of my heart, my love is with you, and God's love, too. But remember, God loves the Tlingit also."

He was surprised. She had voiced an idea that had never occurred to him. But he was in too much of a hurry to think about it or discuss it. He climbed onto the well worn *Olga*, tied alongside, and set sail. Anna and his little Alaskan children waved goodbye. The fleet embarked on the first leg of its journey toward Yakutat. It included the sloops *Alexander* and *Catherine*, sailing like sea shepherds with the bidarkas.

When they sailed into Yakutat Bay, the *bidarkas* beached near the shipways, where the two new sloops were in the final phase of construction. The sailing vessels set their moorings a safe distance from shore. During the mooring activity, men from Kodiak began coming ashore, and Yakutat Russians came out to greet them, including Kuskov.

"Good work," Baranov told him. "The sloops look almost ready."

Kuskov nodded. "I'm short of iron fittings and rigging."

"We'll take them off *Olga*. She's ready to be retired—starting to come apart.

"Still a lot to do to finish these boats. Now that we've brought you the manpower, we'll get it done, and then we're off to Sitka."

"Sitka. Always Sitka. Hanging over our heads."

"Good news," said Baranov. "Two Russian frigates are on their way. Their guns will make us invincible."

"Two frigates coming *here*? Are you kidding?"

"The Tsar sent them on an around-the-world goodwill tour, and they're due here this summer to help us. *Neva* and *Nadezhda*."

"Miraculous! . . . *If* they get here," Kuskov remarked.

Some time later, by the beach of the Russian fort at Yakutat Bay, the two new galley sloops were launched to much excitement and fanfare. Each was sailed around the bay on a test run; then both were moored nearby. With a celebratory bonfire on the beach, to a large crowd of the entire Yakutat Russian community, Baranov gave a short speech.

"What we have done today, launching these two magnificent sloops, proves once again that working together we can achieve anything! Yes, working together—Russians, Aleuts, Kenaitze, Kodiaks—against all odds, we can build ships out here in the middle of nowhere! Imagine that, in the middle of nowhere!"

A serf in the back, yelled out, "That's why we want out of here. . . . It's nowhere!"

Baranov ignored him. "I've written a song for today, which a few of you have already learned. Fellows, come on up. Okay, now we'll sing 'The Hunters Song.'"

He and his little chorus sang the first stanza, then started over, asking everyone to join in. With great gusto, Baranov led the song's first performance:

With iron will we conquer any hardship that's made
and gloriously win Pacific wars of trade.
We fight for the Tsar and dear Russia our home,
we the great fur hunters, so far we roam.
Yet even so far the towers of Moscow we hear,
evening bells and morning guns in our ear.
This spirit of Russia makes us brave and true
following Peter the Great across the blue.
Almighty Lord, we pray thee to aid our quest
to spread Russian rule from east to west,

And we your hunters to bring friendship and peace,

yes let us bond all with friendship and peace.

The moment had arrived. Baranov stood on the beach holding a map and briefing his captains, among them Kuskov, who would skipper the new forty-one-foot sloop *Rotislav,* while Baranov captained the new fifty-one-foot *Yermak,* named for the legendary Cossack hero who had conquered Siberia. The small ships *Alexander* and *Catherine* were also part of the fleet's armed escorts.

The men stood in a circle around Baranov as he explained their route, pointing to the map as he spoke. "We're going right through the heart of Tlingit country to let them know we are back in force and that we mean business. This will weaken any ideas they may have of reinforcing the Sitka Tlingit. To do this, we will take the long way to Sitka, east through Icy Strait by the Tlingit village of Hoonah, then south through Chatham Strait past their big village at Angoon. Along the way we'll hunt otter right under their noses. And down near the end of Chatham, as punishment, we'll burn the two villages that massacred Urbanov's hunters. Then we'll go around the south end of Sitka Island to the Pacific and then north to Sitka Sound. Any questions?"

"Good plan," said Kuskov.

The others all nodded their approval, and the fleet departed from Yakutat and headed south.

***

Having successfully followed his plan, Baranov led his squadron into Sitka Sound fog, proceeding cautiously. They suddenly broke through the scud. Moored ahead were two of his sloops, and the magnificent three-hundred-and-seventy-ton, fourteen-gun frigate *Neva*. Baranov was thrilled.

As he climbed aboard *Neva*, he was greeted with high respect.

"His Excellency, Aleksandr Baranov, I presume?" a young man standing to his right asked.

"Yes, Captain," Baranov replied, having seen the insignia on the man's coat. "And you are?"

"Captain Yuri Lisianski, at your service, sir."

Baranov grinned. "I'd begun to wonder if this frigate was just a legend. How glad I am that you're real!"

"And how honored I am to meet, as my commander-in-chief, the man who built our colonies here against all odds."

"Now we must retake our position on Sitka," said Baranov. "But at a better place to defend—the rock, what they call the *kekur*. There we will build our new fort." Baranov pointed toward the high outcrop a couple of miles distant. "Sitka Sound is the most strategic location in all of Alaska. From here we can keep the British from grabbing the whole American Northwest. Also strategic if Russia is to command the North Pacific in order to protect our fur business here."

"I understand," said Lisianski. "Your plan, sir?"

"First, I meet with the chiefs to make our demands. If we can get what we want without bloodshed, that would be best. They must agree to release all Aleut prisoners and to get off Sitka Island. If they don't agree, then we blast them off. After that massacre, we can't trust them on the island. That's it."

"How will you get the meeting?"

"I've already sent word to the chiefs. They should be arriving in a day or two. We'll meet in that field over there." Pointing toward shore, Baranov asked, "Shall we inspect our troops?"

"Yes!"

On the nearby beach, 800 men, Aleut and Russian hunters, lined up for inspection. It was an ad hoc army, with no uniforms but looking tough and confident. Most were motivated by the desire to punish the Tlingit for the massacre of their friends and families.

Lisianski pointed to the new Tlingit log fort a mile away. "At that distance from the Sound, and situated a bit uphill there, it'll be hard for our guns to reach. We'll have to tow my ship closer to be able to do any real damage."

Soon a hundred *bidarkas* were tied by gut-strings to the bow anchor chains of *Neva* to pull the warship, like worker ants moving a walnut. In amazingly short order, the job was done.

The next afternoon, a dozen hostile Tlingit chiefs and shamans were sitting in a bayside meadow when Baranov paddled over from *Neva* with Kuponek and with Russian hunters as guards. They beached and walked to the line of Tlingit. Baranov and Kuponek sat down on a blanket facing the chiefs as Kuponek murmured, "Their eyes send arrows. Beware."

Baranov nodded almost imperceptibly and began to address them in their own language. *"Years ago, I came to you in peace. I bought land from you. We were good neighbors. Then you attacked and killed my people. I will rebuild here, but on the kekur. I can't trust you, so you all must leave Sitka Island, set free the Aleut slaves, and give me your children as hostages. Then we can have peace."*

"*No!*" exclaimed Katlian. "*Our people are here since the beginning of time. Nobody can take this island from us! You can have the kekur, and we will give hostages and the Aleuts. But we will not leave this island of our forefathers, of Tlingit totems and Tlingit spirits.*"

"*I have spoken,*" said Baranov firmly. "*Tomorrow, if you are still in your new fort on the creek, our mighty guns will thunder.*"

Baranov and Kuponek stood up. Kuponek gathered their blanket, and they turned to walk back through their line of guards to the beach. They climbed into their *bidarkas* and started paddling back toward *Neva*. The guards slowly backed up toward their *bidarkas* and left. The chiefs departed in a dark mood along a path toward their new log fort. As they did, in the back of the line, Chief Katlian conferred with his shaman and three other Sitka chiefs. "*Are warriors coming from the north to join us?*" he wanted to know.

"*No sign yet.*"

Ska-outlelt glanced at him. "*Nephew, as top chief, now it is you who must tell warriors to fetch our gunpowder stored on Cave Island.*"

"*Yes, I'll send a war canoe. We will need that ammunition for a long battle.*"

The chiefs nodded.

One warrior said to him, "*They have many more men than we do, bigger cannons, and better muskets. How can we defeat them?*"

Katlian answered, "*This afternoon I'll show you how.*" The great war chief believed that a successful demonstration was always far more persuasive than even the best argument.

As Baranov and Kuponek boarded *Neva*, Lisianski noticed activity on shore where the Tlingit had left their canoes. He reached for his telescope in its holster near the wheel and with it saw Tlingit warriors launching a large war canoe. Several warriors and an elder got in and headed for a small island out in the bay.

"Sir, what are they doing?" Lisianski asked as he handed the telescope to Baranov, who took a look.

"They're going to the other side of the small island now," said Baranov. "Some islands have caves. Something must be stored there."

"Ammunition?" asked Lisianski.

"*Yes!* They're carrying a sack of gunpowder to the end of the canoe."

Tlingit men kept loading gunpowder bags, small cannon balls, and other ammunition into the big cedar war canoe. One Tlingit warrior asked the elder, *"Should we wait until dark before going back?"*

"No. Their guns can't reach this far out. And we can paddle faster than they can aim."

Lisianski turned to Lieutenant Arbusov. "Send a launch with armed sailors after that canoe. Try to press them within range of our cannon. Then a couple of volleys nearby should scare them into surrendering."

Through the spyglass, he watched the Tlingit launch the canoe from the island. *Neva*'s armed sailors rowed swiftly toward it. The warriors opened fire, and the sailors returned the fire. Suddenly, the Tlingit war canoe exploded.

Lisianski announced to Baranov, *"That* will shorten the battle."

Baranov followed him up to the poop deck, where, to Baranov's surprise, he found Father Nektarios. "What are *you* doing here?" asked Baranov.

"Ministering to our soldiers. I'll hold a baptism service tonight. All heathens will have one last chance to save their souls before battle."

Baranov nodded, headed for his cabin, and said to Kuponek on the way, "I'm going to write orders for each battalion. Then you can deliver them."

"I think tonight I will become a Christian," said Kuponek.

It was a comment that didn't immediately register with the preoccupied Baranov—until he went inside. Then it hit him.

"Kuponek a Christian!" he murmured. "Hmm."

Late that afternoon, a bunched-up clump of branches floated down the Indian River alongside a field where some of the Russian hunter army was camped, and starting to cook their dinner over campfires. Suddenly, Katlian jumped out of the floating brush and onto the shore. A few other warriors followed, and together they attacked the Russians with great fury. Katlian was wearing his fearsome raven helmet, brandishing a long knife, and swinging the blacksmith's hammer. Taking the Russians by surprise, he quickly killed three of them, one by stabbing and two by smashing their skulls with the hammer. The attackers wounded a few others until, with a yelp, Katlian ordered his warriors to run straight back to their fort before the Russians could load their weapons.

Inside Shis'gi Noow, when Katlian returned, he found the warrior who had earlier questioned the wisdom of standing up, outnumbered, to the Russians. The man had been standing on the high platform behind the fort wall, where Katlian had told him and several other warriors to watch, so he had seen everything. Katlian looked him in the eye and said, "That is how we will defeat them."

He had made his point. To those warriors, the great bear killer was the foremost warrior of warriors who could himself do anything he ever asked of them.

But Katlian knew that the loss of most of their gunpowder did indeed put his force at a serious disadvantage.

***

At dusk, many Native hunters gathered on deck, facing aft, where Nektarios had ascended to the poop deck. Kuponek was off to one side, about to join the congregation, when Baranov called him. "My orders for battalion leaders," he said. "Deliver them right away."

Kuponek took the sheaf, nodded, climbed over the side, and paddled a kayak to the onshore camps.

Meanwhile, Nektarios proceeded with his ceremony: "Only baptized Christians are forgiven their sins and may enter heaven and have eternal life. Tonight, all who wish to may become baptized Christians."

Kuponek delivered the messages while Nektarios performed baptisms, with Baranov watching. The priest finished with a prayer, and Baranov bowed his head: "O God, be with our men carrying your righteous sword to the savages. Protect our soldiers. Lead them to victory in the glory of your name. Amen."

"Yes," Baranov muttered to himself sarcastically. "Let us deliver Christianity through the barrel of a gun. Amen."

CHAPTER 23

THE BATTLE OF SITKA

On a rare sunny morning on Sitka Sound, the bay, the mountains, and the forests all shone brightly. It looked like what should be a happy day.

Captain Lisianski and Lieutenant Arbusov conferred with Baranov in Lisianski's shipboard cabin about how best to attack the new Tlingit log fort that the Tlingit called Shis'gi Noow, near Indian River.

Lisianski advised, "There is no way they can feasibly attack four well armed ships. My recommendation, sir, is that we just batter the fort with our cannon until they've had enough and agree to your terms. That way we will avoid any serious risk to our men while getting what you want."

"But at this distance, how much damage can our cannon really do to their fort?"

"That's a question, to be sure. However, three of our ships are smaller than *Neva*, draw less water, and are closer to shore. Their guns are smaller. But even if no single shot from any of our ships is greatly damaging, the cumulative effect of several days of bombardment will take its toll."

"They're very stubborn. They're not going to give up unless we attack with our soldiers, kill a lot of them, and turn it into a rout. We have to do an initial bombardment to soften them, then attack with our troops carrying a couple of small cannon. That should do it."

"There's more risk in that than you may realize," said Lisianski.

Baranov nodded. "But we know that they probably lost most of their gunpowder. So it'll be their bows and arrows against our muskets and cannon."

"As you say, sir."

Two battalions of hunters and sailors were positioned on the shore for the assault. Baranov led the left wing of fifty Russian hunters and several hundred Aleuts. The battalion on the right, led by Lieutenant Arbusov, consisted of about seventy battle-trained sailors backed by a few hundred Aleuts.

It was mid-afternoon when Baranov faced *Neva*, raised his hand overhead, and dropped it as a signal. All the cannon on the frigate's side facing the shore erupted in flame, smoke, and thunder, hurling cannon balls overland that landed short. Fire from the other three ships landed closer. The next volley from *Neva* hit the outer log wall and bounced off with a bang.

Lieutenant Arbusov ran over to confer with Baranov, advising, "Storm the fort at each front corner to force entry. Get two small cannon up there, one on each corner, and we'll win it."

"Then let's go!" agreed Baranov. "I'll signal the charge as soon as you get back."

Arbusov ran back to his men and nodded to Baranov, who raised his cutlass and dropped it. *Neva* and the other ships held their fire as the battalions charged up the gentle slope of the brushy but mostly open field of battle, each dragging a falconet.

Kuponek advanced next to Baranov, musket in hand. Men were soon bogged down in the occasionally soggy brush, struggling much of the way with sodden boots. Half way to the fort, the ground prevented them from dragging the falconets any farther.

In the Tlingit fort, warriors crouched on high platforms behind the log wall with muskets, waiting for the order to fire. Katlian also crouched there, wearing his raven helmet and holding the infamous blacksmith's hammer that had become his favorite weapon. He saw Baranov and grabbed a musket. As the first rank of attackers came within a hundred feet of the palisade, he ordered, *"Now!"* as he rose and fired at Baranov, barely missing.

The warriors all rose, and a musket volley exploded with a great roar. White smoke shot several feet forward from their muskets. The Aleuts, who made up most of the two-pronged charge and had no real battle experience, panicked and ran back toward the beach. Kuponek stood firm, aimed at a bobbing head with a musket behind the top of fort wall, and fired—and the head was gone. A second volley from the fort tore at Baranov's men. Tlingit hidden in the woods, along the flanks of the line of attack, rose then, firing muskets and arrows. The Russians hunkered down and fired back, killing and wounding many warriors. As the Tlingit pushed downhill, Baranov saw that his attack was doomed.

Katlian turned to his warriors on the platforms. *"Jump down now! Go out and attack!"* He dropped from the platform, reloaded, and ran out through a gap in the stockade, looking for Baranov.

"Retreat, men! Fall back!" Baranov shouted into the cacophony of men yelling orders, others screaming with pain, a loud patter of musket shots, and cannon fire from *Neva*. All together it was the roar of battle, the sound of colliding wills gone lethal.

Baranov himself fired his pistol at attacking warriors, slowly backing down the slope. Katlian, now just two hundred feet from him, slid the gun sight of his musket up under his raven helmet, aimed, and fired just as Baranov turned away. The bullet hit his right arm, knocking him down.

Katlian was elated. Soon he would have Baranov's scalp! He ran forward, pulling out his knife. A cannon ball from *Neva* hit the ground twenty feet in front of him, bounced once, and whizzed by his head, missing him by inches before it destroyed two warriors right behind him. He hesitated, looking for the next blast from the ships.

Baranov's arm seemed to have exploded in burning pain. Kuponek rushed to help just as a warrior at the tree line aimed an arrow at him and released it.

The arrow whizzed through the air and struck Kuponek deep in the chest with a bone-crunching thud. His legs froze in horrified surprise, his eyes wide, mouth open, grabbing at the arrow as the searing pain spread through his chest. He grimaced as he realized he was mortally wounded and fell onto his side. Blood began to seep out of his mouth. He crawled toward Baranov, whom some Russians had just grabbed and were dragging back toward the shore. *Neva's* continuing cannon fire at the upper slope killed many more warriors and at last forced a Tlingit retreat. Kuponek, who lay bleeding profusely, struggled to lift his head to see where Baranov had been set down behind a log. Then he spoke his last: "Baranov."

His eyes froze in a stare, and two Russians dragged him to Baranov, who lunged toward him and grabbed his wrist for a pulse he couldn't find. Horrified, he reached over and closed the dead man's eyelids. "Get the priest!" he barked. "Get the priest right now! He must do a baptism!"

A Russian found Nektarios, who arrived quickly. "Baptize Kuponek," Baranov demanded. "Do it right now!"

"I-I can't. He's *dead*."

"He's still warm! He said he wanted to be a Christian."

"I *can't*."

Baranov drew a pistol with his good arm, cocked it, and pointed it at the priest's head. "You baptize him right now," he said evenly, "or I'll blow you to hell, where you belong!"

Nektarios protested, "There are responses—"

"I'll say them for him. *Do* it."

Nektarios opened his baptism kit, and Baranov lowered his pistol. The priest quickly performed the baptism and left. Baranov was left with Kuponek's body, *Neva* behind them in the bay. Across Sitka Sound he saw the tall dormant volcano, Mt. Edgecumbe, and the Pacific Ocean beyond as if they were the subjects of a scenic painting. But in this scene, clouds of white gun smoke drifted by. Baranov pictured it as if from a near hilltop, the din of battle receding and the chaotic activity of the men around him seeming like ants scurrying across the canvas. What did it all mean?

He was carried by his men to a cabin on the *kekur*. At dusk, *Neva*'s surgeon, Dr. Nordhorst, came to remove the bullet. "How you feeling?" inquired the doctor.

"Lousy. My arm hurts like hell. But whatever you do, don't cut it off!"

"Hopefully, I can save it."

"And, hopefully, Captain Lisianski can save this battle. Tell him he's in command now."

Nordhorst removed the bullet and left Baranov with an Aleut. Baranov got up and, with his good arm, reached for his hunting knife in his duffel—the knife of Chief Chokta's suicide that Kuponek had so long before retrieved. He laid it on the table and stared at the gleaming blade as if it might help him understand the end of men. "God," he whispered, "why'd you take such a good man? What use are my prayers, anyway?"

The next morning, he left the cabin on the *kekur*, his right arm in a sling. He saw *Neva* open fire again on the Tlingit, who discharged small cannon at her, damaging the rigging. Lisianski sent Lieutenant Arbusov with an interpreter to offer a parley with a white flag. A Tlingit emissary appeared. A short discussion followed, after which Arbusov rowed to Baranov to report. "They say they'll give you the Aleuts, and the *kekur* for our fort, but they won't leave the island."

"No good," said Baranov. "That's what they said two days ago. If they won't leave Sitka, we'll have to blast them out."

Arbusov took the message and Baranov's reaction to Lisianski, then returned to the parley, which quickly broke up, and the cannon fire resumed.

Inside the besieged Tlingit fort on the Indian River, amidst the thunder of *Neva*'s guns and some cannon balls landing on the stockade and some of the roofs, Katlian was conferring in his longhouse with Shaman Stoonookw. He broke away for a moment to speak with two of his warriors. *"You know the back way up the kekur. Go now, and tonight kill Baranov."*

The warriors left, and Katlian returned to the shaman. *"Do you see our Angoon brothers coming to help?"* he asked.

"No."

"Without gunpowder, bows and arrows won't be enough. What should we do?"

"They can't defeat us if we're not here," said Stoonookw. *"We can make a survival march north, escape, and fight again some other day."*

"We have 800 men and their families here. It will take many days to get everyone out in a survival march. If we leave, they will build a big fort on the kekur. Then what?"

"Our men can hide in woods to stop them from getting food. If they send out hunters or fishermen, we will kill them. We'll starve them out. We kill and survive, then in time we win."

Early that evening, Baranov came on board *Neva*.

Lisianski greeted him. "I'm glad you're back here, sir. You're safer onboard. Just a matter of time now. When they run out of gunpowder, they'll have to surrender. I've moved a big gun from *Neva* to *Catherine*, which draws less water and so is closer to shore. From there, that canon can hit their fort much better."

"It may not be that simple." Baranov looked back at the Tlingit fort, wondering what they were planning. Meanwhile, at the abandoned *kekur*, two Tlingit warriors climbed a narrow hidden trail and, finding that Baranov had left, took up positions overlooking *Neva*.

The next morning, Chief Katlian sat on a log surrounded by other sub-chiefs. *"Today we start a survival march north,"* he said. *"First, old people with grandchildren."*

The others agreed and left to gather children. On *Neva's* deck, Baranov was again considering the fort. Above, on the *kekur*, the warriors shot arrows at him that bounced off the iron mail under Baranov's smock. Musket fire chased them away.

On the main deck of *Catherine,* sailors were joking among themselves while they loaded the big cannon from *Neva.*

Inside the Tlingit fort, children were rounded up and led to the storage hut.

On the *Catherine's* gun deck a sailor asked the gun master, "What kind of load?"

"Grapeshot."

Two sailors picked up a grapeshot ball from the supply and loaded it into the barrel of the cannon.

Tlingit children and their dogs gathered inside the storage hut.

The cannon crew loaded the fuse hole with powder.

Inside the Tlingit fort, a grandmother in a longhouse used a hunting knife to slice a slab of dried fish into small chunks. She put the pieces of fish into a bag for the trip on which she would accompany the children.

The cannon crew stood at attention. "Fire!" ordered the gun master.

One of the sailors tipped the firing torch to the fuse hole. The cannon erupted and jumped back in recoil. The cannon ball, trailing smoke, traced an arc up through the air toward the fort.

In the storage hut, the children were huddling with their dogs when the grapeshot cannonball crashed through the roof and exploded.

Two children and a few dogs were instantly killed. Amid much screaming, barking, and confusion, adults carried all the children out of the hut—dead, wounded, and unhurt—into a longhouse, where all were laid in a corner. Soon two wounded children died. The grandmother who was cutting dried fish came running over with the knife still in her hand and found her seven-year-old grandson mortally wounded. She put her knife down beside him and cradled the boy as he slipped away. She sobbed for a minute, collected her grief, and set it aside for the job she knew she must do for the other children. She rose, grasping her sack of fish sticks, and, with old people and many surviving children, fled through the back gate of the fort, leaving her knife on the floor next to her dead grandson.

The next day *Neva* resumed the siege. Cannon balls crashed down like giant black hail. Katlian watched with the shaman and two sub-chiefs. *"We have to get the rest of the children out of here quickly, or they'll kill them all!"* he warned.

Stoonookw told him, *"Give them as hostages. That will save them and make our escape easier. Later, we will get them back."*

On the beach, under a white flag, a dozen child hostages were sent with the Tlingit emissary. The children were in bunches, holding hands.

Meeting the emissary, Lieutenant Arbusov asked, "Why did you bring these children?" He could see several were weeping quietly. "And where are the Aleuts? When will you leave the island?"

"Children are hostages to stop cannon," said the emissary. "Aleuts come now. We leave high tide tomorrow."

A column of Aleut prisoners was seen starting down the shallow slope.

"Good," Arbusov responded. "We won't fire on your canoes."

The bombardment was not resumed.

The next day there was no sign of the Tlingit leaving by canoes, and the tide was going out. *Neva* fired a cannon at the fort. A Tlingit white flag went up for a parley.

Arbusov told the Tlingit emissary, "You said you'd be gone by now."

"All not ready yet. Will be ready tonight. When ready, I give signal: 'Oola Oola Oola.' Then we leave."

Past dusk, the ululation was heard. Then a sad wailing song caused the hostage children to react with relief, and they hummed somberly along. So mournful was the tune that it unnerved some of the Russians.

The next morning, Captain Lisianski and Baranov came on deck with a telescope and saw no sign of activity at the Tlingit fort. Also, oddly, all the Tlingit canoes were still on the shore. Lisianski handed a conical birch bark bullhorn to Baranov. "Use this to call out in their language. See if anyone is there."

Baranov yelled into the bullhorn, *"Katlian, are you still there? If you are, show us a white flag."* There was no response.

"I'll send an armed scouting party up there to see what's going on," said Lisianski

The scouting party, under Lieutenant Arbusov, went up cautiously and was unchallenged. At the top of the shallow hill, they took a brief look in the fort, and then, with great distaste, came back quickly to report.

Lieutenant Arbusov reported to Lisianski, "Sir, they're all gone. But it's horrible up there. You won't believe it!"

"What is it?" Lisianski asked.

"There are bodies of thirty Tlingit warriors scattered around. Remember, in the main battle, we lost a total of just ten Russians and Aleuts killed. But the situation up there, I just can't describe. It's so awful. You'll have to see it for yourself." He shook his head.

Lisianski hiked up to the fort with Arbusov and a couple of sailors. Inside, they found a room with the decomposing bodies of the five children and the dead dogs. Each child was covered by a small Tlingit blanket, but legs, arms, and hands were sticking out.

"My God! What killed these children?" asked Lisianski.

"Not our cannon," said Arbusov. "This building is undamaged."

Lisianski spotted the Tlingit knife laying on the ground next to one of the dead children.

Lisianski exclaimed, "Look at that knife! They must have killed their own children with that knife! Why would they do that?"

"Maybe. . . maybe they thought the crying would give away their escape through the woods."

Lisianski covered his nose with his handkerchief, and said, "Good God! Now I know what it means to be a savage. Only savages could kill their own children. Drag all the bodies from outside into the fort, and then burn this damned place to the ground!"

Lisianski returned to Neva and found Baranov in his cabin just as the Tlingit fort erupted in flames. They sat down together. "The retreating Tlingit are weak now," said Lisianski. "We could pursue, attack, and kill their warriors, who now have no gunpowder. It would make their defeat complete. And it's what they deserve for the 1802 massacre."

"No, Yuri," said Baranov. "There's no profit in vengeance. No future in it either. And don't underestimate their bows and arrows in the woods. They might outnumber us, too. We've achieved our objective—they're gone from here, so we can rebuild—and that's what matters. Our power is now absolute, but we must use it with restraint in order to keep it."

Lisianski was surprised. But after a moment's consideration, he said, "Indeed, sir. There has been enough bloodshed."

"The truth is," said Baranov, "in this tough place, I've learned to admire them. But I have a job to do, and that comes first. The trick is to apply only enough power to get the job done. Apply too much, and we'll never have peace with them—and we can't survive here, long-term, without peace with the Tlingit."

Katlian was, at that moment, looking through the branches of a spruce toward *Neva* in the distance as the line of Tlingit refugees passed behind him. He muttered bitterly to himself, *"I will kill him. I will kill him and all his kind. It must be done!"*

He led most of his people northeast, to where they had left a few canoes to cross the Peril Strait to the southeast corner of Chichagof Island. There, on a high cliff, they could build a temporary encampment safe from ambush. He led his warriors in the felling of many tall evergreens to build longhouses. As he worked, his wife K'asasee came over and said with tears in her eyes, *"Sitka is my family home."*

He stared at her, and he knew.

"It will take some time," he said. *"We will return to Sitka as soon as we can get enough guns and gunpowder to challenge the*

Russians. We will trade furs to the British to do that. Then we return to Sitka."

She stared at him for a long moment. *"Get it back,"* she said. *"But I don't think you can do it with guns."*

She left him there to wonder, How else could they take it back?

CHAPTER 24

HAWAII FEEDS SITKA, AND YAKUTAT NEWS

Baranov and his men built a high log wall around the perimeter of the site for a new Russian castle-fort on the *kekur* and named the place New Archangel. They used the three old longhouses atop the *kekur* that the Tlingit had built, until they could be replaced. *Neva* left to winter in Kodiak, and then snow fell in blowing drifts. Soon it was New Year's Day 1805.

Three Aleuts left the fort to get clams at low tide. Hidden in the woods, Tlingit warriors killed them with arrows.

Standing near the new log fort, Kuskov told Baranov, "We are woefully short of food, and Kodiak has nothing to send. Scurvy will hit soon. Hunting around here is dangerous, too—Tlingit in the woods pick off our men easily because we have to hunt in small parties to avoid alerting the prey."

"We still have some Tlingit children as hostages from the battle," Baranov reminded him, "yet it makes no difference. Katlian still kills our men. He thinks we won't hurt their children no matter what their warriors do. And he's right, that bushy-tailed red fox. We won't. So they're useless as hostages. How long can we last with the food we've got?"

"With rationing, about two months."

"Then we can't keep feeding these children. Get word to the Tlingit to pick them up. And when they go, be sure to give each child a nice present to remember us by. Maybe they'll be our friends when they grow up."

After a moment's thought, he continued, "King Kamehameha and I exchanged letters and gifts when the Yankee ships passed between us and Hawaii. He once said if I needed food, to just ask. Now, I think we must."

"How? Send *Yermak* to Hawaii? It's too small for such a long trip down the Pacific in winter. And who would skipper her?"

"There's only one man I would entrust with such an important and dangerous mission. You, Ivan."

Kuskov was stunned. He looked across the harbor at *Yermak,* looking barely adequate at fifty-one feet to face the open Pacific and sail the 2,800 miles to Hawaii.

But the sloop sailed south with Kuskov in command, and the voyage was surprisingly easy. Within a few weeks it had entered the harbor at the big island of Hawaii. And then, in short order, Kuskov and two of his men, Dmitri and Mikhail, were ushered into the royal palace, an open-walled edifice lavishly decorated in the floral manner of the islands. In the royal audience chamber, King Kamehameha sat on his throne in native dress attended by his nobles. Kuskov and his men kneeled before the king. The chamberlain motioned for him to come forward and speak.

"Your Majesty, it is a hard winter in Sitka, and our people starve. Governor Baranov remembered Your Majesty's generous offer to send supplies after the Sitka massacre. If it please Your

Majesty, he asks for our small ship to be loaded with food to save Sitka."

"Of course! Of course!" said the king. "It will be my great pleasure to fill Governor Baranov's boat with all that he needs. It's a gesture of my great respect and friendship for him. And let there be no discussion of payment—this is my gift and the gift of my people to a great man."

"Thank you, Your Majesty. Your generosity is so great!"

The voyage back to Sitka was not as easy as the trip to Hawaii. Heavily loaded, *Yermak* wallowed in a storm with waves flowing over its deck. To stay afloat, Kuskov had to jettison some of the precious cargo. His seamanship skills were indeed sorely tried.

But *Yermak* reached its home port—just in time. With a cannon salute, the weary but happy Russians of New Archangel on Sitka Island ran to meet the vessel as it docked, Baranov among them. "Ivan! Ivan!" he called out. "I knew you could do it!"

"King Kamehameha is truly a great and generous man," said Kuskov. "He filled our boat with salt pork, taro, and other food."

"Tonight we celebrate!" Baranov announced.

Three months later, Katlian and his men in the Sitka woods saw that the Russians were building parapets in the corners of their high protective wall. This wall surrounded the base of what had been the cherished Tlingit *kekur* hill on the shore of Sitka Sound.

"They will build a strong fort inside," Katlian said, feeling great remorse for having lost the kekur. *"We must get it back,"* he went on. *"The question is how."*

There was nothing his small group could do at that moment, so he led them back to their temporary camp many miles away.

There, he found that the war chief of Yakutat had come for advice. *"The Russians said that their people at Yakutat would be farmers, not hunters. But they kill all our otter and seal. What should we do?"*

"This must stop," said Katlian. *"Tell them to get out, and that if they don't leave within five days, there will be war. Then, if they still remain, kill them. Yes, kill them!"*

"But what will the Russians at Sitka do?"

"Nothing. They won't dare leave Sitka to attack you, because they know that we would attack whoever remained in Sitka. So do what must be done for your people."

Late in the spring of that year of 1805, Baranov inspected the nearly completed castle-fort at Sitka, passing the parapets overlooking the bay. A sloop had just arrived from the north. Its skipper, with an eight-year-old boy and Kuskov in tow, hurried to find him, bearing terrible news. When they found him, Midshipman Sokorov, skipper of the sloop, began, "Your Excellency! I bring news from Fort Constantine."

"Yes?"

"The northern Tlingit attacked Yakutat three weeks ago and killed almost everyone. But our Kenaitze friends lured the murderers to a potlatch and killed them all. Then, our hunting fleet north of Yakutat was hit by a huge storm that killed two hundred Aleuts."

A stunned Baranov absorbed the news. He grabbed a railing and stared seaward with a tough look that suddenly dissolved as tears started to flow. He was picturing the massacre and the storm. From his own experience, he could see the Aleuts in *bidarkas* being capsized by storm waves. He saw the serf women and men on their knees, pleading to be taken from Yakutat, and, echoing in his mind, the serf Lukin crying out, "Baranov, you will burn in hell for this!" and he stifled guilt-driven sobs.

"God! God! Get me out of here! I should have disobeyed the crown's order about the serfs. What does the crown know about this place anyway? And, oh, my poor loyal hunters, two hundred gone!"

Sokorov waited for a moment, then said, "Sir, I brought with me a young orphan of Yakutat, Samuel Lukin."

Baranov regained his composure and got on his knees to look the young boy in the face and embrace him.

"I knew your parents. You'll live with us now, Samuel—and you'll be safe."

"Thank you, sir," said the boy.

Baranov stood facing the sea again, eyes closed, and held back his sobs.

A few days later, he and Anna were seated across from each other in their Sitka parlor. Agitated, he clutched a glass of vodka, staring into it as he swirled the liquor around. Anna asked, "What help is there for the families of the Aleut hunters who died at sea?"

Baranov looked out the window and turned to face her. "What will the company do? Nothing. The Board of Directors has no fund for families of hunters who die working for us."

He downed the vodka.

"What will *you* do?"

"What will *I* do? I just told you. There is no money for the families."

"My *toyon*, without those men, you would have achieved nothing. What would our faith have you do?"

He slumped onto his chair. "What would our faith have me do? Oh, Christ! And you're supposed to be just a simple savage."

"Am I a savage?" asked Anna.

"No, no. . . . Now I guess the question is, am *I* a savage? Anna, you have never been a savage. In this wild land, you were born with the heart of a Christian, and no church had anything to do with it. It's just you."

He paused as he stared into her eyes. He got up and looked out at the sea for a moment, then back at her, as he agonized over the question. Finally, that place within him that she could always reach spoke. "Yes. We will help those families! With my earnings, we'll do it. And I'll persuade the Board of Directors to create a fund to support them in the future!"

She nodded and smiled, glad now that the right thing would be done.

He reached out and took Anna's hands and pulled her up into an embrace, then said, "You always get me to do the right thing."

Young children burst through the door—Antipatr chasing Irina, and the adopted boy Samuel following. They ran around their parents. Irina hid behind her mother, and Antipatr dove between Baranov's legs to catch her. Baranov pulled his legs together to grab the boy's head in a vise-like grip. Samuel grabbed his legs and tried to pull him out. All giggled in the fun of the moment.

Kuskov and Baranov were conferring in Baranov's office the next day when a letter arrived from Russia. Baranov read it and exclaimed, "No! My good friend Koch, sent to replace me, got sick and died on the way. Too bad. But another man will come. I hope he has better luck getting here."

Midshipman Sokorov knocked on the door and entered.

"Yes?" said Baranov.

"Sir, many of the men have seen Katlian in the woods nearby spying on us with only a couple warriors with him. Our men think we should grab him and then hang him for the Sitka massacre."

"Do the men think I'm crazy? Most of the time here, we are greatly outnumbered by the Tlingit within a day's reach. If we captured and hung him, it would start a full-scale war, which we could not win. No, somehow we must make peace with the Tlingit—and Katlian."

CHAPTER 25

REZANOV BRINGS VISIONS OF EMPIRE

On July 31, 1805, a Russian ship from Okhotsk arrived at St. Paul, Kodiak Island, with the most important passenger to yet land on that shore. The water was too shallow for his ship to tie alongside the wharf except at high tide, so it was moored a hundred yards out in the harbor, and had sent a launch ashore. On the wharf, Banner could barely see the top of a ladder that stretched from the wharf's deck down to the water's surface where the ship's launch had tied on. Looking toward the top of the ladder from mid wharf deck, he could see a plumed tricorne hat come into view, then the handsome, stern face of forty-one-year-old Count Nikolai Rezanov, then his medaled uniform. He stepped firmly onto the wharf, followed by his staff of three, and crossed to where Banner was waiting to meet him and lead him to his quarters.

Nikolai Petrovich Rezanov had arrived in Kodiak from Russia with grand plans of empire. He had also come to inspect Russian America and investigate lingering complaints against Baranov.

He called a meeting in the dining hall with the priests and monks. "I've heard that you have some complaints about Chief

Manager Baranov," he said, decked out in his resplendent blue and gold uniform. "What are they?"

Nektarios rose. "Excellency, that man is evil. He abuses the Natives by keeping some of them as hostages and by forcing them to hunt otters and seals."

"Hostages? They do that themselves," answered Rezanov. "We pay them to hunt for us, do we not?"

"Sometimes, but our payments are often years late."

"But they do eventually get paid?"

"Yes."

"Do you perform mass in their language?"

"Of course not. It would be a sacrilege to perform holy mass in the language of savages."

"Are you out of your mind? How can you possibly convert these people if you don't serve them in their own language? Can you even *speak* their language?"

"Yes."

"But you don't perform mass in it." Rezanov threw his hands up in disgust. "The Jesuits in South America use the native languages! You're not even equal to the devotion of the Jesuits in spreading the faith. You're hopeless! You're useless to Russia! You're useless to God!" He picked up his hat and stomped out of the dining hall.

As he expected, Rezanov quickly saw that the rumors against the Chief Manager were false. After that, he sailed on to Sitka to meet Baranov for the first time.

***

Two weeks later, Rezanov and Baranov were alone together for a drink in the parlor of Sitka's Russian castle. "A toast to you, Aleksandr Andreievich, Lord of Alaska!"

"Thank you, Nikolai Petrovich. But in this great land there is no 'Lord of Alaska' and never will be."

"Maybe so. But without you, Aleksandr, there would be no Russian colony here. By now it would be British. It is your intelligence, your will and courage, that have built Russian America!"

"It's been the Natives—their help, their work, and their sacrifice—that did it. They're the only normal people here, you know, the Natives. All the whites, me included, are people polite society would consider very odd—crazies, criminals, or failures elsewhere. Ordinary white people cannot survive in Alaska. Now it's time for this crazy white man to go home."

After a thoughtful pause, Rezanov said, "Your trials here would test the soul of the greatest of saints. And you have the Natives' trust and respect. If you go, then they go. Without them, the colony goes. Thanks to you, we can now expand the Russian empire to California and gain Pacific bases for trade routes to China. But time is running short. The Americans are coming. Jefferson's sent a large scouting expedition overland to the Pacific coast. We must get moving."

"And where are our navy squadrons of frigates and our legions of troops to accomplish all this?"

"Not needed. . . if we're clever enough. I'll expand His Majesty's empire throughout the Pacific while the European powers are occupied with Bonaparte, and before the Americans can realize their ambitions. Then you'll run our Pacific empire right from here: New Archangel, capitol of the Russian Pacific."

"Send me home for two years with someone else here. Then I'll come back for two years while the other fellow goes home. We'll trade off. That would be good for our families."

"Good idea! I'll propose it in St. Petersburg when I return."

Early March 1806: Baranov and Rezanov stood talking on the wharf at New Archangel, Sitka, as the crew of *Juno* readied the ship for departure.

"We'll be back with food from San Francisco Bay in three months," said Rezanov.

"We'll be out of food here before you get back, unless there's a strong, early run of candlefish."

Rezanov mused, "Negotiating with the Spaniards will be interesting, since they've closed their port at Yerba Buena, in San Francisco Bay, to foreign trade."

"Oh, you'll persuade them, I'm sure," said Baranov as Rezanov climbed aboard *Juno*, and the two men waved farewell to each other.

***

It was a bright, sunny spring day with a gentle breeze driving *Juno* forward as she sailed into the entrance of San Francisco Bay. Rezanov could see the Spanish Presidio ahead on a bluff of the southern side of the entrance, cannon in clear view. He knew he would be expected to stop and get permission before entering the harbor. As his vessel came abreast of the Presidio, he heard a voice from a speaking-trumpet on shore order him to anchor at once. Through his own speaking-trumpet, he replied, "*Sí, señor. Sí, señor*," feigning confusion, and kept on sailing. He knew that, with scurvy now rampant among his men, it would be better to be shot at than risk being ordered back out to sea and certain death.

So *Juno* sailed on toward Ensenada Yerba Buena, the port of San Francisco Bay. It furled its sails and anchored in the cove among other ships and in sight of the small town. Rezanov pulled out a telescope and scanned the town. "Much smaller than I expected," he mentioned to the first mate. "Sitka is probably bigger." He went below and got dressed appropriately as the Tsar's plenipotentiary.

In his secondary blue uniform—he would save his best for the right occasion—he came up, got in the tender, and was rowed toward shore. A group of three Spanish officials, two civilians and one young army officer on a horse, backed by a squad of musket-toting soldiers, were there to greet him.

As he climbed out of the tender onto the beach, it was apparent to him from their stern demeanor that they were prepared to either convey him to higher authority or arrest him on the spot, whichever seemed appropriate—and he knew in his bones how vulnerable he and his great ambitions were in that instant. In just moments, he and his dreams of a Pacific empire based on a strategic alliance between Russia and Spain could be locked up in a Spanish dungeon and never again see the light of day.

He spoke to them with a humble yet confident smile and in fluent Spanish learned on his prior visits to Spanish-speaking countries. "*Good afternoon, gentlemen. I am Count Nikolai*

Rezanov of Russia. I have come from Russian America and wish, may it please you, to speak with your governor."

His dignity and easy charm quickly gained him the welcome he had hoped for. The army officer nodded with a brief smile and signaled for another horse, which Rezanov mounted, and he rode off side-by-side with the young Spanish officer toward the Presidio military fortress three and half miles away.

The apparently successful outcome of the brief encounter on the beach was but yet another confirmation to Rezanov, he believed, that he was a man of destiny. *"Are we going to the governor's office?"* he asked. The Spaniard smiled and looked straight ahead without speaking.

The dirt road wound its way through a series of steep, brush-covered hills that rose nearby on both sides, then climbed to a plateau overlooking the Puerta de Oro and the Pacific beyond. There, atop the plateau, lay the Presidio. They rode through an open gate in the high adobe fortress wall surrounding several buildings within, approached a white stucco main building with a red tile roof, and stopped. The Spaniard motioned for Rezanov to dismount and wait while he himself got off his horse and led it to the building, tied the horse to a hitching post, and went in. Rezanov tried not to look too inquisitive as he stood by his horse and glanced from side to side at the several small buildings around the perimeter of the courtyard. He saw gun stands strategically placed on a platform just below the top of the fort wall, with about a dozen cannon aimed toward the channel.

Five minutes later, another officer came out of the building— Comandante José Darío Argüello, a tall, soldierly man in the uniform of a Spanish army officer. Rezanov put out his hand, and

Arguello took it as he looked Rezanov square in the eye, shaking hands with a serious but respectful expression.

In surprisingly able Spanish, Rezanov said, *"I am Count Nikolai Rezanov, chamberlain to His Majesty Tsar Alexander of Russia, and overseer of Russian America."*

"I am Captain José Darío Arguello, Comandante of the Presidio under the authority of Governor Arrillaga."

"Good to meet you, Captain. I would be honored to meet with your governor."

"He is now at his headquarters in Monterey, but he will be back here at his Presidio office in a few days."

"Then, with your permission, I will go back to my ship and await his arrival. When he comes, please convey my desire to meet with him, and then I would most greatly appreciate it if you would send a horse to bring me to that meeting."

"It shall be done, Your Excellency. Lieutenant Gonzalez will escort you back to the port." Gonzalez's horse was brought over by a soldier.

"Another thing, Captain. We need to make some repairs to our ship that will take a few days. And may I purchase food for my crew in your harbor town?"

"Yes, of course."

The two shook hands again, and Rezanov mounted his horse alongside that of his escort. They began the ride back together to the harbor at Yerba Buena. On their way out of the Presidio, Rezanov noticed a large house tucked into a corner of the fort near the front gate, with several young children of various ages playing in the front yard.

"The children of Captain Arguello," explained his escort.

Now that his escort was talking, Rezanov had a few questions. *"What is your job here, sir?"*

"I am responsible for the harbor," answered Lieutenant Gonzalez.

"To buy food for my crew, I'll need some advice. Can you help me with that?"

"Yes, of course. I'll take care of it for you if you wish, Your Excellency. I'll have a wagon brought over with provisions."

This was an enormous relief, because the crew of *Juno* was starving, and some already had scurvy. Rezanov himself had lost weight, which he hoped wasn't obvious in the drape of his uniform.

The two riders reached the beach, where Rezanov dismounted and passed his horse's reins to Gonzalez, who said, *"Listen for our harbor bell, Excellency. Your ship is number four. If you hear four bells, we want you to come ashore so we can talk, or the carriage has come to take you to the Presidio."*

"Thank you, Lieutenant."

A sailor with the tender was waiting for Rezanov on the beach.

Three days later, Lieutenant Gonzalez escorted Rezanov to the governor's Presidio office. As they entered, the sixty-year-old José Joaquín de Arrillaga was sitting at a long worktable that he used as a desk. A charming Spaniard, he looked up, smiled warmly, and came forward to shake hands. He and Rezanov were immediately *simpático*. The governor offered his guest a seat as he dismissed Gonzalez, and the two sat facing each other.

This secondary office, auxiliary to the governor's main office in Monterey, was decorated with a collection of Mexican bark paintings of the brightly colored birds, lizards, and flowers seen on Spanish *ranchos*. A servant soldier entered, carrying a tray with glasses of freshly squeezed orange juice and cookies, and left it on a low table next to the two men.

"Now tell me, Your Excellency," asked de Arrillaga, *"to what business do we owe the pleasure of your visit?"*

"Russian America—we call it Alaska now—is rich in furs and poor in foodstuffs. We need to purchase food for our people with our furs. You raise much of the food we need here, and in return we offer the finest sea otter and seal furs of the Pacific."

". . . We have a problem, my friend. Spanish law doesn't allow us to trade with foreigners."

"Even when it is to Spain's advantage?"

The governor's bright eyes grew sharper, and he inclined his head ever so slightly. *"Our advantage?"*

"The British and the Americans are pushing west with greedy eyes on this coast, and they are not great friends of Spain."

"And Russia is?" the Spaniard replied with more than a touch of skepticism in his voice.

"Most assuredly! With Russian control of the North Pacific managed by Governor Baranov in Sitka, we can prevent British and American moves on Alta California. And our trade in furs for food is mutually beneficial! Russia and Spain should definitely be allies here."

". . . I see your point," said de Arrillaga with a sigh. *"But, oh, how our Spanish bureaucracy can bury any good idea! And there's*

another problem. With all the turmoil in Europe just now, Russia and Spain could be at war with each other and we not know it yet. . . . However, I am expecting a courier from Spain any day now who may clarify our situation."

"My dear governor, Russia and Spain are so far apart geographically that the chances of them having any dispute worth going to war about are practically nil."

Arrillaga smiled noncommittally. "Tell me, Count Rezanov, have you a family anxiously awaiting your return to St. Petersburg?"

"I have two young children being raised by their godparents. Sadly, I lost my wife Anna in childbirth a few years ago. I do look forward to my return and seeing my children again."

"I can imagine. Now, tell me what you can about your governor in Alaska, Aleksandr Baranov. He is the most famous man on this side of the Pacific, you know. We've heard of his extraordinary victory in the Battle of Sitka. He was up against 2,000 Tlingit warriors with just a few hundred Russians and Aleuts. Yet after several days of desperate fighting on sea and land, he had killed 1,000 enemy warriors in glorious battle and utterly defeated them. What a man!"

"Yes. . . well, I don't think he killed that many, but it was a great victory. He took back our place on Sitka, which has such strategic importance in our contest with the British. Baranov is indeed a most able man of great courage. Without him, we could never have anchored our colonies up there with many cities spread along the coast. And he will play a key role in helping to strengthen the alliance between Russia and Spain that I have proposed."

"How I'd love to meet him, governor to governor. That would be a great honor indeed."

"And it will happen, I assure you, when our countries' alliance is affirmed. Then you and Baranov will be working closely together."

De Arrillaga nodded and rose, signaling the end of the meeting, holding out his hand as he added, *"Come to Casa Grande and be my guest for dinner tonight, Nikolai, and let's see if we can work something out."*

Rezanov shook hands and replied, *"Thank you for your hospitality, Governor. I will be delighted!"*

Rezanov was driven by carriage on his return trip to Ensenada Yerba Buena. On the cobble streets of the outpost town, he could barely contain his excitement. The Spanish governor had been like putty in his hands. Spain needed money, and Rezanov yearned in the end to buy California from the Spaniards so that Russia would own most of the Pacific coast of North America. With Baranov's competent management, he knew it could work. *But one step at a time*, he thought, *and it will all come within my grasp.*

CHAPTER 26

A SAN FRANCISCO ROMANCE

At the state dinner, the Commandant of the Presidio of San Francisco Bay, José Darío Arguello, entered with his wife, his fifteen-year-old daughter Maria Concepción (whom he called "Conchita"), and his two sons. Conchita wore a flowing black flamenco dress bordered in crimson ruffles. Five and a half feet tall, she was slender and beautifully curved in all the right places.

Her oval face had large, startlingly blue eyes accentuated by long eyelashes. She smiled at everyone, sparkling with joy. Her skin was smooth. Every feature of her face looked perfectly formed, her lips inviting. With a red rose pinned to her hair above one ear, most of her long brown curls were pulled to one side, flowing down to her breast. Over her other ear, a curl dangled and twirled with her every move.

Rezanov was immediately struck. She looked right at him with a bright, easy smile. The governor invited her to dance a fandango for the party.

Conchita put on her castanets and, as she clicked them in a rapid Spanish rhythm, threw her hands up over her head and took the floor. Accompanied by two guitars and two trumpets, she executed a fiery solo performance, twirling and stamping her shoes to the passionate beat of the music. As she glided past the Russian, the scent of her rose enchanted him.

After her dance, she took her place at the table, and Rezanov applauded with loud enthusiasm, lifted his glass, and rose to toast his hosts in Spanish.

"To his majesty, King Carlos IV of Spain, long live the king! To Governor de Arrillaga, I offer the felicitations of his majesty Alexander, Tsar of all the Russias. And to Commandant Arguello and his family, I offer my sincere gratitude for the pleasure of your company and the joy of seeing your exquisitely beautiful daughter dance like a Spanish angel. I think when she was dancing, my heart surely missed a beat!"

A titter of laughter rolled around the room.

"Salud!" Rezanov went on, and everyone responded.

Then de Arrillaga raised his glass.

"To his imperial majesty, Tsar Alexander, long live the Tsar! To the pleni-potentiary of the Tsar, His Excellency Count Rezanov, may your great vision of a peaceful and prosperous North Pacific succeed to the gain of both Spain and Russia. And to His Excellency Aleksandr Baranov, who has met every challenge Alaska has thrown at him—truly the master of Alaska."

As the governor sat down, he leaned across to Rezanov and said, *"We'll trade food for furs this once, for humanitarian reasons. Our señoritas are freezing in the fog."*

The two shared a laugh, and Rezanov said, *"Thank you, Governor. You are both kind and courageous."*

They clinked glasses, and the guitars resumed their music. Rezanov leaned to his left and spoke to the commandant sitting next to him.

"Captain Arguello, if I may be so bold, I wonder if I may have the honor of paying your family a friendly visit tomorrow afternoon?"

"Of course. We would be delighted."

Rezanov was happy indeed. He had an idea that could help cement an alliance between Russia and Spain in a manner that would be very pleasant for him as well.

The next day, his carriage dropped him off in front of the commandant's house at the Presidio. He was carrying a gift, and Arguello came down to greet him and invite him onto the veranda. *"Welcome, Your Excellency,"* said Arguello.

"Thank you, Captain. Please, call me Nikolai."

Rezanov stopped to talk privately with Arguello before joining the others.

"Let me be frank with you. At dinner last night, I was enchanted by your daughter. I am myself a widower and a gentleman. I would like your permission to court Maria Concepción."

". . . I appreciate your frankness, sir. I assume you intend to return to your own country?"

"Yes, Captain. And while I am here, I would like to tell your daughter about Russia and the Tsar's court in St. Petersburg, while I try to learn from her how it is possible for her to be so charming. Of course, I expect that our meetings will be chaperoned."

Captain Arguello looked intently at him, briefly considered the diplomatic repercussions of refusing, then said, *"Very well, Nikolai." After all,* Arguello thought, *he's thousands of miles from Russia. Here at San Francisco Bay, I am in control.*

They stepped up onto the veranda, and Rezanov immediately greeted Señora Arguello, Conchita's mother, and kissed her hand.

"Señora Arguello, it is with great pleasure that I am here with you this afternoon. I've brought you a small gift that I beg you will accept with my compliments. Something for cool and foggy evenings."

He handed her the package.

She opened it to find that it contained an otter jacket. She beamed as she put it on. Then she gushed, *"Thank you so much, Your Excellency! It's beautiful, and it will indeed be welcome on cool nights."*

Rezanov turned his attention to Conchita, who was standing off to one side. He took her hand and kissed it. Then he stood staring at her for a moment, as she stared at him. He smiled at her briefly, then turned serious. *"Maria Concepción, I have traveled the world—from Russia to England to Japan to Alaska, and now to California. And in all the world, you are the most beautiful woman I have ever seen."*

She was speechless, especially at being addressed as a woman when she had still so recently thought of herself as a girl.

A servant interrupted with a tray of refreshments brought out to the veranda. They each took a glass of orange juice and sat down.

Commandant Arguello spoke. *"On a beautiful day like this, we always enjoy a horseback ride into the hills, where the views of the ocean are magnificent. Would you care to join us, Nikolai?"*

It will be easier to fend off Rezanov, he thought, *if we are nice to him and put him off his guard.* Then he would surely make a mistake, to which they could justifiably take offense and push him away.

Still staring unashamedly at Conchita, Rezanov replied, *"I would be delighted to join you."*

The Arguello family and Rezanov, all on horseback, took a wide trail up into the hills surrounding San Francisco Bay and overlooking the ocean. Conchita's hair was pulled back in a bun under a small, tan sombrero. Again, she wore her trademark rose pinned to her hat. She also wore tight-fitting blue riding breeches with high black leather boots and spurs. Her parents led the party, she and Rezanov followed—she on a red stallion— and the two Arguello sons brought up the rear.

Rezanov pointed to a precipitous cliff where waves were crashing against rocks and asked, *"Tell me, Conchita, how many men have jumped off that cliff because you refused to marry them?"*

"So many I've forgotten," she answered, laughing lightly. *"Why don't we ride over there and count them?"*

She spurred her horse and galloped ahead on the trail leading to the top of the cliff. She was obviously an expert rider. Rezanov quickly followed. The others continued to canter along. The two galloped up the trail, and she leaned forward and urged her horse with spoken commands to outdistance Rezanov: *"Rápido! Rápido!"* She beat the Russian to the top of the bluff and stopped right at the edge of the cliff, pulling her reins back. Her horse reared up, beating the air with its hooves.

This man Rezanov is so different and interesting, she was thinking. He was much too old for her. But then, he would be gone soon, back to Alaska, so a little fun now wouldn't matter.

He caught up as she steered her mount away from the edge, and he pulled his horse alongside hers, facing in the opposite direction, so he could speak directly to her. *"I see that not only dancing like an angel but riding like a cossack is in your blood!"*

"Not a cossack. A caballero!" she insisted.

Dramatically silhouetted against the sky and sea, they continued to chat, though no one else could hear them.

That evening, in the Arguello dining room, the family and Rezanov were seated at a long supper table. Conchita, in a long, flowing white dress across from Rezanov, was full of curiosity about the Russian court. *"Tell me, Your Excellency, have you ever met the Tsar?"*

"Which one?" Rezanov replied. *"And please, call me Nikolai!"*

"You've met more than one, Your Excellency? . . . I just like the way 'Your Excellency' rolls off the tongue. And it makes me feel more important—that I am privileged to be speaking to a very important man."

"I have met with Their Majesties Tsarina Catherine, Tsar Paul, and our new emperor, His Majesty Alexander, Tsar of All the Russias. And I feel that I should be calling you 'Your Excellency' as well, but 'Conchita' sounds so much more beautiful, so much more fitting."

"You've been to the Tsar's palace?" she asked.

"Several of them. The Tsar has one for every day of the week."

She considered the idea of a Tsar having more than one palace. *"I've never seen a palace,"* she said. *"The parties there must be wonderful."*

"Come to Russia, and I'll show you more palaces than you can imagine, and I'll take you to more parties and more dances with royalty and aristocrats than you can imagine in your dreams."

She replied, *"That makes San Francisco Bay seem so boring."*

"Not with you here," he said with quiet charm.

"Well, this San Francisco is just water, rocks, hills, and fog. What could be more dull? It's a prison for the mind and spirit, and it will never amount to anything."

"On the contrary, my dear," said Rezanov. *"After Russia and Spain seal their grand alliance, we will make this place a crossroads of the world. You know, you amaze me. You have such a happy, outgoing manner, yet your thoughts are so dark."*

"Maybe there's more to this señorita than you think," she said with a smile and a wink. He looked at her, a bit surprised, and nodded slowly.

She began to think there was something really special about this man as well, and that Rezanov might be her one chance to escape this unimportant, boring backwater of the Spanish empire—never mind his wild dreams about its future. She knew the place. But with him, she might reach up to the exciting realm of nobility in a place that mattered.

Arguello lamented, *"So far, he has made no mistakes that I can use."*

The next day, Conchita and her brothers—one older, one younger than she—went riding together to the port at Ensenada Yerba Buena to observe the activity in the harbor. She wore a green riding skirt, a white blouse, and no hat—only a rose pinned to her hair above one ear. Her curls hung loose over her shoulders and fluttered in the wind as she rode. They stopped at an overlook directly above the Russian ship *Juno* and dismounted. The boys took note of a new racing sloop being readied for a test run.

"It has the new speed hull," said Luis. *"Let's go take a look."*

Conchita wasn't looking at the sloop. She was staring at *Juno,* where she saw Rezanov come on deck with a hand telescope. The boys got on their horses and galloped off, unaware that she wasn't following.

Rezanov started scanning the San Francisco hills with his spyglass—until she came in view. He lowered the telescope to look for her with his bare eyes. Seeing her on the nearby knoll, he looked again at her through the telescope and saw that she was staring directly at him.

He set down the telescope and waved. She waved back, and he climbed over the side of *Juno,* jumped into the ship's tender tied alongside, freed it, and started rapidly rowing to shore. When he reached the beach, she was already there dismounting. She tied her horse to a nearby bush, and then, without a word, as he was holding his rowboat on the beach, came over with a smile and climbed in.

"*Hola, señorita. Señorita querida. Conchita, mi querida,*" he whispered over the lapping sound of the water.

Conchita sat down. "*Hola, Nikolai.*"

He pushed off and started rowing north, parallel to the beach, looking over his shoulder every few moments to see where he was going, but mostly looking at her. She looked only at him, almost expressionlessly but with just a hint of nervous anticipation. She had never done anything like this before.

"*I heard you've already been married. Is that true?*" she asked.

"*Yes.*"

"*What happened?*"

"*Sadly, after many years of happy marriage, Anna died in childbirth five years ago.*"

Just as he rowed out of view of the moored boats, a narrow inlet appeared near the northeast end of the cove, and Rezanov rowed into it. With brush at both ends and at some distance from port activity, it was a private place. He tied up to a branch reaching out from shore, crept toward her on his knees, and took her hands in his as they looked into each other's eyes.

He kissed the palm of each of her hands and slowly leaned forward, as did she. Their lips met, and soon their kiss became passionate as thcy fell into each other's arms and onto the floor of the rowboat. As she looked into his intelligent blue eyes, her hands glided over his handsome face and moved up the back of his neck until her fingers swept through his blonde curls and stopped there for a moment.

As they kissed again, his right hand moved up and covered her left breast. She gently pushed it away. A moment later, his hand found that place again, and she did not protest. His hand slid under her blouse and over her chemise. Their kissing became more passionate as their tongues found each other.

Then his hand covered her bare breast as she tilted her head back, and his passion soared on seeing the sensuous arc of her soft, slender throat. He savored the warmth of the smooth skin of her neck and kissed it repeatcdly, then pulled up her blouse and kissed her beautifully rounded breasts and rose nipples, caressing them with his tongue. She made soft swooning sounds, accepting a pleasure she had never known before.

But as his hand began to reach lower, something came over him, and with an enormous exercise of self-control, he stopped. After a moment, he pulled her blouse down to cover her and held her in his arms gently as he whispered in her ear, *"My darling,*

Conchita, you are so young. Too young. And I must protect the honor of your family. But I absolutely adore you." He kissed her again on the lips, untied the boat, and began rowing back out of the inlet as she sat on her seat and composed herself.

This, she thought, was the beginning of what she wanted. And she wanted it with him.

"Nikolai," she murmured. *"Oh. . . Nikolai."*

He rowed back to Ensenada Yerba Buena and beached the boat. They got up and looked warmly into each other's eyes for a moment. He kissed her hand, and she slowly stepped out of the boat, still looking at him. Then she turned and walked to her horse. He sat down in the skiff and started rowing back to Juno. Facing the stern as he rowed, he watched as she untied her horse and her brothers rode up. They dismounted and walked over to her.

"We've been looking all over for you," said Luis. *"Where have you been?"*

She studied them with a blank expression, and with no explanation, she pointed over her shoulder toward *Juno.* Rezanov could be seen rowing toward the ship, and as he saw the boys looking at him, he waved with a friendly smile. They waved back. She mounted her horse and galloped off toward the Presidio, leaving her brothers in the dust.

CHAPTER 27

REZANOV'S GRAND DESIGN

Two days later, in the Arguellos' library, Rezanov again approached Don Arguello. *"I am in love with your daughter,"* he said, *"and am here to request your permission to ask her to marry me."*

". . . Nikolai," Arguello replied, *"I was afraid that was what you were going to say. Do you realize how young she is?"*

"I know. But if she agrees, there will be a long engagement before we can wed."

There was a long moment of silence as Don Arguello looked out the window across the sea to the far horizon. *"If I say yes, that is where I will look for my beloved Conchita—across the ocean. I may never see her again."* He paused, measuring his words, then he looked back at Rezanov. *"I know she cares for you too, Nikolai. Can I stand in the way of the happiness of two wonderful people, just to avoid my own deep sorrow at losing sight of her?"*

Rezanov replied, *"Travel across the sea is rapidly improving, my friend. As head of the Russian American Company, I need to visit its outposts every few years. I would always stop here and bring Conchita to see you."*

Arguello waved that aside as wishful thinking. *"How would*

this even be possible? You are of the Orthodox faith, and we are Catholic."

"I know. We would first have to get permission from the Tsar, from the King of Spain, and from the Vatican. But in love, all things are possible. Something else—I know this is of no importance to you, and it shouldn't be, but I'll mention it anyway. Our marriage would cement a bond between Russia and Spain in the Pacific, enabling Russia to protect Spanish interests in a Pacific partnership.

"And the importance of that bond will drive the approvals we need. Immediately after I go back to Alaska, I will return to St. Petersburg to get the Tsar's permission. And I'm sure I can persuade your governor to request permission from Spain and the Vatican. I'll also deliver to the Tsar the treaty with Spain I have negotiated with your governor. Then I'll be back in two years for our wedding!"

Exasperated, Don Arguello at last said, *"My God. My God! What am I to do? Yes, Nikolai, you have my permission to ask her. May the saints make her refuse!"*

On May 18, 1806, at Yerba Buena Ensenada, several carriages were parked near the beach, having brought Governor de Arrillaga, as well as Captain Arguello and his family, to see Rezanov and *Juno* set sail. The party stood clustered near the edge of the beach as the Russian said goodbye to Conchita. He looked deeply into her eyes and murmured, *"My darling, I carry you with me in my heart and in my mind. Not an hour will pass without my thinking of you, missing you."*

Conchita removed the scarf from her neck and draped it around his. *"Be safe, my dear Nikolai, and bring this scarf back to me with great dispatch! I love you."*

Rezanov held her face in his hands and kissed her longingly. They embraced as the others looked on. Finally, he broke away and stepped into the tender, looking back as he fingered the scarf around his neck. Everyone onshore waved goodbye except Conchita, standing alone in front of them, tears streaming down her cheeks. After he climbed onboard *Juno*, he clutched the gunwale, staring at her on the beach. His eyes were locked on hers, and hers on his, as the ship pulled away. He kept moving back toward the stern so he could keep her in view to the last possible moment when he saw her remove the rose from her hair and hold it in her hand.

***

On Rezanov's return to Sitka on June 19, *Juno* received a three-gun salute. Everyone from Baranov's Castle—as everybody was calling the new fort—ran down to the wharf to see what food was onboard. Even Baranov had lost weight as food became scarce. They were desperate for what Rezanov had brought from California. As she tied up at the wharf, Baranov climbed aboard and greeted him. "You're certainly a good sight for hungry eyes!" he said as he shook hands with Rezanov, who was wearing his secondary blue uniform.

"Sasha! I have a lot to tell you. This has been a most successful voyage. I'll be leaving for Okhotsk and St. Petersburg in just a few days. Here's a letter I wrote to someone at the San Francisco Presidio that I want you to put on the next boat going that way," Rezanov added as he handed the letter to him.

Baranov looked at the name of the addressee, Doña María Concepción Arguello, and at Rezanov with a questioning glance.

"You're wondering what happened at San Francisco Bay? A lot. I'm engaged to be married to the most beautiful woman I've ever seen. They call her Conchita, the daughter of the comandante of the San Francisco Presidio."

"You're a fast worker, Nikolai."

"The point is, this marriage will cement the alliance between Russia and Spain in the North Pacific. I persuaded the governor of Alta California, José Joaquín de Arrillaga, of the benefit to Spain of this alliance to protect their holdings from the English and Americans. He will work with us. You see, it all fits in with our grand strategic plan for the expansion of the Russian Empire. And of course, *you* will be the key to making it all work."

"Amazing! Very exciting!" Baranov responded. "But I fear it will take the cooperation of all the angels of heaven and all the saints to make it work."

Rezanov sailed to Okhotsk as summer began. Upon arriving there with his three aides at the beginning of fall, he started a tortuous overland trip across the frozen wastes of Siberia toward St. Petersburg.

He fell through the ice of a lake, was rescued by his aides, caught pneumonia, and was bedridden for several weeks.

How could it be? he wondered as he lay helpless in bed. "I have a destiny!" he shouted aloud. "It must be fulfilled!"

A nurse ran into the room. "What is it, sir?"

". . . Nothing," he muttered.

Before he was completely well, he resumed his winter trek on horseback. As he rode across a frozen lake, there was steam from his breath and a determined expression on his unshaven face, that was being overcome by a pallor of sickness. Then he fell off his horse onto the ice, struggled momentarily, and became still as the steam of his breath ceased. A gust of wind pulled Conchita's loose scarf from around his neck and blew it away, lifting it high, rolling and tumbling in the wind until it disappeared over the treetops along the shoreline. Behind lay the vast wasteland of frozen Siberia and the distant horizon, beyond which waited Conchita. If there had been eyes on the flying scarf seeking that horizon, the group of men on that lake would have looked like specks of dust on an endless white sheet of lost dreams.

Some believed that Rezanov was a ruthless schemer who had no intention of marrying Conchita. But whatever his true intentions, they expired with him. Also lost was Baranov's champion at the court of Tsar Alexander, as well as Rezanov's expansive dream of a Pacific Russian empire partnered with Spain, with Baranov as its chief manager in the field.

***

Captain Arguello rode on horseback up the road to his *casa*, dismounted, and tied his horse to a railing next to Conchita's red stallion—already saddled for a ride.

"Conchita! Conchita! A letter!" he called out.

She ran to meet him.

"Thank God!"

She took the letter in her hands and kissed it, started to open it, but changed her mind. She got on her horse with the letter and galloped down the trail toward the ocean-side bluff. She galloped right up the trail to the overlook on top of the bluff where she and Rezanov had been so long before. With the surf pounding below, she opened the letter and read it. As she did, little gusts of wind rippled the letter as if trying to take it from her. She kissed the letter again, holding it lightly in front of her as the breeze subsided. She looked dreamily out to sea to the far west.

Joyously, she cried out, *"My darling! My darling!"* At that moment, a gust of wind snatched the letter out of her hand, and it tumbled along the ground toward the top of the cliff. She leaped off the horse and chased after it, but just before she could retrieve it, another gust lifted the letter out over the cliff as she reached out for it, one foot slipping slightly over the edge of the cliff and the ground crumbling beneath her foot.

Her flowing, windblown hair whipped her face as she looked intently at that dear object fluttering in the breeze, her arm outstretched with her fingertips touching the floating letter, the surf crashing on rocks below and behind her. She glanced down at the surf for an instant, than back at the letter. She seemed to hang there in space with the letter just beyond her outstretched hand, her life in the balance. Then she pulled back her hand, slid onto solid ground, and the letter was blown skyward.

It rolled and tumbled in the wind, carried out over the sea. The coastline, the broad expanse of the Pacific, was spread out before her, making her and her horse seem very small. She stared across the sea to the far horizon.

CHAPTER 28

MAKING PEACE

Father Herman had come to Kodiak in 1794 with seven other monks, including Father Nektarios. Spiritual yet realistic, Father Herman became truly attuned to the needs of the Natives. He earned their trust and respect and was highly successful at converting them. They affectionately called him "Apa." With Baranov's help, Herman built and ran a school for Russian and Native children. The two men eventually developed a relationship of trust and mutual respect, though they sometimes disagreed about company treatment of the Natives.

On a visit to Kodiak, Baranov took a kayak to see Father Herman on Spruce Island. He beached the craft at a landing where a trail came to shore out of the spruce trees. Contemplating what he wanted to discuss with Father Herman, he strode along the path toward Herman's shack.

He knocked on the wall beside the open door of the priest's hut and looked in. At that moment, the long-bearded Father, slight of build and dressed in old deerskin clothing, came out of the woods from a side trail to his vegetable garden, carrying some turnips.

Whenever Baranov was at Kodiak, he visited. Since he felt

trapped in Alaska, he had turned to the priest for spiritual guidance.

"Aleksandr Andreievich!" Herman exclaimed, smiling broadly in greeting.

"I thought I'd stop by for some inspiration. You're such an able farmer."

"And I'm trying to be an even better shepherd, but alas, that is hard. So hard for one so lacking as me." He paused; Baranov was staring at him pensively. "What's on your mind, Aleksandr Andreievich?"

"Can we visit your garden?"

Herman studied him for a moment, then put the turnips down on a log and led him along a path to a clearing with his garden.

They walked out into the meadow next to the neat rows of lettuce, cabbage, and squash. Herman noticed that Baranov seemed preoccupied. "I plant my seeds in early May," he said, "and as they grow, they teach me God's way with us. . . . I made a spruce bench here. Let's sit down."

They sat and became silent. Herman knew the man wanted to tell him something. He waited.

"I took this job for five years," Baranov finally said. "But I've been stuck here nearly twenty. Always made a profit. Haven't seen my children in Russia for all these years. Men sent to replace me have died on the way. Seems as if God is keeping me here for some reason. But what?"

"How do you do it? I pity any poor devil who tries to come here to replace you. It seems to be a death sentence."

"What?"

"Are your innermost prayers what you think they are?"

". . . I don't understand. I've had a job to do here for Russia and for the company. I've done my best. I should be allowed to go home."

"But do you really want to leave, Aleksandr Andreievich? Or do you really love it here? In Russia, you were nothing, but here the Tsar made you a nobleman and you became, as some say, 'Lord of Alaska.' Your Russian family is taken care of and doesn't need you there. You have a fine young family here that does need you. . . . So why do you want to go back?"

Baranov stared at him. "Russia is my country. My homeland."

"Is it still?" asked Herman. "Or do you belong to this land now—Alaska? Each of us has a hidden side, you know. And once it is confessed, then the light can come through and triumph. The question we each face is: Are we ready to *confess* our hidden side—what we really want, and what we avoid admitting even to ourselves? It appears you'll never return to Russia if you have your way, and it seems you always do."

". . . If I've prayed for anything, it's to be replaced."

"Yes, in tough times," answered Herman. "But really, if you could, would you have your name written atop Denali? And are you going to stay here until you can figure out how to do it?"

"Oh, come now, I don't care about that. I'm weary of having to make decisions that can cost people's lives. My poor Aleut hunters. Their work is so dangerous. A bad storm, Tlingit attacks, many bad things happen, and then they are lost—sometimes by the hundreds. It's terrible. And we've hunted too much. Large stretches of coastline now have hardly an otter. And how can I make a lasting peace with the Tlingit? This all weighs heavy on me. What is our future here?"

"Your problem is that you're a good man in a bad situation that seems to offer only bad choices. I know that. You have to make a profit here for the Russian American Company for the sake of your family, but the only way to do that seems to be to use large numbers of Aleut hunters and hunt more than you should in too many places. Sometimes this goes against what you think is right, yet you don't seem to have a choice."

"I'm amazed. I didn't think anyone else could see it."

"Prayer, Aleksandr, honest prayer. Let us pray now for truth and humility. And for an answer to your dilemma."

"And then?"

"Listen for the answer. Watch for the answer. It will come when you least expect it, where you least expect it."

Herman bowed his head in prayer. Baranov did also, briefly, then got up and left as the priest continued praying. He looked up above the trees of Spruce Island toward the snow-capped mountains of Kodiak Island behind, then, through an opening between the trees, at the ocean's distant horizon. It occurred to him that he and Herman—all of them really—were just lost specks in the vast wilderness.

Back in Sitka in the late spring, Baranov was on the dock seeing someone off on a ship from Kodiak leaving for Russia. The priest Nektarios was leaving Alaska on that ship. As he stood on deck, he saw Baranov below and called out to him.

"Goodbye, Baranov. I promise you, as soon as I return to St. Petersburg, you will be excommunicated."

"Excommunicated?" replied Baranov. "If that will get me replaced here, then I'm in favor of it. You know, 'excommunicated' isn't even in the Bible. Your version of religion is all form and no substance. Herman's version is all substance and no form—but better for the soul. Why not have religion that is both form *and* substance?"

"Coming from you, that's blasphemy!"

"Have a good sail, priest. I don't want to hear you've become dinner for sharks. The poor fellows would get indigestion." Baranov swatted a mosquito on his arm as he turned away.

"Baranov!" Nektarios shouted at his back. "One thing I know: You can't leave here until you are defeated. Utterly defeated."

Some days later, hundreds of Tlingit canoes entered Sitka sound, and thousands of Tlingit camped on the islands. Sitting in a circle around a campfire, the Tlingit chiefs conferred with their war chief, Katlian.

Chief Naawushkeitl said, *"You lost Sitka for us in the big battle. How will we get it back?"*

"It was the loss of the gunpowder in the canoe."

"You sent the canoe."

"We needed that powder before the battle started."

"In broad daylight?"

Chief Chilkoot of the Chilkat tribe interjected, *"This is pointless. What happened, happened. We have to deal with NOW."*

Katlian said, *"We have a lot of warriors here for the candlefish run. We greatly outnumber the Russians. Why not attack them now and burn them out? We could do it from our canoes in the fog, setting fire to their ships and that damn castle."*

"Not as easy as it sounds," replied Naawushkeitl. *"We didn't come this time prepared for war. Maybe we should meet with Baranov and see if he will let us come back."*

"Ridiculous," said Katlian. *"What could we offer him that would make him let us come back to Sitka?"*

"Peace," answered Naawushkeitl.

Two days later, after sending a message asking for a meeting, five of the chiefs, including Katlian, entered the castle through the main gate, unarmed. As they looked around, comparing what they saw to their prior fort on the *kekur*, they were astonished. There were now several two- and three-story buildings made of heavy spruce logs, whereas they had only had one-story longhouses.

Accompanied by four armed Russian guards, they were led to the main building, where Baranov had his office next to a large meeting room that doubled as a dining hall. On the side walls built from tan logs were hung several examples of Tlingit helmets and armor, and also Aleut *kamleika* rain gear and seal-hunting spears. Hanging on the wall was the big white polar bear hide of *Nanuq*. It hung sideways, the tail to the left, legs spread in four directions, and the head with the snarling teeth to the right, next to Baranov's office door.

There were woven rugs on the hardwood floor, and the chiefs were invited to sit on a rug in a circle around a low table just a few feet from the wall of *Nanuq's* impressive hide. The four guards stationed themselves in the four corners of the room. Baranov and Kuskov entered from the office.

"Good afternoon, noble chiefs," Baranov said in their language as he too sat on the floor cross-legged, though favoring the leg still suffering from an old injury. Kuskov, bearing a small black box, sat next to him. Baranov said to the chiefs, *"Would you like some tea?"*

None of them responded. Regardless, Baranov signaled to one of his men, and a tall, golden samovar was carried in. Tea was poured for each of the chiefs and served with a plate of small sweet cakes. Baranov started sipping his tea, and soon Naawushkeitl began sipping his, watching his Russian host closely.

"I'm glad you've all come for a visit. How is your fishing?"

No one answered.

"You want to come back to Sitka Island," said Baranov as casually as he would say, "We cooked ten loaves of bread today."

"Yes!" Katlian quickly affirmed.

"All right, you can come back. But there must be no more killing of our hunters and fishermen," Baranov said without emotion. *"And you must tell me first where you want to build your village, so I can approve the location. Do you agree?"*

Four of the chiefs nodded to each other; Katlian stared at Baranov. Then Naawushkeitl said, *"We agree."*

Baranov nodded enthusiastically. *"Good! Your people and our people should live next to each other in peace. We should trade and help each other. Do you agree?"*

None of the chiefs responded.

Baranov reached for a teacake and started eating it. *"This is peace cake,"* he said when he'd swallowed his first mouthful. *"It is very good."*

After a minute, Naawushkeitl started eating a cake. He nodded. *"Very good."*

Chief Chilkoot took a cake and started eating, and so did two other chiefs. Katlian did not.

When they finished their tea, Baranov pulled himself up with the help of a nearby chair. Kuskov handed him the box he had been holding. From it, Baranov removed a shiny copper plate engraved with the double-headed eagle emblem of the Russian Empire. He gave one to each chief, and four of them looked pleased as they examined the plates and glanced at each other. *"Thank you for coming to see me, noble chiefs. I give you these copper plates as a gift and as a sign of our friendship."* Then he whispered to Kuskov in Russian, "I'm glad they can't read Russian, because it says 'Property of Empire of Russia' right there under the emblem."

Kuskov gave a knowing nod.

"Come back tonight," Baranov went on, turning to his guests, *"and let us celebrate with a potlatch. We'll have much food, singing, and dancing, because now we have a lot to sing and dance about. . . . My men will guide you out. Remember, please—I always have a good supply of tea and peace cake, any time you wish to stop by."*

Katlian looked at both sides of the copper plate but left it on the low table. The chiefs all got up, turned, and left with the four guards.

After they were gone, Kuskov murmured, "So tea- cakes have become peace cakes. Very clever, Sasha."

"We're well enough fortified now, Ivan, that we can safely let them back onto Sitka. The next challenge will be making friends with them. Our success here really depends on our making a true peace with the Tlingit."

"Yes. Well, we still have a problem with Katlian. We should have seized him and hanged the bastard."

"We'll never make peace that way, Ivan. Even though they are citizens of Russia, we have to treat these chiefs as if they are the royalty of a foreign nation. And royalty has immunity. That is the only way. Now, regarding the location of their new village, I want it close by, so we can easily keep an eye on them."

That evening, Chiefs Naawushkeitl and Chilkoot returned with some of their people for the potlatch held in an open space in front of the castle's main gate. Neither Katlian or any of his *kwaan* came. There was a roaring fire pit in the center, and around the perimeter the Russians had set up a few tables with an array of food—smoked salmon, cabbage soup, bowls of blueberries, and such, together with stacks of wooden plates. Logs had been arrayed in a circle around the fire for seating, but at a distance from the flames to allow space for dancing between fire and audience. The Russians and Aleut sat on one side of the fire, and the Tlingit on the other.

As soon as everyone was gathered, Baranov got up to speak in both Tlingit and Russian.

"Welcome, Chief Naawushkeitl. Welcome, Chief Chilkoot. And welcome to all our neighbors. Tonight we celebrate a new friendship between our peoples. May we live together always in peace and amity. Would you care to say something, Chiefs?"

Chief Naawushkeitl rose and sang a short song that, to the Russians, sounded like a pleasant chant, and sat down. Baranov motioned to the Russian performers to start.

Five Russians with *balalaikas* began playing and singing. Then some Russians performed *kazatsky* dances interspersed with *chastushka* songs, as the Tlingit sat around the perimeter, watching. While they were performing, the Russians moved all around the open circle surrounding the fire.

After a while, Baranov signaled to his people to sit down, then said to Naawushkeitl, *"I'd like to see your dances and hear your songs."*

The chief nodded and led a man with a flat drum, and a few other Tlingit, to an area just in front of the fire. As soon as the drummer began and set the rhythm, the others—some in painted costumes—sang a chant and did a vigorous jumping dance. It mimicked the actions of wolves, bears, eagles, and other animals, conveying the interdependence of nature and humans.

Several days later, from across a small bay, Katlian glared at the Russian castle, arms crossed, as a new Tlingit village was being built on Sitka Island near the castle. He saw Anna emerge with her children, accompanied by a couple of armed Russian hunters, to visit the village.

Anna was carrying a satchel containing many small leather sacks with seeds for gardening. She led the children to a group of Tlingit women wrapped in blankets, sitting on a log at the edge of the construction and watching its progress. She removed a bag of squash seeds from the satchel, showed it to them, and said in her limited Tlingit, *"I, Anna Baranova. These my children. We have seeds for you. Seeds to grow food. Squash, potatoes, beans."*

She poured a few tan, oval squash seeds from the bag into her hand and showed them to each woman as she repeated, *"Squash."* They looked at her with blank faces. She handed the bag to one of the women, who looked into it and then poured the seeds out on the ground and dropped the bag on top of them. She looked up at Anna with no expression. Anna motioned to her Russian guards to leave and sat on the log with the women.

"Antipatr, Irina, and Samuel," she said in Russian. "Come sit here with me." She started them singing a song she had learned in the Tlingit language and had taught to her children. After a couple of minutes, the Tlingit women got up and walked away. Anna looked at the seeds on the ground with the bag lying on top. Motioning to the children, she rose, and they walked back to the castle, leaving the seeds and bag behind.

Three days later, one of those Tlingit women appeared at the gate of the castle with a blanket draped over her clothes, and said to the guard there, "Anna." The Russian guard looked at her quizzically. Again she said, "Anna."

He understood and turned to call to a man behind him, "Get Baranov's woman."

Anna came to the gate and, in Tlingit, said, *"Hello."*

The woman looked at her for a long moment, reached under her blanket, pulled out the bag of seeds, and, handing it to Anna, said, *"Show me."*

She was K'asasee, Katlian's wife.

Anna taught the Tlingit women how to plant and grow potatoes and beans that they could trade to the Russians for iron. It was a very successful project, and as it progressed, she looked upon it with great satisfaction, because it created a partnership between communities to help keep the peace. Again, she had been right.

Not long after this trading got underway, in the woods overlooking Sitka Sound, Katlian and a thoughtful young warrior were considering the distant fort, where Baranov could be seen standing on a parapet.

"There he is, Ayeidi," Katlian said. *"You speak Russian. Get a job in the fort. Get close to Baranov. Then kill him! Our people's future depends on it. He is well guarded, so it will take time and*

patience to get close without others around. It must look like a Russian did it, so they will not blame us. Like hunting a wolverine. Can you do that?"

The warrior nodded. He was slight of build, but clever.

Two months later, a small supply ship from Okhotsk tied up at the Sitka wharf. When Baranov came down to inspect its cargo, a crewman handed him a cargo manifest and letters. He opened a letter from Kargopol, read it, and sighed, "Matrona has died. Poor woman, I never gave her the life she deserved."

He made his way to the end of the dock and, as was his way when he had received sad news, stared across the sea at the distant horizon.

Anna came onto the wharf and, seeing him, smiled.

He said to her, waving the letter, "Now we can get married in church and go back to Russia—if I can get a replacement. Finally."

"How?" she asked, taken by surprise.

"The Russian wife has died."

He pressed her hand to his arm, and they walked home.

A few weeks later, they sailed to Kodiak, where they were married by Father Herman in the church Baranov had built. The groom wore his formal blue jacket with the Order of St. Anne around his neck. Somewhat bald, he had an ill-fitting brown wig secured to his head with a string tied under his neck.

Anna wore the white deerskin outfit she had at their first wedding, which still fit her perfectly. Antipatr, Irina, Ekaterina, and Samuel stood beside them, and the guests included the portly and aging Chief Grigor and many of Anna's family from both Kodiak Island and Kenai. Ivan Banner and other Russian managers attended as well.

At the conclusion of the service, as they emerged from the church onto its frontage, the bell chimed. Hand in hand, Baranov and Anna, with their children, turned to face the bell tower. She and the children were smiling, but Baranov wore a solemn expression as tears of gladness rolled down his cheeks. Yes, he could finally go back to Russia with Anna and their children, once his replacement arrived. What a glorious day that would be!

Father Herman took Baranov aside for a moment. "I know what you're thinking, Sasha—that now you can take your Alaskan family to Russia. Don't. They will have no immunity to urban diseases to which Natives often succumb."

"I won't take them to any cities, just my home village of Kargopol and the countryside around it. But thank you for the advice. And thank you for our marriage in the church. It gives me great peace and joy."

They sailed back to Sitka.

In the Sitka castle office, Ayeidi handed mail from another newly arrived ship to Baranov and Kuskov. Baranov opened an envelope with a royal seal. A triumphant grin lit his face.

"Thank you, Your Majesty!" he exclaimed.

Three nights later, in the grand parlor of the castle, just over a hundred guests sat before the fireplace. On a signal, a drumroll and bugle fanfare silenced the room. Baranov rose and asked Anna to face him. She was wearing a fine European dress that enhanced her good looks and dignity. But she was completely mystified.

He read aloud the Tsar's decree: "By order of Alexander the First, Tsar of all the Russias, Anna Grigoryevna Baranova is hereby recognized as the Princess of Kenai and accorded all of the royal honors thereunto.'"

Baranov beamed with pride. She was both surprised and perplexed.

"Ladies and gentlemen," he said, "I present Her Highness, Anna, Princess of Kenai!" He bowed toward her and led the fanfare and the audience applause.

"Why does the Tsar do this?" Anna asked him. "He has never seen me. He does not know me. What does he want from me?"

Baranov came closer. The audience went silent. Softly, he explained, "This means that, now, our children can go to Russian schools for nobles."

She was unimpressed. "The idea of royal princess is not from Alaska. This idea should stay in Russia. It will make trouble here. I am who I am."

She turned to the audience. "I am your friend, and you are my friends. That is who I am, and that is who we are. So let us now have this *praznyk* to celebrate our friendship!"

Baranov was stunned. Someone in back started to applaud. It spread until the applause was louder than before, and Baranov joined. Then he said quietly, so only she could hear it, "Yes, my dear. You amaze me again."

As the *praznyk* continued, Baranov stepped out onto a porch for a moment to gaze at the moon. Suddenly, a Russian knife whizzed toward him, just missing his head and slamming into a post next to him. Startled, he reached over and yanked the knife out of the post and peered into the darkness. He could see nothing. Someone was after him again, he realized. But he would not let it spoil Anna's *praznyk*. He returned to the party, where many were dancing to *balalaika* music. He hid the knife up his sleeve until he could slip it behind a cabinet, and then he joined the dancing with Anna.

Ayeidi hid in the shadows outside.

A few days later, Baranov was walking along the rocky shore below the castle, as he often did, when the fog blew in. He was on a small beach between a boat landing and the castle. Ayeidi hid in a crag nearby. Just as Baranov passed him, Ayeidi slipped out and noiselessly followed. Baranov glanced at a calm tidal pool and saw the warrior's reflection, but kept walking.

Then Ayeidi rushed toward him, raising his knife. Baranov wheeled around and, with his cane, knocked the knife from Ayeidi's hand. Baranov threw it in the sea and grappled furiously with the young warrior. He whacked Ayeidi with the cane and got him down on his back, Baranov on top of him, choking him with the cane. As Ayeidi gasped for breath, Baranov let up a little.

"You weren't made to be an assassin, Ayeidi. You think too much. Now go back and tell Katlian that if he wants to kill me, he'll have to do it himself."

CHAPTER 29

ASSASSINS EVERYWHERE

After the castle had been built, a contingent of ex-army soldiers had been sent from Russia, whom Baranov had recruited as military guards to man the guns and parapets of the fort. They had been a troublesome lot. In the dim light of a Sitka evening, in a watchtower at one corner of the castle fort, a changing of the uniformed guard was taking place. Corporal Vasilii Naplavkov was relieving Private Lezchinski when he whispered, "Tonight at ten."

"Right. Will the others be there?"

"Yes."

At ten that night, four members of the guard's unit joined Naplavkov in his quarters. As they slipped in, they sat in chairs around a table, or on a bed, or on a couple of chairs at the perimeter of the room.

"Lock the door, Popov," said Naplavkov.

Popov did so.

Naplavkov then cast a long, hard look at them all and began: "We are the Justice Brotherhood, and we have agreed to a three-point plan to seize justice for ourselves. First, we have tried Baranov in absentia for crimes against mankind, found him guilty, and sentenced him and his family to death. Second, we will carry out this sentence. Third, we will seize the ship *Discovery* and a woman for each of us, provision it, and compel its crew take us to Easter Island, where we will settle.

"Before we proceed to carry out the sentence, we must all sign the charter of our brotherhood. It will be ready on Thursday night, two days from now. Any questions?"

Popov asked, "Who will perform the assassinations?"

"I will kill Baranov," replied Lezchinski.

"Each of the rest of you will be assigned names on Thursday night," said Naplavkov.

"Including the Baranov children?" asked Lezchinski.

"Yes, of course," answered Naplavkov. "His seed must end. Any more questions?"

There were none.

"Good, then," said Naplavkov. "We meet again in two nights."

Baranov was working late in his office on Wednesday night. The candle was guttering at his desk and shadows were dancing on the wall when there was a knock at the door.

"Come in," he said.

Lezchinski and another guard, Sidorov, both off duty and out of uniform, were nervously glancing over their shoulders as they entered.

"What's on your minds, men?" asked Baranov.

"Sir, do you know about the Justice Brotherhood?" asked Lezchinski.

"... The what?"

"Justice Brotherhood," Sidorov repeated. "It used to be called the Order of Yermak, but now it's called the Justice Brotherhood."

"Never heard of it."

Lezchinski explained, "It's some guards, and a few hunters, who have met secretly to try you for crimes. They've found you guilty and have sentenced you to death. The plan is to assassinate you and your family, seize the *Discovery*, and sail it to Easter Island with women to colonize there."

Baranov couldn't believe it. "To assassinate my family? You mean my *children*?"

"Yes, sir," replied Lezchinski.

"And for what crimes?" demanded Baranov. "And who are the leaders of this?"

Sidorov answered, "Well, the crimes are imposing unjust punishments on some guards and providing bad food. . . . The leaders are Naplavkov and Popov."

"This is madness!" declared Baranov. "Naplavkov and Popov? Men I've *trusted*? . . . When do they plan to do this?"

"Tomorrow night," replied Lezchinski.

Baranov ran his tongue over his teeth, saying nothing for a long moment, staring hard at the guard. At last, he whispered, "How do you know about all this?"

"... Well, we're members of the group," admitted Lezchinski. "Or at least Naplavkov thinks we are. At first we were part of it just because we were all friends. But now it's going too far. It must be stopped."

"Yes, it must!" Baranov agreed. "Are you willing to help stop it?"

Both the guards said, "Yes."

"Mm. What exactly *is* the plan for tomorrow night?"

"We're to meet at 10:00 p.m., sir, in Naplavkov's quarters," said Lezchinski. "Then we are all to sign a charter binding each of us to the program of the Brotherhood. After that, Naplavkov will give us our assassination orders."

"Assassination orders! My God!" Baranov shook his head. "Well, here's what I want you to do: At the beginning of the meeting, pass around a jug of vodka to loosen them up. Then, after everyone has signed the charter, open a window and sing the Kretchma song. That will be my signal to come in and take them prisoner. We'll tie you up too, then let you loose later."

"All right," said Lezchinski.

Baranov shook his head again. "Justice Brotherhood."

The next night, in the foyer of Baranov's office, eight loyal and armed Russian hunters were gathered. Baranov had just briefed them.

"All right, you know what to do," he concluded. "Now we'll just listen for the signal." He opened the door so they could listen. Not long after, from a neighboring building, they heard Lezchinski singing:

And there is singing, and there is dancing,

and the Russian vodka is all right.

Come to the Kretchma, that's where you'll ketchma,

Drinking vodka every night.

Baranov murmured, "Let's go!"

The nine men charged out onto the boardwalk between the buildings. One of the hunters hammered open the locked door to Naplavkov's room with the butt of his rifle. They found Naplavkov with a cutlass in one hand and a pistol in the other. There was a very tense moment before he surrendered his weapons in the face of six rifles pointed at him. Popov quickly tore up the charter with everyone's signatures, dropping the pieces on the floor. "Seize them," Baranov said flatly.

With the conspirators' hands tied behind their backs and all pieces of their torn charter retrieved, Baranov stared at Corporal Naplavkov. Then Baranov declared, "In the name of His Majesty, Tsar Alexander, I arrest you for treason against the state and conspiracy to commit murder. You will be put in irons, locked up, and shipped to Siberia for trial." As the arrested were led out, Lezchinski and Sidorov were held back, untied, and released.

Baranov said to them, "Thank you for your help. Your loyalty will not be forgotten."

But his confidence and sense of trust in his men, a thing he had known his whole time in Alaska, had been badly shaken. Katlian was one thing, but his own men!

The next day, Baranov and Anna walked into the parlor. He went, as was his wont, to the window overlooking the harbor, and she sat down and picked up some knitting.

He broke the ensuing quiet when he said, "*Yermak* will take you and the children back to Kodiak the day after tomorrow."

"Why?"

He shook his head. "It's not safe here for you any longer. Last night we stopped a mutiny." After a pause, he turned to her, the pearly light throwing half his face into shadow, and said, "I'm going to miss you and the children."

". . . When will you come to Kodiak?"

"I don't know. As soon as I can. Come here, my princess—not the Tsar's or anyone else's kind of princess. Just *my* princess."

She came, and his embrace told her he didn't want to let her go.

It took two years for him to feel confident enough again of their security to bring Anna and the children back to Sitka.

It was the spring of 1812 before they returned. Antipatr and Samuel had grown a lot. They were well into their teenage years, which Irina was just entering—and looking like a copy of her mother. Anna seemed more concerned than ever about where the children were going with their lives. She tried to prepare them with little lessons when they least expected them.

One day they were helping her weed a small garden on high ground overlooking the Tlingit village just one third of a mile from the castle when another lesson popped up.

"Look at the people down there in the village," Anna said. "Each one wants something. So learn what people want, then use the Friendship Rule to make them your friends."

The children straightened up and looked at the village below.

". . . The Friendship Rule?" asked Antipatr. Anna nodded and continued weeding. "Do unto others as *they* would have you do unto them," she continued.

"Like the Golden Rule?" asked Samuel.

"Different. The Golden Rule says treat others as if they want the same things we do. But that's often not true—they *don't* want the same things we do. The Friendship Rule says treat others by what *they* want, not by what *we* want."

"So this rule helps make friends?" Irina asked.

"Yes! And remember, something everyone wants is respect. Give everyone respect, and they will respect you, too. So: Do unto others as *they* would have you do unto them. Then even enemies can become friends and live in peace under the same big sky."

"I like to make friends," Irina immediately replied.

"Let's all say the Friendship Rule," said Anna. They all repeated it, "Do unto others as *they* would have you do unto them."

"Now, let's practice asking friendly questions to learn what others want."

Katlian, K'asasee, and their three children were sitting at a table in their house. Dinner—including fresh salmon he had caught, and potatoes, beans, and carrots K'asasee had grown in her garden—had been served on wooden plates. He stared at the vegetables, stirring them with his knife, thinking about what they meant: growing and eating the Russians' food. She watched his anger slowly rising and said, "We are back in Sitka, my family's home. And we are eating the white man's food. But we grew that food ourselves, and we are at peace. Is that so terrible?"

He realized he had no answer, so he got up and left. He had to think about it.

***

In St. Petersburg in March 1815, a commercial building downtown housed the home office of the Russian-America Company. It was a busy place, with men coming and going. Seven of them passed through a door into a large room and took seats around a heavy oak table. The chairman, Mikhail Buldakov, struck his gavel and said, "The Board of Directors of the Russian-America Company will come to order. First, we'll hear the complaints about Chief Manager Baranov. Andrei Mikoyan, tell us."

Mikoyan began, "We've had many reports from navy men and priests of corruption by Baranov in Alaska. And these aren't just gripes from men disciplined by Baranov and therefore seeking revenge. Some say he steals furs from the company to trade secretly for his own benefit."

"What proof is there?" Buldakov demanded.

"He's too clever to leave evidence," answered Sergei Antonov.

"So it's all hearsay."

Antonov insisted, "We need someone to do an investigation over there."

Mikoyan spoke up again. "Baranov should have been replaced long ago."

Buldakov, known for his tendency to see even the most serious of topics in a humorous vein, needled the man. "You volunteering? If you are, then I'm sure we'll all be happy to give you that death sentence right now." Laughter broke out among most of the board members.

***

Late that spring, in the woods near Sitka Harbor, an American, Wilson Hunt, and two of his men from the Yankee sailing ship *Pedlar*, met secretly with Katlian and two of his warriors. The Americans traded two big cans of gunpowder to Katlian for otter pelt bundles. Hunt worked for the American John Astor but had done some contract work for Baranov. He and his men took the pelts to the harbor shore. Katlian opened a can and rubbed some of the black powder between his fingers. *"Good American gunpowder!"* he said enthusiastically to his warriors.

At the harbor, Hunt's group loaded the bales of furs into a rowboat and started rowing toward their ship. Baranov, sitting on a castle balcony with Stefanov, had his eyes on the harbor, where several sailing ships were anchored. Hunt's rowboat moved in the background, unnoticed. "Everyone's waiting," Baranov said to his companion. "Waiting for pelts from us to buy their cargos of supplies. The *Suvarov* should be back soon from the Pribilofs with a full load of sealskins, so we can start to trade and then sell to Canton."

Stefanov pointed across the harbor and announced, "There it is now!"

The frigate *Suvarov* entered the harbor and began to furl its sails.

On the deck of the frigate, the skipper, Lieutenant Lazarev, and his first officer, Lieutenant Virvo, were supervising. Lazarev put a telescope to his eye and looked toward Baranov's Castle.

"Well, there he is," he said to Virvo. "The foolish old man, already salivating over our load of sealskins. But he'll get none of them."

"What will be done with them?" asked Virvo.

"I'll deliver them right to St. Petersburg. Just watch. *That* should create a stir!"

On the castle balcony, Kuskov and an Aleut hunter joined Baranov and Stefanov.

"Sasha, this man saw something you should know," said Kuskov.

"I hunt birds' eggs in the forest each morning and must not be seen by the birds. So I am well hidden."

"Yes?" said Baranov.

"I sometimes see Katlian in the forest, watching Russians. He does not see me."

Baranov looked at the Aleut with penetrating interest as it dawned on him what the man was leading up to.

"I could kill him for you," said the hunter.

Immediately, Baranov said, "No!" He turned to face the hunter. "Don't even think of it. Ever."

The hunter blinked, glanced at Kuskov, and continued, "This morning I saw men from *Pedlar* trade with Katlian."

". . . What did they trade?" asked Baranov.

"About a hundred otter pelts from the Tlingit for two cans gunpowder."

Baranov pounded the tip of his cane on a floorboard. The leg that he had broken so long ago, and that hadn't healed properly, was bothering him again. "Gunpowder! They broke my *law!*"

He glanced quickly at the anchored ships below, then, leaning on his cane, got up and hobbled off toward the stairs leading down. Even with the cane, he was remarkably agile for his age. He quickly gathered a unit of armed guards and led them to the shoreline to launch *nigilaxes* for *Pedlar*. They pulled alongside *Pedlar* and climbed aboard.

On deck, they confronted the unarmed *Pedlar* crew, who glared at them from across the deck. Baranov had just climbed aboard when Hunt came out of his cabin with a pistol barely concealed under his shirt. He approached Baranov, and just as he pulled the pistol from under his shirt, Baranov swung his cane, knocking the pistol from Hunt's hand. A Baranov soldier grabbed it. Hunt ran across the deck and over the side, his men following. They climbed into a launch and rowed quickly to the nearby American ship, *Franklin*.

"After them!" Baranov commanded.

He and his men went over the side into the *nigilaxes* to pursue. They had soon boarded *Franklin*, whose entire crew was armed and positioned on deck and in the rigging, ready for battle. The boat's skipper, Captain MacLean, challenged Baranov. "What are you doing on my ship?"

"Hunt is a fugitive from the law," Baranov answered.

"What law?"

"Our law against trading gunpowder to Natives. And Russians have exclusive rights to trade for furs here. Turn him over."

MacLean was not about to hand over an American. "On this ship, he stands on American territory under our protection."

Baranov coolly replied, "Then your ship cannot leave port or move without my permission, or I'll blast it out of the water with my guns from the castle." He turned with his men and left the ship.

Soon after, Hunt emerged from where he had been hiding below and handed an envelope to a sailor. "Take this to Lazarev, captain of the Russian ship *Suvarov*, and I'll pay you five dollars American."

When the sailor came aboard *Suvarov*, he handed the envelope to Lieutenant Lazarev, who read it immediately. In amazement, Lazarev said to himself, "What incredible evidence! Baranov will hang for this."

He put the paper back in the envelope and pocketed it.

Early the next morning, as Baranov, in pajamas, was pouring a cup of tea in the castle kitchen, an Aleut hunter came running in, excited.

"*Suvarov* pull anchor at night. Go out with tide."

Baranov exclaimed, "*Suvarov?* I've given no authorization for it to leave! It still has my furs from the Pribilofs!"

He grabbed his cane and hobbled out onto the balcony to see. "Tell the commander of the guard to get every soldier and hunter down to the beach with muskets *right now!*"

The Aleut ran to the guardhouse. A loud alarm bell rang.

Baranov seethed, "That bastard!"

Still in his nightclothes, with his cane, he made his way to the beach and a line of *bidarkas* as his men came running with muskets. At his exasperated direction, pointing at the escaping ship with his cane, they climbed into the boats and took off after *Suvarov.*

Baranov limped along on the sand. "After it!" Baranov cried. "Don't let it get away!"

His men paddled off as fast as they could on the fool's errand, ever loyal to their revered master. When the *bidarkas* were about a hundred yards from shore, *Suvarov*'s sails filled with wind, and it quickly pulled away.

Captain MacLean of *Franklin,* seeing that the big guns of the castle were now temporarily unmanned, saw the chance for his ship to escape with Hunt and took it.

An Aleut aide trudged over to Baranov. "We did what we could. They got away too fast."

Baranov turned to him. "Well, I don't care about *Franklin,* but *Suvarov*—that hurts. After the glory of helping defeat Napoleon, naval officers look down on me and the Alaskan colonies as insignificant and comical. They feel the navy should run Alaska."

"Why?" asked the Aleut.

"As I grow old, their disdain for me makes them want a naval officer to replace me. In fact, so great is their hatred of me, they will stoop to lies to ruin me. And now they even steal our company's furs."

The Aleut, quite puzzled, studied Baranov, turned, and watched the *Suvarov* sail toward the Pacific horizon. Baranov hobbled back to the castle.

CHAPTER 30

ONE PRAZNYK TOO MANY

It never took much of an excuse for Baranov to have a *praznyk*. One winter night at the castle, one such example of that Baranov institution was in progress. Raucous Russian hunters danced with Native women. Baranov was very drunk, as usual. Two tipsy Native girls fawned over him. He soon led them into the hallway, not seeing Anna down the hall. She froze at the sight of a stumbling Baranov leading the giggling women into a guest bedroom, and leaving the door ajar.

"Now, my beauties, get my boots off," she heard him say, followed by more giggling from the women and laughs from him.

Disgusted and humiliated, she dashed upstairs and packed a duffel. She picked up her jade earrings, a wedding gift from Baranov, wrote a note to Irina, and left it next to the sleeping girl. She went downstairs to his office, dropped the earrings on his desk, and left for the Native village below.

Near noon the next day, a very hung-over Baranov entered the kitchen and found the children eating lunch. Sullen, they looked fearfully at him.

"Where is your mother?"

The children glanced again and turned away.

"I said, where is your *mother? Answer* me!"

"She's gone, Papa," Irina said. "She left me a note that something very bad happened last night, so she could not stay here."

". . . Where did she go?"

Antipatr replied, "To the village."

"To the *village?*" stormed Baranov. "*Where* in the village?"

"I don't know," said Irina. "But when she finds a place, she'll come back to get us. . . . What happened last night, Papa?"

Calmly he said, "We had a *praznyk*. That's what happened."

When he went to his office to ponder the mess, he saw the earrings, erupted in a rage, and hurled them at the wall. They fell to the floor, and he rushed over to stomp on them—but stopped himself, picked them up, and put them in his pocket.

Anna had meanwhile found an abandoned hut in the village and moved in. She made her way to the trading post to buy some food. A handsome Kenaitze her age, named Magatoi, came up to her.

"You are Baranov's woman," he said.

She ignored him, but he followed her, intrigued by her good looks and situation. As she bought things at the trading post, he picked them up and carried them for her, and followed her through shallow snow to her hut. She made him hand over the goods, then waved him off, shutting the flimsy hut door.

That evening, she made a fire in the hut fireplace and sat in front of it, staring at the flames. Tears began to stream down her face, upon which her expression gradually flowed from despair to anger. Baranov's infidelity gnawed at the depths of her being, making her question the value of herself and her beliefs. Her world was in turmoil, and she was shaken to her core.

Magatoi returned and knocked on her door. At first she ignored him, but he persisted. In that vulnerable moment, something began to crack within her, and she let him in. She turned away to wipe her tears. He wasted no time in making advances. In an uncharacteristically perverse moment, she played along with him. But when he put his hands on her breasts, she turned and pulled away. *"No!"* she cried. Deeply hurt though she was, she could not betray her children. She could not betray herself.

He decided to slow down—to seduce her gradually.

Baranov had entered the village, looking for Anna. Someone pointed out her hut, and he knocked on the door.

"Anna! Anna, it's me."

He entered to find a shirtless Magatoi facing her. Enraged, Baranov rushed to the fireplace, grabbed a burning stick, and whacked him with it, chasing him out and, from the doorway, yelling after the fleeing man, "I'm not done with you, Magatoi! And there's nowhere you can hide!" Magatoi pulled his shirt and jacket back on as he ran away through the snow.

Then Baranov turned to face Anna.

"Get back to our children, where you belong," he demanded. "Be home soon, or I'll send guards to get you."

"You wouldn't be that foolish," she replied, "unless you were drunk."

He hissed, "Look at yourself here and see who's being foolish."

"If not for you, I wouldn't be here," she replied coolly, without yielding her dignity for even a moment.

Baranov headed back to the castle.

A month before, the Russian frigate *Neva*, traveling from Okhotsk to Sitka, had been heading south through heavy seas paralleling the coast of southeast Alaska about eight miles from shore. It had sailed 3,800 miles through treacherous winter seas, and that afternoon it was less than fifty miles from Sitka. Its passengers were eagerly anticipating their arrival the next day. There was a low, partly overcast sky with a sunset glow on the horizon.

After a late afternoon dinner, passengers sat around the long table of the dining area, some drinking water from mugs. There was a Russian woman with an eleven-year-old son on their way to reunite with her navigator husband, the boy's father. There were two *promyshleniks* too, and Collegiate Councilor Tertii Bornovolokov, the new Chief Manager for the Russian-American Company—Baranov's long-awaited replacement. Forty-nine years old and of stout build, he was reading a book in English about Captain James Cook's discoveries.

"Well, Mr. Bornovolokov," said Mrs. Nerodova. "Soon you will take over from the famous Mr. Baranov. Are you eager to meet him?"

"Yes, I am," he replied. "His work here has been incredible. I hope I can achieve even a fraction of what Baranov has."

At night in the Gulf of Alaska by Cape Edgecumbe, the *Neva* tacked back and forth in heavy seas near the entrance to Sitka Sound, awaiting dawn to enter it. Passengers slept in their bunks as surf crashed on the rocks of the Edgecumbe Promontory, toward which a heavy gust was pushing it yard by yard. The helmsman tried to turn the ship away to seaward—to no avail.

Suddenly there was no more space between the two, and the ship was hurled onto the rocks, passengers thrown out of their bunks. Chaos reigned on deck as sailors tried to cut loose two lifeboats. Waves crashed over the deck and swept people overboard, where they were swallowed up by the dark night sea. Bornovolokov came out on deck with a stunned expression and was immediately hit by a wave that swept him over the side into the cold, churning water. He was never seen again.

Of the original seventy-five souls on board, only twenty-eight made it to shore, where two of them died. From the wreckage swept ashore, they made a crude shelter and somehow survived for a month until Tlingits discovered them. They were loaded into a Tlingit sea canoe and taken to the beach near Sitka Castle, sparking a commotion on shore. The big canoe contained twenty-six freezing, worn-out survivors of the wreck. Baranov came over with his cane as survivors were helped to shore by men from the castle. "What is this?" he demanded.

A *Neva* sailor replied, "We came 3,800 miles from Okhotsk on *Neva*, and then, just twenty miles from here, we hit the rocks during the night over by Cape Edgecumbe. Most drowned, including the captain, Lieutenant Kalinin, and the new governor, Bornovolokov."

"Another one dead!" Baranov moaned. "I'm stuck here."

The survivors were helped to the fort, and as the Tlingit rescuers climbed back into their canoe, Baranov walked over to them and, in appreciation, simply said, *"Gunalchéesh."* The canoe left, and Baranov was left alone to stare out to sea into the fog rolling by and contemplate Anna and Magatoi.

Later that day, Anna still hadn't returned. Baranov ordered

guards to search for Magatoi, who was found hiding in a small boat. He immediately ordered him brought to the whipping post outside the castle, where the man's shirt was ripped off and he was tied to the post. Snow had been cleared from a wide area near the post. When Baranov appeared in his heavy fur coat, Kuskov handed him the whip. It reminded Kuskov of the whipping of Chief Chokta—there was even an Aleut standing to the left of Baranov.

"You know your crime, Magatoi," said Baranov, "and now your punishment: eight lashes."

He set down his cane and uncoiled the whip.

But then he heard the words of Kuponek. . .

"Baranov, *no*."

Startled, Baranov turned to the Aleut on his left. For just an instant, he looked like Kuponek. But Baranov saw that he was not. "Did you say something?" he asked.

"No," the Aleut replied.

Baranov looked back at Magatoi and slapped the tip of the whip on the ground.

Again he heard Kuponek's insistent words. . .

"Baranov, *no*."

"Dammit, Kuponek, I hear you!" said Baranov. He threw the whip on the ground, picked up his cane, and turned back to the castle, calling over his shoulder in a barely audible voice, "Let him go."

Baranov's face was stern and hard as he walked with a slight limp up the trail, yet a single tear of remorse rolled down his cheek.

Halfway there, he found Anna in her tan seal parka where she had stood watching events unfold. He stopped. They stared at each other for a moment.

"I'm sorry for what I did," he said at last. "I let vodka set loose the worst in me. I am *so* sorry. I never meant to hurt you. Now I feel great pain because I did." His gaze fell to the ground. "I'm ashamed that I could carelessly hurt the one I love so dearly. I do not deserve to be forgiven." Another tear rolled down his face. "You can go back to your people now, Anooka."

She thought for a moment about how best to answer him. And then she simply replied, "My name is Anna."

She knew then that she could not escape from her love for him, nor did she want to.

He looked up again, into her calm, strong, yet gentle face.

"Anna. Yes, *Anna!* I *will* get control of it. I *will!*"

From his pocket, he took the jade earrings and put them in her hand. Then, he repeated what she had said to him at Denali: "We are part of each other."

"Yes," she said.

As she put the earrings on, warmth returned to her gaze. She looked him in the eye. Hesitantly, they reached for each other to embrace, then walked up the trail together, through the snow.

That was the day that the great tree that had grown in Baranov's soul, which came from the seed of humility that Kuponek saw planted by the Chief Chokta incident, gave forth the fruit that saved him and his family.

CHAPTER 31

SKIPPING STONES ACROSS CALM WATERS

The next day, Baranov met Ivan Kuskov in his office and said, "Promise me one thing. When I get drunk, make sure a couple of men stay sober to keep me away from women and out of trouble."

Kuskov laughed. "Who do you think would accept such a thankless task?"

"Oh I'll make it worth their while! I have a weakness and can no longer pay its awful price. But I *can* pay for a couple of men to control me."

"Maybe a couple of Tlingit *bucks* would like the job," Kuskov offered with a touch of irony.

"Hmph!"

Kuskov took a deep breath and said softly, "Another solution, Sasha—why not just stop drinking vodka?"

Rage flashed across Baranov's face as he slammed his palm on the table. Then he looked out the window and his rage cooled fast as his rational self briefly considered the suggestion.

"Sasha," said Kuskov, changing the subject, "we have more ships than ever, and our supply warehouse is full."

"Temporary," answered Baranov. "The recent war between England and America was a stroke of luck. The Americans sold cargoes and ships to us cheap to avoid capture by the British. But we have to look ahead."

"Ahead to what?"

"Our biggest problem has always been getting enough food for our people. Farming here is poor. California is much better—a long growing season and good soil. And it's just a third the distance to Okhotsk, by a sea that isn't such a boat killer."

They examined a map of the coast of California.

"You want to put a colony there?" Kuskov asked. "Won't the Spanish challenge us?"

"They're weak in upper California. We'll buy land from the Indians fifty miles above San Francisco Bay, and build a fort there fast. The Spaniards will grumble but do nothing, because that bureaucracy of theirs takes too long to decide anything."

"Very risky," Kuskov objected. "Who will lead this suicide mission?"

"The only man I know who can do it. . . . You, Ivan."

"Oh, not again!"

"But Ivan, you have such an excellent record on dangerous and difficult missions—you *always succeed!*"

***

That fall, Kuskov—tall and thin—stood in front of Fort Ross, California, looking out to sea with his Native wife, and then faced inland. He was wearing the smock of a Russian country gentleman, like those he knew back home. The fort had fields of vegetables and corn facing the southern sun, and a herd of cattle off to the north.

One of his farmers came down to say, "Our first shipment for Alaska is ready."

Kuskov grinned with great satisfaction. "Good, good. Baranov will be very pleased."

Indeed, Baranov was mightily pleased when the shipment sailed into Sitka harbor and reached New Archangel. He came down to the beach while the farm goods were being lightered ashore. There they were, the answer to his prayer for Kuskov's success: hundreds of bags of wheat, potatoes, beans, and barley; piled crates of salt pork and smoked beef.

As they were being loaded onto goat-drawn carts, he said to an Aleut working on the shipment, "What a wonderful sight! Now we have a reliable food source after the American supplies run out. Solves one of our biggest problems."

The Aleut nodded and kept working.

A visiting Russian ship had left behind its ship's surgeon so he could help tend to some injured hunters. Dr. Georg Schaffer, a well educated Bavarian, soon became a frequent dinner companion at the Baranov family table in the castle. After dinner, with a roaring fire in the parlor fireplace, the two men often sat sipping vodka and chatting.

Baranov had a reason for getting to know Dr. Schaffer better. He needed a man for a mission to Hawaii, but his usual deputies—Kuskov and Banner—were occupied at Kodiak and Fort Ross. Nevertheless, he had to get a way station built in Hawaii to service his ships sailing to China, because changes in Chinese trade rules had enabled his agents to trade directly with the them at Canton. But getting King Kamehameha's permission for a way station would be difficult, because the king was loath to allow foreign facilities on his soil. Baranov would have to lean heavily on his long-distance friendship with the king to get permission. This would require delicate negotiations by an able and sensitive emissary. Could Schaffer be the man?

Baranov studied Schaffer during several conversations over several days, when Baranov explained the Hawaiian mission he had in mind. The man was intelligent and knowledgeable; he seemed to have a good grasp of what was needed and was eager to take on the assignment. But Baranov held back for a while, unsure of his capabilities. Finally, he asked himself, "What other choice do I have?" There was none, so he sent Schaffer to Hawaii with a retinue and funds to get the job done.

The Baranov children had been assigned a job of gathering food from the bay for the Russians at Sitka. Mostly adolescents by then, they were quite capable at the task. They finished digging clams from tidal flats and carried their full bags toward shore. It was the spring of another new year, and after being indoors for most of the winter, they were glad to be outside enjoying the shore they loved so much.

Irina said to her brothers and younger sister, "You know what the Tlingit say about this? 'When the tide is out, your table is set.'"

"True!" Antipatr agreed. "Look, the water is so smooth in this cove, we can skip stones. Let's see who can skip the farthest!"

Samuel immediately chimed in, "I can!"

They started doing so. Soon, more stones than theirs were

skipping across the water. They looked up to see four Tlingit youngsters their age joining in. The young Tlingits were strangers to them, but the stone skipping was an icebreaker. One Tlingit was a girl Irina's age. Irina smiled, pointed to herself, and spoke to her in Tlingit.

"Hello. My name is Irina."

"I am Lataka."

Lataka seemed friendly, and so on impulse Irina said, *"Want to play tag? I'll be 'it.'"*

Lataka smiled with delight.

"Yes!" she said with enthusiasm as she turned and ran away, calling out, *"Tag! Tag! Tag! Irina is it!"*

They all enjoyed a spirited game of tag, giggling, while tipping over empty baskets the Tlingit youngsters had brought for clams. Then Lataka's brother Yanledi cried out, *"Look, look! The tide is coming in. We didn't get clams for dinner! We will be punished."*

The kids all stopped playing and stared at the fast-rising tide. Lataka started to whimper.

"Don't worry!" Irina told her. *"You can have* my *clams."*

Irina picked up her bag of clams and poured them into Lataka's basket. Irina's brothers and Ekaterina gave their clams to the Tlingit boys.

"Gunalchéesh, Irina," Lataka said in gratitude. Then she told Irina something that shocked her. *"We had a hard winter with almost nothing to eat. My father says your people took all the food from the bay and left nothing for us. Many times I went to bed hungry and could not sleep."*

Irina stared at her, letting the accusation sink in. Then, her heart spoke in the way that had been so carefully nurtured by her mother. *"We had plenty to eat. We should have shared with you! I will talk to my father and tell him he must never let your people go hungry. In this big bay there is enough food for all of us. We are friends, and friends must take care of each other."*

She took the other girl's hand, and they led the boys up the trail away from the shore as the tide rolled in.

In the nearby forest, hidden behind branches, three Tlingit men armed with muskets watched them, including Chief Katlian. He said to one of his warriors, *"Did you see that? Baranov's girl gave her clams to Lataka, who had none, so that she wouldn't get punished."*

"Yes, so what?"

"Unusual."

Antipatr and Irina paid a visit to the castle office. Baranov was standing by his desk looking over some paperwork. His stance, looking down, emphasized the fact that through the years he had become almost completely bald on top of his head. The teens ambled around restlessly, handling things and then putting them down.

"Papa," Antipatr said, "I want to go to sea on a ship! You have so many ships. Surely some captain can put me on his crew."

"Maybe. See which ship sails next."

Antipatr bounded out the door heading for the wharf.

"Papa," said Irina, "I'm glad we'll share our food with Lataka's people next winter."

"Well, you were very persuasive when you brought this up. How old are you?" Baranov asked.

"Thirteen."

"It's good you understand the Natives—what they need and want. Very perceptive for your age. I must see that your mind is not wasted."

In a few months, he imported two tutors for his children through his American contacts. One was a young man to teach science, mathematics, and history. Another was a German woman who spoke many languages and taught piano. They quickly got the curious and intelligent youngsters working toward a serviceable education. Baranov often visited their classes and was pleased with their progress, especially Irina's French and piano lessons. Eventually, she learned four languages. All of the children read many of Baranov's treasured books.

At midday, a merchant ship from Hawaii arrived at Sitka with a report from a Russian who had gone with Dr. Schaffer to Hawaii. As Baranov sat at his desk in his castle office and read the report, his expression became grim. Schaffer had sided with a Hawaiian chief on Kauai who was an enemy of King Kamehameha. He had virtually destroyed Baranov's good relations with the king, and eventually Schaffer had been forced to leave Hawaii for China. Baranov crumpled up the report and threw it into a wastebasket, then stared out the window with a dark frown. A disaster. All the funds he had given Schaffer for building the way station, lost. He had thought he was through with disasters.

***

Another Board of Directors meeting at the Russian-America Company home office in St. Petersburg had been in session for over an hour. At the head of the oak table, next to Chairman

Buldakov, sat the naval Captain Lieutenant Leontii Hagemeister.

"Gentlemen," said Buldakov, "we've agreed that Captain Lieutenant Hagemeister will go to Alaska with three special powers. First, due to Baranov's advanced age, Captain Hagemeister is empowered to take over as chief manager of Alaska. Second, he is to investigate the charges against Baranov and take proper action. And third, he may appoint another naval officer to the post when he decides to retire from it. Henceforth, the navy shall run Alaska for us, because they have the frigates to protect it. Anything else?"

Chernetsky spoke up. "Certainly all the complaints against Baranov are just the blubbering of incompetent enemies."

"What about the Hawaiian escapade? That was an expensive loss!" said Mikoyan.

"One mistake. And it was a trifle among all the profits he's earned for us over the years. He shouldn't have trusted that politically inexperienced Dr. Schaffer to build a transit station in Kauai. That's all. But there can be no question, we owe Baranov a pension for all his years of service."

Buldakov, ever the miser, replied, "We'll decide that after the investigation. By then, he'll probably be dead of old age, and then we won't have to pay anything. Meeting adjourned."

Chernetsky said to Mikoyan, "What does the navy know about business? Nothing! Baranov is a businessman who knows how to make a profit. Now you can watch our profits sink like ballast thrown overboard while the Imperial Navy sails gloriously on at our expense."

CHAPTER 32

IRINA AND KATLIAN

On a splendid day in July 1816, the frigate *Suvarov* sailed into the port of Kronstadt, Russia near St. Petersburg and berthed next to another frigate, *Kutusov*. Lieutenant Lazarev came down *Suvarov's* gangplank and was greeted by *Kutusov's* skipper, Captain Lieutenant Hagemeister.

"Welcome home, Mikhail!"

"Thank you, Leontii! Great to be home!"

"I'm off for Alaska on *Kutusov* in short order," said Hagemeister. "I'm going to investigate complaints about Baranov and take over as governor there."

"Well, Captain Hagemeister," said Lazarev, now speaking officially, "here's something your investigation needs."

He took Hunt's envelope from his pocket and handed it to him. "Read this. Evidence to hang the man!"

Hagemeister pulled out the document. As he read, he became grave. "My God! My God! I thought this impossible: a bad end for Baranov."

He slipped the damning evidence back into the envelope and put it in his pocket.

***

Antipatr had learned to sail, and on a rare rainless day in early July 1817, he took the whole family for an outing on a small sloop in Sitka Sound. He was at the tiller, Samuel was manning the sails, and Anna and Irina were sitting on one deck bench while Baranov and Ekaterina sat on another. Baranov had coached the boys on some of the finer points of sailing. He was quite pleased with himself and his family. As they sailed out to the middle of the Sound, he said, "Irina, I hear your studies are going well. I'm glad."

"I enjoy languages, though English is hard because some of the grammar makes no sense. That's because it's part Anglo-Saxon and part Latin, which sometimes mix like oil and water. A real hodgepodge."

"I know," Baranov said. "English is a crazy language. Too many words. But I like what Shakespeare does with it. Have you read any of his plays?"

"Oh, yes. I just read *Romeo and Juliet*. Such a sad story."

"The Montagues versus the Capulets."

"Like the Russians and the Tlingit, don't you think?" she asked lightly.

"Are you trying to tell me something, dear?" Baranov replied. "Have you been seeing a Tlingit buck behind my back?"

That amused her. "Oh, yes, Papa. And his name is Romeo-ukatuk, and he serenades me every night under my balcony. But alas, there are no vines for him to climb up the wall."

"Good thing!"

"But I really do have many friends among the Tlingit, like Lataka and her brother."

"I know," Baranov answered. "And I'm glad about your Tlingit friendships. That's the future of our two peoples. But be very careful. Always have a double guard with you when you go to their villages. There are still some Tlingit who hate us."

"Oh, I'm not afraid, Papa."

Anna spoke up. "She takes after you, my *toyon*—afraid of nothing. And smart and stubborn, too."

"I know. But she takes after you also, Anna. She has your heart. I have high hopes for you, Irina, and the rest of you, too. Now that I'm getting old, what I have not accomplished will be up to you."

Just then, Antipatr started giving orders. "Ready to jibe?"

Samuel answered, "Ready."

"Jibe ho!" responded Antipatr.

Samuel moved sails accordingly, and the boat jibed on its downwind run.

As they returned to their mooring, Chief Katlian and some of his warriors were nearby, spying on them and other Russians through the foliage of the forest.

He said to them, *"As I have said before, again and again, the Russians must go, or we have no future."*

One warrior asked, *"But how? They have too many guns."*

Katlian replied, *"There is a way where guns don't matter. Where a single shot won't need to be fired."*

"How is that possible?"

"Baranov's children are often careless outside the fort. I will capture them and tell Baranov I will kill them unless the Russians leave. And I will *kill them if the Russians don't leave!"* After an

angry pause, he calmly added, *"He will get his children back only as the last Russians out of here on the last boat."*

Later that summer, in the grand parlor of the castle, Baranov held a reception party for the officers of the newly arrived Russian frigate *Borodin,* skippered by Lieutenant Ponafadin. The ship's thirty-year-old first mate, Lieutenant Semyon Yanovski, was among them. They all sat facing the piano to hear a recital by Irina, then sixteen. She entered from a side door, bowed to them, and sat at the piano in a French evening gown. She was elegant and breathtaking: Caucasian features with Native accents gave her an astonishing beauty, enhanced by her graceful carriage.

Baranov announced, "Gentlemen, Irina will now play for you the Scarlatti 'Sonata in G minor.'"

Irina flashed a disarming smile and began. Yanovski was instantly captivated. She played with great energy and grace, and at the conclusion received enthusiastic applause. Yanovski couldn't help but jump up and call out, *"Encore! Encore!"*

Graciously, she replied, "Thank you, gentlemen. Now, from Haydn's 'Piano Sonata Number 54 in G.'"

She played, again to great applause. Then she rose and shook hands with all the ship's officers. Yanovski made sure he was last in line, so he could engage her in conversation.

"Semyon Yanovski, at your service," he said. "Your music lifted me to the heavens!"

She smiled at him. "Thank you, Lieutenant. I hope you'll enjoy your stay here at Sitka. Where in Russia are you from?"

"Near St. Petersburg," he replied.

"St. Petersburg, the city of so many palaces," she responded. "Maybe someday I'll see it."

Feeling giddy and impetuous, he said, "Though I can't take you to see a palace now, may I take you on a tour of the harbor tomorrow in our launch? I'd be greatly honored if you accept."

She was quite amused. "You've only been here a day, and already you're giving tours of the harbor? I should come just to keep you from getting lost—or worse, captured by the Tlingit."

Yanovski, dumfounded, blubbered, "Well, I..."

"I'd be *delighted*, Lieutenant," she said quickly. "I'll bring a picnic. Father will insist upon a chaperone, my brother."

"Oh, include him, of course!" Yanovski instantly agreed, delighted that she had accepted.

The next day was a very rare sunny one for Sitka. Yanovski sat with Irina in one of his ship's launches as Antipatr rowed them toward a cove a mile from the castle. They had brought two muskets along for protection, which were leaning against a rear seat. They beached the boat near a meadow. She led the lieutenant to the middle of the clearing and lay out a picnic blanket. He was so intent on her that he left his musket behind. Antipatr stayed by the boat, skipping stones across the cove.

The two sat on the blanket for lunch, engaged in animated banter. But in the forest just uphill from them, four hidden Tlingit were watching. One was Chief Katlian, the other three warriors armed with bows and arrows.

He quietly said in Tlingit, *"If they resist, we kill them."*

They set arrows in the bowstrings.

Irina sensed something, looked up, and saw them. Instead of being startled and afraid, she smiled and waved to the Tlingit, inviting them to join the picnic.

Yanovski turned and was surprised to see them approaching. Irina put her hand on his arm to reassure him. She said in Tlingit, still smiling, *"Hello, Chief Katlian. I'm glad to see you on this beautiful day."*

The chief approached with a stern demeanor, followed by the edgy warriors eying Yanovski and Antipatr as warily as they were watching them. Antipatr, at the boat, evaluated his options.

Katlian barked, *"You're on our land."*

Irina stood in honor of the chief and her smile gave way to a relaxed and respectful expression. *"May I have your permission to sit here for a little while, to have lunch and enjoy the view with my friend and my brother? And will you do us the great honor of joining us—Chief Katlian, the greatest of the Sitka chiefs?"*

He answered by sitting with folded arms at the edge of the blanket, his warriors behind him with their bows at the ready. Irina sat again, ignoring the threat they posed. Antipatr considered the muskets in the boat, then came up unarmed and sat next to Yanovski.

"What's going on here?" Yanovski asked Irina.

"This is Katlian, principal chieftain of the Sitka Tlingit," she told him.

"The chief who massacred Fort St. Michael?"

"That was long ago," she replied. "We're friends and neighbors now."

Then Irina spoke in Tlingit again. *"Chief Katlian, I have the honor of introducing my friend Lieutenant Yanovski of the Russian Navy, who came for a visit on the big ship in the harbor."* She added to Yanovski in Russian, "I just introduced him to you."

The lieutenant tried to look friendly and held out his hand. But Katlian withheld his. Instead, he kept his arms folded and glared at him. Irina laid out more food on the blanket. She motioned to the chief to help himself, but Katlian waited for her. She took some smoked salmon. So did he.

"Chief, what are the names of your companions?" she asked.

"Mogin, Kebuk, and Nerok. My best marksmen."

"Are you hunting deer today?" she asked.

"No. We are protecting our land," he said in an iron tone.

Irina considered the veiled threat for just a moment, then replied, looking him steadily in the eye, *"This is the land of your ancestors, Chief Katlian. Your people have been here since the beginning of time. Your totems stand on Sitka. Your spirits live here. I respect that. And I know it is hard for you to see Russians living and hunting here. The Tlingit are a great people. So are the Russians. And I know that, because the Tlingit and Russians are both great people, we have much more to gain from peace than from war. So much more!*

"In the years to come, more Tlingit will live on Sitka Island than ever before. And your people will prosper, living in peace, partnership, and trust with the Russians. Yes, trust—just as, this very minute, I trust you with our lives. This will be so."

Katlian sat staring at her and recalled the time he had seen her giving her clams to his daughter, Lataka. What she just said gave meaning to what he saw then. *"You are very young, daughter of Baranov. And you are a woman. But there is wisdom in what you say."*

He suddenly rose and, followed by his warriors, vanished into the trees.

Yanovski asked, "What just happened?"

Antipatr answered, "Irina just used Mother's Friendship Rule to save our skins. And it worked."

An angry Kebuk lagged behind in the woods, raised his bow with a mounted arrow and took aim at Yanovski through an opening in the brush. As he was about to release his arrow, a hand suddenly grabbed the arrow's shaft and pulled it away. It was the hand of Katlian.

That was the day Yanovski learned what an extraordinary person was this daughter of Baranov. Fortunately for him, his ship was to be stationed in Sitka for several months. He saw Irina every day that he could.

CHAPTER 33

RED TIDE

A wall of dark green Sitka spruce rose into the mist along the western shore of Sitka Island, near the Tlingit village of Nakina. Fifty yards out from the narrow gravel shore, a squadron of nearly a hundred *nigilaxes*, canoes, and *bidarkas*, with a few Russians and about two hundred Aleut hunters, were cruising northward. Russians in two canoes near shore were throwing out pails of entrails over the side from some seals they had killed that morning. They were seen by a group of Tlingit men and women who had come out of the woods onto the beach to gather shellfish. With baskets on their arms, they waded into the shallows and reached down in the clear water to gather mussels.

Near the center of Nakina stood a fierce, multi-colored totem with an eagle's head, big menacing eyes, and widespread wings. It guarded the women cooking at a fire, where they were stirring a stew in a large black iron pot. The shellfish gatherers dumped mussels from their baskets into the pot as they chatted with the cooks.

Several miles up the coast, the flotilla of Russian and Aleut hunters pulled onto a beach to make camp for the night. Some

Aleuts found an abundance of mussels in the shallows and gathered a large number for dinner.

When dinnertime came to Nakina, the hungry village began to hum with voices coming to the cook fire to eat. They poked large wooden spoons into the pot to ladle clumps of steaming mussels onto their wooden plates. They sat around the fire, cracking open the shells and gulping down the mussels.

At the Russian and Aleut campsite, Aleuts were sitting around campfires eating mussels, too. The Russians chose instead to eat a seal they had killed that day.

At Nakina, within minutes, some Tlingit began to complain of tingling and numbness in their mouths, followed by stomach cramps. Some started to vomit, and others fell over, gasping for air, as their throats became constricted and their lungs were paralyzed. The onset was so sudden and so widespread, in just half an hour everyone who had come to dinner was incapacitated. They began to die at a rate of one or two a minute. Children and old people died first, then even the most physically fit. It was a horror.

Up the coast at the Russian hunters' campsite, the Aleuts quickly fell ill, just like the Nakina villagers.

By the next day, two thirds of the village of Nakina, one hundred and fifty Tlingit, had died. Up the coast, close to one hundred and eighty Aleut hunters had died in the same way. Word of the Nakina calamity quickly reached Chief Katlian, and he rushed by canoe and foot to the stricken village. When he arrived, he asked a survivor, *"What happened here?"*

The young man answered, *"Russians and Aleuts came by in canoes. They dumped something in the water. It poisoned the* clams. *When we ate them, the Russian poison began to kill our people. Now only a few of us are left."*

Katlian glared at the survivor and said, *"This is a great evil! There can be no peace with men who do this. We must return death to them. Death to Baranov and all the Russians! Yes, all of them,"* he said grimly as he thought of Irina.

Several Tlingit chiefs gathered in Katlian's longhouse to hear his argument for war. *"The Russians spread poison over clams to kill our people. Over a hundred died at Nakina. They will use this poison to try to kill us all. We must fight to save our people! All kwaans must join this battle. We need a mighty force of warriors to defeat the big Russian guns. We will attack with hundreds of war canoes and kill them before they can poison all our people."*

Old Chief Chilkoot of the Chilkat tribe was not so sure. *"Maybe they killed our village because you killed their village on Sitka years ago. Now the count is even. How can we kill them now?"*

"Then, we warned them many times. They could have left. But they did not leave, so we killed them. At Nakina, they didn't warn us. They just killed us! They are water rats, and there is no honor in water rats."

"How do you know they did that?" asked Chilkoot.

Katlian clapped his hands to call forward his witnesses. *"Maktal and Okinak! Come tell him."*

Maktal said, *"They poisoned the Nakina clams. Most people of our village died. I lost my wife and two children. Now I have nothing. No future. No joy. I can never laugh again."*

"It was as he said it," said Okinak. *"I ate mussels and got sick.*

But I threw up and spit out the poison, so I live. But most others died."

"*A great evil,*" replied Chief Chilkoot. "*Yes, we must give it back to them. Two thousand of our warriors against 700 Russian and Aleut hunters and guards. We must attack in the fog, when the big Russian ships and cannons are no good, and we will win."*

The other chiefs murmured their consent. Katlian rose from the council with a grim determination and led them out of his lodge to a fire in the center of the village, where he motioned to his drummers to begin the sacred ceremonial dance of commitment to battle.

A Russian sentry pacing the walkway between the Sitka Castle parapets peered through the heavy, slowly shifting fog coming in from the harbor of Sitka Sound. Something was there. He stopped and stared. A sudden breeze cleared a space through the mist—and there in the bay before him he saw a swarming mass of Tlingit war canoes, full of warriors in battle dress, a few hundred yards away and heading for the fort. A bugle hung from a chain around his neck, and he put it to his lips and sounded the alarm. Then he yelled, "Tlingit attack! Tlingit attack!" An arrow came whizzing through the mist, slammed into his chest, and he fell off the walkway to the ground below, dead.

Several guards came running, loading their muskets as they ran. Baranov came too, with a limp and a cane. With his still-powerful arms, he pulled himself onto the high walkway just under the parapet of the stockade surrounding the fort. He saw them. "What the hell is *this*?" he bellowed. He turned and shouted, "Fuse the cannons and fire!"

He always kept the cannons loaded but unfused, so they

would be ready to fire almost immediately. It took just seconds before the cannon roared. A second salvo hit two Tlingit war canoes, destroying their warriors and hurling bloody parts into the bay. The other canoes shifted to the south as the fog again screened the bay from the Russians.

"Katlian. It *must* be Katlian!" yelled Baranov as Yanovski ran toward him along the narrow walkway. "What the hell is wrong with that bastard now?"

"I don't know," answered Yanovski. "It's a complete surprise!"

Suddenly, flaming arrows started raining down on the fort from of the fog, causing pandemonium among the Russians and Aleuts.

"Get water! Pails of water!" Yanovski ordered. "Put out the fires!"

One of the arrows hit an Aleut in the shoulder, and he screamed in terror as he ran toward a water barrel. A captain of the guard came running to Baranov. "We caught a Tlingit warrior sneaking over the back wall. Ayeidi!"

"Bring him to me!" Baranov demanded.

Two big Russians dragged the captive out of the fog.

"Back again for another try?" Baranov snarled.

"This time, *Katlian* will kill you himself!" taunted Ayeidi.

"Why is Katlian attacking us? What's this all about?"

"You poisoned Nakina! You killed the village. Men, women, and children."

"*What?* What are you talking about?"

Katlian led a squadron of war canoes ashore through the fog at Indian River, the old battleground. They pulled their canoes onto the gravel bar and scrambled forward with their muskets, bows, and arrows into the nearby woods. As he looked back over his shoulder, he saw hundreds of warriors following. They marched toward the rear rampart of the castle. Katlian, wearing as always in war his carved raven helmet, grasped his favorite weapon—the Russian blacksmith's hammer he had captured long ago. He thought of how he would soon use it on Baranov's skull. *"Katlian! Katlian!"* barked that familiar hated voice through the fog. *"I did not poison Nakina! I did not kill Nakina! You are making a mistake!"*

Katlian stopped. Making a mistake? As much as Katlian hated Baranov, there was one thing he knew about him. Baranov always told the truth.

"We must talk!" Baranov continued. *"Halt your attack. Come to the beach in front of our fort, and I will meet you there. Just the two of us. No weapons. We will talk. I'll bring you a present— an important present from the Tsar, made of solid silver. Will you meet me there?"*

After a long pause, Katlian called out gruffly, *"I will meet you there. When?"*

"Soon, at sunset. Alone. No weapons."

Katlian shouted an order to his warriors to stop their attack and hold their places.

CHAPTER 34

MEETING OF THE MINDS

Just before sunset, Baranov had three of his Aleuts build a campfire on the beach. The tide was going out, but the loud murmur of the surf was still close. Standing by the fire, he regretted that he didn't get a promise from Katlian to come unarmed, so precautions were needed. Before their meeting, he had to examine Katlian for weapons without his knowing it. He remembered a magician's trick he'd seen long ago.

Through the fog, Katlian soon came along the beach with five of his warriors, heading toward the glow of the campfire. He signaled his men to stop and wait until he called them, and walked on through the mist. As he passed large clumps of seaweed scattered on the beach, he could see the fire more distinctly. He approached it but saw no one there. Through the fog, he could hear a Russian giving commands to someone at the castle and thought it must be Baranov. He circled the fire and walked a few steps toward the fort; his back to the flames, he peered into the fog, expecting to see Baranov approaching.

On the other side of the fire, behind Katlian, Baranov stood up, brushing off some seaweed and looking at Katlian's back. He saw a knife tucked into Katlian's rear belt.

"I said, 'No weapons,' Katlian," he spoke in Tlingit.

The chief wheeled around with a start to face Baranov across the fire, standing there leaning on his cane, like a cunning wolf out of nowhere.

"Throw your knife in the bushes," Baranov quietly demanded.

Katlian flung the knife aside. *"You killed Nakina, even the children!"* he charged as he edged toward the Russian.

"No," Baranov firmly replied. *"The poison came from the sea itself. It killed my Aleuts too who paddled past your people. They ate the mussels a few miles up the coast beyond Nakina. More than one hundred and eighty of them died."*

". . . No one said that. You lie, so you die!" said Katlian with cold determination as he pulled a second knife from inside his smock, jumped over the fire and lunged at Baranov, who leapt out of the way in spite of his bum leg. The furious chief went right after him, and Baranov swung his cane and knocked the knife out of Katlian's hand. But the chief quickly picked it up again as Baranov spread his legs for balance and held his cane horizontally out in front with both hands, to block Katlian.

Katlian held the knife forward and tried to walk around behind Baranov for advantage.

"Nanuq, great white bear, I am Katlian, the great bear killer," the chief growled as he angled for the best position from which to lunge forward in attack.

Baranov had guards waiting out of sight in the fog whom he could call, just as he knew Katlian had warriors nearby in the fog. But he preferred to keep the others out of it. Far better to settle matters with Katlian by himself.

"Kill me, and the Russians will slaughter your people!" Baranov said firmly. *"They'll bring frigates with thousands of soldiers to destroy you! Kill me, or save your people. What will it be?"*

Katlian's eyes were aflame with rage. But he was not stupid, even in the fury of the moment. Baranov's words had sunk in, and he knew they were true. His arm with the knife went slack to his side. He looked across at Baranov, threw his second knife aside, and sat facing the fire.

Thwarted again from fulfilling his hate, he stared grimly into the rising flames.

"That makes no sense—poison from the sea!" he exclaimed. *"We get our life from the sea!"*

"But it's true, Katlian," Baranov insisted, sitting on a rock by the fire. *"How could something we put in the water instantly poison all the mussels along shore? That makes no sense. It must have been a red tide. We can show you the graves of the hunters we lost who were killed by the same thing the same day."*

"Red tide? I have never seen such a thing."

"Red tides happen all over the world. Men of our ships have seen it in many places. Something from the sea turns the water red. When it comes ashore, clams and mussels suck it in. It poisons their meat but doesn't kill them. Soon, the red water disappears, so there is no sign. Then, if we eat the clams, the poison kills us."

"Then it is just like the Russians," said Katlian. *"You come in from the sea and poison our land with disease that kills our people. You destroy our seals and otters, so we starve."*

"That's not the whole truth. A better truth is where we and your people prosper together. You and I must find it." Baranov picked up his cane and used it to turn a burning log, stirring up a

rising flame that flickered upon the two intense faces as they sat staring into the fire.

"*I do not understand Russians,*" said Katlian. "*I do not understand your ships. Why cross the ocean and take our furs? Every land has its own furs. Why not just use furs of your own land? Russians speak of a Tsar who is the great chief of your land and our land. If he is the great chief of our land, why has he never come here? Every chief must see and listen to his people. If we are not important enough for him to see us and hear us, he cannot be our great chief.*"

"*You ask good questions. You and your people deserve the right answers.*"

After a thoughtful pause, Baranov spoke again. "*Long, long ago, Russia was a small place, far, far across the sea.*" He pointed with his cane toward the western twilight glow. Then he used the cane to draw a crude map of Russia, Asia, and Siberia in the sand between him and Katlian. "*Then mighty invading tribes on horses attacked them from the east, killing thousands of Russians and making the rest slaves. The Russians suffered terribly. Then a great Russian warrior led them to push the invaders out of Russia. He became the first Tsar. He was the first Russian to have the sovereignty of a monarch. He knew Russia must never again be invaded and enslaved. So he, and every Tsar after him, pushed the edge of Russia to the east for protection. And that expansion spread the sovereignty of the Tsar over new lands.*"

"*I don't know what you mean by 'sovereignty,'*" replied Katlian. "*We were here long before the Russians, so this land is ours. You say the Russians did not want to be invaded. So they came across the ocean and invaded us, and we do not even know where Russia is to attack it if we wanted to.*"

Baranov continued, *"Russia became too big for the Tsar to see all its parts and hear all its people, so he sent governors like me to see and hear the people for him. I don't really want to be here. I would rather be home in Russia. But I obey the Tsar. I stay until I am replaced."*

"You should just go home," said Katlian.

"I can't. A man is his job. You have yours, and I have mine.

"A man is more than his job," added Katlian. *"He is how well he is prepared for his job, as I was prepared for mine since I was a child. And then, how well he does the job."*

"Yes. Yes, that's true, indeed, it's true," replied Baranov. He paused for a moment to think about that, stirring the fire with his stick. He ran his tongue over his teeth as fatigue began to settle on him, and he thought of how best to engage the mind of Katlian, who he'd just found was surprisingly intelligent.

He took a big breath and went on, *"You ask why Russian ships take furs from here. Russia has more people than good furs. So they must get furs from here. But our hunting of furs has not caused hunger for your people. The opposite is true, because salmon provides more food for your people than otter and seal. Thanks to the Norwegian gill nets we trade to you, your people are now able to catch many more salmon than with the old nets. You can smoke the extra fish to keep the meat through the winter. So now, thanks to us, your people don't go hungry when they can't hunt and fish.*

"And don't forget our religion, to which many of your people have already converted."

Katlian shook his head. *"No, very few—just some old, some sick, and some women. Your religion has nothing for us. We have Raven, chief spirit of our own religion. Raven is good for our people."*

"But if you become Christians, then white men can't call you savages."

The Tlingit chief laughed at this. *"Don't you see, Baranov? Our power is in being savages! The more savage, the better. We don't need your religion. We don't need Russians. We need our land! We need our otter and seal! Russians must go."*

Baranov shook his head. *"The truth is, Katlian, the white man is now here forever—with his idea of sovereignty. If not Russians, then British. If not British, then Americans. If not Americans, then Spaniards. You can't get rid of the white man, because he makes gunpowder and you don't."*

Baranov allowed a little time for this to sink in and then continued, *"The Americans are the worst. To them, killing Natives is a sport that they justify on the basis that Natives aren't Christians. How Christian is that? For you, the Russians are best, because only we consider you equals as men, even as citizens of Russia. You and I must find how to make this work best, for Tlingits and Russians living together."*

Katlian replied, *"How can that be? We are too different."*

"Let's think of what our people really need," continued Baranov. *"One thing you* don't *need is to be a cruel people. Not even Raven favors the terrible cruelty of the Tlingit with prisoners—the torture and slavery. That is mostly why you are called savages."*

"We must make our enemies fear us so they will stay away."

"That is past. Now you can't make anyone *stay away. And as long as you are called savages, the white man has an excuse to harm your people. Think about that, and I think you'll change your mind about a lot of things."*

"I ask again, How can the Tsar be our great chief if he does not see or hear us?"

"But he does hear you. I write letters that are read aloud to the Tsar, telling what you and your people say. He hears you through me. I will get an artist to paint a picture of you for the Tsar, so he can see you, too."

". . . Paint a picture of me?"

"Yes. And to show how important you are to the Tsar, in his name I now give you something of great value." Baranov reached into his pocket and pulled out a large silver medal with the imperial crest inscribed on it—a two-headed eagle with a brass neck chain. He showed it to Katlian. *"Call your men, so they can see this. I'll call mine, too."*

Both leaders shouted to their hidden escorts. Soon a ring of Russian and Tlingit witnesses, muskets in hand, had surrounded them. The features of their solemn faces appeared and vanished in the flickering of the fire as Baranov and Katlian, who had climbed to their feet, stood facing each other.

"Tsar Alexander gives this silver medal to his great allies. In the name of the Tsar, I present to you, Katlian—strong, brave, and intelligent head Chief of the Sitka Tlingit—this Allies of Russia silver medal. Wear it with honor and pride."

Baranov put the chain over the chief's head, and as the medal sank over his chest, Katlian took the round, silver medal in his hands and examined it. It was impressive indeed, worthy as a gift from one great chief to another.

"We must meet again soon to talk more," said Baranov.

"Yes," agreed Katlian.

CHAPTER 35

A WEDDING TO REMEMBER

In the fall of 1817, another Russian frigate, *Kutusov*, sailed into Sitka harbor. On deck, Captain Lieutenant Hagemeister stared at the castle. He took Hunt's envelope from his pocket, looked at it, and again considered the castle before he replaced the letter.

The next evening, Baranov held a formal dinner to honor Hagemeister and his officers. Some Russian and Native hunters were also guests at the table. Years before, Hagemeister had worked well with Baranov. Now, the latter sensed, something was different. "Well, I'm still here since your last trip, Captain," said Baranov. "When I first came, the American president was Washington. Now they're on their fifth, Monroe, but I'm still running Alaska."

"Do you remember the Pugachev Revolt?" Hagemeister asked.

"Of course. I was in Russia then. I remember it well."

"It was the serfs rebelling against the aristocracy."

"I know."

"We learned we must keep serfs tightly controlled," Hagemeister continued. "Give them respect, and they use it to build a revolt." He lowered his voice so as not to be overheard.

"Look at what you're doing here. The Natives are like serfs. Yet you treat them as equals. Very dangerous."

"Alaska is different," said Baranov. "For them to work with us, we *must* show respect. And I must admit, I've been inspired by the ideas of a revolutionary leader."

Hagemeister looked at Baranov in some amazement. "Who?"

"He was often in the company of the most unsavory elements of society. As an advocate for the poor, he had the revolutionary idea that we should have all things in common and give whatever we own to others according to their needs—Acts Chapter 2, Verses 44 to 45. And he taught that we should do not what is best for the 'haves,' but instead what is best for the 'have-nots.'"

"Get to the point. Who is he?"

"Saint Peter denied him three times," Baranov went blithely on. "Do you think *I* should also deny him here, and all that he stood for?"

Hagemeister was speechless, staring at Baranov and then at his plate. He threw down his napkin and fork and rose, glaring at Baranov. "This," he sputtered, "is what happens when a lesser merchant, a mere *mestchannin*, is governor. Good night!"

He strode out of the dining hall, followed by his officers. The remaining men all turned their eyes to Baranov, who looked at his empty glass for a moment before he refilled it with vodka. "Not *mestchannin*," said Baranov, more to himself than to his men. "'Collegiate Counselor,' by order of His Majesty the Tsar. I'm equal to any naval captain. Equal to Hagemeister."

He lifted his full glass of vodka, but his hand was shaking. He looked at the jiggling glass, rose, made his way to the fireplace, stared at the fire, and threw his vodka into it.

The fire flared brightly. "I propose a toast to my right-hand man, whose strength of character has made everything possible," he said as he thrust his glass up and forward. "To Kuskov!" Then he threw the glass into the fireplace—an extravagant gesture for an outpost in Alaska. All the others jumped up, and they too gave the toast.

"To Kuskov!"

They tossed their glasses in the fireplace also.

"How I wish he was here," Baranov muttered as he walked out.

The next day, the navy's artist, Mikhail Tikhanov, took advantage of a rare sunny day on a spruce-capped bluff that overlooked Sitka Sound, about half a mile from the castle—just visible at the edge of the ocean behind his subjects. Katlian and his wife were posing for their portrait, as Baranov had asked. The painter was adding the final strokes to his watercolor, which would be sent to St. Petersburg to be seen by the Tsar. Katlian wore the silver Allies of Russia medal around his neck and a conical copper "peace hat." He came over to see the painting when the artist, dropping his brush into a water jar, motioned to him. After studying his portrait for over a minute, the chief nodded with approval.

"Good. I look defiant," he said in Tlingit.

Yanovski had been seeing Irina as often as he could since July, and when he wasn't with her, he thought about her. Never before in his life had he even imagined such a woman as Irina. She was so special that it would have been impossible to imagine her before laying his eyes on her. His heart and soul had become completely consumed by Irina.

One rainy evening, they managed to emerge onto a covered balcony of the castle without an escort, watching the rainfall on the boardwalks below. It was the moment they had been waiting for. Yanovski took her hand and kissed it. They looked into each other's eyes without saying a word, each seeing love there. In that ecstatic moment, he took her in his arms, and they kissed with all the passion that had been pent up for months. The rain came down in a torrent that pounded everything around them as furiously as their feelings surged.

The next evening, Lieutenant Yanovski appeared before Skipper Hagemeister in his shipboard cabin on *Kutusov*. Yanovski saluted. "Sir, I have a request."

"What is it?" Hagemeister asked.

"May I have your consent to ask Governor Baranov for permission to propose marriage to his daughter?"

". . . Well, Yanovski, this is no surprise. Everyone with eyes sees Cupid at work. Yes, you have my consent. Good luck."

A few days later, Antipatr was rowing the launch with Irina and Yanovski, all of them in winter clothes. They landed at the snowy field of their summer picnic. Irina had a white flag in her hand, and she lowered her parka hood to be easily recognized. Antipatr stayed by the boat as the two crossed the field. Warriors met them. Irina explained what she wanted in Tlingit, and they were led to Katlian's village and his longhouse. They were invited in and led to a fireplace, where Katlian was seated with his wife, K'asasee.

He looked them over with a stern demeanor and asked in Tlingit, *"Why did you come here?"*

Irina answered in Tlingit, *"Great Chief Katlian, we have happy news. Lieutenant Yanovski and I will be married next month. We invite you to our wedding. We would be delighted if you and your wife would join us at this sacred, happy occasion. No one would be a more honored guest at our wedding than Chief Katlian."*

The chief's usually hostile expression melted into surprise, and a slight smile sneaked onto his face. He held out his hand to Yanovski, much to the young man's surprise. They shook hands. Then the chief spoke to Irina with measured gravity. *"I will give you great gifts at your wedding, just as you have given me great gifts."*

Surprised by the mention of gifts, Irina asked, *"What great gifts have I given you, Chief Katlian?"*

"Your trust and respect. . . . And you gave them fearlessly."

On January 7, 1818, in the Sitka Orthodox Church, most of the wedding guests were in place, including Irina's close friend Lataka. Then Chief Katlian and his wife arrived. Everyone rose until the chief was seated. The ceremony proceeded. Afterward, the happy couple left the church between rows of navy men with cutlasses raised in an arch. All the guests then went to the castle for a reception. Katlian and his wife observed the receiving line protocol. And so, like the navy men, the chief kissed Irina's hand. She smiled at him warmly and spoke in Tlingit, *"I'm so glad and honored that you are here, Chief Katlian."*

He shook hands with Yanovski and moved on to the Baranovs—Aleksandr and Anna. Baranov said in Tlingit, *"Well, Chief, I see Irina's charm brings us together again."*

"I congratulate you on the wisdom and courage of your daughter," Katlian replied. *"She is precious to you and special to us."*

CHAPTER 36

THE FALL OF BARANOV, AND NANUQ SAYS GOODBYE

A few days later, Hagemeister and Khlebnikov came to the castle accompanied by six armed sailors who took up positions just outside Baranov's office door. Then Hagemeister and Khlebnikov entered the office. Baranov was seated at his desk, writing a letter.

Hagemeister spoke stiffly. "Sir, I have authorization from the Board of Directors to replace you."

He handed a document to Baranov, who read it with surprise.

"Effective immediately," Hagemeister continued, "I relieve you as governor. You will immediately turn over all records to Khlebnikov here, who will audit your books."

Baranov protested, "How long I've wanted to be replaced, but not like this! As a thief! Why has it been a secret for two months?"

Hagemeister, who paid no attention to the question, continued, "Furthermore, I must place you under arrest on suspicion of grand theft of company assets."

"On what basis?" demanded Baranov.

"I have here a document in your own hand instructing Wilson Hunt to sail to Nootka Sound and deliver a thousand otter furs to the British. In exchange, he was to get a letter of credit in your name to deliver to your bank account in Philadelphia when he returned to America. The value of the stolen furs was thousands of rubles."

"Let me see that!" insisted Baranov.

Hagemeister passed the document to him. Baranov read it quickly, then handed it back in some amusement. "I'm surprised that a naval officer of your standing could fall for such a fraud," Baranov said. "Look at the date."

"June 11, 1814. What's wrong with it?" Hagemeister asked.

"Can't you see?" Baranov pointed out. "Hunt faked this as if I wrote it. But he forgot that in June 1814, England and America were at war! *That's* what's wrong with the date."

"*What?*" Hagemeister exclaimed, not quite understanding the point.

"Hunt's ship was *Pedlar*," said Baranov, "an American ship, and Nootka is a British port. If *Pedlar* had anchored there in the summer of 1814, during the war, the British navy would have seized it as a war prize! So I could never have given Hunt such an order. And who in his right mind would sign such an illegal order? It's not even in my handwriting, which you should have checked. You should know, Hagemeister, that anyone who has power has enemies trying to bring him down. *Always.*"

Hagemeister stared at the document incredulously.

"As Shakespeare said," Baranov went on, "'What fools these mortals be.' At least some mortals. . . . Well, here's your office."

He grabbed his cane, limped to the door, paused, and turned toward Hagemeister. "There *is* something I should tell you," he said. "It may already be obvious to you, but this job involves a dilemma. On the one hand, you have to make a profit for the company, or the Russian government will abandon these colonies. On the other hand, you have to do the right thing for the people who live here, including the Natives. Especially the Natives.

"These two goals are often in conflict, and you have to come up with the best solutions. Not easy, my friend, as you will see, especially in working with the Natives. With them, you have to be enormously patient and calm yet firm in your negotiations. You must respect them as equals. Natives may seem very naive in things where we are smart. However, most of those things don't matter much here. And in anything having to do with wilderness, nature, hunting, they are incredibly smart, and we are incredibly stupid, which is why we need them and their help in this wild country. . . . You should try to keep that in mind."

Hagemeister looked at him with a blank stare. Baranov turned back to the door, went out into the hallway, and saw the armed sailors. "Here for my inspection?" he asked ironically. "You passed."

He continued on to his apartment. Word quickly spread that he had been replaced, and everyone was taken by surprise and consumed with worry, not knowing what to expect.

In the castle library not long after, Anna and Baranov sat reading. "My *toyon*, I'll sail to Kodiak tomorrow to visit family with Ekaterina," said Anna. "I'll come back on the next boat."

Baranov nodded in acknowledgment as he continued reading. Then, what she said sank in, and he said, "Oh. Well. . . Don't be gone long." With a sly grin, he continued, "They might be sending me off to jail, you know, and if they do, I will want you to come along and make sure I get some tea cakes every now and then."

She smiled, "Yes, blueberry tea cakes."

In the captain's stateroom aboard *Kutusov*, Khlebnikov met privately with Hagemeister. "I've finished my audit, sir," said Khlebnikov. "The books balance to the very ruble. Nearly every year had a profit. There's absolutely no sign Baranov stole anything. In fact, he's nearly broke. His money went to pensions for old Aleut hunters, and to support his Russian family and others in need—he paid debts for old Russians so they could go home. Gave big donations to the church, to Father Herman's school for children. . . ."

Hagemeister was surprised. "So he wasn't a thief, just a spend-thrift fool with his own money. What about the complaints of tyrannical brutality that led to the deaths of thousands of Natives?"

"Well, that intrigued me, because as an accountant, I'm a numbers man. I've tallied all the reports of Native deaths during his management here, from several sources. A lot died from diseases, for which he is not responsible. But from storms at sea, battles, and disciplinary measures—the last practically none—the total is about 500 Native deaths over twenty-seven years. That's less than twenty a year. Considering how big and dangerous these colonies are, it's not a bad number. And you know what? There isn't a single jail in all of Alaska. What kind of a tyrant doesn't have a jail?"

Khlebnikov cleared his throat. "Another number that I think is instructive, considering that there are tens of thousands of

Natives in all of Alaska, is that the greatest number of Russians we've ever had here is just a little over 800. Amazing, isn't it? Under Baranov's leadership, just 800 Russians have been able to establish and maintain these vast colonies. Don't you think, with that difference in numbers, that if the Natives had really wanted us out of here, they could have pushed us out? And they have lots of guns from the British and Americans, you know."

"Interesting," agreed Hagemeister, and changed the subject. "Another problem I've got: The Native workers here are loyal only to Baranov. If he leaves, they'll go back to their villages—the colony will collapse."

"I think you know the solution," said Khlebnikov.

"Yes. Resign and make Yanovski governor, because his wife, Baranov's daughter, will hold the Natives' loyalty, and they'll stay. Also, I must get Baranov out of here, take him back to Russia, to end his influence here."

"Exactly," agreed Khlebnikov.

Hagemeister continued, "That will all suit me just fine. Enough of Alaska!"

Baranov's health soon became frail, and, suffering a bout of some unknown ailment that came and went without warning, he was in bed recovering when Yanovski visited him and told him what was happening. "Hagemeister must take you back to Russia, so you can persuade the board to give you a pension and advise the Tsar. We'll send Anna to join you."

"No, don't send her," Baranov said to the man's surprise. "I will die soon, and she'd be left alone in a strange land. Let her stay here with people she loves. I'm falling apart. Piece by piece, parts of the old me are gone. Now I go home while Anna, the part of me I miss most, is in Kodiak."

In a few days, Baranov had recovered enough to see two of the Native chiefs who had been his long-time antagonists but now wanted to say goodbye. Katlian and Naawushkeitl were sitting cross-legged on the rug of the grand parlor. Baranov sat on the rug across from them with his bad leg stretched out. Both chiefs wore the Allies of Russia silver medal around their necks that he had given them earlier.

Chief Naawushkeitl was the first to speak. *"We have grown old as enemies. But in the closing drumbeats of our lives, we must sing the Song of Brothers."*

Baranov nodded. They sat silently as tea was poured. Then he spoke. *"Long ago, I bought land from you to build a village. Then you attacked us, burned our village, killed our people, and put their heads on sticks in the ground. But that is past now."*

"Yes," agreed Katlian, *"it is time to put hate behind us. But we still remember when just we were here, and otter and seal were plentiful, and we alone hunted them."* He noticed the sheathed hunting knife on Baranov's belt.

"Yes," Baranov allowed. *"Then we came, and things changed, not because white men are better, but because we make gunpowder and you don't. That's the difference between so-called savages and civilized men—gunpowder. Not religion, not culture, not government, but gunpowder. And only civilized men make gunpowder. It makes all the rest possible. Now, to survive, you must work with us. But save your own ways, and hold your heads high—where they belong."*

Katlian eyed the knife. Here was the last chance he would ever have.

Baranov stirred his tea and went on. *"Now you are my brothers.*

I gave you the Allies of Russia silver medal. Now may our people live side by side, in amity and peace, forever."

He raised his cup to them, and then drank. They likewise, as Katlian glanced once more at the knife.

Baranov had gifts for them. *"I have another present for you. Here is why your arrows never killed Nanuq: a suit of iron mesh that arrows could not pierce. Brothers should have no secrets. Now it is yours, Naawushkeitl, to protect the spirit of your people. And to you Katlian,"* Baranov said as he removed his sheathed knife from his belt, *"I give my knife, which I need no more."*

He handed it to Katlian, who saw the gift as a sacred sign. And so Katlian made his final choice about Baranov. *"Brother Baranov, don't worry about Irina and Semyon. I will protect them like my own. They can go anywhere on Tlingit lands and be safe."*

"We each came from different people," said Baranov, *"and we each tried to do our best for them. Now they must go on together."*

Naawushkeitl led them in the "Song of Brothers."

In early December 1818, on the wharf below Sitka Castle, most of the residents had come through snow flurries to say one last goodbye to Baranov as he boarded *Kutusov* for Russia. He hugged Antipatr, who was already wearing his sailor's uniform and was about to sail to Russia on another ship.

"I'll see you in Russia, son. I'm glad you'll be going to the naval academy."

Governor Semyon Yanovski said, "We'll do well here. Irina holds the Natives' loyalty. And you showed us what it means to be an Alaskan."

Tearfully, Baranov turned to Irina. He hugged her tenderly and said, "Dear Irina, I have loved you from the first moment I saw you, when you were just born and I held your precious tiny hand in mine."

She replied, "Papa, give me your hand."

She took his hand and put it on her belly. He was surprised.

"Feel your grandchild!" she said. "I wish you'd be here to see our baby—your future."

He answered, "Irina! Now I can leave a happy man! God bless you. Tell your mother I love her. Ekaterina, too. I wish I could wait to see your mother one more time. But I must go now."

He limped up the gangplank and waved goodbye, and then *Kutusov* cast off and sailed away.

From the deck, he saw Alaska recede. He approached Hagemeister, gazing at the Pacific. Again in his mind, he saw Afanassya pleading with him, and he whispered, "Finally, Papa is coming home."

Hagemeister looked at him questioningly.

"Thinking of my daughter in Russia," Baranov said. "Haven't seen her in thirty-one years."

In the next months, *Kutusov* sailed south past Hawaii and then west toward the Dutch East Indies. (Map 7.)

***

On a Kodiak hillside in the early spring of 1819, a bear was loping along the slope. It sensed something, and then saw Anna sitting on a rock in the middle of the meadow. The bear rose on two legs briefly and moved on.

Anna was looking thoughtfully out to sea from that blueberry patch, their special place. The sky was overcast and gray, not the brilliant blue that she still remembered so vividly, that day when she first felt Baranov's innermost love.

She had always known that his being so much older meant he would leave her someday while she was still young. That didn't make losing him any easier. And she had never thought it would be like this—him returning to Russia without her. She understood why he didn't want her to join him there. But her heart still ached for him. Yet knowing him as she did, she knew without a doubt that, wherever he was, he still loved her as she loved him, and that, through their love, they were still part of each other.

***

In April 1819, on the deck of *Kutusov* in the Sundra Straits of the Dutch East Indies, a cabin boy ran to Captain Hagemeister. "Come quick, sir. Baranov has fallen!"

Down in the hold of the ship, the terminally ill seventy-two-year-old lay coughing by a pile of otter furs.

Hagemeister and others came to his side. They pulled Baranov up and leaned him against a stack of otter pelts. He beckoned to Hagemeister, who hesitated and then knelt to listen. Baranov said very softly, "Tell my men. . . my loyal hunters. . . as they ride the waves. . . Nanuq rides with them."

He reached out weakly to stroke the soft rich fur of an otter pelt. His hand grew still, and fell to the floor. A deck hand pulled out one of the furs and used it to cover Baranov's face. As his body was pulled to the side to lay flat on the floor, a large package he had next to him was revealed. The deck hand reached into it and pulled out the polar bear cape.

"I'll take that," said Hagemeister, reaching for it. He lifted it, stroked its white fur, and admired the fearsome head, with the others looking on.

The burly first mate spoke up, "Nanuq. That should go to whoever serves as governor."

"No," said Hagemeister. "It. . . it belongs with him."

The next day, Hagemeister and his officers and sailors were on deck for a solemn burial at sea. Baranov's body lay on a board under the white fur cape of Nanuq tied firmly to it, and covered by a Russian flag with its three white, blue, and red stripes overlaid with the gold image of the imperial two-headed eagle.

Hagemeister faced the draped body, with the ship's uniformed officers and sailors arrayed behind him in rows at attention. He took off his tricorne captain's hat and tucked it under his left arm. In unison, the entire crew did likewise with their caps. Then he lifted his prayer book with his right hand and read aloud:

"Grant, O Lord, salvation and eternal rest unto Thy departed servant Aleksandr. We therefore commit his body to the deep, until the resurrection when the sea shall give up her dead into the life of the world to come, through our Lord Jesus Christ. O Lord, for thy departed servant Aleksandr, known to his Alaskan brethren as Nanuq, make his memory to be eternal with Thee."

The board was raised, and Baranov's body slipped into the sea making his last sound, a splash that was barely heard. Nanuq was gone. Only the flag stayed behind on the board.

Hagemeister and crew remained at attention as a single deep bass voice began to sing the slow and somber tune of the *Vechnaya Pamyat* (Eternal Memory):

"Grant, O Lord, salvation and eternal rest unto Thy departed servant. . ."

The entire crew joined the song in vocal harmony, repeating two words in a slowly rising intonation, "Eternal memory! Eternal memory! Eternal memory!"

It was an intonation that rose from the deck, up through the ship's rigging and billowing sails, and into the sky and heavens above.

***

Six months later, word of his death had reached Kodiak. On that special Kodiak hillside overlooking the Pacific, Anna once again looked southwest at the shimmering ocean below from the meadow of her favorite blueberry patch. It was a beautiful, blue-sky day again. She knew his spirit was free now, and being free, he must be where he most wanted to be—with her. She lay down on the soft bed of moss amid the blueberries and looked up at the blue sky, closed her eyes, and saw above her the strong, good face that she adored. Feeling his presence, she said, "Hello, *toyon* of my heart. My love is with you."

Father Herman made his way up the slope toward her and said gently, "Come, Anna." She followed him down the slope, with the endless expanse of Pacific beyond.

THE END

EPILOGUE

Anna lived to old age at Kodiak with a pension from Baranov, under Father Herman's care. For his selfless service to the Natives, Herman was made a saint of the Orthodox Church. The church's influence ended Native use of torture, murder, and slavery in tribal conflicts, in favor of the spiritual benefits of kindness. More Tlingit eventually lived on Sitka Island (now Baranof Island) than ever before, at peace with the whites, as Irina had predicted.

After two years as governor, Semyon Yanovski returned to Russia with Irina and their two children. At a St. Petersburg palace party, Irina was heard to say, "I haven't seen Alaska again, but I carry it with me still, in my blood." Soon, she died of an urban disease—she had no immunity.

Antipatr Baranov went to the Russian naval academy, married, and fathered at least one child. Then he too succumbed to an urban disease in his early twenties. In 2004 at Sitka, Irina Afrosina, a descendant of Baranov through Antipatr, participated in a commemoration of the bicentennial of the Battle of Sitka that emphasized reconciliation. She gave an icon of a Russian saint to the Tlingit attendees as a symbolic protector of their people.

Chiefs Katlian and Naawushkeitl continued to serve their people for many years after Baranov's departure, maintaining peace with the Russians. Today, Katlian Street in Sitka is named for the chief.

Conchita Arguelo went to live in a convent to faithfully await the return of her beloved betrothed, Nikolai Rezanov. She didn't learn of his death until fifteen years after he left San Francisco Bay.

Baranov's success in building Russian America enabled Russia to keep Alaska out of British hands. In 1867, the USA bought Alaska from Russia for $7,200,000. Some called it "Seward's Folly," but most Americans then approved of this expression of America's imperialist "Manifest Destiny." In 1959, with its wealth of natural resources, Native peoples, and spectacular wilderness, Alaska became the forty-ninth state in the United States of America.

APPENDIX

Aleksandr A. Baranov

August 1818, age 71

Nobility Rank: Collegiate Counselor

Medal: Order of St. Ann

Oil portrait by M. Tikhanov

Note: This is the only portrait made of Baranov during his lifetime.

Shown by permission of the State Historical Museum of Russia, Moscow

This painting can be seen in full color at www.MasterOfAlaska.com

Chief Katlian & Wife

August 1818

Katlian is wearing Allies of Russia silver medal, and hat similar to Baranov's copper "Peace Hat."

Baranov's Castle is in the back.

There are two views of wife to show lip ornamentation.

Watercolor by M. Tikhanov

Note: During Tikhanov's one-month stay in Sitka in 1818, there were only two sunny days. Mostly it rained.

This painting can be seen in full color at www.MasterOfAlaska.com

The Portrait of Chief Katlian and Wife

What makes this August 1818 portrait among the most important paintings in the history of Alaska, as claimed in the Preface? Take a close look. Katlian and his wife look us right in the eye, speaking directly to us. Their body language, their mode of dress, and the context of this painting all tell us a complex human story that the artist surely hoped we would see. The painting subtly communicates several key messages about Chief Katlian, his wife, Baranov, the Russians, the Tlingit, and the state of their relationships, as follows:

1. After leading the terrible massacre of Russians in the first Sitka battle of 1802, and after being forced to surrender Sitka Bay in 1804, Katlian is still alive and back on Sitka Island. Obviously, the Russians have access to him and could have captured and hung him for the massacre. But, following the Battle of Sitka in 1804, Baranov clearly realized that who won the battle would not be nearly as important as who won the peace. And by not punishing Katlian for the earlier massacre and by eventually allowing the Tlingits back onto Sitka Island, he made sure that both sides won the peace.

2. Unlike most paintings of American Indian chiefs, Katlian is not placed in his customary surroundings of a Tlingit village with totem poles. Instead, he is shown on an overlook with Baranov's Castle and the eighteen-gun Russian frigate *Kamchatka* (barely visible by shoulder) in the background. This setting tells us that it was Baranov's will that prevailed over Katlian's in the 1804 Battle of Sitka fourteen years earlier. That battle forced Katlian and

his people off of Sitka Island so that Baranov could replace the Tlingit fort that had formerly sat atop the *kekur* in the bay, a choice strategic position, with his own strong fort. A year later, he let them return to the island. Though Baranov is not physically in this picture, he is there nonetheless, in the form of his powerful fort and what it represents. Perhaps the artist Tikhanov's sensitivity to Katlian's stature led him to put the fort far enough into the background so it wouldn't dominate the scene. But it's there, speaking to us, as are the Katlians.

3. Katlian's wife is well dressed and groomed—not at all a member of a defeated people. From her facial expression and the casual splaying of her right arm over her knee, she appears quite content with her situation. After being expelled in 1804 from the land of her clan, Baranov had eventually allowed her and the Tlingit people back to Sitka Island in peace, and so she is right back where she wants to be, on her family's ancestral lands. This, despite her husband's failure to hold this land in 1804. Note that she is also shown in profile, revealing her lower lip labret, a symbol of her high status among the Tlingit. Due to the matrilineal nature of Tlingit society, whereby Katlian lives with her clan, his political realities may place some boundaries on his freedom of action, a constraint that may weigh on him as much as the power of the Russians. The peace made by Baranov and accepted by Katlian suits her just fine.

4. Katlian, though a man of war, is depicted unarmed and well dressed in upper-class peacetime clothing. But the look on his face says he is not happy here, in front of the Russian fort in the distance that symbolizes his greatest failure.

Is he merely enduring a time between battles, because he must? He wears the Allies of Russia silver medal as an acknowledgment by the Russians of his importance. But both the medal and the hat—like the famous Peace Hat—may be worn not due to a feeling of accommodation with the Russians, but rather because he is a realist. He knows this is a time when he must comply with the terms of peace to keep his wife and her people satisfied. However, in no way does Katlian appear to be a defeated war leader. Instead, he appears to be biding his time until the flow of forces and opportunity return to his favor to enable him to throw the Russians out. If that doesn't happen, he will keep the peace. The fact that he agreed to be painted by the Russian artist, and at the *location* where he is painted, is a testament to his trust in, and respect for, Baranov.

5. Accompanying Katlian and his wife are five of his ever-present warriors, all staring at the Russian fort. Four can barely be seen downhill in back, and one stands just behind Katlian gazing pensively, a thumb to his lip, at Baranov's Castle in the distance. Like Katlian, this man's manner is undefeated. He is not richly dressed but is inconspicuously clothed to be able to lurk in the woods, spying on the Russians. Though unarmed, he represents the Tlingit force—now checked—that always surrounds the Russians, waiting for the call to attack from their war chief and his council.

6. The portrait was staged on a sunny day—rare for Sitka. In fact, during the artist Mikhail Tikhanov's twenty-three-day stay in Sitka, mostly in August of 1818, there were only two sunny days. The blue sky in this portrait, instead

of the usual gray, helps convey a sense of optimism that peace between Russian and Tlingit will prevail.

7. At the same time that Tikhanov was painting this portrait, he was also doing a portrait in oil of a medaled Baranov writing at a table in the castle. He was depicted as a vigorous and intelligent man well satisfied with his accomplishments. This is the only likeness of Baranov made during his lifetime that survives today, and it was painted when he was seventy-one, just eight months before he died. It is significant that it was decided to paint the two men separately instead of together. Such strong characters needed to be portrayed separately, each in his own milieu. But the two paintings belong together as a set, because they are part of the same story. How often do we see portraits of the two key antagonists from a bitter war painted by the same artist in the same vicinity, at the same time, in two very different works of art?

Indeed, the portrait of Katlian and his wife tells a complex and meaningful story of conflict mollified and peace achieved by Baranov and Katlian. A larger, more detailed copy of this painting can be seen in Dauenhauer (110) or Engstrom (128); see bibliography for both.

History vs. Historical Novel

As mentioned in the Preface, there is a difference between a *history* and a *historical novel*. A history relates facts and their interpretation, whereas a historical novel is about the human condition as seen within a historical framework. In a history, the facts and their accuracy have primary importance, and their interpretation is subordinate. But in a historical novel, the interpretation of the human dimensions of events is primary, and historic facts are secondary, providing a supporting backdrop.

Historic events do not necessarily occur with a three-act story structure. But in order for a historical drama to succeed with its audiences, it generally requires the three-act structure, and to implement it sometimes requires reordering historic facts and inventing characters. Also, while history happened, almost nobody was running around recording exactly what people were saying as the events unfolded. So the dialogue, as in a Shakespeare drama inspired by history, is creatively imagined in order to tell the story in a way that is engaging and meaningful to the audience.

Let us refer again to the Native American saying: "This story may or may not have happened this way, but it is true." The truth is in the human dimensions expressed through character interactions, choices, and values. It is within this concept of a historical novel that I wrote *Master of Alaska*.

In a historical novel, it is not the accuracy of an event but rather the validity of an event that is the key to its credibility and meaningfulness. Here are excerpts from some documents, during the time of Baranov's Russian America, that have informed the creation of this story and its quest for validity.

Baranov's policy toward discipline and punishment with Native Alaskans. . .

Baranov's Guidelines to V.G. Medvednikov [manager at Sitka fort]; April 19, 1800 letter by Aleksandr Baranov (Dauenhauer

152—This and subsequent excerpts from Dauenhauer herein are republished with permission of Sealaska Heritage Institute from *Russians in Tlingit America,* edited by Nora Marks Dauenhauer, et al, 2008, Seattle: University of Washington Press; permission conveyed through Copyright Clearance Center, Inc.).

Note Baranov's prohibition of corporal punishment: "Nobody is to be struck at all..."

"All partovshchiki [Native otter hunters], kaiury [former Native slaves], and women are to be treated without rudeness, politely and with kindness. Honorable men [Native chiefs] from amongst the partovshchiki who are hunters are not to be assigned to any task without utmost need, and those who are not adroit (in our ways) are not to be burdened with our tasks too much. Even then, they are to be persuaded by kindness, without swearing or shouting. Nobody is to be struck at all and they are not to be fined on one's own judgement without having consulted Medvednikov [the Sitka fort manager]. [The latter] is to be consulted in all matters and his counsel asked, especially in barter and trade with the Tlingit, when trade goods are on hand. His advice is to be sought how better to obtain profit without causing [the Tlingit] any vexation. Now is not the time to show our limited numbers, a key [that could be exploited by] that conceited people plentifully supplied with arms and ammunition.

"...Russians are to be treated with good will, and in all things you should act as an honest man ought, punctilious in his office, efficient, caring, faithful, and fair, thus perhaps earning personal commendation and approval."

Regarding Baranov's comment above about "our limited

numbers," Russian records from their periodic census taking show that the maximum number of Russians ever in Alaska at one time was 833, during which the male Native population of Russian America was well over several thousand. These Natives included the Tlingits, who were well armed with guns from trading with the British and Americans. Apparently the benefits of trading with the Russians prevented the Natives from uniting in enough numbers to throw the Russians out, which they undoubtedly could have done if enough of them had truly wanted to do so. Baranov seems to have understood this and so had a policy of peaceful friendship with the Natives, as possible, to avoid friction.

Baranov's sympathy for the Aleuts, his main force of sea otter hunters. . .

Excerpt from his letter to Shelikhov and Polevoi, from St. Paul's Harbor (on Kodiak Island), May 20, 1795 (Tikhmenev, *History Vol. II*, 60).

[Speaking from the point of view of Kodiak from which Baranov wrote this report] "Without speaking of other places the route to Yakutat alone is hard on the natives [Aleut hunters]. Imagine the poor natives making this journey both ways, 2,000 versts [1,326 miles—more than the distance from New York to Minneapolis] in narrow bidarkas without sails—using only paddles. They have to endure hunger on the way and often perish in stormy seas because this coast offers no adequate shelter. In places where the natives [Tlingits] are not subjugated they are always in constant danger of attack by the bloodthirsty inhabitants of these regions. It is under these conditions that they [the Aleuts] have to hunt sea otters. For the time being they endure it, but it takes courage and supervision by the Russians, and you can judge for yourself their state of mind."

Baranov's religious beliefs. . .

Excerpt from Baranov letter to Larionov (in Unalaska), July 24, 1800 (Tikhmenev, *History Vol. II*, 120) .

"In conclusion I hope that the Almighty Reconciler will preserve you from all misfortunes and will make the residence of you and your family a quiet and peaceful one (something hard to expect here, but nothing is impossible for God)."

Excerpt from Baranov letter to Larionov (in Unalaska), March 21, 1801 (Tikhmenev, *History Vol. II*, 123) .

"The winter was the coldest remembered and we lost hope of finding anything of the ship [*Phoenix*] or wreckage. Now we rely upon God and you for help and guidance. . . . Thanks to Providence we got more sea otters than we expected and by the generosity of the most gracious and omnipotent Creator we have this year—the third after the last division of furs and the sailing of the transport—almost 4,000. . . . We must consider it the sacred will of the Creator to recompense us for the diminished catch of land animals by increasing our principal catch."

Perhaps not the context in which we may usually think of religious belief, but belief nonetheless.

Baranov's Native mistress, mother of his Alaskan children, and later his second wife...

The story of the Alaskan Native who became Baranov's second wife is sketchy in his letters, leaving it open to broad interpretation.

He mentions two Native women with whom he got involved. The first was from a Kodiak tribe. Then he tells about being given another young Chugach woman as a hostage when he was on the east side of the Kenai Peninsula involved with the building of a ship. His brief description of his involvement with these women has been interpreted differently by his biographers. Hector Chevigny in Lord of Alaska, *and historian Richard A. Pierce in his introduction (xi) to Khlebnikov's biography of Baranov, concluded that Baranov broke off with his first Native mistress and retained the second one from Chugach-Kenai, and that this is the woman who bore him children. Lydia T. Black, one of the most esteemed Alaska historians, has concluded differently, that Baranov left his second mistress from the Kenai area whose connection with him served a political purpose while building the ship, and then returned to his Kodiak mistress. If this were a book of history, it might accept Black's conclusion. But because this is instead a historic novel (a story based on history) the interpretation that Anna was a Kenaitze was chosen, because it better serves the structure of this story. It is likely of little historical importance exactly where in Alaska she came from, only that she was in fact an Alaskan Native involved with a Russian—the top Russian.*

Excerpt from Baranov letter to Shelikhov, May 20, 1795

(Tikhmenev, *History Vol. II,* 68).

"I have for a long time now been keeping a girl, the daughter of Raskashchikov. I have taught her to sew and be a good housekeeper. She can be trusted in business matters, but I found that during my absence she showed weakness. I sin too, sometimes from weakness, and sometimes from necessity, as I did during my long stay at Chugach when the Chugach people gave me a girl for a hostage. On account of that, the Chugach became more attached to me and more confiding."

Some sources equate the Chugach people with the Kenaitze, as in this story also.

The incident in which Baranov's mistress almost loses their boy toddler is described only cryptically by Baranov.

Excerpt from Baranov letter to Larionov, July 14, 1800

(Tikhmenev, *History Vol. II,* 121).

"As a result of my weakness and transgressions I have here a son three years old whose qualities are very promising but whose mother in my absence became affected so that we almost lost the boy. After my return, to cause me vexation the fathers insisted for quite a while that the child be taken away from his mother and tried in different ways to persuade her in this respect. I bear all this calmly but my love for my offspring is offended. I am away very often and he is too small and cannot be without a mother."

The red tide disaster. . .

Excerpt from Baranov letter to Larionov, July 24, 1800

(Tikhmenev, *History Vol. II,* 106).

"I warn you that you must have lots of fortitude and patience in order to read this tale of many successes and of some misfortunes that brought grief to us. . . .

"I did not see our hunting party at Sitka; they left two days prior to my arrival there, but had not gone 80 versts [53 miles] when they met with a sad misfortune. On the day after they left the vicinity of Sitka they stopped overnight at Khutsnov Strait. They had enough provisions with them, but ate some small black mussels. Two minutes later about half of the hunting party had a feeling of nausea and dryness in the throat, and in two hours time about one hundred good hunters were dead. The Russians saved some by giving them powder, tobacco, and spirits of ammonia to make them vomit. This sickness became infectious and even men who never ate these mussels were dying on the way to Yakutat. There was an epidemic at Yakutat also, which started when I was there in June. Some people ate sweet grass that is used for cooking and others who had not eaten anything felt nausea, dryness in the throat and difficulty in breathing and in two days were dead. About twenty died here, and out of the entire party, one hundred fifteen perished."

Tlingit plans to attack New Archangel and Baranov's Castle

Excerpt from Rezanov letter to Minister of Commerce, June 17, 1806 (Tikhmenev, *History Vol. II*, 222).

[From New Archangel, Sitka Sound] "The [Tlingits] lately have ten or fifteen of their men continually coming and going, watching our fortifications closely. Meanwhile, rumors are current that the Chilkhat and Khutsnov [Tlingit tribes] are ready to unite with the Sitkans and capture the port. Mr. Baranov has surrounded his hill with a stockade, with embrasures for cannons, and is on guard all the time."

This account by Rezanov, plus reports in various sources of numerous abortive attempts by the Tlingit to attack Baranov's Castle at Sitka Sound, provide the basis in this story for the final conflict between Baranov and Katlian. Though the conversation between Baranov and Katlian in this imagined incident is fictitious, something like it must have occurred to cause the historically noted complete turnaround in the attitudes of the two men toward each other between the time of the two battles of Sitka and the end of Baranov's role in Alaska.

The character of Baranov...

Added to the impression one gets of Baranov's thoughts, values, and character from reading his letters, there are comments about him in the writings of others, noted here. This evidence does not support the faulty and uninformed modern notion of Baranov having been a tyrannical despot. It should be noted that in all of Alaska during Baranov's time, there is no evidence of the existence of a single jail or prison—"during the Russian period... to the end of 1867, there was not a single jailhouse." (Black, Russians 133). True, there were hostages housed in barracks. However they were not imprisoned like criminals, but instead lived as part of the community where they were held. What tyrannical despot in history survived without a jail?

Excerpt from Rezanov letter to RAC Bd. of Dir., Nov 6, 1805 (Tikhmenev, *History Vol. II*, 154).

[From New Archangel, Sitka Sound] "We live quite crowded here, but the winner of this land [Baranov] lives in worse conditions than any of us. He lives in a sort of plank yurt, which is so damp that the mildew has to be wiped off every day. The shack is full of holes and with the continuous rains it leaks like a sieve. A wonderful man! He thinks only of the comfort of others, but is so careless of his own that once I found his bed standing in water and asked him: 'Perhaps the wind tore off a board somewhere?'

"'No,' he replied calmly, 'it seems to have run in under the floor,' and went about his business.

"I tell you, Dear Sirs, that Baranov is a quite unique and happy creation of nature. His name is heard all along the west coast as far as California. The Bostonians respect and honor him, and the natives, even in the most distant places, fear him and offer him their friendship. His settling down in Norfolk [Sitka] Sound for the second time created such a sensation among them that the famous toion Kau, who lives in ... Prince of Wales Island ... sent his son on a Boston ship this spring to see with his own eyes that Sitka was really occupied by the Russians and to get acquainted with Baranov. I have to confess that I am studying this man with great interest. Important consequences that will follow his acquisitions [of areas of Alaska] will make him better appreciated in Russia. . . . I think that by giving the true picture of his personality . . . taking into consideration human failings and weaknesses . . . It will be unpleasant news for you, in the company's present circumstances, to learn that this man so needed for the company's advantage and for the State, has decided to leave this country. . . . I must tell you . . . it would not be a simple matter to find a new man and by the time this new man adapts himself to the new country the company will suffer great and irreparable losses and can easily lose all the territories it now possesses. . . .

"You must consider the position which Aleksandr Andreevich is in here. He is an outstanding example for the hunters and knows how to endure hardships, but frequent insults by the officers employed by the company have made him and Mr.

Kuskov and some others decide to leave this country. . . . How all this is going to end I do not know. Mr. Baranov still has so much enthusiasm that I . . . hope that perhaps he will stay, provided the company gives him real authority . . . as a sign that everybody here [including naval officers] must be subordinate to him. A report must be made to His Imperial Majesty the Emperor. . . .

"Do not think, My Dear Sirs, that I am prejudiced in favor of Baranov. Not at all. Being a witness and experiencing hardships here myself, I know the many painful efforts it has cost him to retain our American possessions. Knowing the value of his achievements, I see also his shortcomings, and still I will say that his removal now will be very painful for the company, because not only does he have a rare knowledge of the Country, but there is no other man who can get along with the hunters [mostly Aleuts] as well as he can. . . with all his ambition, disinterestedness [pragmatic objectivity] and good qualities, cast by Fate into a mass of violent spirits, in order to win their love and obedience he was forced to feign their way of life to some degree. Having had to force upon himself to adopt ways that were alien to his mind and heart, he has accustomed himself to disregard in others weaknesses which are morally unsupportable."

Kirill T. Khlebnikov, an accountant, met Baranov in 1817, having been sent to Sitka to audit the company's and Baranov's finances and to investigate rumors of Baranov's malfeasance and embezzlement. For a year, Khlebnikov questioned Baranov and others about Baranov's activities in Alaska. Upon this first-hand information, including having known Katlian also, he based his biography of Baranov.

Excerpts from Khlebnikov's 1835 biography of Baranov (Khlebnikov, *Baranov* 111-116, 99).

(111-116) ". . . one of the Chief Manager's obligations is to care for the upkeep and feeding of all the inhabitants, Russians and natives. The natives . . . carelessness, never bothered about the future. But Baranov's good and sympathetic heart was moved for them. He sympathized when there were no fish to be caught, no whales . . . no seals, and so on. He spent sleepless nights when storms delayed the expected arrival of supply ships, or when they foundered and upset all his plans for the general good. . . . But how his heart must have ached when batches of bad news suddenly arrived together, like the loss of the settlement in Sitka and the annihilation of the hunting party. . . .

"Apart from caring for the economy, hunting and trade, Baranov did not neglect his task of educating the young people born in the colonies. In his time Sitka had a school which taught reading and arithmetic. . . .

"Let us say a little more about his nature and character. Baranov never dreamt of amassing wealth. . . .

"Baranov helped not only his friends who were poor but even his enemies who were in distress. There are still many people in the colonies who received his benefactions. Many had a chance to return home with his aid. [He] . . . in this way helped many of his friends who were, by ill chance out of work or in need. . . . Amongst these was Koch . . . with no work or means of support. Baranov, knowing his situation, and the large family he had to support, sent him money regularly. . . .

"Davydov noted that selflessness was not his only virtue, and points to his generosity. To this I must add that his generous spirit was exceeded only by generosity of heart. He was quick to forgive personal wrongs. One of many examples ... In November, 1800, some escaped Aleuts were captured and brought to Kad'iak. . . . they were taken straight to Baranov, and it was by chance discovered that they had daggers concealed under their clothing. . . . they confessed that if Baranov had ordered corporal punishment, they were going to strike him down and then kill themselves. Baranov merely lectured them for running away, but their evil design, as he put it, "he left to God to judge." He knew from experience that for the Aleuts nothing is more shameful than corporal punishment. To escape it, guilty persons had often committed suicide. Knowing this, he usually punished the Aleuts who came before him with shame, or by making them work for a stipulated period. . . .

"[A British ship came calling once, causing] one partner to suggest that they might seize the ship and throw the blame onto the natives: Baranov answered this remark with disgust: 'How could you think that I would break the sacred laws of hospitality and stain these shores with the blood of innocent visitors, leaving on myself the irremovable blot of treachery?' . . .

"The misfortunes and disasters which often befell and tortured Baranov; the boredom of loneliness; the constant isolation from civilized society, and even written contact only once a year; the promyshlenniks from the common folk who surrounded and lived with him; the coarseness of some of his foreign visitors—all this left on him traces of moroseness. . . .

(99) "He had been above all a benefactor, and now, bidding farewell, he left them all forever. Even the Kolosh [Tlingits] who had . . . respected his bold and decisive spirit, parted with

him with a strange mixture of joy and sadness. The famed toen Kotleian [Katlian], respected by Baranov for his intelligence and bravery, and who had harmed Baranov more than anyone by destroying the fort—even he appeared before him, and they made their peace. Baranov bore witness to his successor concerning this man's intelligence and ability."

More descriptions of Baranov's personality and character by other contemporaries who knew him can be seen in Khlebnikov's biography. Those observations on Baranov echo Rezanov's and Khlebnikov's.

Baranov as Nanuq

Excerpt from G. H. von Langsdorff's report of his visit in late October of 1805 with Tlingit people relocated from Sitka to Pt. Craven of Chichagof Island (Dauenhauer 306).

"They [the Tlingit] do not go on land until Nanok, i.e, Mr. von Baranoff or one of his representatives, comes down to the landing and gives them permission [to set foot on New Archangel]. . . ."

BIBLIOGRAPHY

The sources listed below provided much of the historical basis for *Master of Alaska* and are highly recommended. Some are available for free download from the Google collection of public domain writings, such as Bancroft and Lisianski's books.

Bancroft, Hubert Howe

1886. *History of Alaska, 1730-1885*. San Francisco: A. L. Bancroft & Company.

Black, Lydia T.

2004. *Russians in Alaska 1732-1867*. Fairbanks: University of Alaska Press.

Chevigny, Hector

1942. *Lord of Alaska—The Story of Baranov and the Russian Adventure*. Portland, OR: Binfords & Mort.

Dauenhauer, Nora Marks, et al.

2008. *Russians in Tlingit America—The Battles of Sitka 1802 and 1804*. Sealaska Heritage Institute. Seattle: University of Washington Press.

Engstrom, Elton, and Allan Engstrom

2004. *Alexander Baranov—A Pacific Empire*. Juneau: Elton and Allan Engstrom Publishers.

Griggs, Robert F.

1922, *The Valley of Ten Thousand Smokes*, Washington: The National Geographic Society

Hope, Herb

2002. *The Kiks.Ádi Survival March of 1804*. Alaska Native Knowledge Network, http://www.alaskool.org

Khlebnikov, Kirill T.,

1835 [1973]. *Baranov—Chief Manager of the Russian Colonies in America*. Colin Bearne, translator. Richard A. Pierce, editor. Kingston, ON: The Limestone Press, 1973.

This biography was written by the only biographer who actually knew Baranov.

Lisianski, Urey

1814. *A Voyage Around the World*. London: John Booth.

Matthews, Owen

2013. *Glorious Misadventures—Nikolai Rezanov and the Dream of a Russian America*. London: Bloomsbury Publishing.

Owens, Kenneth N. with Alexander Yu Petrov

2015. *Empire Maker—Aleksandr Baranov and Russian Colonial Expansion into Alaska and Northern California.* Seattle: University of Washington Press.

Tikhmenev, P. A.

1861 [1978] *A History of the Russian-American Company.* Richard A. Pierce and Alton S. Donnelly, translators and editors. Seattle: University of Washington Press, 1978. 1863 [1979] *A History of the Russian-American Company Vol. II, Documents.* Translated by Dmitri Krenov. Richard A. Pierce and Alton S. Donnelly, editors. Kingston,ON: The Limestone Press, 1979. *Includes several lengthy reports, letters and a speech written by Aleksandr Baranov from 1793 to 1805. Includes letters from Nikolai Rezanov about Baranov, California, and Conchita.*

Troyer, Will

2015. *Into Brown Bear Country.* Fairbanks: University of Alaska Press.

ABOUT THE AUTHOR

Roger Seiler grew up in King Salmon, Alaska as the son of a bush pilot. He is a graduate of the UCLA Film School and an award-winning filmmaker. His first book in the historical novel genre was Naked Thinkers, which earned Amazon's top reader rating.

MORE PRAISE FOR *MASTER OF ALASKA*

I keep thinking about the story and its characters!

        - Charles Francis, IdeaBank founder

I read it twice. . . a fascinating book!

        - Nelson Page, film exhibitor

I marvel at this book and its compelling story. I felt the energy and compassion of it as though I were there. A great story from Alaska's history that shows how to make peace out of conflict.

        - John G. Haven, solar systems designer & consultant

MAY 0 2 2017

CPSIA information can be obtained
at www.ICGtesting.com
Printed in the USA
LVOW13s2325230317
528320LV00022BA/578/P